for Kay th
mate anyone could
ever wish for.
   Thanks Love ya
      Dee
       xx
   Dee D.B
    25-4-03

Dee D.B. An ordinary 37 year old mother of three. Born Deana Britton, I lived in Hockley, Essex, and was fortunate to have a very happy and privileged childhood, knowing from an early age just what I wanted to do with my life. So after a happy, yet uneventful schooling and hundreds of bald dolls later, I started my first day. Two and a half years later and in true 'Essex Girl' style I became a hairdresser.

By the age of 24, I was a married mother of two, living in North Essex and trying desperately to come to terms with the loss of my Mother, and knowing in my heart I'd make a huge mistake in my life!

On moving back to my home village, I worked in a nursing home for three years, having my third child at 32 and divorcing my husband nine months later.

Happy, but a total wreck, I went in search of some spiritual guidance via a lady named Betty, who suggested I do something 'spiritually creative' such as painting or writing. 'No, not me,' I thought, 'the only painting I ever have time for is the decorating! And the only writing I'll ever be doing is to the Bank, apologising again!' That was five years ago. What an amazing woman!

I now live in a lovely village near Downham Market, Norfolk with my wonderful partner, Dave, three happy kids and my passion – writing.

ROSLYNN

Dee D. B.

Roslynn

Chimera

CHIMERA PAPERBACK

© Copyright 2003
Deana Britton

The right of Deana Britton to be identified as author of
this work has been asserted by her in accordance with the
Copyright, Designs and Patents Act 1988

A CIP catalogue record for this title is
available from the British Library
ISBN 1 903136 24 5

Chimera is an imprint of
Pegasus Elliot MacKenzie Publishers Ltd.
www.pegasuspublishers.com

First Published in 2003

Chimera
Sheraton House Castle Park
Cambridge England

Printed & Bound in Great Britain

Dedication

This book is dedicated to Faye, Lewis and
Megan, my three beautiful children.
For their patience, encouragement and
enthusiasm.

To Dave White, whose love and support made it
all possible, thank you darling, I love you.

To Lee Brilleaux the original Dr Feelgood,
although sadly not with us, I thank you for
watching over me in spirit. Your music lives on.

Chapter 1

Roslynn

Roslynn put her bags on the doorstep and shut the door for the last time. With tears in her eyes she picked up her belongings and crept down the footpath careful not to make a sound. When she reached the pavement she felt a little safer.

"I've done it! I've finally done it," she said, a wave of fear dampening her near smile.

"What if he finds me, what then?"

She started to run blindly down the road not knowing where to go.

At 19 years old she had no home now, no money, no place to go, and she didn't care. She was free from that bastard of a husband her father had sold her to four years earlier. Roslynn shivered, as images of her fat, bourbon-drinking, cigar-smoking, husbands grinning face, as he beat and raped her in front of his friends with his cane, came flooding back She could hear his laughter in her ears as he told his friends.

"This is what you can do if you buy your wife!" as he pushed her over to them and watched as she was passed from one man to the other until they had all had her.

"Never again!" she cried, picking up her speed.

Having walked a good three hours and seeing no one, she sat on a large stone by the road and rubbed her feet. She noticed the sun was rising and guessed it was about half-past five.

"Shit! In two hours he'll know I'm not there and all hell's gonna break loose!" she said to herself.

Sitting there, she thought it best to keep out of the way during the day, and walk some more when it got dark, not knowing where she was going or what she would do. Time was the only thing she had on her side, and that was better than nothing, but time wasn't going to fill an empty stomach.

She stood up and looked around her now there was some daylight. She could see she had walked a fair distance and was on the outskirts of the town east of her home town.

The town was just waking up and Roslynn could smell toast as she walked through the streets to the town centre. She looked at the town clock, 6.45, people were leaving for work, passing her by in their cars. She felt very conspicuous carrying her two bags along in muddy shoes, her hair lank from the dampness of the night. Roslynn came to a crossroads. Standing on the corner she looked every way as panic welled up inside her.

"Which way? Which way?" she whispered.

Remembering the time, she picked up her bags and stepped off the pavement.

The screech of breaks was deafening! Roslynn looked up as an articulated lorry came straight for her.

When she came to, she thought it had all been a dream and she was in bed waiting for someone to tell her she could come down! She was totally confused to find herself in the middle of a road with a kindly face looking in a worried way down at her.

"Are you okay?" the face asked.

"Um… where am I?" Roslynn asked, her voice croaky.

"On the A901," the face said.

"Oh! Am I hurt?" she asked.

"Well, I didn't hit you if that's what you mean!" the face smiled at her. "Can you get up?" she was asked

"I think so," Roslynn replied slowly getting to her feet.

"I'm Ron," the kindly face said.

"And this is Elsie," he said pointing to a huge blue and chrome lorry cab.

"My pride and joy," Ron said smiling.

"And I'm Roslynn," she said, putting out her hand.

"I'm sorry to give you a fright, I didn't see you coming down the road, believe it or not."

"Oh, I believe you! I was watching you. You just stepped out: in a world of your own, weren't you?"

"Well, I was a little lost, still am really," Roslynn replied, biting her bottom lip.

"Hey, listen. Would you like a coffee? Maybe I could help

you out, I live round here so I know the place really well," Ron asked.

Roslynn's stomach grumbled.

"Okay," she said, "but I can't pay for it, I haven't got any money at the moment," Roslynn felt her face flush with embarrassment, then taking a quick breath she said in the coyest voice she could, "But if you buy me a breakfast with that coffee I can pay you back some other way,"

Ron looked at her with total shock on his face.

"Now look here girlie, I've got two girls at home that are about your age and if I thought an old man like me was going to take advantage of them I'd 'ave to find 'im and kill the blighter!"

Roslynn lowered her eyes to the floor and shuffled her feet, wishing the floor would open up and swallow her.

Ron took pity on this young girl, saying to her in a kindly voice.

"Come on girlie, let's go eat and find out your story!" As he took her bags and threw them into his cab, holding the cab door with one hand and Roslynn's hand in the other he helped her up into the cab. Shutting the door he walked to the other side. As he opened his door he raised his eyes to the heavens and thanked God his girls were still tucked up in bed when he left home this morning. 'Oh, what a sorry sight that girl sitting in his cab was,' he thought, 'In a way I'm glad it was me that nearly hit her and she didn't hitch a ride with some of the other blokes I know who drive their cabs and trailers all over the country, notching up the girl hitchhikers on the way.

He had already decided to take her with him if she wanted to go his way, and if his judgement was right she'd be going his way!

Ron turned on the engine, rammed Elsie into gear, gave Roslynn a fatherly smile, and set off for the transport café down the road.

Ron swung Elsie into the café lorry park. Roslynn could smell the bacon fat drifting from the café, and she couldn't remember the last time she was this hungry. Maybe it was the adrenaline that used up the last of her energies, she didn't know, only that she could have one of everything on the menu right at this moment.

"Come on girlie, I thought you were hungry?" Roy shouted up from her side of the cab.

Roslynn jumped as Ron's voice broke her eerie blankness. She was miles away, not thinking, hearing, or seeing. Looking down, she turned and opened her door. Ron's hand guided her down.

"Thanks," she said, rather deflated.

Ron just winked at her and said, "Come on girlie let's get some food inside you."

After ordering their food and the waitress had given them their coffees, Ron said,

"What's your story then girlie?"

Roslynn gave him a look of horror.

"I don't know what you mean!" she said, sipping her coffee.

"So you were in the middle of town, lost, with two bags of clothes, and muddy shoes, just for the hell of it were you…? What happened? Your boyfriend dump you? Lost your job an' you can't tell your ma and pa? You ain't up the duff, are you girlie? 'Cos if you are I know an old dear that can help you, a real lovey she is!"

"NO…! NO…! and… NO…! You wouldn't believe me even if I told you!" Roslynn sighed.

"Try me girlie."

Roslynn took another sip of her coffee and looked at Ron.

"My father sold me to a very rich, eccentric and sick man at the age of 15, he was 50!" Roslynn said, looking around the room at all the faceless people, only snapping back to the present when Ron let out a gasp and said

"Holly Jesus girlie! That's one sick mind you have!" Giving a low whistle as he looked for his food. Surly his intuition wasn't that far out! Jeesus! How could she be telling the truth, it's like something from the dark ages! He thought.

He then caught the look on her face as he watched the waitress walk past.

"Where's our food got to?" he said.

"You don't believe me, do you…? Ha! You should have met my husband! "Now that's one sick mind, and I need to get as far away from him as possible. Please you've got to believe me! I can't go back there, please!!"

"Hey! Hey! I believe you girlie. I don't think you're the type to make-up a story like that and I'm sorry I said what I did, but don't you think you should report him to the police?"

"Oh, and say what exactly?" Roslynn flew back.

"I don't know girlie, I don't know," Ron said, rubbing his chin.

"Listen, have you got anywhere in mind as to where you're going to go?"

Roslynn didn't reply as the waitress placed their breakfasts on the table. Cutting into her sausage, she said,

"As far away as possible," placing the meat in her mouth.

"Well, have you got any people to go to girlie?" Ron asked.

"Not my parents that's for sure! And I don't know anyone else. I guess I'm a self-made orphan!" she smiled at him.

They ate in silence each in their own thoughts. Roslynn wondering where Ron was going and if she could make a new life at the end. Ron wondering why he always seemed to pick up the waifs and strays, and boy had he had some!

"You ready then girlie?" Ron asked her.

"As I'll ever be," she smiled, feeling better with some food inside her.

They got back in the cab and Ron started Elsie up.

"Good old girl this one, had her a good few years I can tell you!" Ron smiled affectionately at the great lump of blue metal.

"By the way, where are you going Ron?" Roslynn asked.

"South girlie, south,"

Roslynn smiled. "That will do nicely Ron, nicely!" as they both laughed together.

Very soon Roslynn was sound asleep. She reminded Ron so much of his two girls, when they used to come on trips with him in the holidays. He smiled to himself and carried on south.

When they got to the town before Ron's drop-off point Roslynn woke, just as they were pulling into a lay-by. Ron jumped out and ran across the road and into a shop. Roslynn sat up, rubbed her face with her hands and stretched. Within five minutes Ron was back, waving a pocket book.

"Afternoon girlie. Were you up all night?"

"Pretty much," Roslynn yawned.

"Look girlie, the next town we come to is my drop-off

point, so we'll be parting company there. I've brought you a map of the area and a sandwich. Oh! And here's a couple of quid to get a roof over your head tonight," Ron said looking down at the foot-well not sure what else to say.

Roslynn took the map, sandwich, and money. "Well, I don't know what to say Ron, but thank you, you've been the kindest person I've ever met."

"Oh, it's nothing girlie," Ron said with a sigh.

Roslynn looked about her.

"By the way Ron, where exactly are we?"

"The island girlie, the island! Actually, there's a caravan park near the sea front. From what I remember they might need someone to clean the vans or something. It's worth a try."

"Thanks Ron, I'll give it a try first, you never know," she said with a smile, her stomach turning over.

"That you don't girlie, that you don't," Ron said, starting the last stage of the journey.

Five minutes later Ron pulled over, and Roslynn slipped from the cab. Ron passed her, her bags.

"Bye girlie, and good luck."

"Bye Ron, and thanks," Roslynn smiled. Crossing the road, she headed to the sea front.

Chapter 2

"Thorn Bay Caravan Park."

"Well, this must be the place!" Roslynn said as she straightened herself up, ran her hands through her hair, checked her shoes for mud, picked up her bags and walked very carefully along the sandy lane that led to the site.

She came across a bungalow by the park and very gingerly walked down the path bags in hand. She rang the door bell and stood back shuffling her feet.

"Yeh, wotcha want?" A man in scruffy clothes stood the other side of the door.

"Oh! Are you by any chance connected to the caravan park further down, only I'm new in the area and…"

"New are ya?" the horrible man said, opening the door and glaring at her chest.

"Well, yes and…"

The man turned his back on Roslynn and shouted.

"Oi Bet, you there? Got a kid 'ere," and promptly walked back in. Roslynn stood on the doorstep with her mouth open. 'What a disgusting man' she thought, and was about to turn and leave when she heard a husky voice call,

"Yes lovey, what can Bet do for ya?"

Still taken aback by the man, Roslynn just stared at this woman.

"Well?" Bet stood with her hands on her ample hips smirking.

Roslynn jumped.

"Oh! I'm sorry but I was wondering if you had anything to do with the caravan park here," Roslynn pointed down the lane.

"Anythin' to do wif it?" Bet laughed

"I own it lovey," she said.

Roslynn swallowed. 'This isn't going too well!' she thought.

'Better just pick up my bags and go.'

But Bet had already seen Roslynn through the front window and knew she could do with someone new. 'Maybe just the one' she thought, watching Roslynn's every move. 'Not bad at all.'

"Now, what can old Bet do fer ya?"

"Well, I'm new to the town and I wondered if you had any work for me. I don't care what it is, anything will do," Roslynn replied quickly.

Bet put her hand to her chin, then patted the back of her well-teased bleached hair.

"I think old Bet can find yer somefin' lovey. Better come in an' we can 'ave a nice chat," Bet's face broke into a big toothy grin.

"Oh! Thank you Mrs?"

"Just call me Bet lovey, everyone else does," she replied walking down the hallway.

Roslynn followed Bet into the kitchen. She felt a little nervous with this woman, but safer than with the man she'd met at the door.

Bet motioned Roslynn to a chair.

"Plop yer bum on that lovey," she said. "Tea?"

"Oh! Yes, please," Roslynn replied, looking around the room.

It impressed her how clean everything was, not a thing out of place except Bet herself.

Bet was a big, brassy, blonde, with a love for bright colours, and deep red lipstick, which she always wore. She'd had a hard life, but had always had a heart of gold. She'd been left the bungalow and land by an old aunt. She had seen it as her way out of the life she had got sucked into.

She soon realised that, that life was where the money was. Now Bet could control her own life and still earn the money!

Bet looked at Roslynn across the table, her big painted eyes staring right into her.

"Got any family lovey?"

"No," Roslynn replied.

Bet nodded

"Got a place ta stay?"

"No," Roslynn said again.

Bet grinned.

"Don't say much do ya lovey?"

"No," Roslynn replied again, but this time a grin crept across her face, and both women burst out laughing.

Bet liked this girl straight away. Yes, she could do something with her. But she knew instinctively that this one would do it in her own time.

"Well, wot's yer name then lovey?"

"Roslynn."

"Welcome ta the island Roslynn. Now what can ya do?" Bet asked, lighting a cigarette.

"Pretty much anything like I said. I don't care what it is, I just need a job. "I'm sorry, I don't want to sound rude or anything only its getting late and I haven't found anywhere to stay yet, and I can't do that until I've found a job! And..." Roslynn stopped in her tracks.

Bet was laughing at her and so was the creepy man who she hadn't seen come into the room.

"What? Why are you both laughing at me? What's so funny? I don't think any of it's funny!" Roslynn cried, standing straight up and picking up her bags.

She was about to leave when Bet said.

"Hey, where ya goin' lovey? Thoughtcha needed a job? Got accommodation wif it, it 'as!"

"Really? Oh! Thank you, thank you so much!" Roslynn cried, putting down her bags she sat down again.

"What kind of job have you got in mind for me?" she asked.

"Well," Bet said, leaning onto the table and licking her lips.

"I've got me this little private club, you see, an' I need a pretty young girl like you ta take the gents coats an' shoes. Reckon yer can do it?" Bet grinned.

"Well, I think I could manage that," Roslynn smiled.

"But where am I going to stay?" she was beginning to feel exhausted and thought she'd have taken a cardboard box by the roadside.

"Well, on the site, of course. I'll take yer rent outa yer wages an' give ya wot's left. How's that sound lovey?" Bet said.

"Oh, that sounds great Bet, thank you."

With a snort the man turned and went back outside.

"Who is that man?" Roslynn asked nervously. She really didn't like him.

"Oh, that lovey, is Jedd, he an' I go back a long way, wouldn't get rid of 'im oh no, no ways. Miserable old sod, smelly too, but when ya get ta know 'im like I do 'is all right. Kinda me protecta if ya know wot I mean," Bet said through a cloud of smoke.

"Yes," Roslynn said.

She didn't really but thought it best to keep her opinions to herself and give Jedd the benefit of the doubt, seeing Bet was giving her a job and a place to live.

"Right Roslynn. Let's go find yer new 'ome shall we?" Bet said, standing up, and doing a deep bow she waved her hand to the front door.

When they stepped outside it was getting dusk. They turned left and headed to the caravan park. Some of the vans had lights on and Bet explained to Roslynn that some of the caravans had permanent residents in them and that's what she called her "bread and butter," Roslynn had never heard that saying before and got Bet to explain some more as they walked on.

"Well, lovey. Me "bread an' butter" is them residents that stay all year, you know live 'ere. I get me regular income from them an' they get a cheap place ta stay."

"Oh! I see now," said Roslynn.

They walked in silence for about another five minutes until they came to some older vans.

"Sorry it ain't a new van lovey, but it's cheap, it's clean an' dry and yer only a stones throw from yer new job."

Bet opened the door of the little grey caravan and said.

"Welcome ta yer new 'ome lovey."

Roslynn stepped in and looked around, tears ran down her face.

"Wot's up lovey?" Bet looked concerned.

"Its lovely," she cried, "just lovely."

Bet raised an eyebrow and gave her a quizzical look.

"It's only a van lovey."

Roslynn nodded and smiled at Bet. For the first time in four years, she felt safe.

"I'm sorry Bet, I think I'm a bit tired, that's all."

Bet nodded saying, "Well, I was goin ta take [
club, met the rest of me girls before we open."

Roslynn looked at Bet.

"Well, okay," Roslynn smiled weakly "Just let 1
hair and we can go," she said. Really all she wante[
sleep, her clean little van was so cosy. But, Bet had b[... so] good
to her in such a short time she didn't want to upset her.

'How strange to meet two of the nicest people I've ever met
in my life in one day!' thought Roslynn.

Putting her bags on the little table, she turned to Bet and
said nervously, "Right, I'm ready."

Roslynn shut the little van door and Bet gave her two keys.

"One fer the van, an' one fer the club," she said.

Roslynn put them in her bag, and they walked down a
sandy path lit by two rows of lights either side.

"As ya can see," Bet said,

"Me club's way out the back 'ere, all me customers 'ave ta
drive up past yer van an' park then walk down this path. There
ain't another way in or out!"

Roslynn nodded.

At the end of the path was a very plain square building with
one door and no windows. Roslynn was confused now.

"This is your club?" she asked hesitantly

"Yup," grinned Bet.

"Com'on," she said, putting the key in the lock and turning.

What Roslynn saw next took her breath away. They walked
into a foyer out of a time past. Roslynn thought of her so called
husband for some strange reason and shivered.

Bet caught Roslynn's look of sadness and pain, logging it in
her brain to ask questions very carefully with this one.

Bet walked across the black and white marble floor. It was
so clean you could see your reflection in it. There was a hat and
coat stand on the left hand side, and several gilded chairs with
red velvet cushions scattered around, but the most impressive
thing of all was the big central staircase that, at the top, went to
the left and right. There were double doors on the left past the
hat-stand, two doors that faced to the front, either side of the
staircase, and two sets of doors on the right hand side.

Bet opened the first doors on the left.

"This…" she said, "is where our gents leave their belongings, and where you'll be workin'.

"When they come in the first person ta greet 'em will be you. So tamorrow you an' me, we're gonna see what glam rags ya got.

"I haven't got anything glamorous!" Roslynn panicked.

"Ah, not ta worry lovey, one of me girls'll 'ave sumfink. Now, where was I? Oh, yeh our gents. Right, see these keys 'anging up?"

Roslynn looked to where Bet was pointing. At the end of the room were about twenty keys hanging up with gold oblong tags on them.

"Yes," replied Roslynn.

"Right, when the gents come in you give 'em one of the boxes on the right an' they put their shoes, car keys, money and any other valuables they 'ave on 'em in one. Now, each box 'as its own number. When they give you their box, you give 'em the key wif the same number. Got it?"

"Yes. Got it."

"That's it lovey. Now, let's go meet me girls."

They came out of the room and Bet led Roslynn into the next set of double doors. She flung them open, at the same time winking at Roslynn.

"I like ta surprise 'em sometimes!" she laughed.

A group of girls turned towards the doors as they crashed against the walls.

"Girls, meet Roslynn," Bet called still laughing.

They all eyed Roslynn up and down and nodded at her. Roslynn couldn't help but stare; not one girl had all her clothes on! They were doing each other's hair and nails, walking around in see-through negligées or stockings, bra, and panties. Some had just go hot pants on, no top! Not one girl seemed in the least bit embarrassed when Roslynn caught herself staring at them. They just smiled a knowing smile that confused her all the more. She looked at Bet.

"What do these girls do?" she whispered.

"Why, they entertain me gents, that's wot they do lovey. You'll see soon enough tamorrow," Bet laughed.

Bet told the girls to have a good night and walked Roslynn

out the door, past the stairs, and into the double doors opposite the room where she would be working.

"This…" she said, "is the games room," with a grin.

"What do you mean?" Roslynn couldn't work out what games were played in this room.

There was an odd looking table, and mirrors. Ropes and chains were hanging from the ceiling, straps came out at her from the walls, belts, cat'o'nine tails, golden pegs, chains, and sticks hung around the room.

"Oh, my God!" Roslynn gasped.

"It looks like a torture room.

"That it is lovey!" Bet chuckled.

"Our gents like this room! So much so, as ya can see, we've 'ad ta knock these two rooms through ta fit 'em all in together. Yep, we've 'ad a few wild parties 'ere I can tell ya!"

Roslynn's mouth fell open. It slowly dawned on her what she was standing in.

"My God it's a brothel isn't it?" she cried, covering her mouth with her hand.

"Well, done lovey! You've finally cottoned on. Now we've got one more room down 'ere. And that's the room ya gotta take 'em to once yer give 'em the key."

Bet opened the doors. Facing them was a huge bar stretching the length of the room. The walls were a deep red with gilded paintings hanging everywhere the only lighting was table candles and back lighting at the bar. It felt as if Roslynn was in a different world. She liked this room she didn't know why, but she did. Bet was studying Roslynn's face, she could see the girl liked the room.

"Nice ain't it?"

"Yes, very," Roslynn replied, thinking, 'I wonder what goes on in here!'

"Right you've seen the downstairs, that's all ya need ta see. Upstairs is me girls' space. There's twenty keys an' twenty doors. Get me drift lovey?"

"Oh, y… yes I understand," Roslynn stuttered.

"I'll let ya get some sleep now lovey. Be 'ere at seven pm sharp tamorrow."

And with that, Bet ushered Roslynn out of the red room

across the foyer and out the door saying, "I got a meetin' wif me girls lovey, so I'll see ya tamorrow night," promptly shutting the door before Roslynn had a chance to answer.

Chapter 3

Roslynn woke to a banging noise outside. Coming to she jumped up and stuck her head out of the window, and squinting her eyes through the morning sun, she saw what was making the noise.

Across the site, Tommy was trying to start his old Bedford van.

"Come on you little fucker, start!"

Tommy tweaked a few more tubes and wires, slammed down the bonnet and got in the van once again. He put his hands together as if in prayer.

"Come on, come on, and come on!"

Nothing, just a whirring noise. Tommy slammed his arms down on the steering wheel.

"You fucking bastard bit of shit! Why taday eh? Fuck it!!" Tommy got out slammed the door, kicked the side panel of the van and walked off.

Roslynn watched him walk off and laid her head back down again.

Tommy really didn't need this today, his first job since going it by his self.

"Jesus fuckin' Christ. I don't believe me fuckin' luck! This is the last thing I fuckin' needed! Jeees, don't look very fuckin' professional when the fuckin' builder you've employed turns up on the bus does it!" he muttered to himself.

It was three in the afternoon when Roslynn woke again. She washed, dressed and brushed her hair, then went in search for food.

She brought some currant buns with the money Ron had given her.

Walking out of the shop, her head in her bag, she slammed straight into Tommy. Her currant buns hit the pavement and rolled in every direction. Roslynn was dumbfounded as to what had happened.

"Jeesus!" Tommy said, rushing to pick up two of the buns.

"I'm… really… sorry!" stammered Roslynn rushing to retrieve the other two buns that were just rolling in the road.

Walking back to the spot where she had collided with him, she picked up the ripped paper bag that had carried her buns. Tommy walked over to her and gave her a quizzical look.

"New 'ere, ain't ya?"

"Well yes, how do you know?" she questioned.

"Know most the people on the island, me!" Tommy answered.

"Where ya stayin'?"

Roslynn looked up from the buns Tommy had given her,

"Oh, the Thorn Bay Caravan Site, do you know it?"

Tommy grinned.

"Know it, I bleedin' live there, don't I!"

He looked at Roslynn. 'Bet she's one of old Bet's girls' he thought.

"Wot end ya stayin'?" he asked eyeing her.

"Quite a walk really. I'm right down the end. The caravan goes with my job," Roslynn replied.

"Yeh! You ain't got the little grey van 'ave ya?"

Tommy's mind was working over-time. 'Might just go to old Bets club an' 'ave a look at this one,' he thought.

"That's right, I take it you've seen it?" Roslynn said.

"See it every mornin', noon, and night! I got the van wif the old blue Bedford outside," Tommy said proudly.

"So it was you who woke me up this morning?" Roslynn said with her hands (two buns in each) on her hips, giving Tommy a stern look.

"Shit! Sorry. Fuckin' thing wouldn't start, would it!" Tommy said, throwing his hands in the air, making Roslynn laugh.

"Hey, listen, want a coffee ta go wif them buns?"

"Okay, why not," Roslynn smiled, and Tommy took her to the café just down the road.

"Two coffees mate," Tommy ordered from the doorway.

"Righto' Tommy me lad," the man behind the counter replied.

Tommy led Roslynn to the window seat and sat opposite her.

"Yer can eat yer buns in 'ere babe. Pr'aps old Reg'll get some more people in if they see you eatin' in 'ere!"

"Cheeky bastard!" Reg shouted back, shaking his fists in mock anger.

"So wot's yer name then?" Tommy asked, leaning forward.

Roslynn told him

"Fuckin' 'ell! Bit of a gob-full, ain't it?" Tommy said, raising an eyebrow and smiling.

"Don'tcha prefer Ros or Lynn?" he asked.

"Well, nobody has ever called me either, so I've never really thought about it, but if you want to call me by one you can choose," she said smiling back, thinking how cute this denim clad guy was.

"I recon it's gotta be Ros! Goes better wif Tommy don'tcha fink?"

"What do you mean, it goes better with Tommy?" Roslynn said, a little taken aback.

"Well, I recon you an' me are gonna be one 'ell of an item babe!" Tommy grinned, picking up his coffee.

"Oh, really?"

"Yeh, really!" Tommy said, grinning over his mug.

Roslynn gave a little smile and looked around the café. She caught sight of the clock on the café wall.

"Shit! Is that the time? I've got to get back," she said getting up from the table.

"Hey! Wait, I'm goin' 'ome now, I'll come wif ya," Tommy replied standing up.

"An' you can tell me wot yer job entails," he said his blue eyes shining.

'Shit!' Roslynn thought. 'What if he knows it's a brothel! What can I tell him? He seems a real nice guy, with his cute grin, curly black hair and bright blue eyes. Shit! shit! Shit!'

"Well, okay, but I'm in a bit of a rush. I was only going to be out half an hour and I've got a lot to do," she said quickly, remembering Bet saying that she was going to pop round to see what clothes she had. 'God, what if she's waiting outside the van for me! What am I going to tell Tommy?' she thought.

What Tommy came out with next nearly put Roslynn on the floor.

"So you one of old Bet's new girls then?"

"W… What did you say?" she whispered, her face white.

"Well, you said the van went wif the job, yeh?"

Roslynn nodded.

"Well, all old Bet's girls get a van. An' I know wot 'er girls do! Christ I practically built the fuckin' club single 'anded! Decorated the inside an' all. Been round it yet?" he said grinning at her.

"Yes, as a matter of fact I have, Bet gave me a tour and showed me my job last night."

"I bet she did!" Tommy scoffed.

Roslynn strode ahead, tossing her hair in the air.

"I'm not one of Bets girls! And YOU don't know what I do," she cried.

Tommy smirked. 'If I play me cards right I won't even 'ave ta pay!' he chuckled to himself.

"God, you're pathetic!" Roslynn spat, and marched away from him.

Tommy watched her go. She wasn't pretty, but she wasn't ugly either, there was just something about her. He had to admit he was intrigued.

Roslynn opened the door of her little van, and a cloud of smoke hit her in the face.

"Met our Tommy then lovey?" Bet grinned through the smoke.

"Saw the two of ya 'aving a natter. Upset ya did 'e?"

"Yes, I mean no! Bet, did I leave the door open or something?" Roslynn frowned.

"Nar lovey, got me own set ta all me girls' vans, just in case like," Bet replied, putting her cigarette to her lips.

Roslynn was about to ask Bet if she'd been waiting for her long when Bet pointed to the other end of the little van.

"I took the liberty and 'ad a look at yer gear, an' I 'ave ta say ya don't make the most of yerself do ya lovey? I mean look at yer clothes, if yer was forty, an old forty mind, then fine! And yer 'air needs a bloody good seein' to if ya ask me. Not that ya 'ave! Anyway, I couldn't believe me eyes when I saw this lot. So

I got a couple of me girls ta 'ave a butchers an' we've decided before ya start ya job. You me girl are gonna 'ave a make over!"

Bet took a gulp of air.

"An ya can look at me 'ow ya like, I ain't takin' no nonsense from ya.

Now shoo, go on out ya go," Bet said, as she turned Roslynn to face the door and gave her a little shove.

Roslynn didn't have time to think, let alone speak. Bet shut the door grabbed Roslynn's hand and half skipped her down the path towards "The Club". The door was open this time. When they entered there was a group of girls talking and giggling on the stairs.

"'ere she is girls. Now do yer best, I've every faith in ya," Bet boomed across the foyer.

Bet shoved the petrified Roslynn towards the girls and shouted.

"Don't ferget, shop opens at seven girls, an' I want ta see 'er before that."

"Okay Bet," the girls called in unison, as they headed towards Roslynn like a pack of lionesses after their prey.

They circled Roslynn lifting her hair and poking at her body. Roslynn began to feel very intimidated.

"Bet was right with this one!"

"Annie, you take this little mouse through and get one of those dressing gowns on her. Oh! and wash her hair, would you darling, please."

"No problem Rose," Annie jumped up and down, clapping her hands together.

"Come on babe," she breathed

Roslynn followed Annie, a very petite bleached blonde with a beehive nearly as big as her, into the girls' leisure room.

"Right Jude. I want you to give that girl a complete restyle, I think she needs it to her shoulders with a full fringe and a bit of height at the back," Rose said, holding up her hand.

"I know what you're going to say darling. I know she's tall, but she's got a lot of face and a bit of fullness is needed onto it, don't you think?"

"Put like that, yeh, yer right!" Jude laughed, nodding,

"I'll go sort out me scissors an' rollers, and get ta work on

29

the poor lamb!" Then, shaking her ample breasts and backside into a shimmy, she kissed Rose on the cheek and turned to leave.

Rose put her arm out to Jude

"Better take our Sal with you Jude. She can do Roslynn's nails. Okay with you Sal?"

Sal, a tall leggy natural blonde with straight hair to her backside, small breasts, iridescent blue eyes and ghost-like skin, looked at her own nails and said.

"That's fine by me I think I'll do the same as mine. What d'you think?" showing the other four.

Jude put her big thick arm around Sal's waist and said.

"Com'on you dozy tart get yer arse in that room," Making Sal giggle as Jude slapped her backside.

Rose turned to the other two girls, Misty, a dark skinned amazon type, with a mass of afro hair, and Kel, a natural titian with a peach complexion and a naturally fit body due to her love of dancing.

"Right, you two, we've got the make-up and clothes left. I think Misty, you can do the make-up, what with your artistic eye. And Kel, you and me, we'll find the clothes. We can't keep her in the bloody things she's got! "Christ, she'd scare the old boys away!"

"I'll go and adjust my artistic eye. Call me when she's ready," Misty said, heading for the bar.

"Okay Rose, what look do we want?" Kel said, heading up the stairs.

"Do you know what I mean when I say "All fur coat an' no knickers!"

Kel looked at Rose and collapsed on the stairs in a fit of laughter.

"Well, I have now! But believe it or not I think I've got an idea," she giggled, pulling herself up the stairs.

An hour later Rose walked into the girls' room.

"How's it going, girls?"

"Not bad at all," Jude shouted from the corner.

Annie ran over to Rose like an excited puppy.

"Oh, come and see her Rose, you were right as usual."

Rose hugged Annie like a child and followed her over to Jude and Roslynn. Jude turned to Rose her short silky black bob swaying on her head.

"Well, whatcha think?" she asked standing back from teasing Roslynn's head.

"Not bad at all," Rose grinned.

Roslynn felt she was caught up in a whirlwind of activity and she was in the middle with no control. She hadn't said a word since Bet had pushed her out of her little van and in to "The Club". She looked down at all the hair on the floor and panic welled up inside her.

Rose pulled her up

"Well, babe, what an improvement!" she said, twirling her around.

"Now for your nails and make-up!"

"Annie go get Sal and Misty, would you, darling?"

"Sure thing Rose," Annie said, running off to the bar.

Roslynn was standing hands clasped in front of her, with a hideous pink robe on and her hair all teased and lacquered.

"Right Jude, great job, now go get yourself ready babe. Oh! and tell Doughy dinner in an hour, would you?"

"Sure," Jude said putting her comb down, and bounced out of a door disguised as a wall panel.

Roslynn stood staring with her mouth open.

"What's the matter babe?" Rose asked looking concerned.

"Well. When Bet said she had a job for me, I didn't expect my clothes to be examined while I was out, my hair chopped off, make-up done, not to mention nails! And to top it all... and I hate to think what it's going to be? A new outfit!" Roslynn cried, taking a deep breath "and now I find you've got secret doors in the wall!"

Rose could see the panic on Roslynn's face.

"Woow there babe!" Rose butted in before Roslynn could carry on.

"We've got a reputation to keep up here, and Bet saw potential in you."

"What's a little bit of girlie fun! I mean we're not going to make you any worse!"

Roslynn felt as if she'd been slapped in the face by Rose's remarks.

Anger rose in her.

"I'm not a doll, you know. Don't I get a say? It's my hair, face, and clothes you're changing. If I knew I was going to have to go through this kind of humiliation, I would never have taken the job!" Roslynn spat. She wanted out NOW!

"Okay babe, I'll get your clothes and you can scoot. But just remember three little things. No job = No money = No place to stay! Think about it. You got anywhere else to go Roslynn?" Rose hissed at her.

Roslynn looked down, deflated.

"No," she said.

"Right, now let's get your face and nails done, shall we?"

Sal and Misty were standing in the doorway, watching the drama unfold.

"Come on, Ros. Can I call you Ros?" breathed the ghost-like Sal.

"Y… yes," Roslynn nodded, following her over to a table.

"Right Ros, you sit here," Sal pointed to a straight-backed chair.

"Then Misty and I can work on you together," she said pointing to the two swivel chairs either side of Roslynn's seat.

On the white Formica table in front of Roslynn was an assortment of nail varnishes and make-up. She took a deep breath and closed her eyes.

The two girls got to work on their task in hand.

"I'm just going to see what Kel's come up with," Rose said to the little group as she walked past. The girls nodded and smiled, their attentions totally on their subject.

Rose heaved a great sigh.

"You've got to hand it to Bet, she knows one when she see's one!" she tutted, gliding out the room and up the stairs.

Rose tapped on Kel's door.

A muffled "Come in," came from the room.

Rose entered the room to find Kel with her head in a huge travel chest.

"Think I've found just the thing Rose. Look on the bed!" Kel said, jumping up from the chest and moving to the bed picking the dress up with two fingers and twirling it around the room, as if she was dancing with it.

Rose clapped her hands together.

"Perfect Kel. Perfect," she said, smiling.

"And in that chest I've got just the thing to finishing it off!" Kel exclaimed.

"Well, when you've found it, bring it all down would you babe?"

"Course I will. Oh! Isn't it exciting?" Kel said, burying her head back in the chest.

Rose smiled 'no wonder that girls always busy!' she thought as she closed the door on Kel's backside sticking out of the old chest.

Going down the stairs Rose checked her watch, 5.30 half an hour to finish their prodigy, get Bet to see her, then the girls can eat, an' while they get ready, I can show Roslynn the ropes once more. Oh and I must remember the meeting with Bet at 8 o'clock.'

As rose walked into the room, Kel came bounding in behind her.

"Found it!" she to Rose running over to the four girls.

Misty was just finishing Roslynn's false eyelashes.

Sal and Annie their faces made up as well, were sitting on the edge of the Formica table, watching intently. Seeing Kel come running over to them, they jumped off to meet her.

"What you found then Kel?" Misty said, standing back to admire her work.

"Ta! Da!" Kel said, as she swung the dress from behind her back.

"Oh, yes!" they exclaimed grinning.

There hanging on Kel's fingers was a shimmering gold lamé dress, very low cut with shoe-string straps and a split all the way up to the hip on the left hand side.

Roslynn turned to look at their excitement.

"I'm NOT wearing that! Oh no, no way," Roslynn cried, shaking her head.

"Three little things babe!" Rose reminded her.

"Now, go try it on, there's a good girl."

A dejected Roslynn took the dress from Kel and followed Annie over to a screened-off area. There was no mirror to be seen, so she didn't even know what she looked like, she could only guess. She slipped off the robe and stepped into the dress. It

33

felt cool and heavy on her body, she felt very conspicuous with no bra or panties on. Very hesitantly, she stepped out from the screen.

There standing in front of her were the six women. Jude had brought a full-length mirror with a sheet over it back in with her. Roslynn stood in the room staring back at them.

"Gold strap sandals don't you think?" Rose said, with her hand on her chin.

"Definitely!" they all replied.

"What size shoe are you babe?" Rose asked her.

"A six."

"Good, good, we've got loads of sixes,"

"And I know just the pair," Misty said, running out of the room to a big cupboard under the stairs.

"Here we are!" she said, bringing the shoes with her.

Roslynn slipped them on.

"And now the finishing touch!" Kel squealed, producing a long gold chain with an amber pendant hanging from it. She slipped it over Roslynn's head.

"Perfect!" she breathed.

The others nodded.

"Go get Bet, Annie," Rose grinned.

Annie ran from the room and the others fussed over Roslynn, putting a stray hair back, and touching up her lipstick.

"Fuck me! Is it the same girl?" Bet said, as she strode into the room.

"Well, girl ya tart up good I can tell ya!" Bet laughed.

"Right let 'er see 'erself girls."

Jude unveiled the mirror, and the four girls pulled Roslynn over to it.

She stared at the person in the mirror. Her mouth fell open. Where was she? Where was the long straight hair, the big face, and figureless body she was used to looking at gone? Instead she was looking at a big haired, big eyed, shimmering gold mist, and she loved it!

Roslynn turned from one side to the other, then all the way around. She looked at the others and her face broke into a huge grin.

"I can't believe it's me! Really I can't!" she cried, her face beaming.

"I fink she likes it girls," Bet said, her hands on her hips, a cigarette hanging from her mouth.

Rose clapped her hands together.

"Girls, you've done a great job. Now go get something to eat and get yourselves ready. Oh! And can one of you ask Doughy to keep Ros's dinner warm. I just want to show her the ropes one more time," Clapping her hands together once more she dismissed them.

Roslynn was still staring at her reflection 'no one would recognise me now!' she noted and it gave her a bit of confidence.

Bet disappeared, and Rose ran through Roslynn's job with her.

"You should be all right tonight babe, we only got a few in tonight. Now any questions?"

"Nope," Roslynn smiled. "Only, when can I have something to eat, I'm starving!"

Both women laughed and Rose led Roslynn through the concealed door and into a big homely kitchen.

"Doughy, I'd like you to meet Ros, she's our new box hostess."

Doughy wiped her hands on her apron.

"Nice to meet you Ros. Hungry?"

"Oh, yes, I am," Roslynn replied.

Doughy motioned her to the table and chairs, and got a plate out of the oven placing it in front of her, saying,

"When you've finished leave your plate on the table and the girls will be waiting for you in the bar. Know where that is do you?"

"Yes, thank you," Roslynn replied, tucking into her meal. She didn't realise how hungry she was until she started to eat.

It was 8 o'clock and The Club had three gents in. Rose popped her head around the door to Roslynn.

"How's it going Ros?" she asked.

"Oh, fine," she smiled.

"I didn't realise the gents were so nice!" she said, in a whisper. An image of her husband flashed before her and she shivered. Rose took note of her expression, but didn't say a word.

"I'm going to see Bet. I'll be back in a while," she said, with a smile as she left her.

Rose knocked on the door.

"That you Rose?" Bet shouted from behind the door.

Rose opened the door and went inside.

Bet was sitting behind a huge old oak desk, obscured by a cloud of smoke that always surrounded her. She pushed her face through the cloud, red lips in a smile.

"Just been lookin' through the bookings, not bad, not bad at all. Bit quiet tonight but all in all not bad. You seen the new one yet? 'ow's she doin'?

"I was right about that one weren't I? Tarted up good, ain't she? Don't talk much at the moment but she will. Recon that one'll be quite an asset later on!"

Rose just smiled; she knew not to open her mouth when Bet was on a roll.

"Saw 'er an' our Tommy together taday! 'ad a row from wot I saw."

"Proberly trying ta get in 'er draws if I know Tommy! Don't waste much time does 'e?" she said, shaking her head.

Rose tutted saying, "She's doing fine babe, just let her get a bit more confident and in time!" she raised her hands to the ceiling. Both women chuckled.

Tommy sat in his little van, party seven and a bag of chips on the table. He couldn't believe what a stroppy cow that Roslynn was.

"Wouldn't mind but she thinks she's above Bets girls but she ain't!" he muttered to himself.

"Might go an' give old Bet's place a visit, see what madam's up to, yeh that's what I'll do!"

He poured himself another beer and raised his glass into the air and toasted the image of Roslynn stomping off earlier.

It was 10 o'clock when Tommy put his key in "The Clubs" door, greeting him was Roslynn.

"Fuck look at you!" he slurred.

"What are you doing here?" she spat.

"Thought I'd give ya a visit," Tommy grinned standing up straight.

"You look fuckin' shit hot babe!" Tommy was in love.

"Really? Visit much, do you?" Roslynn hissed.

"Nar. First time I've used me key. Never 'ad ta pay fer it yet babe. An' I ain't gonna start now, I must say the girls done a fuckin' brilliant job on ya!" Tommy said, undressing her with his eyes.

"So when you an' me goin' on a date? I know, 'ow about tamorrow afternoon? I ain't got nothing on an' I can show ya round the island,"

Roslynn looked at him. "Okay but only because I don't think I'd get rid of you until I've agreed to you."

Tommy smiled

"It's a date then. 'Ow's about lunchtime. We can go an' 'ave a pub lunch or sumfing?"

Roslynn laughed at him.

"It's a date."

"I'll give ya a knock tamorrow then about 12.30, okay?"

"Fine," Roslynn replied.

"Now, are you coming or going?"

Tommy raised his eyebrows.

"Both babe, both!" then walked away.

Roslynn shut the door. She looked like the cat that had the cream.

'Tomorrow' she thought.

Roslynn woke and looked at herself in the mirror. 'Oh my God! What do I look like?' she thought. Staring back at her was a make-up smudged face, with one spiders leg eyelash hanging at a peculiar angle from her eye, topped by a tangled mass of dark hair.

"How the hell am I going to do my hair! Let alone my make-up," she cried, running her hands over her hair and on to her face gently tugging at what looked like a dead spider from her eye. Suddenly she remembered her date.

"Shit I need help!" she groaned.

'Who?' she thought,

"Who can I ask without feeling a total fool?" she said, lifting her hair up. She slumped down on her bed,

"No one. That's who!" she said, aloud sighing.

Getting up from the bed, she put some water on to heat and looked about her.

The girls had given her another dress and shoes for tonight, also some brushes, rollers, combs and make-up.

Kel had given her a bag of "day" clothes to try. Roslynn tipped the bag up on her bed, an assortment of clothes fell out.

Roslynn picked up each garment and examined it, eventually choosing a pair of black trousers, a pink fluffy top, and a pair of pink pumps that she found in the middle of the pile.

She washed and dressed, then sat down to tackle her hair and make-up. Placing the mirror Misty had given her on the table, she picked up a brush and started detangling her hair. She looked at the special comb Jude had given her "To get height!" she'd said. Roslynn picked it up and taking a clump of hair on the top of her head started to knot her hair up again.

She smoothed over the tangled lump she'd done with the comb, dragging it down the back, flicking up the ends, and combed her fringe down. 'Not bad!' she thought, turning from side to side and pouting. "Now for the face!" she said to herself in the mirror.

Roslynn found some black khol for her eyes and some pink lipstick. She looked at the end result and couldn't believe what she saw. She, Roslynn, actually looked good! She blew herself a kiss in the mirror, and did a little Marilyn Monroe routine, gaining more confidence with every minute.

12.30 on the dot Roslynn got a knock on the door. Her stomach flipped and all her confidence drained from her body. Carefully she opened the door. Tommy barged in.

"All right babe? Ready?"

"As ever," she said, feeling a little hurt that Tommy hadn't noticed the way she looked.

"Thought we'd go 'ave lunch in a pub I know called "The Admiral". Got a room out back that all the local bands practise in. Never know, might be lucky taday an' see me favourite band called "The Jug Band" they are. Like music d'ya babe?"

"To be honest, I don't really listen to music," Roslynn replied, remembering her husbands' ban on music and radio's in the house.

"Well, maybe Tommy can change yer mind eh?"

"We'll see," Roslynn said.

The pub was along the island's sea front, they walked into a crush of people just on their way out.

"Hey! Steady guy's!"

"Aright Tommy, 'ows it goin'?" one of the lads said.

"Well, John. You?"

"Yeh mate. An' a nice bit of arse wif ya! Fuckin' got it all taday ain'tcha?

"The Jug Bands" in there! 'aving a right old jam they are!" John laughed.

Tommy grinned at John, and held the door for Roslynn leading her in, not giving her time to retaliate.

The pub was dark, smoky, and smelt funny to Roslynn. Tommy's face was alight when they heard the distant thudding coming from the back room.

"You get us a table, and I'll get the drinks in. Wotcha like?"

"Just an orange juice. I haven't eaten yet today."

"You got it babe."

Roslynn found a table, sat down, and looked around her. The thudding was getting louder and louder suddenly the door at the back of the pub flung open.

"An fuck you too, arseholes…! Sorry love! I didn't see you there!" the man said, grinning at her.

"Here. Don't I know you from somewhere?"

"I don't think so," Roslynn replied giving him a smile.

Suddenly she went scarlet when she remembered where he'd seen her. He came in last night at about 10-30, spoke to Rose and went. He was only there half an hour top's. Roslynn prayed he didn't recognise her!

"Yeh! That's it. You were at "The Club" when I popped in to see Rose last night. New door girl, ain't you?"

The shock ran through her and her red face drained. She took a deep breath 'Come on Roslynn it's only your job' she told herself. Sitting up straight she smiled at the man.

"That's right. I only started last night," she said, trying to sound as casual as possible.

Tommy looked over to Roslynn. Seeing her talking to the man a pang of jealousy swept over him. He turned to the barman.

"Bung a large vodka in that juice would yer mate," the barman done as he was asked and took Tommy's money.

"Well, I suppose I'll see you tonight then love," the man said to Roslynn.

"Got a party of us coming over you have," the man chuckled.

"I was just asking the lads in the back room if they wanted to come but they've got a gig on."

Roslynn sat staring at this man not knowing what to do. She was about to open her mouth when Tommy reached their table.

"All right babe?" he asked eyeing the man.

"Y... yes fine Tommy," Roslynn smiled, glad to see him.

"Well, I'll be off then love, see you later," the man said, with a wink. Tommy clocked the man's wink and the jealousy came over him again.

"Don't fink so mate," he said, sitting down next to Roslynn.

"Wotever mate!" the man said, smiling as he walked away.

"Who was 'e?" Tommy demanded.

Roslynn's head snapped back.

"I beg your pardon?" she said.

"That bloke who was 'e?" Tommy replied.

"I haven't got a clue. He just came out of the back room and spoke to me, that's all," Roslynn said, trying to dismiss the conversation they'd had, and sipped her juice. She turned up her nose.

"This juice tastes really funny. It's not off, is it?" she asked taking another sip.

"Nar babe. 'Ave ya 'eard anyfing from the band?" Tommy replied, trying to change the subject.

"Just some thudding that's all," Roslynn said, taking another sip of her drink.

"Oh, well! Probably just warming up at the moment. Come on babe, drink up and I'll get ya another one," Tommy said, gulping down his pint.

By the time Roslynn had, had three "juices" she was feeling very relaxed and her confidence came flooding back.

"Fancy creeping into the back room and seein' the band?" Tommy asked a now grinning Roslynn.

"Okay, but just let me use the ladies and I'll be ready," Roslynn said, trying to stand.

"Wow there! You okay babe? Ya seem a bit wobbly."

Tommy asked grinning.

"Just fine Tommy," she grinned back.

"But I could do with another one of those juices if you wouldn't mind," Roslynn slurred, then giggled.

"Comin' up babe!" Tommy said, rubbing his hands together. 'One more and she'll be so pissed she won't be able ta stand let alone fuckin' walk!' he thought.

By the time Roslynn had returned from the ladies, Tommy had got the drinks in and was standing waiting for her.

"Ready babe?" he asked, handing her, her drink.

"Yep!" she giggled.

They walked over to the door at the back of the bar. Tommy opened it a crack and peered in. the noise was deafening to Roslynn's alcohol-laden ears, but she had a huge cat-like grin on her flushed face. Tommy put his finger to his lips, signaling for her to be quiet and Roslynn giggled.

"Shhh!" Tommy said seriously, knocking the smile from her lips. They crept in.

There were five of them in all. Two were playing the guitar. One on the drums, One singing and playing the harmonica. The fifth was sitting down, legs crossed tapping with the beat, with paperwork all over the place.

He jumped up.

"No! No! No!" he shouted. "Try it again guys, this time from the top!" he turned and saw Tommy and Roslynn standing there.

"Yeh, wot can I do fer you people?" he asked, walking over to them.

"Nufing mate just wanted ta watch the guys play! Their No.1 fan, me!" Tommy gushed at the man.

Roslynn giggled at the way Tommy was acting all starry eyed and big smiles.

"Oh, really?" the man said, smirking.

"Well, I'll tell you what, you can sit in fer 5 minutes an' then yer have ta go, ok?"

"Brilliant mate! Cheers fer that," Tommy said, taking Roslynn's hand and leading her to a set of chairs in the corner.

"All right with you guys if they sit in?" the man shouted as they stopped playing.

The band looked up from their conversation and nodded, not taking much notice of the two strangers.

"Right, ready guys, like before and from the top again," the man shouted as he went back to his seat.

The drummer counted them in and Roslynn watched unthawed, time had no meaning any more, she was totally engrossed in the music. They'd played about three songs, when the man sitting down, jumped up waving a sheet of paper.

"Okay, which one of you is responsible fer this?" he screamed at them poking the paper with his finger.

"What?" they said, grinning and looking innocent.

"Don't you fuckin' 'What!' me," the man shouted back.

"This," he said, shaking the piece of paper at them.

"Say's 'ere that we've got to pay for the repairs on last week's venue! Fuck me! I stay away one fuckin' night and it costs me fuckin' hundreds! No wonder you lot never said much about it!" the man screamed at them pacing up and down getting redder and redder. Tommy sat on the edge of his seat.

"'Ere mate," he interrupted the man

"Maybe I can 'elp ya," he said.

"What!" the man stared at him.

"You don't know anything about it!" he said.

"Well, it sounds ta me thatcha need someone ta do the repairs. On the cheap I mean!" Tommy grinned.

"May...be," the man said, coming to a halt in front of Tommy.

"What can ya do?" he asked.

"Oh, name it mate, I'm fuckin' red 'ot!" Tommy said, proudly standing up.

"Well, give me yer number, an' I might give ya a call," the man said, calming down a bit.

The guys in the band saw Tommy had calmed things down. so started playing out some new chords to each other.

Tommy motioned to Roslynn to get up. Finishing the last of her drink, a drunk Roslynn tried to stand as lady-like as was possible.

"'ope ta see you guys later," Tommy gushed at the band members, and taking Roslynn's hand walked her out the room and into the bar.

Tommy was on a high.

"Yer're a good omen babe! Yer know that?" he said, twirling Roslynn around.

"Now, another drink, or do ya wont ta get outa 'ere?" his blue eyes shining.

"I think I need a bit of fresh air actually Tommy," she said, in a heady voice.

"Okay babes, 'ome it is!" Tommy said, dragging Roslynn to the door. As soon as the air hit Roslynn everything spun. Tommy put his arm around her waist.

"Com'on babe let's getcha back!"

"Okay Tommy," she said, snuggling into him. Tommy smiled to himself. John was right. It is his day taday!

The two of them staggered into the site, laughing and giggling with each other until they reached their vans.

"Well, ya gonna invite me in?" Tommy asked, leaning against her van.

"Why not!" she said, with a grin.

Roslynn went in first, Tommy followed closing the door behind him. As soon as the door shut Tommy grabbed Roslynn around the waist and started to kiss her neck. Roslynn gasped but then relaxed turning until their lips met. Roslynn pulled away first and stared at him.

"I just want you to know I've never been in this situation before! I'm not always like this!" she cried.

Grinning, Tommy pulled her to the bed.

"I believe ya babe. I believe ya!" he said, kissing her mouth hard.

Roslynn didn't resist as she lay down beside him. Tommy ran his hands down her body making her tense every muscle he touched. Kissing her neck he ran his hands up to her breasts, he could feel her nipples getting harder through her top. She wasn't wearing a bra, and Tommy felt his cock jump to life. Taking her hand he placed it over the bulge in his trousers. Roslynn hesitated for a moment before running her hand up and down Tommy's now hard cock. He pushed her top up and released her breasts, pinching one nipple and sucking the other. Roslynn arched her back towards him, breathing heavily. Tommy ran his other hand down to her trousers, tugging at the fastening.

43

Roslynn had both hands working on his jeans. He pulled open the zip and slid his hand down to Roslynn's crotch, he ran his fingers over her, she was so wet. He ripped down her trousers. Roslynn sat up, kicking off her garments. |She turned to Tommy and tugged at his jeans, releasing his rock-hard cock from its confines.

Tommy watched as she stared at his manhood. He sat up and pushed her down on the bed. Leaning over her he kissed her mouth, letting his hand run over her body. She clasped her hands around his neck pulling him down towards her breasts again. Tommy, not having to be told twice, started to lick, suck, and pinch her now very erect nipples. Running her hands down his back and around to his front, she cupped his balls in one hand and was stroking his cock with the other. Tommy thought he would explode if she carried on much longer! He pushed her legs open with his other hand and started to run his fingers over her wet lips, he ran his tongue down across her belly to her bush burying his face in her mound. He rubbed her clit with his finger. Roslynn gasped and Tommy could feel her swelling under his touch. He pulled her lips apart and ran his tongue along the inside, circulating and sucking her clit. Roslynn's body shook as he slipped his fingers into her hot, wet, hole. She started to pump onto his now dripping fingers. Roslynn guided his cock into her mouth running, her tongue around the tip and then down the shaft. Tommy grabbed her hair and pushed his cock to the back of her throat. She could feel it pulsating in her mouth, she sucked hard. Tommy let out a groan. Pulling his cock away from its snug fit, he rolled in between her legs pushing them apart with his knees. He rubbed the tip of his cock along her wet lips until he found her hot, wet, hole, pushing himself as far into her as he could. Roslynn shuddered as he started to pump into her, grunting with every stroke.

Roslynn opened her eyes, visions of her husbands' friends, hands all over her jumped out from every angle of the little van. Catching her breath and with all the strength she could muster, she pushed the oblivious Tommy off her.

"What the fuck! I was nearly there then!"

Roslynn jumped off the bed grabbing a sheet.

"Get out! Just get out will you!" she yelled.

"Are ya 'aving a laugh? Yer can't just stop like that! Don't start getting' all frigid on me, yer fuckin' bitch!"

"Just go, will you!"

"Too fuckin' right I will!" Tommy said, pulling on his jeans and shirt.

He turned to her and put his hand in his pocket, took out some money and threw it on the table.

"Yer not get the full rate yet babe," he said, slamming the door behind him.

Roslynn slumped on the bed, Tommy's scent still on her. Floods of tears ran down her face as she could hear Tommy shouting.

"Fuckin' prick tease! What's the matter, didn't give ya the fuckin' money up front? Fuckin' bitch!"

She put her hands to her ears to stop the barrage of abuse.

Reaching his van Tommy punched the side panel of his beloved Bedford in frustration.

"Fuckin' bitch!" he groaned nursing his already swelling knuckles.

As he entered his van the phone was ringing.

"Yeh?" he barked down the receiver.

"That Tommy?" the voice on the other end asked.

"Yeh 'ow's this?" Tommy was not in the mood for chit chat.

"My names Ben Rooke, we met out the back at "The Admiral"."

"Yeh mate, wot can I do fer ya?" Tommy said, in a lighter tone.

"Well, I might have some work for you. Interested?"

"Sure. Wotcha want done?" Tommy asked, very interested. 'Could be the break I need,' he thought.

"Oh, just some repair work, and a bit of decorating," Ben replied.

"Sure, no problem," Tommy said, looking at his swollen hand.

"When and where?"

"Well, I need to go over what damage the guys done! An' what damage was already there when they arrived! Could we meet tonight and go over the details and maybe work out a price?"

"Yeh sure mate. You tell me the place an' time an' I'll be there!" Tommy said, quickly.

"Well, I know it's a unusual place, but do you know "The Club"?"

"Know it?" Tommy said, with a smile.

"Who don't!"

"Good. I'll let the girl on the door know you're coming, and I'll see you there say 9.30 ta 10 o'clock tonight. That okay with you, only it's the only time I can fit you in?"

"Fine mate! But ya don't 'avc ta worry about lettin' the girl know. Got me own key, ain't I!"

"Fine, fine," Ben said, a little put out.

"Tommy, can I ask you one question before I go?"

"'Corse mate, wot is it?"

"How the fuck did you get a key when they're like rocking horse shit?!" Ben asked, his curiosity getting the better of him.

"Well, practically built the fuckin' thing by me self didn't I!" Tommy said proudly. "The keys one of me perks fer maintaining the place. Not that I ever use it mind! Don't 'ave ta pay fer it when I wan' it!"

"I'm sure," Ben said, replacing the receiver.

Tommy sat down, lit a cigarette, smiled, and wondered what the look on Roslynn's face would be when he walked through "The Club's" door tonight.

Roslynn stopped rocking herself and uncovered her ears. Nothing. All was quiet. She peered out of the window, there was no one in sight. To say she felt confused was an understatement!

"Is this the way it's going to be the rest of my life!" she cried as she thought about what had happened and wondered if Tommy was right.

"God I can't stay here!" she said to herself.

She opened the cupboard and pulled out the two bags she'd brought her clothes in. She shoved her clothes back into them, and got dressed. She threw the clothes that the girls had given her back in their bag, grabbed her key to "The Club", picked up her belongings and went out the door.

Chapter 4

Bet saw her walking up to the bungalow. 'Shit! She looks rough!' she thought, as Roslynn rang the bell.

"I'll get it," Bet shouted to whom ever was listening.

"All right lovey? Wanna come in?" Bet asked, clocking Roslynn's bags.

"No, I won't Bet. I've just come to give you your keys, and the girls stuff back."

"Why's that?" Bet asked, a concerned look on her face.

"Because, I think I've made a big mistake and, and…" the tears came flooding back to her.

"Com'on in ya come lovey 'ave a nice cup o' tea, an' you can tell old Bet all about it!" Bet said, pulling Roslynn in and shutting the door. "Ere we go!' thought Bet.

"Sit yer bum down there," Bet said, leading Roslynn into the front room.

"Bung the kettle on Jedd!" she shouted from the doorway, and walked over to where her cigarettes were.

"Right lovey ya gonna tell me wot's up?" she said, plopping into the chair opposite Roslynn.

"There's nothing to tell…" Roslynn said through sniffs.

"Really?" Bet said raising her painted eyes and taking a puff on her cigarette.

"Yes, really!" Roslynn said, trying to compose herself.

"I think I've just made a big mistake that's all. Don't get me wrong, you've all been wonderful to me it's just…"

"Ere we go!' Bet thought, 'story time!'

"It's just wot, lovey? Can't be that bad, surely!" she said with a smile.

"Well, it is, and I'd rather not talk about it if you don't mind… I'm sorry if I've let you down tonight, but I just can't!" she said breaking off her speech with a huge sniff.

"There, there lovey!" Bet said, handing her a box of tissues and checking the clock above her at the same time. It was 4 o'clock. 'Three an' a 'alf hours at the most! I'll kill that fuckin' Tommy when I get me 'ands on 'im!' she thought.

Bet had been in her front room when Tommy and Roslynn came back to the site earlier that day, so she had a good idea what had happened.

"That fuckin' Tommy 'as 'e upset ya lovey?" Bet asked as Jedd walked in with the tea.

He placed the two mugs down and looked Roslynn up and down, smirked and walked out again.

"It's not just him," she whispered.

"Wanna start at the beginning lovey?" Bet questioned.

"I doubt you'd believe me even if I told you," Roslynn sighed.

"Try me, 'eard 'em all me!" Bet smiled at her.

Nodding Roslynn started playing with a piece of cotton that had come loose from her shirt.

"It started when I was fifteen," she said, looking at the floor.

"My father met a very rich man, who had a liking for young girls. This man offered to buy me from my father for an extraodinary sum of money.

My father, realising he wouldn't have to work again agreed. I had no say. I just had to go with him."

Bet nodded and lit another cigarette from her previous one.

"Go on lovey," she said.

"Well, I went to live with this man as his wife. He was very eccentric and he liked to live his life in a time gone by. I mean it's 1969 not 1869! His house looked like something out of Sherlock Holmes! He'd leave me for days just wandering around the house. I was never allowed out except in the back garden, and I wasn't allowed to contact my family. Not that I wanted to after what my father had done.

"He'd hold parties," Roslynn said with a vacant look.

"I had the clothes he'd want me to wear laid out, and I would have to sit in my bedroom in them until he called me down," Roslynn swallowed hard.

"I'd pray that he'd forget me but he never did!" she said

with a sigh. "I'd have to go down to the room where he and his cronies were..." tears spilled down her cheeks.

Bet got up and went over to Roslynn, sitting on the arm of her chair, she put her arm around the girl.

"Your doin' fine lovey, just fine."

Roslynn looked up at her and blew her nose, sniffing she said.

"I'd be paraded around the room with them all glaring and grinning at me. Then my "husband" would sit down in his big leather chair, light one of his huge cigars and give a nod. That's when I would have to stand in front of him and his "friends" and strip. Oh God! God! God!" she cried running her shaking hands through her hair. My Husband would then make me stand in front of each one of those men and say "This is what you can do if you buy your wife!" He would then put me over his knee and spank me with his cane, sometimes he'd rape me with it! In front of his friends! When he'd had his fun, he would then tell his friends that they could use me at their will! Because when he'd had enough he could always go and buy another one! I was no more to him than a piece of furniture!"

Bet leaned out of her cloud,

"So you ran away," she said, quietly nodding.

"Yep, that's right," Roslynn said with a sad smile.

"But I messed up so I'm going to have to move on I'm sorry Bet."

"But why's that lovey?" Bet asked frowning.

"I had a date with Tommy today. We went to the "Admiral" do you know it?" Bet nodded.

"Well, it was all going well and I was enjoying myself, anyway Tommy came back with me because I felt a bit funny. I still think that juice was off!" Roslynn said, frowning at how the drink made her feel.

Bet gave a knowing smile. 'That Tommy's a cheeky bastard!' she thought.

"Well, we started kissing, and one thing led to another, and I have to admit, it felt good for the first time ever! Then all of a sudden the visions of my "husband" and his friends came rushing back and I froze! I told Tommy to go and he got angry threw some money on the table as if I was some common whore,

49

and slammed out calling me a prick tease! God I can't face him again. Really, I can't!" Roslynn felt completely deflated, sobs racked though her body. "And do you know the worst bit? I really liked him!"

"You leave Tommy to me lovey," Bet said in a motherly way. 'I ain't gonna lose this one, because of that fuckin little prat Tommy! Fuckin' spikin' 'er drinks, an' trying ta get 'is leg over! Don't waste much fuckin' time d'ya Tommy me lad!' Bet thought with a smile saying.

"Listen where else ya gotta go lovey? Don't worry about that little shit, I'll sort 'im out. Now drink ya tea an' 'ow's a nice 'ot bath sound? You'll feel a lot better. Then you an' me can do ya face 'n' 'air, getcha ready fer tonight. Com'on, whatcha say?" Bet said giving her a warm smile.

Roslynn smiled. She felt a lot better telling some one. She felt safer. Yes, that's it! She hadn't felt that feeling for so long she'd forgotten what it was like.

"What am I going to do Bet?" she asked, blowing her nose.

"MY advice ta ya lovey is USE IT!" Giving her a knowing smirk. "Now com'on bath!"

Roslynn got up still wondering what Bet meant. It was 7.30.

"There ya are lovey. Yer look a million dollars! Now, let's getcha ta "The Club". We got a big group in tonight an' I need ta see Rose," Bet said, applying another layer of lip-stick to her already stained lips.

Bet and Roslynn walked through the door at a quarter to eight.

"There you are babes!" Rose greeted them.

She was wearing an all-in-one green cat suit, with a plunging neckline to her waist, and backless to her bottom. She'd thrown a long chiffon scarf around her not so young neck, and the ends danced on her bottom when she moved.

"We're nearly set. The girls are just adding the last coat of lippy!" she declared, pouting her own lips.

"Go an' see them if you want Ros. Then I can have a quick word with Bet."

Roslynn took her cue to leave them and wandered into the girl's room. As she entered, she could smell that same funny smell that was in the pub earlier. Jude saw her first and jumped up.

"Over here Ros," she called, motioning her over to where the five girls that helped her yesterday were sitting.

"Thought you'd done a runner, didn't we girls?" Jude said, taking a puff on her cigarette and passing it to Sal. Roslynn smiled.

"Oh! I came with Bet, she let me have a bath at hers,"

All five girls fell about in fits of laughter.

"What?!" Roslynn asked grinning at them.

Rose led Bet to her office. Shutting the door behind her, she went and sat behind the big oak desk.

"So?" she asked.

Bet sat opposite her, lit a cigarette, blew out the smoke with pursed lips and said.

"Fuckin' unbelievable, but I fink she's stayin', ain't got anywhere else ta go that's fer sure! Now wot's 'appening tanight, looks like the girls are ready ta party!"

"We've got a group of ten coming in at about 8.30, a work party can you believe? They want to talk business first in the bar for an hour, then have the girls sent in. That okay with you Bet?" Bet nodded. "I've told the girls it may be a very late night, but we'll make it worth their while,"

Bet nodded again.

"We got anyfing else on tonight?" she asked, putting her cigarette out.

"Got a couple of the girls up there at the moment with there regular gents. Apart from that unless we get them coming through the door, it's just the party."

"Fine, ain't bad fer mid week is it? Make sure yer get 'em ta pay fer the girls before. An' we'll send 'em the bill fer drinks, smokes, an' any extras after. Talking of smokes 'ow much yer get in fer tonight?" Bet asked, always the business woman.

"Six ounces, all weed. Sal's already rolled a few for the girls to get them in the mood, and bagged up the rest in eighths."

"Fine, sounds good, thanks Rose. Now I'll just go an' see the girls, get some sounds on, an' try out some of the gear!"

Bet and Rose stood up.

"See ya later lovey," Bet said, lighting another cigarette before she walked out the door.

Bet walked into the girls' room to find Roslynn looking a lot more relaxed, sitting in a cloud of purple smoke.

'That's a girl!' She thought grinning to herself.

She walked over to their table. Sal passed Bet the cigarette, she took a lung full of the smoke in passing it to Kel.

"You girls ready fer work?" she asked exhaling the smoke.

"You bet Bet!" they all said, collapsing into a fit of giggles.

"Oh, yeh very funny! Move yer arses," Bet said grinning.

Roslynn stood with the others, and they all dispersed in different directions.

Walking to her room, Roslynn couldn't help but giggle. 'I don't know what's in the girls' cigarette! But it was a lot better than that old bastards cigars!' she thought, stifling another giggle.

Roslynn had just got herself organised, when the key went in the door. She greeted the party of ten men as they entered, taking their coats and giving them each a box. As the boxes came back Roslynn gave each gent a key. Then led them, like a mother duck and her chicks into the bar. When Roslynn returned she was kept busy with the regular gents leaving, and the odd one or two popping in to see if their favourite girl was busy or not.

She was just saying goodbye to one of their regulars when, all of a sudden a huge roar came up from the bar as the music started up. The men were all cheering and whistling. Curiousity got the better of her, and she walked over to the bar room.

Peering in she saw Kel. She was doing an erotic dance with a chair in front of the men. Roslynn leaned against the door frame and watched.

Kel started to take her clothes off and throwing the garments at the men. The noise was so loud that Roslynn could hardly hear the gyrating music being played. Kel was now down to her panties, as she knelt on the chair facing its back, her panty clad backside level with the men's faces. Very slowly she eased them down over her very taut cheeks. The men's eyes nearly popped out on stalks. When she had pushed them down to her knees, she sat down on the chair, lifted her legs to her head and pulled them off, throwing them at one of the men. The red faced man grabbed them and put them in his top pocket.

Kel then ran her hands down the insides of her legs parting them as she went. When she reached her crotch she dramatically threw an arm up, palm facing the ceiling. One of the other girls placed a banana in her hand.

There she was stark naked, sitting on a chair, her legs in the air slowly peeling a banana. The men urged her on. She threw the skin behind her, and clasping it like an erect cock, started to lick and suck it. She then took it out of her mouth and pushed it between her legs, and started to move the banana in and out. Roslynn couldn't believe her eyes!

Kel motioned to one of the men to kneel in front of her and eat the banana from her fanny. The man buried his head between her legs, while Jude started to rub and kiss her nipples.

A noise behind Roslynn made her jump and turn from the scene.

"Good little mover that one. Wotcha doin' babe, takin' notes?" It was Tommy.

Roslynn went white.

"How long have you been standing there?" she hissed.

"Long e'nuff babe, long e'nuff," Tommy said, walking past her and into the bar, joining in with the clapping as he went. He sat down next to the man Roslynn recognized from the pub earlier that day. The man put his hand out to Tommy and they shook.

He motioned Tommy to a quieter part of the bar and Roslynn went back to her room seething.

Ben and Tommy sat down and one of the girls came over to take their order. When she'd gone Ben said.

"I'll make it quick as, as you can see I'm entertaining some heavy business here tonight and it could be the break the guys need," talking to himself as much as Tommy.

Tommy nodded and said,

"Well, mate, tell me wotcha want done, an' I'll give ya a rough estimate now. Then we'll both know wot's 'appening!"

Ben told Tommy what work was needed and Tommy started grinning,"'ad a good time then didn't they?" he said.

Ben gave him a scornful look.

"That may be, but it's my job to get them gigs! An' if they go smashing up each venue I get them, we'll soon run out of places ta play! Look, tonight could mean a record deal in the near future, so I can't stay talking long."

Have another drink, work out a price an' when you can do it, and I'll give you an answer tonight."

Tommy nodded. This could be the start of something good if he played his cards right and did a good job. Maybe this Ben could give him some good contacts!

"Right, I'll be getting back to the group. When you're ready we'll sort out the business. Oh! And after please feel free to stay, could get a bit hairy! And we've got some first class weed Rose sorted out for us," Ben said laughing.

'I know she has,' Tommy grinned to himself, as Ben walked back to the group of men and Kel.

Ben had already decided, after looking at Tommy's work in the club, to hire him, but he wasn't going to tell him that!

Roslynn sat in her room seething.

"How dare he!" she hissed to herself.

"He knows nothing about me! I'm glad I stopped him now," she said tidying the boxes.

Suddenly there was a commotion out in the hall.

Roslynn peered out of the doorway to see Bet and Rose bending over one of the girls.

"She'll 'ave ta go ta 'ospital Rose," Bet said.

"Fuck me! 'ow many times do I 'ave ta tell these girls not ta run in them fuckin' 'eels! They're supposed ta be fuckin' ladies not fuckin' footballers!" Bet said standing up and lighting a cigarette.

"Give Jedd a ring an' get 'im over 'ere, 'e can take 'er. That all right wif you lovey?" Bet said to the girl sat crying on the stairs.

She nodded wiping her eyes. "Good. Now move yer arse off the stairs an' let's getcha on that chair by the door," Bet said, pulling the girl to her feet, and helping her to the chair. Rose came rushing back.

"Jedd will be here in a couple of mos. You all right babes?" Rose asked the girl, stroking her hair.

The girl looked up at the two women.

"I'm truly sorry Bet, Rose. I won't ever run again!" she said through sobs.

"Well, yer 'ad ta learn the 'ard way didn'tcha Carol?" Bet said.

"'Ere Rose can I 'ave a word?" Rose followed Bet into the girls' room.

"Right!" Bet said. "We're completely fucked now all the other girls 'ave been given the night off an' we're one down! Whatcha suggest?" she asked.

Rose sat at the table rolling a joint. She looked up at Bet.

"How about we get Ros in to serve the drinks, then Annie can step in for carol, she's better anyway!" she said, licking the tobacco papers.

"Umm!" Bet said, taking the joint Rose had rolled and lighting it.

"Not a bad idea that. We'd 'ave ta loosen 'er up a bit. Ya know give 'er a glass of wine, an' a couple of puffs of this!" she said passing the cigarette back to Rose.

"I don't fink she'll be shocked wif wot she see's! she might be a bit jumpy wif our gents though wif out a bit of Dutch courage in 'er!" she said, remembering the tale Roslynn told her earlier that day.

"Never know could be the makin' of 'er!" Bet finished.

"Go sort it Rose will ya. I'll be in the office wif Doughy if ya need me."

With that she took the joint back and ambled off to the office, leaving Rose with the job of telling Ros her position had been changed for the night.

Rose wondered what Roslynn had told Bet about her past, and smiled as she rolled another joint. 'Whatever it was Bet would tell her later, she always did!'

Bet liked Rose to know everything about her girls, so any problems that came up never became a shock, and could be dealt with quickly!

Rose lit the cigarette and went in search for Roslynn. She found her just shutting the door on Carol and Jedd.

"Ah Ros! Just the person," Rose said blowing the smoke from her joint at her. Roslynn turned inhaling it.

"What's wrong Rose?" she asked, waving the cloud of smoke away.

"We've got a bit of a problem, all the other girls that work have got the night off. So we're one girl down due to Carol," she said, taking a long drag of the joint and purposely blowing it in Roslynn's direction.

"So Bet has decided you've got to serve the drinks so Annie can take over from Carol. Okay?"

Roslynn eye's widened with horror as a vision of Tommy grinning jumped out at her.

"No I can't do it! Rose please! Don't make me please!" Roslynn pleaded. Rose threw her hands in the air.

"I only run the Club. Bet has the final word seeing it is hers. And if she wants you in the bar, then in the bar your going! No arguments babe sorry. Now go tidy yourself up, you've got five minutes!" she said, blowing another cloud at Roslynn.

This time Roslynn inhaled the smoke deeply into her lungs. Exhaling, she looked at Rose and smiled not saying a word. She didn't smoke herself but she loved the feeling that the joint gave her when she had inhaled it earlier, so she said.

"Rose will you show me how to smoke one of those?" pointing to the cigarette in Roses hand.

"Sure thing babe, I'll roll one up while you're sorting yourself out. And before you go in the bar, me an' you'll have a little smoky and a glass of wine! What you fancy, red or white?"

"I don't know!" Roslynn said. "I've never had any wine before!"

Rose whistled.

"You telling me the truth?"

Roslynn grinned and nodded. "But I've got a funny feeling I'm going to like it!" she said, walking out the door. Rose shook her head 'How does Bet do it!' she said to herself smiling, as she followed Roslynn.

Roslynn saw Rose sitting at a table in the girls' room. She walked over and saw two glasses of red wine on the table and a joint, perfectly rolled, waiting for her in the ash tray.

"Sit down babe," Rose said pointing to a chair.

"You ready for your lesson?"

Roslynn sat down and put both elbows on the table and said, "Show me what you do!"

Rose picked up the joint and put it to her lips. She took it out straight away when she saw Roslynn really didn't have a clue.

"Watch me! You light it, and suck on the end, now you inhale through your mouth, not your nose. Like this," she said.

Rose lit the joint, and a swirl of purple smoke drifted to the ceiling. Rose blew out the smoke.

"Now you try," she said handing Roslynn the cigarette.

She placed it to her lips and inhaled. As she did she started to cough. Rose handed her the wine.

"Here drink this," she said forgetting Roslynn had never tried it before. She sipped the wine giving another little cough then beamed at Rose. The joint had hit her immediately. She felt great!

"This is nice," she said, raising her glass to her lips again.

Rose grinned. 'A couple more puffs and that glass of wine will just about do the job!' she thought. Taking another puff on the joint, she passed it back to Roslynn, who put it straight to her lips and sucked. She didn't give a damn about Tommy sitting in the bar any more!

"You ready to face the hounds?" Rose asked, looking at her watch. Roslynn growled and they both laughed.

Rose led a now very high Roslynn into the bar room. Things had moved on since Roslynn had been watching from the door. The girls were entertaining the gents as they knew best. They were all in different stages of undress and some of the men had their shirts and trousers off.

Roslynn's glassy eyes scanned the room. Kel, having finished her show, was now straddled on one of the gent's laps, her head thrown back so her hair touched her backside, her arms around the gent's neck. The man was running his hands all over her body, he had his head buried in Kel's breasts sucking and biting her nipples. Not being able to control himself any more, the man pushed down his trousers and let his cock spring out, then lifting Kels arse up with both hands, he pulled her cheeks apart and lowered her onto his throbbing cock, pushing her down as hard as he could. The man shuddered. Kel brought her head up grinning and kissed the gent's neck.

She saw Sal and Misty together. Sal, her long slender body almost ghost-like, on the floor, her legs spread as far as they could go! Misty was on top of her, her head buried in between them, her dark bottom hovering just above Sals face. Sal had an empty wine bottle and was fucking Misty with it.

Big Jude was on her hands and knees in front of a gent, her glossy black hair swaying as she moved her mouth up and down a bulbous cock. Another guy came up, dropped to his knees and entered Jude from behind. Every time the guy slammed his cock into her the other man filled her mouth.

Annie, whose job Roslynn was taking over, was laying spread eagled on a table, her head hanging over the edge licking another girl's pussy, while one of the gents fucked her. He pulled the other girl over on top of Annie, pushing her head down to where his cock was thrusting into Annie. The girl immediately started to lick Annie and the gent, while Annie fingered her!

Roslynn had never seen anything like it! A couple of the other girls she didn't know, were bent over tables, sucking one gents cock, while being fucked by others. Roslynn felt her nipples tingle and she felt wet between her legs.

"Well, what do you think?" Rose asked, standing behind her and watching the scene.

"I think," Roslynn said, "I need another drink!"

Rose laughed and led the way to the bar. Roslynn felt confused at how very conspicuous she was, being dressed!

She looked about the room at all the girls and gents either half or completely naked. The funny thing, all the girls seemed to be enjoying themselves! Rose handed her a glass of wine and smiled.

"Welcome to the wonderful world of "The Club," she said holding her glass up and watching Roslynn's reaction.

Roslynn held up her glass.

"To the girls," she said grinning.

'Yet again Bet was right!' Rose thought smiling to herself as she took a sip of the wine.

In the corner a gent raised his hand for the waitress to take his order.

"That's you babe. Go take his order, and remember if he gropes you, please smile! If you can do this, I'll give you a bonus this week for your trouble, how's that?" Rose added quickly as she saw Roslynn's face drop at the mention of the gents groping her. The air was thick with the smell of sex, sweat, and cannabis.

Roslynn moved slowly over to the corner where the fully-clothed gent was sitting with his back to the room. Roslynn thanked the heavens that the gent wasn't naked.

"Yes, sir. May I take your order?" she said, smiling at the mans back. Roslynn's smile soon faded when she saw who the man was. Now it was Tommy's turn to smile.

"Well, well, well, thought you weren't one of old Bet's girls!" he said with a smirk.

"Liked the idea of getting paid did ya? Well pr'aps we can finish wot we started. Wotcha say babe?" he said as he ran a finger down over her breasts.

Roslynn stepped back as if she'd had an electric shock.

"I don't think so buddy," she said icily, her body reacting the opposite way as her nipples pushed through the flimsy material where Tommys finger had been seconds earlier.

Tommy grinned, nodding towards her breasts.

"Well, it looks ta me like they don't agree wif ya," holding up his key he carried on.

"You mine tonight or ya promised ta someone else babe?"

Roslynn was about to tell Tommy what she thought of him when Bet's advice, "Use it lovey" suddenly made sense. Looking at Tommy she grinned.

"Look, I'm sorry about today, maybe tonight I can make it up to you," It was out before she had time to think.

"'Ats a girl!" Tommy said grinning back. "Now 'ows about a drink? Oh, an' a bag of weed babe," he said, not looking at her as he spoke.

Roslynn smiled politely.

"Bastard," she hissed under her breath, as she turned and headed to the bar. Rose had been watching the whole thing and smiled to Roslynn when she reached the bar.

"Got him on the run, haven't you? Look, if you want to carry on with him it means, whatever the gent wants the gent gets. Understand? But I must say our Tommy's never used his key before except to do the repairs!"

Roslynn gave Rose a weird look as she nodded. Taking a gulp of her wine she looked over to where Tommy was sitting.

"I had a talk with Bet today about my problems, and her advice was to use them to my advantage. But I don't know how!"

she said, taking a deep drag on Rose's joint.

"Just do what comes naturally babe, an' I'm sure you'll do fine," Rose said, taking the joint from her.

"Okay," Roslynn said in thought.

As she headed back to Tommy she gave Rose a wiggle of her backside.

"That's my girl!" Rose called after her laughing.

'Here we go!' she thought, 'out of the frying pan into the fire as they all do!' she smiled shaking her head.

"I'd best go and let Bet know what's going on," she muttered to herself, slipping off the bar stool and wandering out the room.

Some of the girls had taken the gents to the other room or upstairs, and Rose could hear their giggles above the music as she went in search of Bet.

Tommy looked up as Roslynn returned with a tray containing their drinks and a bag of weed. She sat down opposite him and smiled, placing the drinks on the table.

"I don't fink so babe. Get yer arse over here so I can play!" he said, licking his lips.

Smiling, Roslynn did as she was told, remembering what Rose had just said at the bar. Tommy turned to her as she sat down and slid his hand down her top, pinching her nipple.

Roslynn flinched with the pain!

"That's pay back time fer earlier taday babe! Now let's party," he laughed.

Roslynn wished she could run from the room, but it was her decision no-one else's. So she accepted the pain, and toasted Tommy.

The room was nearly deserted by the time they'd drunk their drinks and smoked the joint Tommy had put together. Roslynn felt as if she was floating and couldn't stop grinning. Her cheeks ached. She draped her arm around Tommy's shoulder, and ran the other one down his chest. He relaxed back in the chair, as Roslynn ran her hand down to the bulge in his trousers.

Tommy suddenly jumped up, startling her.

"W... what?" she asked surprised.

He grabbed her arms, pulling her from the chair. As she

stood up he ripped open her top, and her breasts fell out, bouncing with the force. He then spun her around and bent her over the table holding her with one hand. He undid his trousers, letting them drop to the floor, then pushed her skirt up, spreading her legs and rammed himself into her. Roslynn gasped, then started to push her backside out so he could get deeper and deeper with each thrust. Tommy suddenly stood up straight and shuddered, Roslynn lay across the table, not moving.

"Jeesus, I needed that!" Tommy said in a husky voice, pulling away from her. Helping her to her feet, he kissed her full on the mouth, pushing his tongue deep inside. Without saying a word, he pulled up his trousers and walked out of the room.

Roslynn was left standing there, her top pulled apart, exposing her breasts, skirt bunched up around her waist, and her mouth open. She really didn't know how she felt. Part of her was excited, horny, and happy, the other part confused and degraded.

She looked around the room, rearranging her clothes. Bet was sitting at the far end of the bar, a cloud of smoke about her head. Putting her glass down and lighting another cigarette from the previous one, she watched Roslynns every move. Her painted lips curled at the edges, as a slow clap came from her hands.

"Not bad lovey, wotcha getting dressed fer? All me girls are in the ov'er room earnin' loads of cash. Fancy 'avin' a go wif 'em in there?" she said, pointing her thumb over her shoulder.

Roslynn couldn't believe her ears and Bet saw the look of shock on her face.

"Oh, com' on lovey after wotcha told me taday yer used ta men seein' an' usin' ya. 'ow's about turnin' the tables an' get paid fer it?" Bet said, raising her glass to her lips.

"Because!" Roslynn cried, going over to where Bet was sitting. "I'm not a whore!" she spat, pulling her top around her.

"Well, I'm fuckin' glad of it!" Bet said, pouting her lips and putting her head to one side.

"Cos nev'ers any of me girls!" her mouth growing into a big grin.

"They're just me gents 'ostesses! You seen any of them gents payin' me girls?" she said laughing.

Roslynn took a joint from the bar and lit it smiling at Bet.

"No. I can honestly say I have not seen any money pass hands," Roslynn giggled. She sat down next to Bet.

"I think if I'm going to have a go, I need another drink and a few pointers. I mean! I couldn't do what Kel does!" she said hopping on to the stool and sticking her backside out at Bet and pouting her mouth. Bet slapped her arse, and laughing, said.

"Oh! Old Bet thinks you'll do just fine. Now get this down ya," passing Roslynn a glass of wine.

"Then get yer arse in there," pointing behind her again.

Roslynn looked as if some one had slapped her.

"What the fuck's wrong now," Bet asked sternly.

"I can't go in there naked by myself!" she cried.

"Oh! Fuck me! Yer can be shagged over a table in a bar! But ya can't walk into a fuckin' room naked, pleeese!" Bet cried in a shrill.

"Tell me yer jokin' yeh? Fuckin' 'ell Roslynn, you walk in that room an' one of the gents'll be straight over, no probs!" Bet said, nodding her candy floss head. Roslynn thought about it.

"Are you sure Bet?" she asked biting her nails.

"As sure as shit comes out yer arse lovey," Bet said.

There was silence in the room, then both women collapsed over the bar laughing.

"'ere," Bet said.

"Wrap this round yer neck! Yer won't feel so bare then!" handing Roslynn a scarf.

Roslynn dissolved on her stool, wrapping the scarf around her head in a turban. Bet was laughing so much that she fell off her stool in a heap on the floor.

"'ere Ros."

"What?"

"Fuck off next door, me fuckin' belly's killin' me! I can't laugh any more it hurts!" Bet cried nursing her stomach.

Stripping off her clothes, leaving only her heels and scarf on, Roslynn flicked her head at Bet, stood up straight and walked towards her future.

"That's me girl!" Bet shouted after her, getting up from the floor. Tommy walked down the path of "The Club" with a stern look on his face.

"That'll teach the bitch. Fuckin' mess me around earlier!" he muttered to himself. Walking up to his van and kicking it.

"Fuckin' piece of shit!" he growled, as he entered his caravan. Sitting at the little table he poured the last of his party seven into a mug, lit a joint he'd rolled and left in the ash tray inhaling deeply, he leaned back in his seat and ran his hand through his dark hair.

"Why'd I do it?" he muttered

'Because she's a prick tease, that's why!' the voice in his head answered.

"Yeh. But…"

"No 'But'," the voice said.

Tommy exhaled and let the drug flood over him.

"Whats she expect workin' there!" he suddenly burst out.

"Fuck, wot a mess!" he sighed.

"Least I got meself a fair job outa tonight! Could be yer lucky break Tommy me boy. Yeh!" he answered himself.

The vision of Roslynn across the table jumped before him, and a mixture of emotions welled up. Tommy felt confused, no one else had ever had this effect on him. "Love 'em an' leave 'em" that was his motto. 'So why am I wanting to find out more about this one? She ain't the cutest bit of arse I'd ever 'ad! All the same I want more!' he thought, sighing deeply.

Roslynn's debut went well and Bet was pleased. She knew a good one when she saw one. But even she was amazed at how Roslynn fitted in and what a natural she was.

Chapter 5

Roslynn woke, stretched, and looked at her watch on the side.

"Shit!" she cried, as she jumped out of the bed.

"Jude's going to kill me!" she said, pulling her dress over her head and looking for her keys.

Grabbing them off the little table she went out the door and headed down the path to "The Club".

She rushed into the girls' room and over to where Jude and Annie were waiting for her.

"Where the hell you been? Yer look like shit babe," Jude said grinning at her.

"Absolutly nowhere! I just overslept that's all. I haven't even washed yet, so I wasn't any more later than I am now!" Roslynn cried.

"Wondered what the stink was," Annie laughed, giving her a peck on the cheek.

"Well, seeing you've cocked me whole time table up. How's about we 'ave a coffee first, an' I'll do Kirsty's hair while you 'ave a shower an' you can 'ave her spot?"

"Sounds good to me," Roslynn grinned.

"Are you sure she won't mind?"

"Nar, she ain't doin' anything else today, an' she ain't working tonight unlike us poor souls," Jude replied, rummaging through her bag of rollers.

"Coffee all round girls?" Annie asked the room, jumping off the table and heading to the kitchen.

"Doughy's been baking again, so I'll bring us something nice back," Annie called, as she had her hand on the concealed door.

"Where she get all her energy from?" Roslynn grinned, shaking her head.

"Speed, girl, speed!" Jude sighed, and they both laughed.

Roslynn had been with Bet and her girls for just over six months now, she'd only seen Tommy a few times getting in or out of his van. They hadn't spoken since that night, and she was glad of it.

Roslynn had done a lot of growing up in the past months. She wasn't as naive as she had been and Tommy didn't bother her any more.

She'd been put on duty with the five girls she'd first met. The six of them had made quite a reputation for themselves and 'Ros' as she was now called, had come into her own on the entertainment side.

So when Bet decided to expand the business to doing private parties outside "The Club", the six girls had constant bookings.

Annie came bursting through the kitchen door, a look of panic on her face.

"You'll never guess who's in the office with Bet 'n' Rose," she blurted out.

"Well, they'd better be more fuckin' important than our coffee an' grub!" Jude moaned, grabbing her throat and looking up from her rollers into Annie's stricken face.

"Oh, Christ Jude that's coming. It's Ros I was talking to not you anyway!" Annie cried, sticking her tongue out at her.

Jude put her hands on her hips,

"Ooh, get you!" she said, flicking her hair and grinning at the miffed Annie.

"Oh, fer fucks sake Annie spit it out, will ya," Jude cried.

Ros felt the panic rise in her. Who was in the office that would concern her?

"Well, I was helping old Doughy out by taking a tray of coffee up to the office to save her legs bless her…"

"Annie who the fuck's in the office?" Jude butted in.

Ros really didn't know if she wanted to find out who the stranger was in the office. Panic waved over her again, 'could he have found me?'

"Tommy, that's who! Tommy," Annie blurted out.

Ros let out a sigh of relief.

"Yeh darlin?" Tommy, all suited and booted, stood there grinning at the entrance of the girl's room.

Annie dived towards the kitchen her face scarlet. Ros stood motionless with her mouth open, leaving Jude to do the talking.

"How ya doin' Tommy? 'Haven't seen ya fer wot about six months ain't it?" she said, giving Ros a knowing look.

"Er yeh! Must be babe," Tommy grinned looking over at Ros.

"Been a bit busy lately, got meself a bit of a side line ain't I,"

"Oh, yeh?" Jude said, trying to sound interested.

Ros stifled a giggle and turned away from them.

"Yeh in fact, just sorted out some business wif Bet 'n' Rose seems I'll be seein' ya later!" he said, smirking.

"Really?" Jude looked amused at him.

"Yeh, booked ya fer tonight actually!" he said smugly turning in the door way and catching Ros' eye.

"Later babe, later," he laughed walking out. Jude looked at Ros

"You all right sweetie? ya look a bit pale," she said, holding her cold hand.

"Well, he sure knocked the smile off our faces didn't he?" Annie said, coming through the kitchen door with a tray of coffee and pastries. Jude looked at Ros and they burst out laughing.

Rose breezed into the girl's room just as Jude was putting the finishing touches to Ros' hair.

"All right babes, where's the others?" she asked, plonking down in the chair opposite the two women.

"Fine," Ros said, turning to see the sides and back of her hair.

"Like it?" she asked, twirling round.

"Looks bloody cracking babe! Only I need to have a word about tonight."

Jude caught Rose's glare, saying,

"They're about somewhere, I'll go give 'em a shout," And putting her comb down, walked out the door before Ros had a chance to open her mouth.

Rose motioned Ros to sit down again and shouted at Jude,

"Bring some coffee back with you babe."

Jude put a hand back around the door frame, gesturing that

she'd heard her.

"I'm glad it's just you an' me Ros, I wanted a quiet word with you about tonight," Rose said.

"Oh, really, why?" Ros smiled, resting her arms on the table, an amused look on her face.

"Well," Rose said, clearing her throat and lighting a cigarette. "Bet has done a bit of business with Tommy, for Ben. An', 'erm, he wanted you girls for tonight! I told him there's no way, but when he said Ben would pay double Bet agreed I'm afraid. I'm really sorry babe, I really tried, honest I did!"

"Why's that Rose?" Ros asked, not at all concerned.

"Well, you haven't seen him since 'that night' have you? An' to then be told you've been cancelled from one booking to do this! I didn't think you'd take it very well, that's all," Rose said, looking concerned.

"Oh, Rose, you big softy, thank you. You know if it wasn't for our Tommy, I wouldn't be here today. You see, Tommy was the last man to ever use me! Since then I've been in control and tonight will be no different! In fact, I think I'm going to quite enjoy myself!" she said, a big grin spreading across her face, knowing that Tommy was in for a shock.

Rose just stared at her, open-mouthed, her gaze fixed as the other five girls came bustling in, their voices coming to a crescendo and abruptly stopping as they saw Rose's face.

"What's the matter darling?" Sal asked, as she floated over to Rose, putting a comforting arm around her.

"Oh! There I was worrying about this one, an' seems I was wrong!" she said pointing to Ros.

"What?!" they all asked.

"Oh. No, nothing," Rose said smiling.

"Right, grab a seat girls, I want a word about tonight," she said giving Ros a knowing look and a slow smile.

Jude brought a tray of coffee in, and sat on the table.

"Okay, I'm ready now," she said passing the cups round.

"Right, we've got a change of plan tonight. Kirsty and her girls are going to take on your job 'cause Bets got you booked for some band. I can't remember their name, but I do know their local lads. I want you all tastefully tarted up! Sounds like it's gonna be one hell of a party! A late one as well. Now, anyone

67

got any questions?" Rose asked business like.

Ros grinned. She still couldn't get used to this side of the business, it seemed so far removed from what they actually did.

"Yeh, I have," Kel piped up.

"Where we going tonight?"

"It's a house party. Something about the manager buying a new one," Rose told them.

"No. Is it still on the island or wot?" Kel said, giggling.

"Oh, I see what you mean! Yes, still on the island, somewhere along the sea defences. Now, anything else?" she said, looking at the group.

They all shook their heads.

"Right!" Rose said.

"Get your arses in gear, you've got," she said, looking at her watch, "about 4 hours to get yourselves and your gear together.

A car will be waiting for you at 9 o'clock. Oh and girls… Get some food inside you. I reckon you're gonna need it tonight," And getting up, she threw a bag of grass on the table with a wink.

"Enjoy ladies. Enjoy!"

"God bless you Rose," Misty said, retrieving the bag and getting a pack of papers from the tray permanently on the tables.

"How's about a neat one girls?" she grinned.

Rose shook her head and left them to it.

By a quarter to nine the girls were sitting having a drink with some gents in the 'bar room'. The 'Club' was starting to come to life with scantily clad girls flitting from one gent to the other, touching and kissing them on their way.

Bet walked in and motioned them to the bar, taking her usual spot at the end. The girls excused themselves and walked over.

"You girls ready?" she asked.

They all nodded. Bet waved to the topless girl behind the bar.

"Top the girls' drinks up, Lucy. An' go get us a couple of joints, there's a lovey," then turning to them she said, "Right you lot, yer me best girls an' I don't wont any trouble comin' back from tonight! Understand wot I'm sayin'?" they all nodded, and Bet continued. "I got a lotta money on ya so give 'em a fuckin'

68

good show an' there'll be a bonus fer ya."

Again they all nodded mutely.

"Fuck me! Wots wrong wif ya tonight? Cat got yer tongues?" Bet burst out.

"No, we're just listening to the boss," Kel piped up smirking.

"Fuckin 'ell that's a first!" Bet said putting her hands to her chest and giving them a shocked look. The girls started laughing.

"Now, give me the last of that joint an' piss off, the lot of ya," she said in a loving way.

"Yes mam!" they all said saluting her and heading for their tools of the trade in the hall.

Rose came out of the box room with one of the gents.

"Wow! Look at you lot!" she whistled.

"Behave yourselves girls, and have a good night," she said, blowing them a kiss.

Nine on the dot there was a knock on the door. Jude opened it and came face to face with a grinning Tommy.

"You ready girls? I gotta say 'ow classy you all look. Wot a treat!" he grinned looking them up and down.

"Fuck off, you prick," Jude hissed.

"Ooo. Now, now!" he laughed patting her backside as she passed him.

"Arsehole!" Jude glared at him.

Tommy shrugged his shoulders and turned to the others as they filed past. The last one was Ros. Tommy's face dropped. He didn't know she would be with them.

"Well, you did say later babe!" Ros said, her head held high as she walked past.

Tommy's face was a picture. Jude and Annie (the only ones that knew about Ros and Tommy in the bar) looked at her and put their thumbs up and Ros grinned.

'I'll show you, you bastard, just you wait and see.' She thought as she got into the car.

Tommy hadn't expected to pick Ros up. He didn't know she was one of Bet's girls. He was totally taken aback, the way she was acting towards him. As if nothing had happened between them.

"Just you wait Tommy, my boy," Ros said under her breath,

and grinned.

Tommy pulled up outside a newly built house. They heard the thudding of the music in the car.

"Nice house. Whose is it?" Misty asked Tommy.

"He's the manager of the "Jug Band". You girls 'ave met 'im before. Ben's 'is name. Nice guy, been doin' some work for 'im, 'aven't I," he said proudly

"Done all the décor in there!" he pointed to the house.

"An' I've built a fuckin' great studio out the back fer the guy's ta practise in. That's why we're 'avin this party! Bit of a 'ouse warmin', ain't it," he said, getting out of the car.

"Com'on girls, let's go party!"

As they walked down the drive past the numerous cars Tommy said,

"We're gonna go round the back so you girls can get sorted in the studio,"

Annie looked up at Sal and raised her eyebrows.

"Seems our Tommy's got himself well in here, don't it," she whispered, Sal stifled a giggle.

They walked down the side of the house and came across a door. Tommy took hold of the handle and opened it.

"Ere ya go ladies!" he said, standing back to let them past.

As they walked in the sound of music became muffled. Shutting the door behind him, Tommy said.

"The guys 'ave laid on some puff 'n' booze over there, 'elp yerselves. I'm just gonna let 'em know yer all 'ere," And walked out another door into the house.

The girls looked around them. The room had a distinctive electric smell about it. There were three guitars and a set of drums laid out surrounded by speakers, wires, papers and mics. Laying on a bar stool by the front mic was a harmonica. Kel danced around everything, running her hands over the drums. She plonked down on the kits stool and very dramatically kicked her legs up in the air.

All five girls collapsed in a fit of giggles.

"Trust her ta take the nerves away," Annie said, dabbing her painted eyes so as not to smudge anything.

Jude broke away from them

"Right girls, let's get ourselves ready an' see what that puff's like!" she said, unzipping her bag. They all followed suit.

They had just poured themselves a drink when there was a commotion outside the door, and Tommy burst in eyes shining.

"Girls, meet Ben and the band," he said, waving them in.

Five guys tumbled into the studio all shouting and pushing each other.

"Well, wot we got here, Tommy, old son?" one of them said grinning at the girls.

"These young ladies are your entertainment for the night," Tommy cried, always the showman.

"Well, go on Tommy!" another guy laughed.

"Wots yer names girls?" he asked.

Sal glided over to the man.

"I'll introduce you," she breathed.

"I'm Sal, and this is…"

She motioned them closer and they stepped forward when she said their names.

"Well, ladies, shall we?" Ben the manager said, pointing to the party now in full swing.

"Yeh! come on my darlins, let's see whatcha can do," the fourth guy said, grabbing hold of his cock through his trousers.

The fifth guy pushed him.

"Wot's the matter John, lost sumfin 'ave ya?" he asked slapping him on the shoulder as they went through the door laughing.

The girls followed them out, Ros being the last. Tommy grabbed her arm and she swung round to him, eyes glaring.

"What Tommy?" she asked, through clenched teeth.

Tommy stepped back.

"Hey, only gonna say ya looked good enough ta eat!" he said, hands in the air.

"Ha! You'll be lucky!" she spat, and walked through after the others.

Tommy grinned.

The girls walked in. The room was dimly lit and heavy with smoke. The beat coming from the stereo was throbbing through the room, everyone was having a great time.

The five guys stood in a line with their hands in front of them. Tommy turned down the music and everyone turned to the line of men. When they had every one's attention Tommy put the pulsating music on for them.

The five men spun round to the girls pointing their fingers at them and fell away. Everyone cheered.

A skimpily dressed Sal and Misty stood in the middle with Jude on one side, clad in black leather and little Annie on the other side dressed in nothing, but a dog collar and a chain lead attached to Jude's hand.

Kel and Ros were behind them. Kel on her chair, and Ros, on her table.

The sight was quite orgasmic to the viewers.

Sal kissed Misty full on the mouth and the others followed cuc. Annic dropped to her hands and knees crawling over to Jude who was waving a cat-o-nine tails about her body in a seductive way. As Annie reached her, Jude held the lead tight pulling Annies head back and whipping her bare backside. Annie squirmed and her nipples went hard. Jude straddled her and kissed her upturned mouth, pulling at Annie's nipples. She then turned herself around to face Annie's arse and slapped each cheek. Grabbing them in both hands Jude spread her cheeks and ran her tongue down Annie's crack to her lips and back again. Annie pushed her arse out more. This stopping Jude, got Annie a whipping again. She pulled Annie up to a standing position and bent her over, wrapping the lead around Annie's legs so she couldn't move Jude then strapped on a dildo and fucked Annie from behind.

Kel was well into her routine with her chair, loving every minute of it. She got so turned on watching the other girls that she got off her chair and went and joined Jude and Annie.

By this time Sal and Misty had taken their clothes off and were exploring each other's bodies. Misty had Sal laid on the floor, and was kneeling over her sucking her breasts and rubbing her clit and lips. Sal had her back arched on the floor one hand dissapearing up Misty's hot wet fanny and the other pulling on her nipples. Misty could stand no more and straddled Sal burying her pussy in her face, while Sal was licking, sucking, and fingering Misty. Misty was fucking her with a candle up her backside.

Ros looked over and seductively winked at Misty. She was

laying on her table knees up with her legs apart and back arched her huge tits wobbled as she writhed about one hand opening her lips the other fucking herself, she brought her fingers to her mouth and licked them. Then reaching behind her she produced an empty champagne bottle and ran it down between her breasts and across her stomach, arching with its coolness. She ran it down between her legs, running its neck along her lips. She was so wet the glass glistened. She took the bottle to her mouth and licked her juices while turning over and squatting on the table. Her silver heels giving her height, she ran the bottle down her body again and slid it between her love lips lowering herself on to it, pumping up and down her arse cheeks and tits bouncing with the force. She leaned forward, grabbing a full bottle, shaking it as she bounced. She undid the foil and wire with her teeth, she then replaced the empty bottle with the full one gripping the cork with her fanny lips. Slowly she eased it from the bottle, the golden liquid exploded up into and over her. She dropped to her knees and released the cork from her swollen wet lips.

Tommy was totally gobsmacked! His mouth hung open. Ros turned to face him, slid across the table on her belly taking the cork in her mouth, then keeping her eyes on him, swung herself off the table and walked up to him. Releasing the cork from her teeth she dropped it in his top pocket, pecked him on the cheek and sauntered away to join the others, who were just unfolding a square plastic sheet. They laid it on the floor and reached for their baby oil. They got into pairs and squirted the oil over each other's bodies, rubbing it in all over. The girls formed a circle on the floor, every other girl laid on the plastic their partner dropping to their hands and knees facing their feet. Sliding on to the girl on the floor the girls started to explore one another.

A cheer roared from the room. All six girls grinned and were soon joined by the audience. As the girls' show came to an end, the party started to really get hot. The music throbbed into the night along with the girls and party movers.

Chapter 6

A week later Tommy couldn't get the vision of Ros out of his mind, his thoughts swung from wanting her badly, to absolute disgust at what he saw. He couldn't take much more; she seemed to take up most of his waking life, and all of his sleeping, when he could!

"Right, I can't take much more of this. I've gotter go an' 'ave a word wif 'er," he said, looking at himself in the mirror.

"Fer fuck sake Tommy get a fuckin' grip will ya!" he muttered.

He paced up and down his little caravan and looked out of the window over to Ros's van. The curtains had been drawn open. Tommy knew this meant she was in. She always drew her curtains when she went out even in the day. He ran his hands through his hair and lit a cigarette taking a deep drag.

"Right 'ere goes," he said grabbing his keys and walking out the door he marched over to Ros's van. Taking a last drag, he flicked his cigarette away and knocked on the door.

Ros opened the door, the smile on her face disappearing when she saw Tommy standing there.

"What do you want Tommy?" she asked, her hands on her hips.

"You Ros! I want you!" he blurted out not thinking.

Shock registered on his face when he realised what he'd said. Ros stood there just as shocked, her mouth opened to say something but nothing came out.

They seemed to stand there for an age. Tommy broke the spell.

"God! Shit! I'm sorry Ros. I didn't mean it. Well I did mean it, but I didn't mean it to come out like that!" he rushed looking like a little boy who'd been caught stealing some sweets.

Ros raised an eyebrow.

"I think you'd better come in don't you?" she said standing aside to let him past.

Tommy meekly walked past her into the van and sat down at the table his head in his hands. Ros sat down opposite him, amusement danced over her face.

"What's all this about then Tommy?" she asked clasping her hands together and resting her elbows on the table.

Lifting his head Tommy looked into her eyes.

"I want you Ros," he said quietly.

"Oh, really?" Ros replied, a smirk on her lips.

"Yes really!" Tommy said, raising his voice.

"Since the party. And before! All I can think about is you. And I don't want anyone else to have you. I want us, you 'n me ta get married!"

As soon as he'd said it his little voice slapped his head 'Fuck why'd ya say that! Where the fuck did marriage come from! Wotta tosser.'

Slowly Tommy looked up at her, he didn't expect to see such a look of horror though.

'Shock yeh. But not horror!' he cried inside.

"Look I'm not that bad Ros. I've saved enough money fer a down payment on a nice little 'ouse I've seen. Needs a bit of work though! But that ain't no problem, an' work's comin' thick an fast since I done that bit of work fer Ben!"

"Woo Stop! Stop right now Tommy!" Ros said laughing at him.

"Whatcha laughing at?" he said looking hurt.

"Well, for a start, we're not even seeing each other and your talking of marriage! Secondly you don't want anybody else to have me! That's my job, my life. And thirdly I couldn't give a shit what you want Tommy!" she spat at him.

"W... What! But Ros," Tommy pleaded.

"Don't you fucking 'but' me. You! You were the one that pushed me overboard in the first place! It's your fault I'm what I am! You were the last person who'll ever use me, do you know that? Ha! I suppose really I should thank you. I like what I do and I'm good at it! Plus I earn plenty of money. So you see you can't offer me anything I haven't already got!"

She finished, a victorious smile spreading across her face.

"What about love?" Tommy said slowly.

"I mean it Ros. I think I loved you the first time I saw you before all the hair, make-up, clothes and attitude," he said, swallowing hard and fighting the tears threatening to burst through.

"I know I did a terrible thing to you, and God knows I've regretted it ever since. I was just so confused."

"Oh! So that makes it all right then does it? You were confused. Ha! I suppose it never crossed your mind as to wonder why I stopped you, did it?" Ros sobbed

"What was it Tommy, your male ego get hurt, did it?" Ros yelled through sobs.

Tommy put his head down, grabbing Ros's hands.

"I'm really sorry Ros, really I am. I don't know what else to say!"

Ros pulled her hands from him and curled up into a ball. Sobs wrecked her whole body as she rocked herself.

Tommy jumped up and went round to her, putting his arm around her and burying his face in her hair.

"Oh, baby, I'm so so sorry," he said, clasping her face in his hands. He kissed her forehead. Ros just stared at him, her eyes a million miles away, tears flowing down her face. Tommy gathered her up close to him, rocking her slowly. Everything seemed to have come to a crescendo that day and Ros couldn't hold it in any more. The tears kept coming, Tommy held her tightly until her sobs subsided.

It was getting dark when Ros finally lifted her head up. Tommy looked deep into her eyes and smiled.

"How ya doin' babe?" he whispered.

Ros gave him a slow smile. Her body ached and her head was thumping.

She ran her fingers under her eyes; they were sore and swollen.

"God, I feel like shit!" she said, licking her lips and sitting up.

"Want me ta stick the kettle on?" Tommy asked, getting up and moving to the little stove.

Ros nodded, stretching her back and neck.

"Please I'll have a coffee," she croaked.

"Okay babe, one coffee comin' up!" Tommy said busying himself with his task.

He put the two mugs on the table and sat down opposite her.

"Ya sure yer okay babe?" Tommy asked tenderly.

"You know you ain't so bad Tommy me boy!" she grinned, nodding.

Tommy bowed his head, "Why thank you mam' nice of ya ta say so," he said looking up at her and they both laughed.

From then on they were an item. Tommy showed Ros the little house he wanted and she agreed with the potential it had. He opened Ros's world to music and they'd go and watch Tommy's favourite band play in the local pubs. Tommy was getting more and more involved with the band and they spent some wild nights with them. The only thing they disagreed on was Ros's job. Tommy hated it, but was careful when the subject came up. Ros would tell him he had no right to tell her what to do, and if he didn't like it he could go. So he seethed inwardly and bore it. They bought the little house together and moved in. Tommy spent every spare moment he had on it, and with Ros's flare for interior design they had the house done in no time.

Tommy threw himself onto the sofa grinning from ear to ear and looked around. Ros padded in wearing one of his shirts, a bottle of wine in one hand and two glasses in the other.

"Finished babe! We've finally finished," he said, making room for Ros on the sofa.

She plonked down and tucked her feet under her, passing a glass and pouring the wine. She put the bottle down, turned to Tommy and said.

"To us!" clinking her glass with his and taking a sip.

Tommy sat forward and started to roll a joint while Ros tipped her head back and closed her eyes. She felt safe, happy and secure, but the best of all in love.

Tommy bit the end of his joint and lit it.

"I've been thinking babe, you an' me we've been tagever wot nearly a year now an' I was wondering if ya fancy getting hitched, wotcha say?" he said, grinning at her.

"I don't know Tommy," she sighed, sitting up and taking the joint he passed to her.

"I mean if we got married, would you expect me to give up my job?" she asked, taking the smoke deep into her lungs waiting for it to hit her brain. Tommy looked at her. She knew he hated what she did.

"Look babe, you know how I feel about it, but like you say it ain't any of me business, an' the only time I'd definitely want ya ta give it up is when we 'ave a kid." He grinned shyly.

"Kid!" she cried open mouthed.

"You haven't even asked me if I want any kids yet!"

"Well, do ya?" Tommy asked, amusement in his eyes.

"Well, I don't know. I haven't given it much thought. Maybe, later, but not right now," she said, seriously.

"So will ya babe?"

"Will I what?" she asked.

"Marry me Ros. Marry me?" Tommy asked, on his knees in front of her.

"Yes, I'll marry you Tommy," she said, wrapping her arms around his neck, pulling him to her and kissing him full on the mouth.

"Thank you darlin', thank you," he breathed into her ear.

Roslynn was lying in bed eyes staring at the ceiling. Tommy was peacefully sleeping beside her. Panic gripped her again. 'What am I going to do? I'm already married! How am I going to tell him? God I'll have to tell him everything. Shit I can't! It's no good, I'll have to say I've changed my mind. Fuck he'd want to know why then wouldn't he. Fucking hell what a mess!' She slipped from the bed and got dressed. 'I've got to get away from here. I've got to think,' she told herself.

She picked up her handbag, scribbled 'At the Club' on a piece of paper, leaving it on the table for Tommy and walked out the little house. Memories of running away flooded her head.

Ten minutes later she was walking down Bets path. She rang the bell.

"Ros wot's wrong? It's fuckin' four in the morning!"

"Tommy asked me to marry him," she blurted out.

"What! Well, I'm fuckin' pleased fer ya! But fuckin' 'ell, Ros, look at the bleedin' time!" Bet yelled through a yawn not at all happy for her broken sleep.

Ros collapsed in a flood of tears and Bet opened her door

waving her through. She shut the door and looked to the heavens. 'Ere we go!' she thought.

"Go through to the kitchen an' stick the kettle on will ya?" Bet said, yawning again, heading for the toilet.

"I'll 'ave a coffee, won't be a tick," she called, disappearing through a door. Ros went through the motions as if she was a robot, her mind swimming. Bet sat on the toilet wondering why Ros was so upset. Then it dawned on her.

"She ain't told 'im 'as she!" she muttered to herself.

She walked through the kitchen door reaching for her cigarettes on the side. Lighting one, she sat down flattening her tangled hair with both hands. Taking the cigarette from her mouth she watched Ros pouring the water and said.

"You ain't fuckin' told 'im 'ave ya?"

Putting the mugs on the table, Ros shook her head, tears flowed down her face. "What am I going to do Bet? I can't tell him the truth!" she cried flopping onto a chair and taking the cigarette offered.

"Well, ya can't tell 'im a fuckin' lie! The past always 'as a funny way of catchin' up wif ya! Believe me I should know!" Bet said, lighting another cigarette from her last.

"Nar, I fink the best fing ta do is tell 'im," she put her hand up to stop Ros and carried on, "Yer can always divorce the old bastard, fuck knows yer got enough against 'im! Unless... Unless you ain't even married! Listen Ros did ya 'ave a service or sign any papers? Mainly the papers. Think real 'ard Ros, 'ave ya ever 'ad ta sign anyfink? Cos if I know anyfink about dirty old bastards like 'im it's 'is money that signed everyfink, know wot I mean?" she said, raising her eyebrows.

"I can't remember ever signing anything, but I was only 15 Bet! Jesus, he paid my dad for me!" Roslynn's voice rose to a shrill.

"Yeh. But was there any paperwork?" Bet demanded.

"No, no, I don't think so," Ros sighed.

"Well, the only way ta find out is give the registrar a buzz an' see what they say."

"I can't Bet. I can't ask if they know if I'm married or not! They'd think I was mad!" she cried in a panic.

"Well, I'll fuckin' ring 'em," she said, passing Ros a pen and paper.

"Now give us yer parent's address an' the old bastard's. Oh an' all their names, an' I'll see wot I can do. Might take a couple of days. Yer can keep Tommy sweet fer a while can't ya?"

"I'll try. Thanks Bet, I owe you," she said, feeling a bit more in control. She'd never even thought that perhaps she wasn't even married, and she gave Bet a smile.

"Right emergency over I'm fuckin' off to bed. Wot cha gonna do?" Bet asked, lifting her ample backside off the chair.

"I left Tommy a note saying I was at the Club so if it's okay with you I'll go and have a bath an' slip in with one of the girls."

"Okay wif me lovey," Bet replied stretching.

"Now sod off, I'll talk to ya later," she said, walking as far as the bedroom door with Ros. "Yer can see yerself out can'tcha lovey?"

"Sure and thanks," Ros said giving her a peck on the cheek and heading for the door.

"See you later," she whispered closing the front door quietly.

Tommy woke to an empty bed. He sat up with a jolt.

"Ros babe, where are ya?" he shouted, expecting to hear her in the kitchen, making a drink.

When no answer came he got out of bed and nipped down the stairs to the kitchen.

"Ros, where the fuck are ya?" he called, getting a little worried.

He walked past the little Formica table and the piece of paper with her note on it caught his eye. Reading it he looked at the clock on the wall, it was 7.30. Running his hand through his hair and reaching for the kettle he wondered why Ros had gone over so early. He couldn't remember her saying anything about going last night. Tommy grinned slowly to himself remembering the night. 'Didn't give the poor cow a chance really, did ya old son!' he thought smiling to himself and shaking his head.

"I'll give 'er a ring before I go ta work," he muttered throwing his coffee spoon in the sink and picking up his cigarettes, he wandered into their little front room, grinning as he stepped over their scattered clothes. Ros didn't sleep when she left Bets and was sitting at the big old kitchen table in "The

Club" dressed in a pink ostrich feather trimmed robe, both hands clasped around her tea mug, staring in to space.

"Fuck me girl, you look like a flamingo contemplating laying an egg!"

Doughy bustled in, fastening her pinny around her.

"W… what?" Ros jumped and Doughy pointed to her robe.

"Oh, I know," Ros said, smiling, looking down at the robe.

"It's all I could find when I got out of the bath."

Doughy frowned.

"You been 'ere all night?"

"Pretty much," she said, putting her cold tea on the table and giving her a slow smile.

"Fancy a 'ot one?" Doughy asked, pointing to her mug and lighting the huge stove, blowing out the match, saying.

"You an' Tommy 'ad a row?"

"No, he asked me to marry him," Ros replied, miles away.

Doughy mouthed an 'O', turned and busied herself making a fresh pot of tea, leaving Ros to her thoughts, wondering if she should congratulate her or not. Putting the large teapot on the table she went to the fridge to get the milk.

"Oh, fuck it! That bloody milkman 'ad better 'ave been!" she cried waddling off to the front door.

As she passed the stairs Rose was just on her way down, her long wavy red hair swinging as she descended.

"Good morning Doughy, and how are we today?" she asked breezily.

"Oh, I'm fine thanks Rose. More than I can say fer Ros," she said raising her eyebrows.

"What'd you mean Ros?" Rose asked, looking a little shocked.

"Is she here?"

"Been 'ere all night from wot she said," Doughy replied.

"Right… She okay?"

"Nar, not really Tommy asked 'er ta marry 'im," Doughy explained shrugging her shoulders.

"I thought she'd 'ave been 'appy but she ain't!" she carried on. "She's in the kitchen staring into space. Don't think she's up the duff do ya?" Dpughy asked concerned.

"No not Ros but I'll go an' see her. Give us a five minutes

would you darling?"

"Yeh fine with me," Doughy replied

"Better take the milk with ya. If 'is been that is," she said walking to the door fingers crossed in the air.

Rose smiled. Doughy was like everyone's Nan and she truly loved the old girl. She took the milk from her and headed for the kitchen.

Ros looked quite a sight in that robe and Rose couldn't help but smile even though Ros looked so bloody miserable.

"I know," Ros said, looking up and seeing Rose walking in.

"It's all I could find," she said, holding her hands up.

"I didn't even know we had such an awful thing on the premise," Rose replied grinning.

"Well, actually, it was a toss up between this one or a canary yellow one we've got!" Ros said trying to act as if nothings wrong.

"Well?" Rose said, putting the milk down.

"Well, what?" Ros said frowning.

"Why have you been here all night Ros? I know Tommy asked you to marry him. I thought you'd be pleased not bloody suicidal!"

"I am! It's just that I needed time to think."

"About what? I take it you said yes?"

"Well, yes, I did," Ros smiled.

"But it's a big step, that kind of commitment," she answered trying to hold herself together.

"No, it isn't!" Rose said, eyeing her.

"You live with him now, pay the mortgage together, the bills, sleep in the same bed, you do every thing a married couple do but with out the piece of paper. How much more commitment do you think there's gonna be after you're married eh? None. I'm telling you. Look, Bet told me a long time ago about your, shall we say 'problem'" Rose held up her hand for Ros to let her finish.

"And l really don't think you were actually married to him."

Ros sat there open mouthed.

"W… when, how long ago, how long have you known?" she gasped.

"Oh, the day after you told Bet," Rose said waving the

subject away.

"But I asked her not to tell anyone. Who else knows?" she demanded.

Rose sighed deeply.

"No one, just Bet and me. Look stop worrying no one else knows honest Ros, and the only reason Bet told me was because if that old bastard came looking for you I'd know what to do. So for fuck sake calm down will you.

Panic rose in Ros.

"Has he ever come here?"

"No, that's why I personally don't think you're married to him," Rose replied, putting a hand on Ros's feather clad arm.

Ros looked at her.

"Bet's going to find out for me in the next couple of days. I've got to keep Tommy from knowing anything Rose. I mean it!"

"Hey, I didn't even let you know did I?" Rose said smiling.

"No, I suppose not," Ros said, playing with the feathers on her robe.

"I'll tell you what though. If any of the girls see you in that get up they'll know something was up!" Rose said, flicking the feather collar.

"Oh, I don't know, it's kinda growing on me," Ros said, pouting.

"Yeh like the plague! Go up to my room and get yourself dressed before the girls come down an' see you. Wear what you like, but not that!" Rose retorted with a grin.

"Oh, an' Ros. Stop worrying, will you or Tommy will think something's wrong. By the way, does he know where you are?"

"Yeh, I left him a note," Ros said getting up from the table

"Just to let him know I'm here. Listen if he rings tell him I came in early to help Doughy would you. Only I don't think I can speak to him at the moment, without him knowing some things wrong."

"Okay darling. Now get your arse upstairs!" Rose said slapping her backside.

"Go on move it!"

As Ros headed for the door Doughy put her head round it.

"Okay ta come in now?" she asked raising her eyebrows to

Rose.

"Of course it is," Ros said giving her a peck on the cheek as she passed her.

"Thought I'd do pancakes this mornin' you want some?" Doughy asked as she bustled into her kitchen.

"That sounds bloody wonderful," Ros called from the girls room "I'll be a couple of minutes," she said, heading for the stairs.

"What's all that about?" Doughy asked Rose, waving her thumb over her shoulder.

"Oh, nothing that Bet can't handle darling," Rose said, leaning against the now hot stove.

"She can certainly handle most things!" Doughy muttered, as she retrieved the flour from the larder.

"True," Rose agreed.

"Want a hand with anything?" she asked, changing the subject.

Doughy had been with Bet and Rose long enough to know she wasn't going to get anything else out of Rose, so she said,

"No love. Old Doughy can manage thanks. But you can give the girls a shout for me an' tell 'em breakfast in twenty minutes, save me old legs."

"No problem I'll do it now," Rose said, knowing it was her cue to leave Doughy to it.

She picked up her mug, topping it up as she went, and headed out the door to give the girls a call and go over some paperwork in her office.

Rose had just opened the desk drawer and pulled out her papers when the phone rang. She picked it up knowing it would be Bet and shouted

"Hang on Bet, I'm coming…" as she dropped the phone to catch the papers about to fall on the floor.

"Hello."

"Mornin' ta you. You all right?" Bets voice crackled through the phone.

"Yeh, I am, Ros isn't though," Rose said, getting straight to the point of the call.

"No, I know. That's why I'm callin'. She still there?"

"Yep getting dressed. You want her?"

"No. Fuckin' got me up at fuckin' four this mornin', 'avin' a panic up about 'er an' Tommy. She told ya 'e asked 'er ta marry 'im?"

"Yes she did Bet, I also told her I know about her problem. What the fuck you going to do?"

"Well, I'll 'ave a phone round first an' see wot I come up wif. Recon the old bastard's me best bet, wotcha fink?"

"Jesus! I don't know Bet!" Rose said, concerned.

"Well, the way I see it 'er old man ain't gonna say much is 'e? So the old bastards next on me list. Might as well go straight to the 'orse's mouth so ta speak," Bet said with confidence.

"Then if I don't get any joy from 'im I'll 'ave ta ring the registrars, but I don't fink they're gonna tell me much if ya know wot I mean."

"Well, yes, I even said that to Ros this morning, I really don't think she's married. Bet have you thought about speaking to her mother?

"No I 'ave ta admit I ain't but I will. The old bastard's proberly gone an' bought another one by now ain't 'e?" Bet answered, giving a little chuckle down the phone.

"Fuckin' sick bastard," she said as much to herself as to Rose.

"Well, let us know when you've found out anything won't you. And Bet, be careful," she said.

"Always am lovey, always am!" Bet said, putting the phone down.

Chapter 7

Two days later, Ros was a bag of nerves. She hadn't heard a thing and Tommy kept asking her if she was all right. Every time he asked panic would well up inside her and she'd want to scream at him to leave her alone. She was glad she was working every night that week and only saw him for a couple of hours when he came home from work each night.

She was pacing their little house like a caged animal, unable to keep her mind on any thing else longer than five minutes. The phone rang and the blood rushed from her face. She seemed to take forever to get across the front room and pick it up, her voice barely a whisper.

"H… hello," she felt is if her lungs were going to explode.

"Ros that you?" Bet asked, straining to hear the voice on the other end.

"Y… yes," she whispered, flopping to the floor and reaching for her cigarettes.

"You all right lovey?" Bet asked in a concerned voice.

"Yes I've just been waiting in a daze for you to ring, an' now you have, I don't think I want to know," she rushed, taking a puff of her cigarette.

"Is it bad?" she asked changing like the wind.

Bet, hearing that Ros was in a bit of a state, said,

"Look lovey I'm sendin' Jedd over ta pick ya up. That okay wif you?"

"Okay, fine. How long?" she asked, not really listening.

"I'll tell 'im now, so in a couple of mins all right?"

"Yep, fine," Ros said, replacing the receiver, not even saying good-bye.

Looking at the phone Bet put it down and yelled.

"Jedd get yer arse round ta Ros's, pronto mate!"

Jedd grunted, picked up the car keys and went out the back

86

door.

Picking up the phone again Bet rang Rose at "The Club".

"Rose, it's Bet. Couldn't come over 'ere could ya? Jedd's just gone ta get Ros, an' I fink she's gonna freak when I tell 'er wot I've found out."

"I'm on my way," Rose said, and putting the phone down grabbed her jacket and headed for Bet's.

Rose turned up just as Ros was getting out of the car. She looked pale and drawn.

"Come on babe," Rose said, taking her arm and leading her around the back to Bet's kitchen.

"Let's get you inside, shall we?"

Ros didn't say a word, she simply let Rose lead her. It didn't even dawn on her as to why Rose was there. Rose opened the back door and guided Ros in, raising her eyebrows at Bet. Bet glared at Rose to say nothing, and Rose put her hands up to acknowledge her.

All three women sat at the table looking from one to the other. Bet waved the cloud of smoke from her face.

"Right you ready fer this Ros. Only I fink it's gonna be best if I just come out wif it."

Ros looked away from the other two and slowly nodded. Rose motioned with her hands a 'T', and Bet nodded, waiting for Rose to get up to put the kettle on. Bet touched Ros's arm to get her attention, handing her a cigarette and lighter.

"The reason it's taken a couple of day's lovey, is 'cause I 'ad ta take a little trip up Norf," Bet started.

Ros's mouth fell open, but nothing came out she was totally dumb struck. Bet had said she'd ring around, not go up there!

"Why'd you have to go up there Bet. I don't understand!" Ros blurted out, her eyes, staring deep into Bet's, searching for answers.

"I fink yer'll understand why when I carry on," Bet replied, taking a deep breath.

"I went up an' 'ad a long chat wif yer mum, an' she told me wot really 'appened!"

"But I didn't lie to you Bet! Honest I didn't. How can she tell you what really happened! She wasn't there, I was!" Ros screamed at her.

"I know Ros, but let me finish will ya!" Bet said calmly. 'If she don't keep control we're be 'ere all fuckin' day!' she thought.

Ros nodded to her, taking the coffee Rose had made, placing it on the table staring at the little bubbles spinning on the top.

"She told me she 'ad a fling wif a man older than 'er when she was sixteen. She was engaged ta ya dad then, but this bloke offered ta give 'er a sum of money fer 'er services so ta speak. Fings were tight an' yer mum 'ad seen a little flat fer sale. So she told yer dad it was given ta 'er by an old aunt who'd died. An' they used it as a down payment. She didn't see the bloke again.

When you were fifteen years old. Yer dad 'ad met this bloke in the pub, an' 'e invited 'im back 'ome wif im. Can ya remember anyfing about that night Ros?" Bet asked.

"No, I was always in bed when dad came home from the pub, he wasn't very nice when he'd had a drink," Ros said, drifting back to all the times she'd hid under the covers to block out the arguments downstairs.

"Umm," Bet nodded to her, remembering her own childhood. She understood Ros perfectly.

"You want me ta carry on?" she asked, bringing Ros back to the present.

"Oh! Yes. I suppose so," she said knowing that Bet was going to tell her, her dad sold her to the bloke that night and she went in the morning to him.

"Right," Bet said, leaning across the table to Ros and looking into her eyes.

"When yer dad an' this bloke came 'ome. Yer mum took one look at 'im an' went white. Yeh!" she said nodding to the open mouthed Ros, "Yer guessed. 'E was the bloke that 'ad given 'er the money. She 'oped 'e didn't recognise 'er, but, when yer dad went out the room 'e made it quite clear he knew who she was, an' yer dad soberin' up a bit took one look at 'em from the door an' knew sumfink weren't right. So 'e came straight out wif it an' asked 'em. Yer poor mum ran out the room an' left 'em to it, knowing wotcha dad was like. But that night 'e didn't lose 'is temper 'e sat down opposite the man an' asked 'im outright 'ow 'e, a man of 'is status knew yer mum. An' yer know wot that bastard told 'im? Fuckin' everything. Yer dad got yer mum back in the room an' sat 'er down, 'is mind tickin' over.

Well, yer poor mum was beside 'erself, she didn't know wot was 'appening. Yer dad was far too calm fer a start. 'e asked the bloke 'ow long ago all this 'appened, an' when 'e told 'im. everythin' made sense ta yer dad."

"She ain't mine is she, ya fuckin' whore?" he spat atcha mum. "An that fuckin' old aunt yer'd never met. It was 'is money weren't it?" All yer mum could do was nod. Scared yer dad would 'it 'er!"

"The bloke looked from yer mum ta yer dad. "Who's she?" he asked enjoying the scene.

"Yer fuckin' kid that's who!" Yer dad jabbed the man.

"'old on just one minute. Are yer sayin' that I've gotta daughter up yer stairs?" the bloke asked yer mum.

"All she could do was nod, an' yer dad told 'im ta go an' 'ave a look atcha. Which 'e did. When 'e came back ta the front room 'e said 'ed got a proposal for 'em. That 'e'd buy ya from 'em givin' 'em enough money not ta 'ave ta ever worry again. A lump sum the next day! All yer dad 'ad ta do was take yer ta the 'otel 'e was stayin' in an' leave ya there an' collect an envelope from the desk. Yer mum didn't want ta let ya go, knowing wot 'e did ta 'er at sixteen, but yer dad told 'er if yer didn't go 'ed kill ya anyway. An' knowing 'is temper she letcha go wif 'im the next day. Not only 'as she never seen you again, she ain't seen nufing of the money or yer dad either!"

"So Ros yer 'usband is really yer dad!"

Ros sat at Bets table shaking her head, not accepting any of it. The shock of what she'd just heard hitting her like a sledgehammer.

"NO! No it's not true! She's lying! Bet she's got to be not my f...father!

"Sorry lovey she ain't," was all Bet could say to her, looking helplessly at Rose.

"But what he did to me!" Ros whispered.

"How could he? How?" she screamed, running out of the kitchen.

"Leave 'er," Bet said to Rose, who was going after her.

"She needs time ta think," she said sighing.

"S'pose the one good fing ta come outta it, is she ain't gotta tell Tommy!" Bet said, getting up an' putting the kettle on again.

"True," Rose sighed.

"Bet. Are you sure, I mean 100% sure the old girl was telling the truth?"

"Positive Rose. I wouldn't say anyfing uverwise, would I!" Bet said, taking the cups from the table.

Ros came back to reality, finding herself sitting on a bench facing out to sea. She didn't know how she got there. How long she'd been there, or where she'd been before. Her head was pounding and she couldn't think straight. Bets words kept swimming in and out of her head and ears. She clasped her hands over her ears and shut her eyes tightly, trying to block out everything. Nothing helped. She ran her hands through her wind swept hair and the tears started to fall. They came thick and fast not letting up. It was as if her body was squeezing every bad memory from her body.

It was getting dusk by the time her sobs subsided. Her ribs ached and her body felt heavy as she stood up and took a deep breath of salty air and exhaled. Looking out to sea her eyes hardened and she made a promise to herself.

"One day," she said.

Then she turned her back on the sea and walked away to her life now. Ros never spoke to Bet or Rose about that day, and they never brought the subject up again.

Chapter 8

Come on Ros, get yer arse outta that room an' let's 'ave a look at the bride!" Annie yelled, jumping up and down, excitement in her eyes.

"Yeh, come on Ros, we've gotta get yer face on yet!" Misty said, rummaging in her cosmetic box trying to find a tube of foundation and tapping Sal's hand as she went to dive in, giving her a grin.

Bet and Ros sat at a table drinking their Bucks' Fizz and sharing a joint.

"I 'ope all goes smoothly taday fer 'em," Bet said smiling at Rose.

"Right, you lot, ready?" Ros shouted from the "Box Room" laughing.

She hadn't let any one see the dress.

"Fuckin' get yer arse in 'ere will ya!" Bet yelled, grinning at the girls as she and Rose stood up and went over to them.

They were all stood in a row when Ros came through the door. You could hear a pin drop. No one said a word, they all stared at her open mouthed.

"What?" She asked, looking down at her dress a frown on her face, trying to figure out what was wrong.

"Well, fuck me! We got ourselves a fuckin' virgin in the house!" Big Jude piped up covering her eyes.

The rest collapsed in a fit of giggles.

Ros grinned.

"I thought I'd give Tommy a treat," she said laughing.

"The best bits when I turn around," she cried, showing them.

"I dunno about Tommy but the vicars gonna get an eye full!" Bet boomed, wiping the tears from her eyes.

The dress was long, straight, and very plain, with a high

neck and long sleeves at the front. But when Ros turned around the whole of the back was cut away down to the crack of her backside. Her veil fell to her shoulders covering her face and she was carrying a dozen long stemmed red roses.

"So what do you think?" she asked grinning, taking the joint passed to her, and inhaling.

"You look wonderful babe, really you do. Doesn't she?" Rose said, asking everyone in the room.

They all smiled and agreed with her.

"Right, get over here an' let me put your face on. We haven't got much time left," Misty said, motioning Ros to a chair.

Tommy was already at the church when they arrived and the ceremony went without a hitch. Bet gave Ros away and Rose was maid of honour. The other five girls were bridesmaids. Tommy's best man was Ben the manager, and the guys from the band were witnesses. Tommy was the proudest person on the planet.

The reception was held out the back of a pub called "The Haystack" where the guys from the band played.

After all the formalities of the speeches were over, the lights were dimmed and the party began. The guys played a slow ballad for Tommy and Ros's first dance, and then they changed the tempo, giving them a private gig. No one could knock the grin from Tommy's face. He was the cat that got the cream.

Everyone was just getting in the party mood, when the manager of the pub asked them to wind it down. Sal and Misty ran over to Bet

"Would it be okay to suggest we all go back to the Club?" Sal breathed, draping a long white arm over Bets shoulders.

"Please Bet," Misty said, a glint in her eye. She'd met one of the bands roadies.

Bet, always the business-woman, said, "Go on then, but make sure they all know they 'ave ta pay fer their drinks!"

Misty jumped up and down clapping her hands.

"Oh, thank you Bet," she said, giving her a kiss on the cheek.

Bet raised her eyes at Rose.

"I fink I'm gettin' old Rose," she said, grinning.

"Me too," Rose sighed, raising her glass and toasting her. The two women looked at each other and laughed.

Everyone piled through "The Club" door, Tommy carrying Ros over the threshold first and straight up the stairs to a cheer.

Kel lit the candles in the bar room, putting on some music as she went.

Jude and Annie went behind the bar and started serving their guests. Sal disappeared to the kitchen and brought back some nibbles, knowing that pretty soon people were going to get the munchies. One of the guys from the band stopped in the hall and asked.

"Ere beautiful, wot's in there then?" pointing to the "Entertaining Room".

Sal glided over, took out her key and opened the door pushing it all the way back. She didn't say a word, and walked off, leaving the guy with his eyes nearly popping out. Grinning as she heard him let out a low whistle.

Going over to Misty she said with a wink,

"I think it's going to be quite a party. I've just opened the Entertaining Room!"

"Oh, go on Sal!" Misty laughed.

The guy came into the bar and went over to the other band members and Roadies.

"Fuck me! 'ave you seen that fuckin' room next door?" he said, pointing out of the door.

"Yeh mate," Ben the manager said, looking up from rolling a giant joint and grinning.

"Well, don't fuckin' keep it ta yer self!" another one said.

"Fuck me! You name it! It's in there!" The guy said.

"Go see fer yer self," he finished picking up his drink and taking a gulp.

"Nar later. Looks like things are hottin' up over there," he said pointing to Sal and Misty dancing together across the bar.

"Those two were at your place, weren't they Ben?"

"Sure were my man," Ben said, looking over to the girls as he licked the tobacco papers.

"Right little ravers from what I remember!" he added.

"Lucky old Tommy," another said, and they all laughed.

Annie and Jude came out from the bar and joined Sal and

93

Misty on the dance floor. The girls smiled and danced closer together running their hands over each other and gyrating their bodies.

Kel, seeing the girls together thought she'd step things up a pace. She put some slow rhythmatic music on and climbed up on to the bar, moving her body with the music. A cheer came up from the room as Kel slowly started to strip, ripping her buttons off one by one instead of undoing them. Running her hands around her breasts until she reached her nipples, pulling on them as she leaned back so they were pointing to the cciling, letting her arms drop, and her top dramatically fell to the bar. Kel flicked her long hair over so when she straightened up her hair made a veil over her face.

Turning her back to the crowd, she flicked it back, pushing out her skirt covered backside. Running her hands down she reached for the button and zip fastening, slowly sliding the zip down and letting her skirt fall as she wriggled out of it.

Wolf whistles and cheers came from around the room.

The girls looked at each other and grinned.

"Trust Kel," Sal breathed.

"Shall we girls?" her long arm leading them to the bar.

"Oh, isn't this fun," Annie beamed, letting Jude pull her up onto the bar and kiss her.

Sal and Misty were helped up on the bar by two of the bands roadies, and stood the other side of Kel. All four girls started to strip. Annie danced around Jude, delicately kissing every bit of her flesh as it was exposed. She started at the nape of Jude's neck and ran her tongue down her spine as she slid the zip of Jude's dress down. Jude danced trance-like to Annie's touch. Annie came round to Jude's front and wiggled her body on to Jude's. Taking hold of her dress at the shoulders she very slowly peeled it away letting Jude's huge breasts tumble onto her upturned face. Letting the dress fall to Jude's feet Annie licked and kissed the underneath of Jude's breasts, running her tongue to Jude's huge nipples and down again.

Jude could take no more and pushed Annie's head down to her crotchless panties. Annie didn't need showing twice, she ran her tongue across the top of Jude's panties then straight to the slit in them embedding her little tongue deep inside Jude.

Jude grabbed her hair, pulling her up and kissing her full on the mouth, while ripping her clothes away, grabbing Annie's little breasts in one hand, and her backside in the other.

Sal and Misty were up the other end of the bar, stripping in perfect unison back to back. They undid their tops button by button with one hand, the other spread at their side staring into space. They revealed one breast at a time. Sal's pert white breasts with rose bud nipples mirrored by Misty's big chocolate breasts with dark brown nipples. They turned to face each other nipples touching. Letting their tops fall, they pushed their breasts together and tilted their heads back unzipping their skirts, letting them fall down. They then pushed their hands together, lifted their heads and started to explore each other's mouths with their tongues. Kel danced around them, letting her hands wander over the iridescent and dark bodies.

When all the girls were wearing nothing but their shoes, stockings, suspenders and panties, they turned their backs on the wedding party, bent over, sliding their fingers down each side of their panties and peeled them down wriggling their backsides as they went. A roar came from the party of people encouraging them all the more. Kel turned first, taking a handful of ice as she went. Kicking her shoes off she let her legs slide apart on the bar until she did the splits, both feet pointing to the ceiling, her fanny kissing the bar. She rubbed the ice cubes down her neck letting the melted liquid run between her breasts, past her belly and down over her fanny lips ending with a pool of water on the bar.

Misty and Annie stood over Kel's feet and let the heels of their shoes guide them in to the splits on to Kel's upturned feet, the muscles in their legs contracting as they pumped themselves on her toes. Kel reached for the two girls' nipples, twisting and pulling them as they moved up and down on her.

Jude and Sal by this time had slipped off the bar. Jude was bent over it, licking Kel's clit. Sal was pulling Jude's voluptuous arse cheeks apart and burying her face deep into her while a man from the party was sucking Sal's nipples, and another was licking and finger fucking her.

The girls seeing a couple of the men 'helping' Sal, and a few of the girls from the reception dancing topless finished on the bar and danced erotically around undressing everyone as they went. No-one objected and soon a few couples ventured to the 'Entertaining Room.'

The girls grabbed a guy each and took them into their wonderland.

Ross and Tommy could hear the wolf whistles and shouts from downstairs.

"Fuck me! They're goin' fer it, ain't they?" Tommy grinned kissing Ros's forehead as she snuggled up to him.

"Well, no-one'll be able to say they don't remember our wedding if the girls have anything to do with it!" she said, kissing Tommy's chest and laughing.

"True babe. 'Ere don't fancy showing' me wot ya job entails do ya?" Tommy joked slapping her backside.

"I would but you know what you gents are like! Still it gives us a tea break I suppose!" she retaliated, taking hold of Tommy's flaccid manhood.

"Fuckin' cheeky bitch!" Tommy grinned, his cock jumping to life again.

"Go on Tommy, my man!" Ros laughed, letting Tommy's tongue go to work on her body again.

Chapter 9

Tommy came through their back door.

"All right babe?" he said, giving Ros a kiss and tapping her backside as he passed her in their galley kitchen.

Ros reached for the kettle and shouted after him.

"I'm fine. What's the rush for?" she said flicking the switch for the kettle to boil.

"Oh! Sorry babe," Tommy said, coming back into the room, grinning

"You workin' tonight? Only Ben's invited us over ta 'is place fer a drink, an' I really fancy goin'."

"As a matter of fact no, I'm not. What time do you want to go?" Ros asked, pouring the water into two mugs and stirring the coffee in.

"I dunno. 'E said 'e'd give us a ring later, about six'ish. Said 'e wanted ta 'ave a word wif me about some work 'e wants done. Plus the guys are 'avin' a practice over there tonight," Tommy said, taking his coffee and following Ros into the front room.

Ros sat down.

"Look, Tommy, do you really want me to come with you if you're going to talk business with Ben, then watch the guys play?" she said, trying to get out of going.

In the past six months they'd been married, unbeknown to Tommy the girls had "entertained" Ben and the band round the house every time Ben had a private party, and although it was only a job to Ros when she went, she didn't know how she'd feel going round on a personal basis with Tommy. Especially as she'd stopped going with Tommy on their wild nights out.

"I 'ad'nt thought about it like that babe. I'll go by meself if ya don't mind then. I just thought you'd like ta 'ear the guys that's all!" Tommy said, lighting his cigarette and handing Ros the lighter.

Ros couldn't really tell Tommy she'd probably heard them more times than him!

"I would but what if you an' Ben take longer than expected sorting out your business. I mean it must be more than your usual runs. What if he wants a major job done?"

"True babe," Tommy said, sitting up proudly and puffing his chest out.

"Yer right, of course, as always. Wotcha gonna do while I'm out?"

"Well," Ros said, getting off her chair and sitting on Tommy's lap.

"I'm going to take a long bath and get myself ready for your return."

"That's me girl!" Tommy said, tweaking her nipples through her jumper and biting her neck.

"If you carry on doing that, you won't be going anywhere!" she said, enjoying his touch, tutting as the phone rang. She got up and answered it.

"Hello?" she said looking across the room at Tommy and teasing him by running her hand over her erect nipples and smiling.

"Oh, hello Ros," Bens voice came through

"Oh, hi Ben," she said, motioning Tommy to the phone.

"I'll get Tommy for you," she said her tone light.

"I'd rather have you!" Ben breathed down the phone.

Ros caught her breath.

"Here he is. Bye Ben," Ros handed the phone to Tommy and went out the room seething. 'How dare he! This is our home not my work, the bastard. He'd better not say anything to Tommy about his parties,' she thought. Pulling herself together she went back in the room.

"Yeh, see ya later. Bye mate," Tommy replaced the receiver and turned to Ros.

"I'm goin' round about eight. That okay?"

"Fine with me I'll go and get dinner sorted out," she replied quietly, smiling at him.

"You okay babe? Did Ben upset you?" he asked, looking concerned at her.

"No! Why d'you say that?" Ros asked, quickly giving him a

reassuring smile.

"Oh, I dunno ferget it," he said tapping her backside as he headed for the stairs.

"I'm gonna go get washed an' changed okay babe?"

"Fine, dinner won't be for about half an hour yet," Ros told him as she headed for the kitchen.

Tommy headed down the drive and round the back. He tapped on the kitchen door before opening it.

"Ben, you about, mate it's Tommy," he called, as he went through the doorway.

Ben's voice found its way to him.

"In the front Tom!" he shouted back.

Tommy walked through.

"Evening you lot," he said, as he entered the front room and grinned.

"All right Tom 'ow's it 'anging?" one of the roadies said, passing him his joint as he sat next to him.

"All right mate. You?"

"Yeh, fine. Wanna drink?" the roadie asked, pointing to the table up the other end of the room.

"I fink I might, yeh. Anyone else want one?" Tommy asked the other nine men.

They all shook their heads and Tommy went and got a beer. Plonking himself down again he looked around. He really felt part of this elite group of men and music. He took a swig from his can and let himself relax.

"'Ere Tom, can't get 'old of some gear fer us can ya? Only we're runnin' a bit fuckin' bare fer my likin'!" Paul the drummer asked, as he rolled a huge neat spliff, lighting it and letting the purple haze of smoke fill the room, he carried on.

"You guys wont anyfing different than wot we got 'ere?"

Everyone shook their heads.

"Wot we 'ad last time Tom, fuckin' surperb mate! An' those 'blues', fuckin' first class!" Al the guitarist piped up and the others agreed.

"Well, thank you fer sayin' gentlemen!" Tommy said in a posh voice grinning.

"Seriously though 'ow much of each we talkin' 'ere seein' Pauls rollin' neat now!" he said, giving Paul a wink and accepting his joint.

"Fuckin' cheeky bastard! Don't see ya turnin' it down!" Paul joked with Tommy.

"I may be fuckin' cheeky but I ain't fuckin' stupid!" Tommy replied, in the same manner, taking another deep drag on Pauls joint, before passing it back.

Ben leaned forward taking the cigarette from Paul

"I think what we had last week will do fine, but double up on the 'blues' seein' the boys play better when they're wizzin'!"

"An that's our fuckin' manager!" John yelled, laughing.

"No. We're havin' a big promotional do next week so we need 'em for entertaining," Ben said, seriously

"Actually that's why I wanted a word with you Tom. I need some work done on a bar I've just bought. Let's go into the kitchen and sort out the business, then we can relax. That's if you're interested?" Ben said, raising his eyebrows in a questioning way.

"Too fuckin' right I am!" Tommy answered, his brain going into overdrive.

"Shall we then?" Ben said, standing up and heading to the kitchen followed by Tommy, beer in hand.

"See ya in a mo boys," Tommy called over his shoulder, pushing the kitchen door open.

"Take a seat Tom," Ben said pointing to a chair.

On the table in front of him were the blueprints of the bar, and notes on the alterations Ben wanted done. Tommy studied the prints while Ben went to the fridge and poured himself an orange juice.

"What d'you think?" he asked, sitting down opposite Tommy.

"Not bad mate," Tommy replied, rubbing his chin, not taking his eyes off the plans.

"There's a lot of work 'ere. It ain't gonna be cheap, ya know!" Tommy said, looking up at Ben.

"I know. But can you do it?" Ben asked, taking a sip of his juice.

"I can do it mate, but when d'ya want it ta open up?"

"Oh, I recon in about three months time. Can you finish by then?"

"No probs. Prob'ly 'ave it finished in eight ta ten wif no 'old ups," Tommy said, looking back down at the plans.

"Great! I'll get everything tied up with the solicitors, and if you give me a list of the materials you need, I'll have them ready for, let's say, what a week Monday?"

"Yeh mate, sounds great, it'll give me time ta finish up all me uver jobs," Tommy said, trying to make it sound as if he had a lot on.

"Good. D'you want to take this copy with you now?" Ben asked, rolling the plans up.

"Yeh, that'll be great. Cheers fer this Ben," Tommy said, taking the plans from him, tapping them in his other hand and nodding.

"Hey, you're good at what you do Tom. If you weren't I wouldn't hire you!

And if you can get it done in eight weeks there be a nice little bonus for ya mate," Ben said, getting up from the table with Tommy.

"Now let's go an' relax!" he said, shaking Tommy's hand and heading for the kitchen door.

"Sounds good ta me!" Tommy grinned, following Ben to the door and into the front room.

The guys were all chilling, talking, and listening to the music pumping from the stereo. As Ben and Tommy entered the room, they hesitated with their conversation. Tommy being Tommy noticed the atmosphere straight away. Ben had also noticed, and guessed the guys had been talking about the party they had, had a couple of nights back with Bet's girls and a few of the groupies.

"Ere Tom where's yer gorgeous wife tonight then? Not working, is she?"

John the lead singer piped up as Tommy sat down across from him.

"What? Nar mate she's curled up at 'ome waiting fer us ta get back," Tommy replied his head down, rolling a joint.

He didn't see John's reaction, but the others did and tried to cover up their acknowledgement, smirking to each other. Tommy looked up catching a couple of roadies, their smirks fading fast. He slowly looked around the room. No one would look him in the eye, except a young boy Tommy hadn't noticed was there before. He just stared deep into Tommy eyes, a knowing look on his face. Tommy felt a shiver run down him, and pulled his eyes away from the boys. Casually lighting his joint and acting as if he hadn't noticed anything wrong, he poured the last of his beer in his mouth and said.

"Thinkin' about wot I got back 'ome, I fink I'll make a move boys. I'll pop me list in later on tamorrow, all right wif you, Ben mate?"

"Yeh sure Tommy, see you later," Ben replied, nodding.

Tommy stood up and made his way to the front door. He looked across to the corner of the room where he saw the boy watching him, taking everything in, his expression never changing. Tommy made a mental note to ask Ben about him, and went out the door his mind on Ros. 'why'd the guys act so oddly when she was mentioned? Come ta think of it 'ow did John know Ros was gonna come tonight! It was Ben that invited us!' he thought, his mind ticking.

Arriving home, he found Ros as he'd imagned she would be. A book in one hand, a cigarette in the other, a glass of red wine down the side of the sofa and Ros curled up on it, stark naked except for one of Tommys checked shirts.

'She seemed ta jump when I came in!' he thought. Then shaking it off he said.

"Hey, babe, you waitin' up fer me?"

"Oh, Tommy!" Ros said, looking up and smiling.

"I didn't expect you back for a while yet. How'd it go?" she asked, sitting up and reaching for her wine.

"Do you want a glass darling?" she breathed, reaching to their sideboard to get a wine glass for him, and pouring without waiting for an answer.

Taking the glass and nodding, Tommy said.

"Not bad. Ben wants me ta redecorate a bar 'e's just bought on the island."

"Oh, Tommy!" she grinned jumping up and running to him.

"That's wonderful darling! I'm so pleased and proud of you. It's superb!

Really, it is!" Ros cried, kissing his face all over.

"Hey. Hey babe, calm down, 'ow much of that you 'ad?" he

said, laughing and pointing to the bottle of wine on the floor.

"Not enough!" Ros said, running into their kitchen and bringing another bottle and corkscrew with her.

"I think a celebration drink is in order, don't you?" she said, handing Tommy the bottle and corkscrew.

She plonked down on the sofa tapping next to her with her hand for Tommy to sit. Tommy pulled the cork from the bottle and placed it next to the other one on the floor sitting next to her.

"John said sumfing real weird tonight," he said as much to himself as to Ros, but as the words fell from his lips so he felt Ros tense, making him even more suspicious of her.

"Ros you not tellin' me sumfing?" he asked, looking deep into her eyes.

"Telling... you... what... Tommy?" Ros asked slowly.

"Well, if I fuckin' knew that! I wouldn't be fuckin' askin' would I?" he bit back, not really knowing why but letting his gut feeling lead him.

"Tommy, I don't know what you mean!" she cried, panic welling up in her.

"Fer fuck sake Ros, d'ya fink I'm stupid! You went like a fuckin' board when I said about John actin' weird. Wot's 'e know that I don't eh?" Tommy hissed, grabbing the top of her arms.

"Tommy, you're hurting me! Please. How am I supposed to know what John said! You haven't told me! And I wasn't there!" she gasped, trying to wriggle from his grip.

"Don't give me that crap! I know sumfing's goin' on Ros! Wot's 'e one of yer regulars eh?"

"Y... yes. Yes I'm sorry Tommy. Yes he is. I'm truly so sorry... But anything that goes on in the Club, is strictly confidential between... g... gent and girl... Please Tommy I'm so sorry!" Ros sobbed her head bowed.

"I fuckin' knew it! That's it Ros, you ain't doin' it no more! I've 'ad enough, you 'ear? I ain't puttin' up wif it any more. An' anyway I want a kid!"

"WHAT! You knew what I did when we married. You know it means NOTHING to me! You can't tell me what I can and can't do! And as for kids! Don't you think I have a say in it? You chauvinistic bastard! You don't complain about the money each week coming in when you've not got any work on! Oh no! I suppose now you're'in' with Ben you think you're one of the big boys, do you? Well, you're fucking WRONG, do you hear me Tommy?"

Tommy stared open mouthed at her, seething.

"I mean it Ros, NO MORE! Tamorrow you tell Bet yer 'anging up yer fuckin' stockins! You hear me? I'm not gonna 'ave uver blokes fucking me wife ANY MORE, you got it Ros? You got it?" he screamed, shaking her by the arms.

"Jeesus fuckin' Christ I love you, don't you understand? I 'ate it when ya go ta 'work'! I wont us ta 'ave a normal life, wif kids an' all that shit!"

Tommy sighed, releasing his grip and running his hands through his hair.

"Please Ros I'm beggin' ya only this once. Please, no more," Tommy said, tears running down his face,pleading in his eyes.

Ros caught her breath.

"Okay Tommy... I'll talk to Bet tomorrow, see if I can go back to my old job. How's that? I can't not work Tommy I'd go insane! But I'll stop 'entertaining'. And if a baby means that much to you, then, okay, I think we should think about it seriously. I must admit now I know you feel that strongly about it, the idea does sound more attractive," she said, wiping away her tears, sniffing and smiling at him her body shaking.

"But one thing I want to know Tommy?"

"Wot's that Ros?" he asked, quietly, gazing into her eyes, and rubbing the spot on her arms where he'd grabbed her earlier, shaking his head slowly.

"Will you still love me when I'm fat!" she said stuffing a pillow up her shirt.

"Love ya, I'd fuckin' adore ya babe!" he said, leaning over and kissing her neck.

Roslynn rested her chin on his shoulder and stared straight ahead.

Tommy pulled away and looked at her.

"'ow's about we start practising now fer our kid?" he said with a glint in his eyes Ros had never seen, as he slid his hands up under her shirt running his fingers down her spine and up again Ros went to jelly.

Nothing mattered anymore when Tommy was with her.

"Tommy Carter, you're gonna be doing a lot of that from now on!" Ros said, grinning at him, undoing his shirt buttons and sliding her hands across his chest.

"Oh, keep goin' babe. I fink I'm gonna like all this practising!" Tommy said, closing his eyes.

Ros pushed him back against the sofa running her tongue over his chest where, seconds earlier her fingers were. She moved her hand down to Tommy's trousers, circling the top of his leg with her nails. Tommy moved his hips hard against her fingers and groaned. Running her hand across to the fastenings she felt a large bulge in his trousers, straining to be set free.

Ros ran her nails up and down Tommy's rock-hard cock through the material, and sucked on one of his hard nipples.

"Please babe. I can't take much more!" Tommy pleaded in a husky voice, undoing his trousers with one hand and pushing her head down with the other. Ros willingly received his cock into her mouth. Tommy sighed and pushed himself deeper down her throat. She lifted her head and ran her tongue around the tip of his cock, flicking the rim of it, then took him deep into her mouth moving up and down in a rhythmic pattern, then releasing him, she ran her tongue down his cock over his balls and flicked the tip of her tongue over the swelling under his balls, circling them one at a time, rubbing his cock up and down with her hands. Tommy pulled her up by her hair, kissing her deeply, holding her head in his hands. Ros kissed him back, straddling him and rubbing his cock between her hot wet lips, pushing her clit into the tip of his cock. She pulled away from their kiss, lowering herself slowly onto him slipping his cock in inch by inch.

She threw her head back and pulled her shirt off releasing her heavily aroused breasts into Tommy's face.

Tommy grabbed them with both hands, rubbing his face in them, biting and sucking. Ros ground herself on to him time and time again. Tommy lifted her off of him and bent her over the sofa her backside sticking up in the air, he buried his tongue deep between her swollen wet lips, tasting her, her juice's running down his chin. He ran his tongue from her clit all the way up past her arse and up her spine, biting her neck as he entered her from behind. Ros pushed her bottom out meeting

Tommy with every stroke until they came together. Collapsing over her Tommy kissed her neck and said, a big grin on his face.

"I fink this is one job I'm really gonna enjoy! I love you Ros."

"I love you too darling," Ros said turning her head and kissing him, returning back to reality. She felt a wave of dread roll over her. She really didn't know if she could do it. She really loved her job!

Chapter 10

Ros knocked on the office door.

"It's open," Rose called from within.

She walked in and plonked down on the chair opposite Rose.

"You look like you've got something to tell me!" Rose said, leaning her elbows on the old oak desk and lighting a cigarette.

"Rose I've got a real problem!" Ros said, sitting forward pushing her face across the desk at her.

"Tommy wants me to give it up!" she cried, "And he wants a baby! And I! Me the stupid cow agreed to it!"

By the time Ros had finished, she was lying across the desk her face inches away from Rose pleading in her eyes.

"What am I going to do Rose? Please help me sort out this mess. I really don't know what to do this time!" she finished, slumping back in her chair rubbing her face with her hands.

"Fucking hell Ros! When you have a problem, you really have one. Jesus Christ! Why can't you just tell him you've changed your mind for the time being? Say you want to move!" Rose beamed pleased with her problem solving.

"Yeh that's it say you'd rather have some money behind you, an' if he wants kids you'd rather move now instead of two years down the line with two babes in tow!"

Ros's face was a picture, her eyes were out on stalks

"Two? Who said anything about two!!" She said horrified.

Rose laughed.

"Not really you silly bitch! You really have got to learn how to play your man, or any man for that!" Rose replied, very much the willing teacher.

"It's no good. He knows one of the 'gents' I entertain, an' he's found out by the 'gent' saying something weird. Don't ask me what I haven't got a clue. All I know is he's fucking shit mad about me entertaining this guy!"

She cried in a panic.

"Look. Will you just calm down!" Rose said putting her hands in the air.

"Tommy knows what you do. He knew before you were married, but his pride's hurt! Does he know this guy? Is this guy close to him?" Rose asked as if she was coaxing information from a child.

"Know him! It's his fucking hero!!" she cried jumping out of her chair, taking a cigarette from the desk and lighting it, she blew out the smoke

"He was so mad with me Rose, I felt I had to agree!" she said pushing her sleeves up showing her the bruises Tommy's fingers had left.

"Did… he… hit you?" Rose demanded.

"No, no of course not! But he made it quite clear that he'd had enough of my 'entertaining'. He's agreed to let me stay on here if I take my old job back. But only until I get pregnant then he'd really like me at home running the house and being mother for fuck sake! Me a mother!" Ros said pacing the room, the smoke from her cigarette following her like the vapour of a plane.

Rose picked up her phone.

"Who you ringing Rose?" Ros asked in a panic.

"Only Bet darling. Who do you think I was going to ring?" Rose asked giving Ros a concerned look and putting down the receiver.

"I don't know really," she said giving Rose a little smile.

"It's just me being paranoid sorry!" she said sitting down again. Jumping up as soon as her backside touched the seat.

Rose raised her eyebrows and half grinned at her.

"Look Ros why don't you go fetch us some coffee, Oh and ask Doughy if she's got any of those apple turnovers left, I really fancy one, an' I'll give Bet a ring. You'd better fetch one for her and bring an extra mug back with you. Rose said picking up the phone again and dismissing Ros.

Ros had just shut the door as Bet answered.

"Bet it's Rose. Get your arse over here will you. We've got us a stroppy husband on our hands!"

"It's that fuckin' Tommy ain't it?" Bet demanded.

"Is 'e there?"

"No, but Ros is she's in the kitchen getting the coffee."

She know yer ringin' me?" Bet asked looking around her kitchen for her house keys.

"Yeh I told her. See you in a mo," Rose put the phone down and lit another cigarette.

'Why do these girls always think their mans 'different' They're all the bloody same! Get a ring on their finger an' they think they own them! Fucking bastards!' Rose thought to herself, shaking her head and getting up from her chair. She wandered over to the little window opening it to let the stale air out and the fresh come in. Rose stood there for a moment, eyes closed inhaling the cool fresh sea air.

The door opened breaking the moment. Rose gave a sigh, 'back to the grind!' she thought to herself, making a mental note that she needed a holiday.

Ros came in backside first, carrying a large tray containing three mugs, a milk jug and coffee pot, also a plate with an assortment of cakes and pastries Doughy had made. She walked over to the desk, Bet walked in just as she placed the tray down, making Ros jump when she heard her voice.

"Mornin' all!" Bet called like an unannounced whirlwind.

"Right wot's all the fuckin' trouble about then?" she asked plonking herself down on the old desk choosing a chocolate éclair from the plate and lighting a cigarette.

"It's Tommy," Ros said pouring the coffee out.

"He want's me to stop entertaining and have a baby."

"Don't wont a fuckin' lot does 'e!" Bet said putting down her éclair and excepting the mug of coffee

"Cheer's lovey. An' wotcha say ta 'im about it then?"

Ros looked into her mug, then looking to Rose for some support, she said very quietly.

"I agreed to it!"

"You fuckin' what!" Bet jumped off the desk and paced the floor no one said a thing.

"Ros it's fine if that's wotcha wont. But if it ain't, ya gotta tell 'im," Bet said patting her bleached hair and trying to sound motherly.

"I can't Bet! He really meant it this time," Ros sighed tears welling up in her eyes.

"I don't fuchin' believe this!" Bet yelled looking at Rose, who simply shrugged her shoulders as if to say, "I told you".

"So that's it is it? Cos fuckin' Tommy opens 'is mouth you fuckin' jump! You surprise me Ros!" Bet said glaring at her.

"Answer me this. Do ya wont ta stop entertaining? An' do ya wont a kid? You Ros not fuckin' Tommy YOU?" Bet said her face inches from her.

"NO and NO!" Ros screamed at Bet burying her head in her hands and sobbing.

"She's got bruises all over the tops of her arms Bet," Rose said nodding towards Ros.

Bet pulled up Ros's sleeves and ran her fingers over the purple marks very gently, shaking her head she pulled the sleeves back over Ros's limp arms.

"Right we've gotta fink about 'ow we're gonna go about this!" Bet said picking up her coffee and sitting next to Ros, she looked across the desk at Rose.

"Got any idea's?" she asked.

Rose's mind had been ticking away while Ros told Bet what had happened and the only thing she could come up with was.

"Only one. An' that's, lie to him!" Rose said putting her hands in the air.

"What else can she do?"

Bet sat there nodding slowly.

"True," she agreed

"But wot about the 'private parties'?" Bet asked Rose, as if Ros wasn't even there.

This was business and Bet had a lot of money on Ros and the girls with the 'parties'

"There's one booked fer next week. Ben and his crew want them. Entertaining some big wigs from out of town, some kind of promotion.

Said the girls might even get some photo shoots out of it! Then there's the stag do at the rugby Club a couple of days later. Then next month they're.," Rose stopped in mid sentence.

Bet waving the cloud of smoke that was permanently about her head away.

110

"Wot! Wot the fuck she say?" she asked Ros sobbing in the chair.

Staring wide eyed at Rose waiting for an explanation.

"I… if Tommy knew I was entertaining for Ben! He'd kill me I know he would!" Ros rushed between sobs.

"Wot! You've fuckin' entertained 'im enough times before! Why the fuck now?" Bet looked confused.

"Because… He… he doesn't know I entertain for private parties! He thinks that first time was my only time and I've never told him any different! He knows one of the gents I entertain here and the guy's mentioned it to Tommy in some way. Anyway he knows! And he's not happy one bit."

"Hold on one minute! Who the fuck we talkin' about 'ere Ros? Give us a fuckin' name will ya fer Christ sake!"

"John," Ros said lowering her eyes away from Bet and Rose stifling another sob.

"Yer mean the singer?" Rose asked, her brain putting two and two together.

Ros nodded unable to speak.

"Fuck me it all make's chuffin' sense now! Your fuckin' Tommy's idol right?" Bet said triumphantly slapping her hand on the table. Ros dissolved once again.

"'ere blow on this an' suck on that!" Bet said throwing her a box of tissues and a cigarette.

Bet leaned back in her chair and licked the cream that was oozing out of her éclair, then bit into it. Rose could see Bet's brain working over time and smiled, knowing that in five minutes Bet would have come up with something, she always did. Bet gave Rose a smile and Rose began to relax. She had known Bet long enough to know what every expression on her face meant. All she had to do was wait. After Bet had eaten her éclair the two older women drank a fresh coffee Rose had poured for them in silence. Ros's sobs slowed and came to a halt. Bet looked at Rose and placed her empty mug on the tray, then lighting a cigarette passing the pack to her.

"I've got it. It ain't that 'ard really when ya fink about it," Bet said to them.

"Well, firstly, Wot our Tommy don't know ain't gonna 'ert 'im is it?"

"You mean the private parties?" Rose asked nodding in agreement.

"I can't lie to him!" Ros blurted out grabbing another tissue and blowing her nose.

"'ow can ya lie when 'e don't know anyfing about it in the first place? Fer fuck sake Ros get a grip will ya! As fer yer workin' 'ere, if yer wont ta go back ta 'box 'ostess' ya can. Or… Yer can carry on entertaining an' I pay 'box 'ostess' money to ya an' bung yer entertaining money in a bank account fer ya. As fer the baby, that ain't nufing ta do wif us. All our gents 'ave ta use a condom even though you lot are on the pill! That Ros is down ta you lovey. But even if ya did get preggie, a baby ain't gonna be a problem wif all us lot 'elpin' out. Least yer married! Most me girls who 'ave a slip up ain't!" she said softly, her mind going back over the years.

Ros stared open mouthed at Bet.

"Wot the fuck I said now?" Bet cried.

"Oh, don't tell me ya thought you'd be the only one of me girls ta ever get in the Club if ya pardon me pun!" Bet said amused.

"Fuck me 'ave we seen some come an' go eh Rose?" Bet said.

"You remember Brenda?" Rose said a grin on her face.

"Fuck me 'ow could ya ferget 'er!" Bet said starting to chuckle.

"Now she was a one weren't she Rose?" Bet said looking in to space.

"Sure was," Rose agreed nodding her head in agreement and smiling, picking up an apple turnover.

"Found 'erself up the duff. So know wot she did?"

Ros shook her head.

"She only slept wif five of 'er richest gents wifout any condoms tellin' 'em she was on the pill! Then a month later she told each one of 'em when they came ta see 'er that the kid was 'is! Well each gent gave 'er a sum of money ta keep stoom about it, cos as usual they were married, an' she left 'ere wif quite a little nest egg didn't she Rose?" Bet chuckled shaking her head.

"She sure did. Little Isabelle's what two an' a half now. Doughy looks after sometimes actually," Rose said looking through her desk for a photo. Finding it she said passing it first to Bet.

"There she is quite a little character that one!" Her eyes softening.

"Umm an' wotcha expect wif a muver she's got!" Bet replied grinning at Rose and handing the photo to Ros.

"So wotcha say Ros?" Bet asked.

"Oh! She certainly is lovely!" Ros gushed.

"Nar ya silly tart! Not the kid. Me proposition about work. You wanna do it or not? The choice is yours lovey!" she said standing up and lighting another cigarette.

"Fink about it an' let us know later yeh?"

Bet then asked Rose.

"Anyfing else I need ta know?"

"Nope, all running smoothly," Rose replied tapping her paper work and smiling.

"Good, well I'm off then, an' let us know tonight wot ya wont ta do Ros. See ya about eightish lovey," Bet blew Rose a kiss and marched out the door leaving a cloud behind her.

Rose turned her attention to Ros.

"Well, what do you think?"

"I think I'm going to give it a go, and not tell him especially if he wants a baby. I mean it would be nice if I did ever get pregnant to know that I'd have some money saved up, just in case," she said, not taking her eyes from the photo of the little girl, the thought of having a baby getting more appealing.

Ros smiled to herself, then tearing her eyes away from the child handed it back to Rose. Rose took the picture and placed it back in her drawer saying "Business as usual then Ros?"

"Business as usual Rose."

"Well, thank Christ for that!" Rose finished toasting her mug at Ros and taking a sip.

Chapter 11

"I can't bear this any more!" Ros shouted covering her eyes

"Just tell me will you! The suspense is killing me!"

"Oh, fer fuck sake! Put 'er out of 'er misery will ya!" Bet called to the others in the kitchen laughing a deep croaky laugh.

"Oh, stop it Bet," Rose dug her in the ribs.

"Well, we 'ave this every fuckin' month!" Bet chuckled.

Rose was about to reprimand her again, when Annie burst through the door jumping up and down a huge grin on her imp like face.

Bet and Rose sat up in their chairs.

"Nar she ain't gone an' done it 'as she?"

Bet grinned at Rose.

"I think may be she has," Rose replied her eyes soft.

By this time the others had bounced through the door and they were all huddled around Ros congratulating hugging and kissing her. They pulled her up dancing around the room with her cushions shoved up their tops.

"Well, bugger me!" Bet said grinning.

"If 'e'd done that she wouldn't be like she is now would she!" Jude shot in as she twirled Ros past them.

Everyone froze then collapsed laughing.

"Only from our Jude!" Rose cried wiping away her tears of laughter.

When they all calmed down Ros started to cry.

Annie ran over to help Jude comfort her.

"Hey, wot's up sweetie?" she asked full of concern.

"It's just a bit of a shock to know I've got another life growing inside me every minute," Ros let out.

"Well, it ain't too late if yer know wot I mean>" Jude whispered in Ros's ear giving her a hug.

"I think we've all done it a least once in this room!"

Ros smiled at Jude and gave her a kiss on the cheek.

"It's okay I do want it. It's just after being told for the last six months a big no every time. I was kinda expecting the same result again!"

Annie gave Ros a cuddle then beamed.

"I'm gonna be a Auntie!" she called to the other girls.

"I've never been a Auntie before!"

"Stick in the business a few more years, an' your be an Auntie ta 'undreds!" Jude said sullenly.

Annie looked hurt. Seeing her face Jude burst out laughing followed by the others.

"Ere Ros. When ya gonna tell your Tommy?" Bet shouted across the room.

Everyone fell silent. They all knew about Ros's problem with Tommy and her work. Seven pairs of eyes were on her. Ros looked at Bet and then Rose lowering her head shaking it from side to side.

"I don't know!" she said lifting her head and sighing.

"Want my advice?" Sal breathed gliding over to Ros's side slipping her backside onto the table so she was facing her.

"Go on," Ros said running her hands through her hair.

"Don't tell him!" Sal said lifting her ghost-like hand for Ros to let her finish.

"Well, think about it darling. Your only just preggie anything could happen! God forbid it did. But until your three months gone there is a chance! Plus if Tommy knows now, even though he's working away at the moment, he'd expect you to be at home with your feet up wouldn't he?"

"True," Ros said nodding.

Life for Ros and Tommy seemed to be getting better and better. Ben was so impressed with Tommy's work on the bar he'd brought, that he'd put the word around for him and for the past three months Tommy had been working away on some studios in Buckhamshire for a big producer Ben knew and was loving every minute. Ros didn't feel so guilty lying to Tommy about work seeing that he wasn't at home knowing her every move. Bet had, had a quiet word with John about the confidentiality of the Club and her girls. She had also made it clear to Ben that if he wanted the girls to entertain privately for him, that Tommy was not to know! Ben understanding perfectly made a deal with Bet for a cut in fee's for his silence. Bet agreed knowing better than to cut her nose off to spite her face. Ros being blissfully unaware of Bet and Bens deal just accepted it as coincidence when every 'private party' Ben held Tommy was working away. The girls however weren't so naive and had asked Rose outright what was going on. Rose made them swear not to let Ros know anything. The girls agreed as Ben always gave each girl a bonus before she left the party making it worth their while to keep quiet.

"When's 'e back Ros?" Bet asked through her cloud.

"Oh, he's nearly finished so late Friday night. I'm so excited but scared as well! I don't know if I'll be able to keep my mouth shut. He knows I'll be doing the test this week," Ros replied smiling at the thought of Tommy's return.

"Well, it's up ta you lovey ain't it!" Bet said eyeing Rose.

"Umm I know, but Sal is right. If I tell him now he'll expect me to stop working. That was the deal!"

"Haven't we got a party booked Friday night?" Rose asked to who ever was listening.

"D'you want me ta go get the book?" Misty asked Rose.

"I'm heading that way," she added halfway out the door.

"Could you babe that'll be great," Rose said giving Misty a smile and catching Bets glare.

"What?" she hissed at her.

Bet raised a finger at Rose to be quiet, then shouted over to Ros.

"So do we 'ave ya workin' or not lovey? Only I'll 'ave ta let Kirsty know Thursday latest!"

"I'm talking to Tommy tonight, so I'll know for definite when I come in later," Ros called not looking in Bet and Rose's direction.

Rose raised her eyebrows to Bet to let her know she understood Bet's glare, and lit a cigarette.

Misty came back with the book and dumped it down on the table in front of Rose.

"I didn't realise how bloody heavy that thing is!" she exclaimed wandering off to the girls.

Rose opened it up on the date they were talking about.

"Yup I was right! Oh fucking shit! You'll never guess?" she whispered to Bet.

"Don't 'ave ta fuckin' guess!" Bet replied looking over at Ros and sighing.

"Don't look like she's gonna 'ave ta tell 'im this weekend!" she said shaking her head.

"Fuckin' men I 'ate 'em," Bet hissed.

Rose looked at Bet open mouthed.

"She's really got to you that one hasn't she?" she said quietly.

"Yep," Bet sighed.

"Ya can see it's gonna all end in tears can't ya? I really 'ope fer 'er sake it don't, but she enjoys 'er work too much ta let it go. She's like me that one. Mark me words if 'e 'urts 'er she'll come back fightin'."

Rose nodded. She didn't have to say anything she knew Bet's history.

"Who's the party booked for Rose?" Kel asked looking over Rose's shoulder as she passed to the kitchen.

"Want anything brought back?"

Both Rose and Bet put their hands up to say no thanks and Rose said in a business voice.

"Ben Johnson. A birthday party for one of the band members," she said non committal.

"He didn't say who then?" Kel asked curiously.

"Nope the only requirement is you six as usual and a naked buffet!!"

Rose said reading the notes by the booking frowning.

"What the fucks a naked buffet?" Jude boomed across the room.

Rose looked at Bet in amazement Bet started to laugh.

"Got ears like fuckin' Dumbo ain't she?" she said breaking into a cough.

"Well, considering where she is. I think I'll have to agree with you," Rose smirked.

"I heard that an' all!" Jude grinned at them.

"Heard what?" the others stopped to find out what was going on.

"Nufink," Bet shouted

"Just got a naked buffet ta do fer Ben Johnson on Friday night. One of the guys birfday an' before ya ask we don't know who!" Bet finished.

"And who's the buffet?" Sal asked wrinkling her nose and sticking it in the air not fancying it at all.

"Wot about Kel an' Ros, or Kirsty if yer can't make it lovey," Bet said to Ros.

"See if Ros 'ere ain't gonna make it Kirsty ain't gonna 'aft ta learn any of yer moves 'as she!" Bet explained.

"Good idea," Rose agreed.

"Oh, thank God for that!" Sal said covering her long neck dramatically with her hands.

"I really didn't fancy being covered in cheese and egg mayo sarnies!" she gasped.

"I dunno, I think I'd quite enjoy it!" Jude replied licking her lips.

The rest of the girls raised their eyes to the heavens and giggled.

"That's why it's Kel an' Ros you gutsy bitch!" Bet shot back laughing at Jude.

"Well, save us some grub girls!" Jude said rubbing her stomach.

"Right so it's sorted. Kel and Ros if not Ros then Kirsty. An' yer gonna let me know tonight latest Ros yeh?" Bet said getting up from the table looking at a nodding Ros.

"An congratulations lovey. I 'ope you an' our Tommy'll be very 'appy!"

"Yeh!" all the girls breathed at Ros their coffee morning ending.

Bet put her hand on Rose's shoulder and whispered in her ear.

"'ow much ya willin' ta bet 'e don't come 'ome Friday? The only fing is I can't work out who's got the 'ots fer 'er Ben or John!" she chuckled walking out the door.

Ros went home after the coffee morning. She felt so restless, half of her wanted to tell Tommy to get his arse home he's going to be a Dad! The other half felt she should keep it to herself for the time being just in case Sal was right. She looked down at her belly cupping it with both hands, still not quite believing there was another person inside. Rubbing her stomach she grinned as she daydreamed about her and Tommy pushing the pram down the high street, Tommy the proud father strutting along his head held high like a cockerel. Ros giggled to herself at the thought. Wandering into the hall she noticed the postman had been and picked up the letters tapping them.

"Even you horrible bills can't knock the smile off my face today!" she said sticking her tongue out at them and throwing them on the hall table.

She headed up the stairs to have a bath and a nap before she went to work.

Ros woke to the phone ringing down stairs. She jumped out of bed taking the stairs two at a time, jumping the last three. She dived into the front room grabbing the phone as much to stop the noise as answer it.

"Hello," she gasped down the phone rubbing her eyes.

"Ros that you babe?" Tommy asked not sure he'd dialled the right number by the sound of the voice on the other end.

"Oh, Tommy it's you! Sorry darling I was having a nap. Are you okay? What time is it?"

"You really 'ave just woke up ain't ya," Tommy chuckled down the phone.

"An fer your information Mrs Carter it's quarter ta six me sweet. An' yeh I'm fine!" He said grinning, remembering Ros when she first wakes up. "Any fing else before ya take a breath?" he asked joking.

"No. I didn't realise it was that late that's all and I was worried there was something wrong at your end," Ros replied her voice softening.

"Nar not really babe."

"What do you mean not really?" Ros asked quickly panic washing over her.

"It's just that I don't fink I'll be 'ome on Friday babe," he said quickly.

"Oh, Tommy why? I've missed you so much darling I was really looking forward to seeing you!" Ros cried disappointed.

"Me too babe! But the guy told me taday 'e wont's the job done as early as poss. Got some big band comin' next week ta stay. Said 'e'd make it worf me while if I worked the weekend

119

an' finished mid week next," he explained.

"Oh, darling! So when am I going to see you?" Ros asked quietly.

"Probably a week ta day," Tommy said thinking of the work he'd got left to do.

"So next Wednesday! God it seems like forever away!" Ros cried pouting like a child.

"Yeh I know babes but just fink. When I get me arse back, you an' me are gonna 'ave a 'oliday on me bung 'ow's that?" Tommy said proudly.

"Oh, Tommy that sounds wonderful darling, but I'd rather have you back Friday," she smiled down the phone.

"I know babe I know. I miss you too but 'ows a week in the sun sound ta ya just me an' you fer a whole week," Tommy breathed down the phone.

"What abroad?" Ros cried.

"Yeh abroad where d'ya fink fuckin Skegness?" he laughed "You go get the brochure's an' 'ave a look while I'm away an' we can choose when I come 'ome 'ow's that sound? An' if yer really lucky I might be able ta get 'ome fer Tuesday!" He said excitement in his voice.

"Tommy Carter I love you truly I do!" Ros cried down the phone.

"An I love you too babe," he replied.

"Listen babe I've gotta go in a mo me money's runnin' out. I'll give ya a ring Friday cos I'm gonna 'ave a good kip tonight an' work all day an' night Thursday, cos we got the sparkies in on Friday, doin' all the sound systems. So I've gotta 'ave me arse outa there by then. Listen gotta go babe love ya speek ta ya Friday bye love you."

"Bye darling I love you tooo," Ros said tears welling up in her eyes as she heard the pips go.

Wiping away the tears she went into the kitchen and put the kettle on opening the fridge to get the milk out. It suddenly dawned on her that Tommy hadn't even asked if the test was positive or not. Running her hands through her hair and down her face Ros gave a deep sigh for him. 'God he must be really pushed up there!' she thought looking down at her flat belly saying.

"Don't worry darling daddy'll be home soon."

Ros walked into the Club to the sound of riotous laughter coming from the girl's room. She walked in to find Kel laid out on a trolley stark naked but for a pair of sandals and a smile. The girls were standing around her each with different fruits in their hands on the table beside Kel was an assortment of whipped cream, pastries, chocolate sauces, jams, nuts, ice creams and a couple of bottles of champagne. Ros went over to join the fun.

"I don't know what your laughing about Ros that one's for you!" Kel giggled pointing to another identical trolley to hers.

Ros's face was a picture.

"Isn't it a bit cold lying there?"

"Not half as much as it's gonna be when those cows slap on that ice cream!" Kel said grinning.

"I wish it was me gonna be lyin' under all that shit," Jude boomed sticking her finger in the chocolate sauce and seductively sucking it off.

"Yeh well you wouldn't be under it fer long ya gutsy bitch!" Bet piped up from behind Ros her deep crackling laugh filling the room.

"Ow's it goin' then girls? Recon that lot'll cover 'er?" she asked pointing to Kels prostrate body.

"Are you sure this is what was requested?" Sal breathed holding a banana between two fingers as if it would bite her if she held it any tighter.

"Nar ya gotta peel it ya dosey tart!" Bet said seriously.

The girls collapsed and Kel jumped off the trolley.

"It's no good I gotta 'ave a wee that trolley's gone right through me!" she said running out the door, making the roar of laughter louder.

"One fing," Bet said above the laughter.

"Yer can't say yer don't enjoy yer job!" Chuckling and shaking her head as she followed Kel out of the room, turning as she reached the door way she said

"You know if yer workin' Friday yet Ros?"

Ros looked over and nodded.

"Tommy's got to work all weekend to finish, but he'll be back Wednesday week," she said wiping her eyes.

"Surprise surprise!" Bet muttered to herself giving Ros a

nod and leaving them to it.

"Com on Ros get yer kit off. We've only really got tonight ta work out how we're gonna dress ya an' Kel with all this food," Misty said pushing the other trolley next to Kel's.

"Oh, thanks!" Ros said grinning at them starting to undress.

"Don't I get it warmed up for me!" she said putting her hand on the metal top.

"Don't be such a baby! As soon as you lie on it it'll warm up. Just don't move once you're there!" Sal said placing the Banana back and poking the other fruit with a long finger nail and wrinkling her nose.

"Oh, thanks for your sensitivity!" Ros said hopping on to the trolley top and pulling a face.

As she stretched out so Kel came trotting back in and laid out next to her giving her a wink.

"Right what's the plan of action then?" Jude asked the other three picking up a jug of sauce and holding it first over Kel then Ros.

Annie jumped up and down clapping her hands like an excited child.

"Oh, can I pour the sauce over them please Jude, I'm not tall enough to place the food on them, but I recon I could do a good job with that!" she finished pointing to the jug in Jude's hand.

"Who said I was gonna pour it over them? I quite fancy keeping it to meself it taste's fuckin' wonderful!" Jude said to a pouting Annie and grinning she passed it to her.

"Oh, thanks!" Annie beamed

"Now where should I pour it?" she asked the others a glint in her baby blue eyes.

An hour later.

Sal when you've finished putting the finishing touches on them I think they'll be ready!" Misty said standing back to admire their work.

"I'll go get Bet and Rose," Annie said running out the room her blonde hair bouncing behind her.

"Right don't move now girls," Sal breathed taking a glacier cherry between two finger nails and hovering over one of Kels brown nipples piped with cream.

"If you move now you'll look like your tit's are odd so

122

don't!" Sal said judging where to place the cherry, one eye shut and the tip of her tongue poking out of the corner of her mouth in concentration.

Sal placed the cherry on each nipple and one in their crotch. Jude got up from rolling a huge joint to see the finished result. She walked from one end to the other of each trolley rubbing her chin.

"Not bad! Not bad at all. Well it's made me 'ungry anyway!" she said taking the finished joint to Misty, who inhaled deeply letting the smoke drift from her nose.

"You girls want a puff?" she asked waving the cigarette across their noses and laughing.

She slipped the tip of the cigarette first in Ros's mouth then Kels both took a long drag on it

"Hey, be careful will you! If you breath too deeply the food might fall off you!" she said covering her eyes.

"Fer fuck sake don't fart!" Misty burst out.

"You'll pebbledash the walls!"

The room fell silent. Then they all burst out in fits of laughter.

Ros and Kel's bodies shook where they tried not to move. The more the girls looked at them the worst they got. Their breasts were giggling all over the place making the cherries look as if they had a life of their own, bouncing about the trolley. Ice cream shook on their bellies like a first timer on the ice rink. The bananas placed in the ice cream bounced up and down like a vibrator turned on full. Annie came through the door with Bet and Rose to see the bouncing bananas do a final shake then slap one in between Ros's legs. The other over Kel's left leg. Both Ros and Kel's eye's shot open their mouth's making an 'O'. they held their position for a couple of seconds as the shock of the cold banana hit their bodies making them look like a couple of blow up dolls.

"Fuck me! That's the fuckin' funniest fing I've ever seen in me life!" Bet burst in clapping.

"Oh, no don't I'm going to pee myself if you don't stop!" Ros screamed tears rolling down the side of her face and dripping in her ears.

"Pleeese!" she begged laughing.

"Arr! You cow!" she laughed as Jude sploshed another huge dollop of ice cream on to her stomach making her want a wee all the more. She sat up scooping a hand full of grapes ice cream and chocolate sauce in her hands and chucked them over Jude. Jude stood motionless for a few seconds the ice cream and sauce slipping down her face, three grapes balancing on top of her head.

The room fell silent as the food hit Jude. No one knew what to do they didn't know how Jude was going to react. She simply stuck out her tongue and licked as much of the ice cream she could reach off. Kel jumped up from the trolley and shouted.

"FOOD FIGHT!" scooping an armful of now crushed fruit and melted ice cream, and flung it around the room.

She managed to get all of them with one swipe. Every one froze as the goo hit them. Kel and Ros high fived each other on their trolley's and burst out laughing. By the time the eight of them had finished the room looked like the insides of a knicker blocka glory glass! There wasn't a bare piece of skin left, they were covered from head to toe in the sticky goo and they'd loved every minute of it.

"Ere who fancies a night out tamorrow?" Jude piped up from under a table.

"I do!" Annie called from behind a chair slowly standing up her hands in the air surrendering.

Eventually all the women came out from their hiding places flopping onto the nearest chair or stool.

"You fancy it Bet? Rose?" Kel asked lighting a cigarette.

"Wot after tonight! Nar thanks loveys," Bet said wiping some kiwi from her eyebrow and grinning.

"Nor me thanks girls!" Rose panted.

"I think I'm going to spend all of tonight laying in the bath," she gasped reaching for a bottle of lemonade and unscrewing the lid.

"So it's just us lot is it?" Jude said slipping over to Annie and a chair a big grin on her face.

"God 'elp the island tamorrow night!" Bet quipped chuckling.

"Yeh! Where do you lot fancy going?" Sal ever the lady sat down crossing her legs, wiping away some mashed banana from

124

her shoulder.

"Oh, I don't know. How about we start at the local an' see what happen's shall we," Annie said looking at Jude for support. She'd fancied the barman for ages.

"Yeh why not," Jude said sealing the plans for the night.

"Okay why not!" they all agreed

"Now who's going in the shower after Bet and I?" Rose said looking over her shoulder as she headed for the door.

"Oh, I don't fink I will! I taste goood!" Jude grinned giving herself a lick as the others watched on and giggled.

Ros woke in her 'room' she hadn't bothered to go home last night. Looking at the clock on the wall she couldn't believe her eye's. It was half past twelve, she'd slept like a baby! Moving her legs she still felt sticky from the night before. She thought back to the food fight and grinned touching her hair and wincing, it was still stiff from all that sauce. Getting out of bed she stretched and headed for the shower rubbing her neck as she went. When she was dressed she went down stairs to the kitchen. Walking through the door she said.

"That smells good Doughy what you cooking up today?"

"Oh, thought I'd do you girls a nice stew tonight you in later?"

"No I'm not," Ros said in a disappointed voice.

"An that smells so good as well!" she said walking over to the huge saucepan and lifting the lid.

"Ere 'ave a taste," Doughy said passing Ros a spoon.

"I can give ya the recipe if ya want?" she said getting a pen and paper, scribbling as she walked back to her and handing it over.

"See you lot 'ad some fun last night!" she said her hands on her hips and an eyebrow raised.

"Poor old Mary 'ad a bloody awful time getting all that crap off the walls an' carpets!" she said tutting and grinning at Ros.

"We did make a bit of a mess didn't we!" Ros said giving Doughy a guilty look.

"Umm," Doughy agreed.

"You stayin' 'ome tonight then?" she asked changing the subject.

"No actually we're all having a girls night out tonight."

"Oh, Christ! God 'elp 'em!" Doughy whistled looking to the heavens and crossing herself.

Ros laughed and poured two cups of tea from the pot. It never stopped amazing her that no matter what time she came into the kitchen the pot was always hot!

"Here Doughy come and sit down with me and I'll give you a hand with those vegetables after," Ros said pointing to the two cups on the table sitting down in front of one of them. Doughy wrung out her hands on her pinny and waddled over to the other chair and cup plonking her ample backside on the chair.

"You're a darlin' Ros me old legs are givin' me a right old toof ache taday!" she said rubbing her calves.

"Hear you got some news ta tell me young ladie!" Doughy said not looking up from the biscuit tin she was trying to open.

Ros grinned

"Yep I have Doughy but if you already know why do you want me to tell you?" she asked still grinning but a little confused.

"Cos I like ta be told meself not by gossip then I can't get in ta any trouble can I!" she replied passing the opened tin to Ros and smirking.

"Oh, Doughy you're quite a character you know that?" Ros said laughing and leaning across the table, planted a kiss on Doughy's powdered cheek.

"Aw go on wif ya!" Doughy said proudly giving Ros a motherly squeeze on the arm.

"'ow far ya gone then?" she asked putting her cup to her lips.

"Only about six weeks," Ros said looking down at her belly.

Doughy nodded.

"Early days yet girl," she said giving her a motherly warning.

"Oh, don't I know! I haven't told Tommy yet. I'm taking Sal's advice and going to wait a few more weeks. I don't want to get his hopes up then disappoint him do I?" she asked rather than told the older woman.

"Look lovey when ya meant ta tell 'im ya will," she replied looking like Gypsy Rose Lee reading the tea leaves.

Nodding Ros got up from the table.

"Right where are the veggies? I'll start on the potatoes shall I?" she said heading for the pantry.

"Okay lovey," Doughy replied heaving herself up saying.

"Pot's are on the left hand side Ros. An' bring out that swede and collie will ya," As she waddled over to the sink, turning on the tap.

"So where you lot going tonight?" she asked picking up her knife.

"I think we're starting at the local then seeing what happens," Ros said diving into the sac of potatoes.

"Umm know why yer startin at the local don'tcha?" Doughy asked a mischievous look on her face.

"Noo why?" Ros stopped what she was doing and put her hands on her hips as if she was the mother and Doughy the child.

"Come on tell me?" she said raising one eyebrow.

"Little Annie!" Doughy said grinning.

"Little Annie what?" Ros said.

"The bloke behind the bar! Annies crazy about 'im. Goes all bloody gooy when she see's 'im. Come's in 'ere twirling around like a love sick fairy!" Doughy said taking hold of the cauliflower and cutting off its outer leaves.

"Nooo! No one's told me!" Ros looked shocked.

"How long our Annie been after him?" She questioned.

"Oh, a couple of months from wot I gather," Doughy looked up a questioning look on her face.

"What?" Ros said concerned

"Well, you'd fink wif wot she does fer a livin' she'd 'ave the balls ta ask the guy out wouldn't ya?" Doughy said shaking her head and tutting.

"So she's got it real bad then?" Ros said smiling.

"Yup," Doughy replied attacking the vegetable.

"Well, we'll have to see what can be done for our Annie tonight then won't we!" Ros said a gleam in her eyes.

"Some one's gotta do sumfing wif 'er, the poor gels just a jibbering wreck. When she see's 'im fink wot she's gonna be like if 'e speaks to 'er! Poor cow'll pee 'erself!" Doughy giggled.

"Oh, we'll sort her out don't you worry darling," Ros said putting the last of the potatoes in the sauce pan.

"Well, if there's anything else I can do for you say now!" Ros grinned giving her shoulders a squeeze.

"Nar ta. You run off now an' 'ave a good night you 'ear," Doughy said pecking Ros on the cheek.

"See you Friday before we go out. Bye darling," Ros said heading for the door, then giving Doughy a wave she was gone.

Chapter 12

Draining the last of the wine from her glass, she walked over to their stereo and lifted the needle. The house fell silent. She took a last deep drag on her joint dropping it into the ashtray dramatically doing a little wiggle at it. Opening her bag she pulled out her lipstick taking off the lid she walked over to the mirror above the fireplace and re did her lips pressing them together she pouted then blew herself a kiss. Turning on her heels she placed the lip stick in her bag, patted the back of her hair down, checked her backside in the mirror, picked up her keys, turning the light switch as she went out the door. Shutting it, she took one more look in the dinning room and kitchen, checking the windows and doors before opening the front door and walking out, pushing the door to make sure the latch had caught. She checked her earrings were straight, put her keys in to her bag, slipped it over her left shoulder and walked down the path heading for the local.

As Ros walked into the pub a group of lads leaning against the door frame looked her up and down, giving her a wolf whistle as she passed them. In return Ros gave them a wiggle of her backside grinning over her shoulder. She headed to the girls table, Annie, Jude and Misty were already there. Annie the best she'd ever looked hiding in the corner seat looking coyly towards the bar, where the object of her desire was serving. Ros grinned.

"Boy has she got it bad!" she said nodding towards Annie as she got level with Jude and Misty.

Both girls looked up at her grinning nodding into their glasses.

"You didn't 'ang around though did ya!" Jude said shaking her bobbed head in the lads' direction making the others laugh. Ros grinned.

"Well, I had to give them something back for their

appreciation!"

"An you the only fuckin' married one amongst us!" Jude shot back waving her index finger at her.

"Oh, sorry mum!" Ros said sucking her thumb.

"Any one want a drink seein' I've got to get one?" Ros asked looking to each of them and memorising what they wanted.

"Come on Annie you can help me carry them back," she said leaning across the table grabbing Annie before she could slip back out of her grasp.

"Go on Ros pull her!" Misty jumped off her chair to make way for a protesting Annie, sitting straight back down so she couldn't get back.

Ros took her by the arm pulling her towards the bar.

"Annie's bein' dragged closer and closer to 'er dream bloke an' all she keeps doin' is look at us with pleading in 'er eyes. What the fuck's wrong wif 'er Misty? You'd never believe wot she did would ya? I fink she's the most unrealistic hooker I've ever known!" Jude said laughing at Annies face.

"Don't Jude!" Misty giggled resting her elbows on the table.

"I think it's really sweet!" she said staring at Ros and Annie at the bar. Ros ordering the drinks. Annie standing next to her looking every where but in the barmans direction.

Misty caught her eye and gestured for her to turn around to face the bar.

Annies face was such a picture of panic that Misty and Jude collapsed in a fit of giggles. Sal and Kel glided in straight over to them demanding to know what they'd missed out on. All Jude and Misty could do was point towards the bar at Annie, her big hair following her head as she shook it, waving her hands at her side trying to stop them bringing attention to her, but it was too late. As she turned to the bar the guy was leaning across the bar inches from Annie's face, then cupping her face with both hands, kissed her puckered lips. Releasing her, he looked in to her eyes and said.

"Hi gorgeous I'm Greg," And smiling at her, he walked away to serve some one else leaving Annie paralysed at the bar her head stretched forward over the bar still with her lips puckered, her eyes wide open. Ros gave her a little shake to bring her back to earth. She looked at Ros in a startled way.

"Did I just dream that?" she asked pointing to the bar, then at Ros, round to the girls, who were all laughing so much that there were tears rolling down their faces dripping on to their tops.

"It's not funny you lot!" Annie called over to them trying to look hurt, but couldn't keep the grin from her face.

"Thanks Greg!" Ros called over to the barman.

"No thank you for tellin' me!" He said with a wink.

"W... what but!" Annie stood speechless.

Ros pecked her on the cheek

"Greg's a friend of Tommy's so I just happened to mention earlier today when I saw him that I knew a lovely person who was very interested in him, and that I'd bring you up to the bar with me tonight. You must have made some kind of an impression for him to do that!" Ros grinned.

"Oh, Ros you moo!" Annie bounced back to the girls her imp face all smiles. She flopped down on the nearest chair and did a dreamy sigh raising her eyes to the ceiling. They all reached over to her giving her a comforting squeeze on the arm and shoulders trying to contain their giggles.

"It's okay girls you can laugh if you want to I don't care!" Annie said taking a sip of her drink and sticking her nose in the air.

They all collapsed in a heap.

"Here's to a girls night out," Sal said delicately raising her glass with two fingers and a thumb.

"Girls night out!" they all toasted together.

"Right what do we all fancy doing?" Kel asked placing her empty glass on the table.

"Ow's about another round then girls?" A dark voice they all knew broke in.

"Oh, Al you angel! Mines a brandy and Babycham," Sal breathed turning and placing a ghost-like hand on his forearm looking back over her shoulder at the others, who nodded.

"Better make that six darling," Sal said giving him a smouldering look.

"Six Brandy and Babychams coming up girls," Al said tapping Sal on the shoulder.

"Fancy givin' us a 'and beautiful?"

Sal smiled sweetly, then elegantly uncrossed her long legs and glided from the chair to Al's side.

"Ow the fuck she do that?" Jude said nudging Ros in the ribs.

"I don't know but I wish I could!" Ros said shaking her head and grinning.

"Wot you boy's doin' 'ere?" Jude asked the other three as they took their seats.

"We got a gig down thc road an' thought we'd 'ave a jar 'ere before we went over," Gary the bass player explained sliding in next to Kel slopping his beer on the table.

"You fuckin' sloppy bastard!" John called to him sitting down next to Ros.

"All right darlin'?" he said running his fingers up her thigh and giving her a cheeky grin.

"I'm fine thank you!" she replied removing his hand from her leg and crossing them away from him.

Paul the drummer went round the table sitting in the corner where Annie had been earlier, putting his glass on the table he leaned forward across the table.

"Ere any of you girls wont a spliff?" he said pulling out a plastic bag and some papers, making a valley with the crease of denim at the top of his legs.

"Paul you are a top man!" Misty grinned blowing him a kiss.

"You tellin' me babe!" Paul said winking and turning his attention to his task.

Al and Sal arrived back at the table Sal carrying a tray of the girl's drinks and Al carrying four pints of beer for the guy's.

"Ere Sal an' I 'ave been 'avin' a natter. Why don't you girls come ta the gig an' watch us, free booze! As our guests 'ow's that?"

The girls all gave the thumbs up and Jude being the protector said

"That'll be great fellas but can we make one thing perfectly clear?"

The guy's all nodded, smirking.

"We that is us six, are on a girls night out. We are not

working now! Understand?"

"Ya mean we ain't gotta pay fer it?" John piped up. The rest of them girls as well burst out laughing.

Annie excused herself.

"Don't leave without me you lot I'll only be a mo!" she cried, heading towards the bar.

"Where she goin' all of a sudden?" Kel asked composing herself and sitting off of Gary.

"Think she's got a bit of Dutch courage in 'er!" Jude said lifting her glass and drinking the last of her drink down.

"Com on girls drink up. We've gotta make a move in a while, an' we wont ta get another round in yet!" Paul said lighting the huge joint in the corner a cloud of smoke eloping him.

"Sounds good to me!" Sal giggled leaning on Al.

John stood up.

"Same again girls?" he asked nodding towards the table.

They all agreed.

"I'll get Annie ta give us a hand," he said placing a hand on Ros's shoulder when she moved to stand up.

She looked up to him the bulge in his trousers inches from her face. He looked down into her eyes smiling. Ros felt something stir deep in her belly as a red flush crept up her neck, the moment seemed to last an eternity. Pulling her eyes away she looked around the table. No one seemed to notice what had taken place.

Annie came back from the bar desperately trying to control the tray of drinks in front of her.

"Oh, girls," she gushed putting the tray on the table.

"Look what I've got!" she said sliding her hand from under the tray.

Entwined in her fingers was a piece of till receipt. Waving it in front of their faces she pulled it out straight showing a name and number.

"He's sooo sweet!" she clasped the paper to her and spun round.

"You'd better let yer new guy know where we're gonna be so 'e can come an' see ya later!" Paul said grinning in the corner

"Ere ya'd better get 'is full name so we can bung it on the

door," he said passing Annie a pad from inside his jacket pocket and she disappeared to the bar again scribbleing something down as she went.

"That girls so sweet and excitable!" Jude said shaking her head always looking out for her.

"You two got a fing goin' girl?" Al said leaning across the table for a lighter and nudging Paul. The two of them giggled like a couple of school boys.

"Jeesus it don't take a lot ta please ya does it!" Jude threw back grinning.

John had just finished telling them a joke, when a blonde haired lad of about fourteen came striding up to the group determination on his face, attitude in his step. John looked up giving the kid a wink.

"All right Dan mate?" he asked running his hand down Ros's leg.

Dan looked at John's hand moving up and down, looking straight into Ros's eyes making her shiver and move John's hand. The child seemed to be able to look right into her and she felt as if all her skeletons were being dragged from her. Blinking, Dan broke the stare saying something in John's ear. John flicked him a cigarette and he strutted out the pub.

"Five minutes guys. Drink up will ya ladies, we gotta hit the road!" John said draining the last of his beer and taking the joint from Al and lighting it up.

"Where you playing boys?" Kel asked draining the last of her drink and picking up her cigarettes lighting one, she dropped the packet in to her bag along with her lighter.

"About a ten minute drive off the island along the front," Gary said taking the last drag of the joint and stubbing in out with his thumb in the ashtray.

"Shall we?" Paul said standing up from the corner and shrugging his shoulders back into his slipped black jacket.

They all stood up and Annie ran back excited as a puppy passing the pad to Paul.

"He's gonna come over when he's finished," she told the girls clapping her hands together as if she was praying to God.

"Thank you Ros," she said squeezing her arm.

"Come on ladies, move yer arses will ya!" Gary said

slapping Misty and Kels backsides as they passed him following John, Ros, and Annie to the door.

Once outside they were faced with an old 'Plaxdon' coach, the doors flung open at the front, the smell, of diesel coming from the engine. The four guys motioned to the girls with their arms to climb aboard. Ros climbed up first followed by the others. As she reached the last step and looked down the end of the coach, she noticed the lad sitting near the back, feet up across the seat. Their eyes locked again for a few seconds before the noise of the others made her move. Dan smiled slowly and turned around to talk to the roadies.

The girls sat two to a seat behind the driver chatting and giggling like a group from an all girls boarding school escaped for the night.

The four guy's bounced on to the coach.

"Right listen up ya fuckin' 'orrible lot, are we gonna 'ave a right fuckin' good time or wot!" John shouted down the old coach.

Everyone cheered and whooped.

"Any one who ain't 'ere ain't comin'!" he shouted again running up the back of the coach and leaping on to the huge bunk at the back.

"Who's got the blues then?" he shouted as he reached in to a compartment pulling a yellow liqueur bottle out and opening it. Taking a swig he replaced the lid, threw it on the bunk and slid off heading to a roadie with his arm up. Taking a small package he said.

"Cheers Sam me man!"

Opening it he pulled out a little blue tablet and placed it in his mouth, passing the package on to Al, who took out three then, standing up said,

"Any of you girls won' one?" waving the bag in the air.

All six shook their heads.

"No tar," Misty called.

"But if ya got any of that green stuff it would be most appreciated!" she said in a posh voice accepting a small package from Paul and a pack of red papers.

"You're a gent," she said blowing him a kiss.

"Let's get some fuckin music on in this old heap can we

135

someone!" Gary shouted from the back, catching a can of beer that had been thrown to him.

"Fuckin' nearly took me 'ead off yer bastards!" he cried laughing.

A roar came from the back as the music shook the coach as it bombed up the hill.

"If we don't sort this piece of shit out soon, we'll all be fuckin' pushing it off the island!" John shouted from the front, a huge grin on his face, his feet tapping in time with the beat of the music.

"Leave the old road runner alone will ya!" the driver Dick called taking his eyes off the road for a couple of seconds to look down the back of the coach at them.

"All right girls we're gonna be there in about five minutes so get yerselves lookin' good fer us me darlin's," John joked as he walked back to the other end again, checking everyone knew what they were doing when they got there.

"Has any one seen this lot play in a gig, apart from Ros's wedding an' our private parties?" Sal breathed climbing up on her seat and looking down the coach.

"I have," Ros said nodding.

"They're really good!"

"When you seen 'em then?" Jude asked leaning over Ros's seat.

"Tommy and I often go an' see them play. They do loads of local gigs and have just got their first album out actually," she said sounding very knowledgeable about them.

"Plus, I suppose having John as one of ya regular gents you hear it all then as well!" Annie burst in a bit louder than she expected.

Ros poked her head around her seat and looked down the aisle. The only person that was watching and listening was Dan! He stared straight ahead at her. Ros sat round quickly as if she'd been slapped.

"You okay honey? I didn't mean it to come out so loud honest!" Annie whispered to the white Ros.

Ros put a hand up and forced a smile.

"It's okay Annie. I shouldn't have turned around so quickly after all that drink and smokies! Ijust went a little dizzy that's all," she lied getting her lipstick out and a small mirror. Smiling she said.

"Better do what the man said. Want some after me?" she asked, showing Annie the colour of her make-up.

Annie nodded giving Ros a concerned look.

By the time Annie had given herself a last look in Ros's mirror the coach had arrived at its destination.

"Right 'er we are lads! Are we gonna kick arse tonight or wot!" John shouted walking to the front.

"You girls follow me an' the guys in. Then you'll 'ave ta entertain yerselves until we've set up okay wif you?" he asked.

"Fine by us," Kel spoke for all six, as they stood up and arranged their clothing.

"Com'on then you lot! Looks like we've quite a welcomin' party tonight!" John shouted at the guys and roadies, who all cheered back laughing and joking as they moved down the coach.

The gig went really well and the girls were totally exhausted by the end.

They had, had such a great time letting their hair down and screaming at the guys like a bunch of groupies.

When the guys came off stage they were all hyped up on the adrenalin still pumping.

"I fink it's party time!" Paul shouted to them as he took a pint of beer from the barman.

"Wot ya say girls!" he said grabbing Misty's backside and squeezing it.

"Well, I'm up for it!" she said running a finger down his cheek and winking at him.

Paul grabbed hold of her pulling her close and kissing her full on the mouth.

"You're a horny bitch you know that?" he said smiling down at her.

Misty seductively kissed her finger and placed it on Paul's lips, giving him a wink she turned to the bar and picked up her drink.

"Right all back ta the 'ouse then!" John said rolling a joint on the bar not giving a shit who saw him.

Annie ran up to the girls.

"Look Greg an' I are going back to his. So I'll see you lot tomorrow," she said jumping up and down.

"Go girl!" Jude kissed her.

"I wanna hear all about it ya 'ear me!" she said laughing.

"Have a wonderful night darling!" Ros said grinning remembering how her and Tommy used to be.

"Oh, I will!" Annie said blowing them all a kiss and running off.

The coach pulled up at the house and everyone clambered down the steps piling onto the pavement outside.

"Come on you lot let's get this party on the road or in the fuckin' 'ouse. Oh fuck ya know wot the fuck I'm on about!" Al said grinning and running down the drive.

"I thought this was Ben's house!" Ros said to John as they walked around the back.

"Let's just say it's communal shall we!" he said laughing.

"Now get yer arse in will ya!" slapping Ros's backside then gently rubbing it in a circular movement.

Ros felt a shiver run down her spine and she closed her eyes as he gave her a gentle push through the back door.

Every one crashed into the front room. The candles were lit giving the room a warm sensual feel. One of the roadies turned on the stereo and the deep crackling of the record filled the room before the silence was replaced with a deep full bodied beat. Someone placed a crate of beer on the floor and put the spirits and mixers on the table by the kitchen.

Paul pulled Misty on to his lap as he fell on to a chair, making her spill the drink she was holding straight down her front taking her breath away.

Paul gave her a cheeky grin and licked from her neck to her cleavage.

Misty threw her head back laughing, draping her arm around Paul's neck.

She slipped her hand into his top pocket, pulling out his rolling material and waving it. Paul looked up at her hand and grinned.

"Give us it 'ere darlin' an' I'll roll us one ta go ta 'eaven wif!" putting out his hand. Misty dropped the stuff on to Paul's upturned hand.

138

"You stay just as ya are fer me an' I'll roll it on yer lap babe," he said pulling two papers from his pack and sticking them together.

Kel dragged Gary by his tie into the middle of the room letting her body feel the beat. She began to dance around him holding his tie in one hand letting the other travel over his body. Kel slipped his tie off draping it around her neck. She then pressed her body up close to Gary's wiggling in time to the beat. Kel could feel the bulge in his trousers growing.

Looking into his eyes she smiled pushing herself harder on to him. He grabbed at her but she broke free laughing as she gyrated around him.

"Come 'ere ya little prick tease," he laughed rubbing his cock through his trousers.

"You got a problem mate?" Al shouted laughing from the kitchen door way. Sal drapped a long white arm on his shoulder, smiling at Kel and Gary.

"How about I tease your prick?" she whispered in his ear running her hand down his shirt to his trousers.

"How about it babe! Follow me," he said grabbing her hand and leading her through the studio door locking it after him.

"Christ your mate's eager ain't she?" Sam one of the roadies said to a very stonned Jude.

"Call that eager!" she said dropping to her knees and pulling down his jean zip with her teeth. When she'd accomplished her task she looked up at him, growled, pinching her finger and thumb together.

"You crazy bitch!" Sam laughed pulling her up and kissing her.

"Yer friends seem ta be 'avein' a good time!" John said smiling at Ros.

"Umm I know," she said turning to face him but keeping her eyes from his.

"Wots the matter Ros not enjoyin' yerself?" he questioned raising an eyebrow.

"Of course. I'm just coming down a bit that's all," she answered.

"Well, we can't 'ave that can we!" he said going over to Paul whipping the joint from his mouth and giving him a wink.

He passed it to Ros, who laughingly took it along with a glass of what John was drinking. 'Whatever's in that yellow liqueur bottle. It tastes a bit like coffee.' She thought. But after a couple of puffs on one of Paul's joints you didn't know what planet you we're on, let alone what you were drinking!

"Com on Ros drink up! Let's make a punch wif all this booze. Might taste a bit better all in together. Whatcha say?" John said a mischievous grin on his face.

"I say you're mad!" Ros cried stifling a giggle.

"Too fuckin' right! Ain't no point bein' normal! Too fuckin' borin' don't ya fink?" he laughed dragging her over to the table.

"Ere Dan. Do us a favor will ya. Go get me a huge bowl outta the kitchen. Cheer's mate!" John called to the lad, as he started to take the lids off of all the spirits.

Dan came back with a bowl placing it on the table between John and Ros.

He gave Ros a knowing smirk and disappeared into the room. Ros felt exposed again. 'Who is he?' she thought, turning her attentions back to John and the punch. When every bottle was poured into the bowl he threw in a whole apple and an orange for good measure. Turning round he shouted into the room, holding up a glass of the deadly liquid.

"Listen 'ere you fuckin' miserable lot! We've just mixed up a fuckin' rockin' potion fer us now let's get this room movin'! Someone fer fuck sake bung some livelier sounds on. Al! get yer fuckin' arse out 'ere will ya! We're gonna 'ave a bit of fun!" swigging a mouthful of the punch from the glass.

"Jeesus that's fuckin' shit!" he said passing it to a laughing Ros, who taking a sip coughed and splattered.

"Ere 'ave some more it tastes better after two!" John said pushing the glass towards her again.

Sal and Al emerged from the studio. Sal looking as if butter wouldn't melt and Al, looking hot and flustered.

Ros took one look at them and burst into a fit of giggles.

"See told ya this gears good!" John called to the others who were by now dragging themselves up and over to the bowl.

Ros started dancing around the room in a world of her own. The beat of the music carrying her away.

By the time three songs had finished everyone had, had at

least two glasses of the powerful concoction and were in the mood. The atmosphere started to get hot and smoky. Misty complained she was hot and started to strip her clothes off followed by the rest. They ripped at each garment tossing it into the room. Within minutes all the guys had on were their smiles and the girls their shoes. Everyone started to grind their bodies. You could feel the tension in the air. Sal and Misty moved closer together rubbing their bodies against each other. Paul and Al pressed themselves up against their backs. The girls could feel their cocks pushing in the crease of their backsides.

Jude grabbed Sam the roadie and pushing him down on a chair straddled him. He pushed her huge nipples together sucking them both at the same time. Jude bounced up and down on his hard cock. He grabbed her full arse cheeks, pulling her harder on to him.

Gary had Kel in the corner of the sofa her legs draped over his shoulders, his head buried between her legs. Kel threw her head back and arched herself towards him holding his head with both hands as she came.

Al by this time was lying on the carpet with Sal straddled on top of him, her body facing his feet. She leaned back so Al could pull on her hard nipples as Misty on her hands and knees licked her clit. Paul was on his knees fucking her doggy style. Replacing his cock with his fingers, he slipped himself into her arse pumping in slow rhymatic movements until she was pushing him deeper and faster into her making him explode.

John sat Ros on a dining room chair lifting her head she looked into his eyes. He held her head with both hands pushing his cock into her mouth inching deeper with each stroke. Ros cupped his tight balls in one hand, grabbing his backside with the other pulling him deeper down her throat.

John pulled away from her before he came. Turning Ros over so that she was kneeling on the chair holding the back, he entered her from behind.

Grabbing her breasts he thrust deep and hard into her. Ros's body shook as she came again and again. Lifting her head reality suddenly hit her.

She opened her eyes to see Dan give her one last knowing smile before he left the room for the night!

Chapter 13

When Ros woke the next morning her head was pounding, she turned over letting out a cry. Some one was next to her. She very slowly lifted the covers. There, sleeping like a baby, was Kel, her long red hair covering the pillow, she disturbed and turning over, she flung her arm across Ros.

Smiling more through relief that it was Kel she lied back on her pillows.

Rubbing her eyes she tried to remember how Kel managed to be in bed with her! Turning her mind back to the night before she shivered. If Tommy ever found out he'd kill her. She slid father down the bed under the covers, only her eyes and nose were exposed. Ros tried desperately to remember. 'God I must have been totally wrecked!' she thought, visions of the night before slowly coming back to her. 'Why'd I go back to the house, when I knew what would happen!' she thought questioning herself. The face of Dan came to her mind and a wave of apprehension washed over her. 'Who was he? He seemed to be able to look right into me and I don't like it! He's too unnerving that one!' she thought feeling cold. Closing her eyes a picture of John grinning came to her. She squeezed them tighter to block everything out. Nothing helped! She felt so guilty.

"Poor Tommy doesn't deserve this!" a voice in her head told her

"I know!" she sighed aloud to herself.

Kel turned opening her eyes and blinking. She sat up in bed covering her body with the covers.

"Ros! How the fuck did I get here?" Kel said her eyes wide with bewilderment and confusion.

"I thought perhaps you could tell me!" Ros said giving Kel a smile.

"Don't ask me!" Kel said stretching and shrugging her

shoulders.

"Shall I go an' put the kettle on?" she asked swinging her legs out of bed and padding over to the bedroom door.

"I might be able ta tell you then!" she said grinning back.

Ros nodded still confused about the night before. She slipped out of her side pulling on a robe.

"Kel use T... Tommy's it's on the door," she said pointing to the bathrobe hanging behind the door and smiling weakly at Kel.

"Cheers Ros," Kel smiled unhooking it and wrapping it around her tiny frame.

"You comin' down or d'you want me ta bring it up?" she asked cupping her hands to look like she was carrying a mug of tea.

"No it's okay I'll come down," Ros replied walking over to the curtains and drawing them.

"Right you are," Kel called trotting down the stairs heading for Ros's kitchen.

Ros looked out of her window the light hurt her eyes. Squinting she looked in the mirror.

"God I look like shit!" she said aloud to herself turning and heading for the bathroom.

By the time she'd got downstairs Kel was just taking their drinks into the front room. Placing the mugs on a plastic scatter table she went to open the curtains.

"No don't!" Ros shouted grabbing her head and diving on to the sofa.

"How the fuck are you so God dammed bouncy after last night?" she winced.

"Oh, sorry Ros you feeling a bit worse for wear?" Kel asked grinning and passing her a cigarette.

"Just slightly!" she said taking the cigarette offered and rubbing the back of her neck.

Kel laughed.

"Well, you were going fer it in a big way wern'tcha?"

"I don't know, I can't remember that much!" Ros said looking horrified.

"Just as well really!" Kel grinned sipping her coffee.

"Why what did I do Kel? You've got to tell me!" she cried

143

panic in her voice.

"Hey, calm down babe you didn't do anything you didn't want to!" Kel replied, looking amused.

"It's not funny I'm a married woman!" Ros cried.

"Yer also a fuckin' good hooker!" Kel cried back going over to the stunned Ros.

"What did I say?" she asked handing her the lighter.

Taking it Ros lit her cigarette with a shaking hand

"Nothing. It just felt as if some one had slapped me when you said that," she said exhaling the smoke.

"See I've never thought of us as common hookers before! But I suppose we are really aren't we?" she sighed.

"Talk fer yer self!" Kel said looking hurt then smiling.

"Were good at our job. That's all it is Ros a job! You've proved that with Tommy an' you getting' married! I know he doesn't really like it. But he hasn't exactly locked you in the house until he comes back has he?" Kel told her.

"The difference is I wasn't working last night, was I! We went for a girl's night out, and I end up not knowing what I've done! I mean I keep having flashes but can't piece any of it together! Was I completely out of order Kel?" she asked frowning "You've got to tell me or I'll go out of my mind!" she said leaning over to pick up her coffee and flicking her ash in the ashtray.

"That depends what you call out of order, bein' married an' all that!" Kel said thoughtfully.

"What! What d'you mean Kel?" Ros asked panic in her voice.

"Well, you an' John!" Kel said giving Ros a clue.

"What about me an' John?" she asked going white trying desperately to remember the night.

"I can remember going back to Ben's and helping John with the punch then it all goes blank… except," Ros paused putting her hands over her face. An image of her on a chair and John behind her flooded back.

"Oh, fuck!" she cried.

"Fuck! Fuck! Fuck!"

"Yup you could say that!" Kel grinned putting out her cigarette in the ashtray.

"Look Ros Tommy ain't gonna find out if that's what yer worried about," Kel said trying to ease her mind.

"It doesn't matter any more!" Ros cried.

"Don't you see!" she said sobbing into her hands.

Kel looked confused.

"No not really Ros! I thought you were scared Tommy would find out! You know about last night!" she said quietly not knowing what was wrong with her.

"Yes! but it should never have happened. I slept with someone else because I wanted to! Not because of the job. Don't you see?" Ros said looking at Kel her eyes wide.

"What aren't you telling me Kel?" she asked seeing Kels face.

"Well, it wasn't just John!" Kel replied quietly looking to the floor not able to meet Ros's stare.

"What!" she cried jumping up.

"Who? When? Where?" she asked pacing the floor.

"Umm… things got a bit wild after we took our clothes off!" Kel said trying to jog her memory.

"What things Kel? Tell me?"

"Well, we all ended in a mass on the floor. I don't know who you were with! I was enjoying myself too much to watch you! But I know you were there when John and I… anyway after a while you suggested you, me, John an' Gary have a foursome that's why I'm here from what I remember!" Kel told her

"What! Noo. What back here?" Ros screamed waving her arms around the room.

Kel nodded lighting another cigarette.

Ros collapsed on the sofa again in total shock and disgust with herself.

Looking at Kel she said.

"Why didn't you stop me?" as if it was Kel's fault it all happened.

Kel feeling no remorse for what she'd done last night said.

"I did! But you insisted we come back here don't ask me why I was just going with the flow! At one point I was getting quite jealous! You were on top form if you know what I mean! You had 'em both panting fer more! She told an already devastated Ros.

"That's it Kel no more I can't handle it! Just answer me one more question though," Ros cried her mind a mess.

"Sure what's that?" Kel asked with out malice.

"Did anyone mention Tommy?"

"No why should they have done?" she answered frowning.

"No... no it doesn't matter darling. I'm not angry with you Kel just myself for doing it!" Ros said sighing and giving her a painful smile.

"I don't see what your problem is Ros. You do it in the Club most nights, why was last night so different? I mean I know we were on a girls night out an' all that," then it dawned on her what Ros had said earlier

"Oh, I understand. It's because they weren't payin' an' you enjoyed it isn't it? Oh... darling... you... enjoyed... it!" Kel said.

Ros crumbled into her robe, sobs wrenched her body.

Kel sat beside her cradling her head.

"It's all right Ros. It's gonna be all right, your just feeling guilty at the moment but when your head clears a bit you'll see it's not that bad really!"

"You don't understand! I think I've fallen in love with John!!" Ros blurted out staring at Kel open mouthed.

All Kel could do was stare straight back she didn't know what to say or do. She was completely gobsmacked!

"Fuck where the hell did that come from?" Ros whispered to herself as much to Kel.

"Don't ask me!" Kel said hunching her shoulders. Getting up she picked up their mugs.

"I think I'll go put the kettle on," she said eager to leave the room.

Ros nodded lost in her thoughts.

Kel came back in the room.

"Look Ros I think you need time to think by yourself. I've put the kettle on and I'm just gonna go and get dressed. I'll see myself out and I'll see you tonight okay darling?" she said quietly.

Not waiting for a response she went upstairs.

Ros came to as the front door shut. Getting up she shuffled to the kitchen pouring the boiled water into her mug and stirring the coffee and milk in.

She opened the kitchen draw pulling out a packet of cigarettes and unwrapped the box. She picked up her mug and wandered back into the front room.

'Why'd I come out with that!' she questioned. 'John why John? I love Tommy don't I? Christ what a mess!' a wave a sheer horror washed over her. 'The baby!' She'd completely forgotten she was pregnant!

"Oh, my God!" she said aloud sitting forward on her chair.

She buried her head in her hands and closed her eyes. John's grinning face came immediately to her. Her eyes shot open as if she'd seen a ghost. She compared the two men. Both were total opposites. Tommy was a rock. A hard worker, a good friend and lover, but set in his ways.

All he's ever wanted was to settle down and have a family with a homely wife. Homely Ros wasn't!! So what was the attraction? Tommy did have his moments, and was very masterful when he had to be. He loved his music and he did have an ambitious streak, but only with his work. John on the other hand couldn't give a dam. Loved life to the full, and was passionate about everything especially his music. But that was all Ros knew about him. That and the fact that when she was with him any other time but for last night, he paid! She was in control. Last night was different. She willingly slept with him. Not only him by the sound of it either! So she must have really enjoyed it! Which disgusted her even more.

"Poor Tommy doesn't deserve this!" she said aloud running her hands through her hair.

John jumped into her mind again.

"Jeesus!" she screamed trying to rid him of her.

She felt sick and confused. Panic welled up in her as she realised she'd have to see him tonight. Taking a deep breath to clam herself down, she tried to think straight. 'I've got to keep away from him! I'll tell Rose I can't do it, say I'm ill or something!'

"No you won't!" the voice in her head said.

Grabbing her hair she tried to pull the voice out.

"You love the way he makes you feel!" it went again.

"Nooo!" she cried pulling her hair even more.

"It's no longer business now though is it? It's gone past that, you let it last night!"

"Noo!" she screamed slapping her own face trying to bring herself out of the nightmare. Exhausted she laid curled up on the sofa staring into space.

The next thing, she woke to the telephone ringing in her ear. Jumping up she answered it.

"Hello!"

"Ros it's Kel umm, I'm umm just wondering how you're, er, feeling now?" Kel asked in a quiet voice.

"You okay darling, you looked so upset earlier?" Kel added concerned.

"Oh, Kel tell me it's all a nightmare! Please!" she said desperately.

"I'm sorry Ros. I only rang to see you're all right darling! I didn't know whether to stay or go this morning. I hope I did the right thing!" Kel said down the phone.

" Oh Kel you know it's not you don't you."

"Of course darling. Listen I'll see you tonight yeh," Kel said trying to close the call not knowing what else to say.

"Okay," Ros answered

"Kel what time are we being picked up?" she asked

Kel took the phone from her ear and looked at it. She couldn't believe her ears. 'Ros really has lost it!' she thought.

"Ah I think we're gonna be taken to the house about eight. It's gonna take about an hour to get ready once we're there. Ros are you sure you're okay?"

"Yes honestly I'm fine," she said slowly.

"I'll see you at the Club about seven. Oh and Kel.

"Yes?"

"What I said this morning…"

"It's forgotten," Kel said replacing the receiver and shaking her head.

She thought for a moment as to whether she should let the others know or not. Then dismissed it. It was between her and Ros. If she wanted anyone else to know she could tell them not Kel.

"Ros all right?" Jude called from their kitchen.

"Yeh fine," Kel smiled as she walked into the room.

"You got the list sorted out?" she asked leaning over Jude's

148

shoulder.

"Yup all sorted!" Jude said looking up and waving a piece of paper.

"We've got fucking loads ta do before tonight girl, you ready?"

"Let me grab me jacket," Kel said wandering through to the hall and lifting it from the hook.

"Ready," she said checking herself one last time in their hall mirror.

"Tart!" Jude said as she got level with her, giving her backside a tap and winking.

Kel blew her a kiss and they both walked out the door together heading for the shops.

Chapter 14

Ros decided to go in earlier than what she told Kel she would that day. She needed to see Rose about some money she wanted out of her savings account seeing Rose held her book so Tommy couldn't find it. So she had to ask for it a day before she needed it. Then Rose could bring it in for her.

She wanted to go shopping before Tommy came home on Wednesday and give him a special meal and a special night, just to say how much she'd missed him, and tell him he was going to be a daddy. Doughy had given her the list of ingredients she needed to get from the shops. Ros felt more in control of herself than she had that morning. 'What's the saying we've got?' she thought as she sat in the girls room rolling her first joint of the day, telling herself before she'd even lit it, that she was going to need a few more before the night was over.

"Oh, yeh that's it 'Business as usual'," she muttered to herself.

"Business as usual!" she said toasting the air with her coffee cup.

She'd had a long think after talking to Kel on the phone and had decided that last night was a mistake and she was going to put to behind her, forget it ever happened! For her and Tommy's sake. Not to mention the baby he didn't even know she was carrying in her belly. She'd also wanted to see Rose about something else. She'd decided she was going to do tonight, then that was it no more. The night before had made up her mind.

Tommy may be set in his ways but all he wants is the best for her and no one had ever put her first like him. He deserved more than Ros's deceit.

Rose accepted Ros's reasons graciously and wished her well saying that if she ever wanted to come back to the entertaining side she would always have a place there.

Rose sorted out different hours for her, because as much as she loved the girls, when she was with them she couldn't say 'no'. So both Ros and Rose thought the best way for Ros to work as a 'box hostess' was to change shifts.

"You supposed to be smoking that in your condition?" Bet asked as she whizzed through to the kitchen.

"What! Oh this?" she said raising her joint.

"Not really but no more after today," she said unsmiling.

Bet stopped in her tracks.

"You got the fuckin' ump?"

"Rose'll tell you," she replied flatly.

"Fine if that's 'ow ya wont it!" Bet said carrying on to the kitchen.

"Wot's up wif 'appyness in there?" she asked Doughy poking her thumb over her shoulder.

"Don't ask me been like it since she walked in. she seems a bit 'arder don'tcha fink?" Doughy said not looking up from her pastry, but knowing exactly who Bet was talking about.

"She's 'ad a word wif Rose that's all I know," she added.

"But no ones told me anyfing."

"Great wot we got a fuckin conspiracy on our 'ands!" Bet moaned pouring out some tea.

"Won't one?" she asked.

"No tar I've just 'ad one.

"Know where Rose is?" Bet asked dipping her little finger into a sweet concoction.

"Office last time I saw 'er," Doughy replied tapping Bet's hand away.

"Okay see ya later babe," Bet said turning on her heels and going out the door again.

Doughy put a floured hand up and Bet was gone.

"Sure ya don't wanna tell me Ros?" Bet asked as she came into the girl's room her tea in hand.

"Tell you what?" Ros said not looking at Bet.

"Wot the fucks wrong wif ya that's wot!" Bet said her patience running thin.

"I've quit!" Ros said in a toneless voice. Taking another drag of her joint she sadly said,

"The funny thing is it's because I like what I do too much!"

"Wot the fuck you talkin' about?" Bet said, as she sat down opposite her.

"We went out last night yeh? Well I fucked John and a few others from what Kel tells me!" she said the sad smile still on her face.

"And you know the worst thing I enjoyed it!" Ros cried.

"I'm doing tonight then that's it, no more, it's not fair on Tommy any more, he deserves better than that. So today is the last time!" she said holding up the joint.

"Call this my leaving present if you like, but to be honest I don't think I'll be able to get through tonight without a few more!" she looked sadly at Bet.

"I'm sorry Bet, but it went past girl and gent last night. It's time I stopped."

"Okay girl! Was all Bet said putting a hand on her arm and giving her a smile. 'She'll be back on it!' she smiled to herself saying to her.

"I'll see ya later I got ta go through some paperwork wif Rose now," getting up from the table, she picked up her mug and lit a cigarette, the cloud of smoke, engulfing her as always, and she was gone.

Ros took the last drag of her joint and tossed it into the ashtray. Checking her watch. 'Five good I think I'll go have a bath.' She thought to herself. Getting up she picked up her rolling material and wandered into the 'bar room'

"Open a bottle of red wine would you please Sue?" she asked the girl getting the bar ready for that evening.

"I really fancy a long soak in the tub," she said making conversation.

"Are you sure you should Ros?" Sue asked concerned.

"Bloody hell! News travels fast in this place!" she said taking the bottle of wine from her, and reaching over the bar, unhooked a glass from above.

"Look I'm really sorry! I didn't mean anything by it," Sue said.

"Yeh what ever!" Ros said quietly walking out and heading up the stairs.

Ros ran a bath and poured the wine, she took a sip the acidity burning all the way down her throat. Putting down the wine she sat on the wicker chair in the corner and rolled herself a joint taking another sip of her wine half way through. This time it tasted a whole lot better and she nodded to herself a little smile creeping on her face.

"It's true what they say it tastes a lot better after the second sip!" she muttered biting the end off her joint and lighting it. She slipped out of her clothes, pulling the chair over to the bath. She placed her ashtray, lighter, wine bottle and glass on the seat. Then sat on the edge of the bath both feet on the other edge. Carefully she dipped a toe in, to check the temperature lifting it out as soon as it touched the water and leaning over to add some cold. Visions of her little caravan came to her making her shiver when she remembered how she had to heat the water on the stove to have a wash. Turning the water off and swirling the water with her foot, she slid in letting the warmth envelope her. Closing her eyes she took a deep breath and exhaled. It was the first time that day she'd felt at peace and she just lay there for a few minutes letting some of the tension slip away with the water. She reached over for her wine and joint, taking a sip of one and placing it back on the chair. She retrieved the lighter and inhaled deeply as the flame came in contact with the cigarette. Ros laid her head back and blew out smoke rings towards the ceiling and thought about the days events, she definitely felt more in control knowing tonight would be the last time, but there was also a sadness in it. It was true she loved her job and she was good at it. She'd also miss all the girls changing her shifts, but she had to do it. She couldn't lie to Tommy any more. 'Things have gone too far, some one might say something to him! Thank God he wants to go away when his finished this job. At least we'll have time together away from here!' she thought. Then suddenly she remembered Tommy was going to ring tonight.

"Shit!" she said aloud.

"Oh, he'll guess I'm here and ring here if he doesn't get any answer at home," she answered her panic.

And sorting out at least that little problem she treated herself to another sip of wine and tried to relax her body and mind for the night ahead.

A knock on the door startled Ros back to earth.

"Ros you okay in there?" it was Kel.

"Christ what's the time Kel?" she asked sitting up the cold water splashing up her back.

"Quarter to seven darling. How long you been in there?" Kel asked chuckling as she came through the door.

"Bloody ages," she said shivering and passing her wine glass to Kel, who thanking her finished it off with a smile.

"God is nothing sacred!" Ros said standing up and taking the bath towel from Kels out stretched arm.

"Thanks darling," she said stepping out of the bath and giving her a grin.

"How you feelin' now?" Kel asked pouring some more wine into the glass and taking a sip before passing it to Ros.

"To nights my last night. I've told Rose, and Bet knows. I can't see him any more and that means having to stop working. Anyway Tommy'll be home Wednesday an' I've decided to tell him I'm pregnant when he gets back. So I feel more in control than this morning," she said giving Kel a sad smile.

"Plus I won't be able to carry on much longer anyway will I?" she said looking down at her belly with a little smile.

"So you're leaving altogether?" Kel asked shocked at how Ros was so calm especially after how she was this morning.

"No darling I'd go mad! But you lot are too incorrigible. So I've taken a different shift pattern as 'box hostess'," she said slipping on her room robe.

"Oh!" Kel said nodding.

"Here you wanna see wot Jude an' I 'ave brought today for tonight!" she said changing the subject.

"We've even found some plastic fruit and attached them to our sandals, how's that?" she said laughing.

"Umm lovely!" Ros said smirking.

"Very classy for my last night!" she said looking at Kel and burst out laughing.

"That's what I love about this place no matter what your problem you always end up laughing! Come on," she said taking Kels arm.

"Show me my out fit, I can't wait!" she smiled walking out of the bathroom arm in arm with her, heading to Kels room.

There sitting on the bed were two pairs of sandals an assortment of cherries, grapes, lemon slices, orange segments, and greenery adorned the foot wear. Ros took one look at them turned to Kel placing her finger on her chin and said.

"Umm very tasteful!" she commented, then collapsed on to the bed in a convulsion of giggles.

"Oh, and that's not all!" Kel said moving her eyebrows up and down.

"No more please!" Ros said putting a hand up and holding her stomach with the other.

"Noo I'm not wearing that!" Ros burst out laughing as Kel pulled on a turban adorned with more of the plastic fruit, a huge plastic pineapple right on top.

"Who did that?" she asked through giggles.

"Jude!" Kel laughed.

"Huh typical! The cow!" Ros said shaking her head.

"Some one call me?" Jude called from the doorway.

"No we didn't you bloody cow!" Ros grinned.

"How'd you like to wear a sodding fruit bowl on your head?" she carried on pulling the turban over her head so that only her nose and mouth were exposed.

"You crazy bitch!" Jude boomed tugging at the back of it.

"Well, I suppose we don't have to do our hair tonight. Which is a bit of a bonus!" Kel said slipping into her sandals and dancing around the room.

Suddenly she stopped in mid flow.

"Ere I hope the rooms gonna be warm tonight."

Both Ros and Jude stared at her a look of bewilderment on their faces.

"Why's that?" Jude asked intreged.

"Well, when I get cold my teeth chatter an' I'll look like I've got fuckin' St. Vitus dance with all this lot on me head!" she said seriously.

Ros and Jude looked at each other unable to contain their fits of giggles any more. As Kel demonstrated what she'd look like and all three of them slid to the floor tears running.

"Oh, shit! I'm gonna wet meself if I carry on!" she cried running to the toilet not knowing whether to hold her belly or head wear. The other two could hear her laughing all the way down the hall.

Suddenly Ros's tears of laughter turned to tears of sadness.

"Hey, wot's the matter babe?" Jude asked going over to where Ros sat sobbing.

"I'm going to miss you lot! I love you all dearly you know that," she said the wine kicking in.

"Wot the fuck you on about?" Jude pulled away looking into Ros's face.

Ros shook her head.

"I'm quitting. To nights my last night with you lot an' I'm going to miss you so much!" she sobbed pulling off her turban and wiping away her tears with the back of her hand.

"Fuck me Ros. When this 'appen?" Jude asked shocked.

"I went too far last night!" she sighed reaching for her wine, she took a large sip turning she sniffed and smiled at Jude.

"I'm sorry it's this!" she said holding up her glass to Jude then taking another sip before placing it back on the side.

"Listen will you tell the others I'll only get upset again."

"Wot you goin' fer good?" Jude questioned about work, knowing it was best not to ask about last night. She'd be told soon enough.

"No just changing shifts as 'box hostess' your far too incorrigible!" she said sniffing then giving Jude a smile.

Jude gave her a hug.

"Well, we'll 'ave no more of this!" she said wiping Ros's face with a tissue and kissing her cheek.

"Encourageable eh! Well I'll let the others know and we'll have one hell of a night tonight. Send you off in style! 'ow's that?" Jude said getting up and running her hand over Ros's head.

Ros looked up giving Jude a smile, then pulling herself together she pulled her turban back on her head and said.

"You call this style? Gee, thanks!" and getting up she did a twirl pulling a face at her.

Both women grinned at each other and hugged.

"I'll see ya down stairs in a mo then," Jude said pulling away from Ros heading for the door.

She met Kel in the hall way.

"You know about Ros?" she whispered as they got level.

Kel nodded giving her a sad smile.

"I'm gonna miss her," she said quietly.

"Me too. 'ere keep 'er up 'ere fer about five minutes will ya. I'm gonna tell the others."

Kel went to stop her.

"It's okay she asked me to, and we'll have a bit of a drink before we go off. It'll only take us a little while to dress you two up when we get there, whatcha say? I mean we know where all the foods gonna go an' we know we've got plenty of the stuff we made sure of it!"

"Okay darling," Kel said placing a hand on Judes arm and smiling.

"We'll see you in a little while," Withdrawing her hand she skipped off.

Ros and Kel wandered down the stairs carrying their turbans and sandals in their hands. Both girls were dressed in a pair of black trousers a white shirt and a black waistcoat. They wandered into the girl's room to a cheer from the others. There was two pops as Jude and Misty uncorked two bottles of champagne pouring three glasses a piece. Jude handed Ros the first glass then the others took theirs.

"To Ros. I'd just like to say on behalf of all of us here. That we will all truly miss you darling!"

"Your health. Cheers!" Sal breathed and they all joined in holding up their glasses to Ros.

"Cheers!" they said.

"Oh, bleedin' 'ell yer started 'er off now!" Jude beamed.

"Ere girl 'ave a puff on that," she said passing Ros the joint.

"It's so so sad," Annie cried into her tissues, sniffing she took a sip of her champagne.

"You will visit won't you?" Annie asked Ros quietly.

"Oh, of course. I'm only changing shifts, I'm probably going to see you a couple of times a week anyway!" Ros explained smiling at her.

The girls sat around talking, crying, giggling and laughing until it was time for them to make their way to Ben's house. Ros started to panic as the girls turned down the road to the house.

"I really don't think I can do this!" she whispered to Kel in the back of the car.

"Don't worry I'll keep an eye on him. But Ros think, what if it's his birthday, an' what if he wants to fuck you! What do I do?

You are working tonight!"

"Yes. I am working aren't I?" Ros stated sitting up straight her nerves gone, being replaced by her old confidence.

She was in control tonight he was going to have to pay.

"Don't worry darling this is like you said work! I want you to have a great time, not look out for me all night!" Ros said pulling her waist coat straight and giving Kel's hand a squeeze taking a deep breath, she looked out the window.

"We're here!" she said holding her head up high and getting out of the car. She held the door for the others giving her a little more time to get herself together.

Chapter 15

Ben was waiting for the girls as they came round the back to the studio door.

"Hi girls how you doin'?" he asked getting up from a stool and laying some music sheets on it.

"No ones here yet. They're still all at the restaurant. I've just nipped back to welcome you and tell where we've put all the food. Come this way and I'll show you," he said wandering past them and opening the other door leading out to the front room and kitchen.

"In here girls. Help your selves to a drink. We've put all of what was delivered earlier in that fridge there and the freezer next to it," he said pointing to two white cabinets standing next to each other.

"Thanks Ben. I didn't see the trolleys when we came in. don't tell me Jedd didn't bring them!" Jude said helping herself to a scotch from the side.

"Yeh there in the other room," he said with a grin. Then turning to all six of them he carried on.

"So whos the lucky ladies going to be?"

"Me and Ros!" Kel said taking her head out of the fridge and putting a grape in between her front teeth and bit.

"Umm nice!" he said looking Kel up and down.

"Save one for me won't you," he nodded to the grapes in her hand.

Kel gave him a gracious nod and went back to the fridge pulling out the plates and bowls, passing them to the girls.

"Well, we'll all be back here in about an hour. Will you all be ready by then?" he asked checking his watch then looking at them.

"That will be just fine Ben," Sal said.

"Can you tell me who the birthday boy is!" she whispered

in his ear.

"Now that would be tellin'!" Ben grinned giving her a wink walking to the back door and pulling out some keys. As he reached it he turned.

"Have fun ladies," he said blowing them all a kiss and was gone.

"Well, I think we've just got time for one of these!" Misty said holding up a small package of hash.

"Before we start on you two that is," she said pointing to Kel and Ros by the drinks.

"Too bloody right!" Jude called sticking her finger in some whipped cream and sucking it off.

"Ere go put some music on Annie will ya. An' I'll sort out the trolleys wotcha say?" she asked.

"I don't know how to turn it on!" Annie squealed.

"What if I break it?" she asked.

"Fuckin' 'ell Annie! Ya turn the fuckin' thin' on. Bung a record on it. Bung the needle on the record... Da da!!" Jude said tapping her fingers on the work surface.

"Okay I'll give it a try," Annie said nervously.

"That a girl!" Jude said putting an arm around her and leading her to the front room laughing.

The other four took all the food into the studio splitting it into two equal piles. Jude pushed the trolleys one at a time in to the room singing as she went about her chore. Ros and Kel sat on the little stage sharing a joint and a glass of wine.

"I suppose we're gonna have ta strip off in a minute! I'm really not looking forward to sticking my arse on that cold metal I can tell you!" Kel giggled.

"Oh, I don't know about that wait until the ice cream hit's your belly!" Ros joked.

"No don't! That really does me!" Kel said hugging her body.

Sal and Misty walked over to the girls looking down at them. The two girls each gave them their 'costumes'.

"Come on, we've only got half an hour to cover you," Sal breathed stretching an elegant arm towards the trolleys.

"Yeh and you've got to change!" Misty added going into fits of giggles as the girls stood holding the sandals in one hand

160

and the turban in the other.

"Oh, yeh very funny!" Kel said poking her tongue out at her as Jude and Annie wandered in.

"What's funny?" Annie and Jude asked together as they walked through.

"Madams taking the piss out of our 'costumes'!" Kel grinned pointing to Misty.

"I'll 'ave ya know it took all my artistic talents ta do those masterpieces!" Jude said pouting.

"Christ I feel sorry for you two. Living with that talent in the house!" Sal said cupping Kels turban in the palms of her hands examining it with her head to one side.

They all laughed as Jude pretended to be a stroppy artist. Five minutes later Ros and Kel were sitting on the edge of their trolleys having their hair tucked into their turbans.

"There perfect!" Sal said stepping back to admire her work on the two women.

"What d'you think girls? Do they need adjusting or not?" she asked the other three.

Jude turned both girls from one side to the other.

"Perfect! Now get yer arses up on there girls! It's nearly party time! An' I'm getting' the munchies wif all this grub about!" Jude finished licking her lips.

"Oh, some one throw her a fish!" Sal said tapping Jude's stomach and giving her a kiss on the cheek as she glided past to get the cream and glacé cherries.

About twenty minutes later the girls heard the birthday party come into the house.

"Hurry up girls!" Annie said excitedly as she peeked through a crack in the door.

"Ben's coming over how long you gonna be?" she called over to them jumping around like a scared rabbit.

"Tell him ta give us Ten will ya Annie," Misty called back not looking up from placing the banana in Kel's pyramid of ice cream and chocolate sauce belly.

Kel sucked in some air.

"Fuck that's cold! I hope I don't start shivering!" she said giving Ros a wink.

"Don't start Kel!" Ros said sternly trying to stop a giggle.

Ben opened the door and a barrage of music, laughter and voices filled the studio until the door clicked shut again.

"Wow you two look good enough to eat!" he said laughing at his own joke.

All six stopped and looked at him.

"Okay I'm not funny!" he said putting his hands up in surrender.

"Can you lot be ready in five?" he asked spreading his hand wide.

"When you get a knock three times would you wheel the girls out singing 'Happy Birthday' and leave them at either end of the room please ladies."

Ben said in a business manner.

"Do we get ta know who's birthday it is now?" Jude asked in a huffy voice fed up with not knowing.

"It's no big deal darling, only John's," Ben replied pulling six envelopes out of his jacket.

"So why weren't we allowed ta know before if it's only John?" Jude questioned her hands on her rubber-clad hips.

"If any one knew, it might have come out that's all!" he said looking straight at Ros.

"And I wanted ta give the guy a real surprise an' you're it!" Ben said in a flattering manner.

"Huh really?" Jude flicked her bobbed head at him.

"Yes really! Now here you go girls a little extra for your services," he smiled passing Jude the six envelopes.

Jude took them with out a thank you tapping them in her hand.

"Five minutes you say?"

"Please!" Ben answered smirking. Walking to the door he turned.

"And three knocks!" he said.

"Sarcastic bastard!" Jude muttered under her breath. She looked at Ros then inclined her head.

"Is it my imagination or are 'er nipples pissed?" she asked prodding the left cherry on Ros's nipple.

They all giggled and the mood was lighter again.

Knock. Knock. Knock.

"Ere we go girls ya all ready?" Jude called standing behind

Ros's trolley.

"Ready," Misty said standing behind Kel.

Sal eased the door open slowly draping a long leg outside the door. When she heard the wolf whistles she pushed the door wide open slowly pulling, as Misty pushed Kel out the door, followed directly by little Annie pulling and Jude pushing Ros. Sal moved the trolley elegantly down to the other end of the room. Annie and Jude manoeuvred Ros at the studio end. Leaving the trolleys the four girls sang 'Happy Birthday' as they danced seductively around the room.

John and the other band members all came to the middle of the room cheering and whistling. Ben came up to John stretching out his hand.

"Many happy returns mate!" he said clasping John's hand and shaking it.

Then the two men slapped each other on the back and roared into the air shaking their heads like two wild animals.

"Enjoy man enjoy!" Ben shouted pushing John to a trolley. The other three charged towards the other one pushing and shoving each other.

Tommy had worked all through Thursday into Friday non stop trying to get the studio ready for the electricians to get in. Then the last thing they all needed happened. Nine thirty on Friday morning the electric went off. Tommy couldn't finish and the electricians couldn't start. Tommy rang the electric company to be told a major power plant was having difficulty with striking workers and there's a possibility the electric would only be on for a couple of hours a day for at least over the weekend. He decided to surprise Ros and went out buying her a huge bunch of flowers, wine and the biggest box of chocolates he could find. Placing them on the passenger seat of his old Bedford he headed home, hoping to get there by about half eight that night with a couple of stops. He knew he'd be exhausted by the time he got there but he desperately missed her and needed to be home.

Tommy pulled up at their little house and smiled.

"Great I'm home!" he said his heart doing a little flip.

"Fuck I love that woman!" he muttered to himself as he

retrieved the flowers, wine and chocolates from the front seat and shutting the van door with his foot. He put his key in the door carefully turning. It clicked and he slipped in shutting it behind him by lifting the latch. The front room door was shut. Tommy crept over to it grabbing the handle he pulled it down and jumped into the room with a "Tommys home babe!" only to be faced with an empty room.

"Ros you upstairs babe? It's me I'm 'ome!" he called from the bottom of the stairs.

When he got no answer he ran up them two at a time. With the vision of her in bed with another man in their bed! He flung the bedroom door open to find an empty room and bed. He turned calling her name looking in every room in the house. When he was quite sure she wasn't anywhere in the house he threw the flowers in the sink and dumped the chocolates and wine on the side. He took out a packet of cigarettes from his top pocket. Opening the pack he bit one out lighting it with the other hand. Flicking the lid shut he slipped the packet and lighter back into his pocket. He took the cigarette from his mouth exhaling the smoke into the air.

Grabbing his keys he left the house and got in his van. Turning it on, he swung it around in the road and took off in the direction of 'the Club'. 'If anyone knows where Ros is, some one there will.' He thought flicking his cigarette out of the window and winding it up.

Tommy pulled into the Club car park and janked up the hand brake up. Dismounting his vehicle he slammed the old door shut and wandered down the path using his key to open the door. Josie the 'box hostess' tottered out of the room in a blood red tight fitting cat suit held together with a few gold chains. Her smile froze when she saw him.

"Tommy! Wot you doin' 'ere!" she asked surprised to see him.

"All right Josie. Ros 'ere?" he asked letting his eyes run down her fit body and smiling.

"Dunno Tommy," she said wandering back to the 'box room'

"Any one in that would know?" he asked her impatiently.

Josie hunched her shoulders saying.

"Go 'ave a look!" without looking back she disappeared into her room.

Tommys mind started to click into over drive, he wandered over to the 'girls room' and poked his head around the door. He expected to see Ros and a couple of the girls having their break if she was here working.

When he only saw Rose, Bet and Sue the bar girl in the room, Tommy really wanted to know where Ros was! He'd guessed already she was with the girls. 'They're probably down the local or some thing.' He thought trying to calm himself as he walked over to the three women. No one saw him until he was level with them. When they looked up from the table to see who was there Rose went white! Bet collapsed into a coughing fit, waving her permanent cloud from her head and Sue sat frozen to the spot.

"You ladies all right?" he asked in a suspicious voice.

"Anyone would fink you'd seen a fuckin' ghost!" he said lighting a cigarette.

"Any one know where Ros is?" he asked exhaling the smoke, knowing damned well they knew where she was by their reactions.

Tommy was getting nervous.

"Wot she up to Bet?" he demanded staring into her eyes.

"T… Tommy wotcha doin' 'ere?" Bet stuttered.

"It don't fuckin' matter wot I'm doin' 'ere where's me wife?" Tommy shouted, anger showing in his eyes as he leaned over only inches from Bets face.

"Tommy, she isn't here! Really she isn't!" Rose broke in getting a little colour back in her face. She squeezed Bets leg under the table.

"Yeh that's right she ain't 'ere they've all gone out ain't they Rose?" Bet said looking to Rose for support.

"Umm, they might even all be back at Jude, Kel and Annies place with a couple of bottles of wine!" Rose said.

Both Bet and Tommy stared at her open mouthed.

"Ya can't fuckin' lie ta save yer life can ya Rose!" Tommy grinned.

"Now where is she ladies? Stop pissin' around an' tell me," he said banging his hand down on the table making their drinks

165

jump.

Bet looked at Rose and Sue. Then looking up at a now pacing Tommy she whispered.

"Ben's!"

"Wot I didn't 'ear ya?" Tommy lept over to Bets side, putting a hand to his ear.

"BEN'S!" she said loud and clear.

"Ben's."

Rose threw her hands up to her face burying her head in them.

"Wot she doin' at Ben's?" Tommy hissed into Bets face gripping the table with both hands.

Bet looked down at the table and shook her candy floss head.

"Fuckin' tell me Bet!" he screamed making all three jump out of their chairs.

"Workin' Tommy! That's wot she's fuckin' doin' WORKING!" Bet screamed back.

Tommy stepped back his eyes wide shaking his head from side to side, shock showing in his face.

"No," was all he could say slumping into the nearest chair the ash of his cigarette falling to the floor.

He could feel his chest tightening and he wanted to be sick.

"How could she? She promised me!" he whispered into his hands running them through his hair. He looked over at the three stunned women.

"Wot's 'appenin' over at Ben's?" he demanded slowly.

"Party," Bet said quietly.

"Someone's birfday party. Tommy she's only doin' ta night!" Bet shouted hastly as he marched across the room to the door.

"Yeh! Well that's one fuckin' night too many Bet!" he hissed as he reached the door opening it and slamming it behind him.

Ros lay there praying that John wouldn't come to her trolley. She already had a crowd around her drooling, not daring to touch. She heard a cheer go up from the other end. Every one turned to the noise and laughed. Ros started to relax and even had a grin on her face. She had to admit she did feel good with all the food over her. It was a very sensual feeling having chocolate sauce drizzled over your body. Suddenly the crowd around Ros started cheering and clapping. The crowd parted and John was standing there cheering back at his friends. Turning their eyes locked. John caught the smile on her lips before it faded as she realised it was him. He leaned over her body never taking his eyes from hers, bending his head he bit the cherry from her nipple. Ros shuddered closing her eyes, opening them to John's grin.

"Are you me prezzie then darlin'?" he asked running his index finger down in between her cleavage and licking his finger, allowing his eyes to wander over her body.

Ros's body deceived her by giving a little shudder again. 'I can't believe this is happening!' she thought trying desperately to be professional, smiling politely and not saying a word.

"I fink I'm gonna 'ave..." he said turning to his crowd of friends and rubbing his chin.

Some one shouted.

"Crotch Cream!"

And the rest started to chant and shout.

"Crotch cream! Crotch cream! Crotch cream!"

John did a twirl holding the ends of his jacket out as he went, then lept on to the trolley burying his face deep into Ros's pussy and pushing his tongue as deep as he could. He lifted his head keeping his tongue out covering it in whipped cream, the banana hitting him on the nose as he came up! Ros couldn't contain her shock or pleasure any more, and seeing Johns face as the banana hit she burst into a fit of giggles. The crowd roared with laughter as he began to work his way up her body eating the goods as he went. By the time he'd reached her breasts his face shirt and jacket were covered in fruit, cream, ice cream and chocolate sauce. Ros by this time was laughing as the crowd cheered him on. He looked into her eyes and they locked for just a few seconds but enough for Ros to feel the bulge in his trousers grow and see the lust in his eyes. John knelt up and ripped off his jacket and shirt flinging them into the crowd. A couple of girls scooped up some fruit and cream and rubbed it down their fronts encouraging their partners to lick it off. John reached down and rubbed the palms of his hands in a circular movement over Ros's breasts, then pushed them together bent his head over and rubbed his face in whipped cream. He then laid on top of her wriggling his body onto hers. He kissed her full on the mouth running his tongue along her teeth and grinding his hips into her. Ros felt as if she was in heaven, the crowd seemed to stop cheering and disappeared. There only seemed to be her and John in the room.

***

Tommy pulled into the turning for Bens house. As he neared the property he could here the music pumping into the air and cheers rising above the music. His stomach churned as he pulled up and got out. Booting the van door shut, he stormed up the driveway. The front door was open a crack Tommy noticed as he got level with the house. He walked across the drive stepping over a flowerbed and stood in front of the door. He gave it a little push, the noise flew out into the night. He walked in drawing the door back to how he found it. The two glass-panelled doors dividing the hall and front room were closed. Tommy started to sweat the anger welling up inside him. Behind that door his wife was entertaining "On the job" against his wishes and while she thought he was way sneaky little bitch!

Tommy pushed one of the doors open blinking his eyes a couple of times to get them adjusted to the light and smoke. He stood by the door not wanting to go in any farthur. He heard a cheer roar up from a group of people surrounded by what looked like a hospital trolley in front of him.

He looked away catching some one sitting in the corner rolling a joint. Before he could draw his eyes away the head lifted and it was the kid. He looked deep into Tommy's eyes, as if drawing out his thoughts as he licked his paper. Rolling up the joint, never taking his eyes from Tommy. Suddenly Dan pulled away slowly smiling and nodding a knowing look in his eyes, then blinking as if to end what ever had happened he lit his joint and nodded his head to the music.

Tommy felt as if he'd been drained of something and shivered. He walked over to the crowd in front of him robot like, he pushed his way threw the partying people partially dressed in their party gear and horny as hell. Tommy couldn't believe his eyes when he got up to the trolley. There were about four guys and a couple of girls licking and sucking a knickerbocker glory from Kel,s body. Kel seeing Tommy standing there gasped and immediately looked in the direction of the other trolley. Tommy instinctively knew Ros was in the middle of the other crowd. He turned on his heels giving Kel a pitiful look and stormed ahead to the cheering and screaming people. Tommy barged his way through the first couple of people then the others seemed to fall away and the room fell silent.

"You dirty fuckin' little tart!" he hissed at Ros still with John on top of her covered in cream and fruit.

Tommy turned to John.

"You wont me wife? Well ya can fuckin' 'ave 'er!" he spat. He ran his finger down Ros's face slowly.

"Bye babe," he said and turning his back on her heading for the front door, his head spinning. As he reached the divider doors he looked into the corner and met Dan's eyes. He nodded slowly to Tommy taking a drag of his joint. He looked over to where, John, covered in the table concoction, and a stark naked Ros, except for what cream was left on her, were scrambling off the trolley. John touching the floor first called across to Tommy.

"Hey, Tom I don't want yer fuckin' wife! She's only a bit of arse mate!" then burst out laughing flicking a squashed orange segment from his chest.

"Yer wanna fink yerself lucky least ya didn't 'ave ta pay fer it!" he called taking a drink from one of the roadies and swallowing it in one.

Ros ran across the room falling at Tommy's feet.

"Tommy pleeese!" she begged grabbing hold of his jeans.

Tommy looked down at her disgust in his eyes.

"Tommy you don't understand!" she cried.

"I'm pregnant!" she sobbed onto his legs.

"Yeh and?" Tommy said pulling his legs from her grip and brushing off some cream from his jeans. Without looking back he walked out.

"Noooooo!" she screamed getting up and running to the divider doors straight into Bets arms. Turning like a caged animal Ros scanned the room. Dan's eyes locked with hers for a couple of seconds breaking the stare with a victorious smirk. The room spun and Ros fell to the floor. Jedd stepped from behind Bet and wrapped her in a sheet lifting her like one would a sleeping baby and walked out the door with her. Bet turned to the silent crowd saying.

"Don't let a little fing like that spoil ya evenin' consider it a extra!" smiling she followed Jedd with Ros.

As they got Ros in the car they heard the sound of music and laughter come from the house.

"Business as usual!" Bet muttered getting into the front with Jedd and he started the engine.

"Better take 'er ta mine lovey!" she said giving Jedd's leg a little squeeze.

Smiling she lit a cigarette filling the car with smoke before opening the window. Ros came to in the back of the car not knowing where she was. Lifting her head she saw Bets candyfloss head in the passenger's seat. Bet turned and looked over her shoulder.

"You all right lovey?" she cooed into the back.

Ros pulled a hand out of the sheet and dragged the turban from her head.

"That's it then we're finished!"

"What the fuck am I going to do Bet? We're finished!" she whispered through a husky voice her eyes wide and starey.

"Oh, lovey it ain't that bad! Tommys a stroppy little bastard, but he'll come round you'll see. Now you wont ta stay at mine or the Club ta night?" Bet said giving Jedd a little prod as he huffed.

"I want Tommy that's what I want!" Ros sobbed.

"You wanna go 'ome?" Bet asked arching her neck to see Ros's face.

"Yes. No Oh fuck! I don't know! I need a drink! Fuck what a bloody mess!" she cried dragging at the sheet to free her other arm and lighting a cigarette Bet had given her.

"Change that to the Club," Bet said to Jedd turning back to face the front of the car.

Jedd pulled around the back of the Club where the delivery lorries did their drop off's. He got out of the car and unlocked the goods door giving Bet a wave to say all was clear. Bet got out opening Ros's door for her. She slipped out of the back seat shrugging the sheet over her shoulders. They walked into the kitchen to be met by Rose.

"Hello darling I've got a nice hot bath waiting for you want to go hop in?" she said to Ros as she came in behind Bet.

Ros gave a little smile and nodded letting Rose lead her through the kitchen door to be met by Sue. She gave Ros a sisterly hug and led her to the bathroom. Jedd made his excuses and left leaving Rose and Bet in the kitchen facing each other.

"Tea?" Rose asked going to the tea pot.

"Fuckin' tea!" Bet barked.

"I need a fuckin' proper drink! Pass us that bottle over there," she said plonking down on a kitchen chair.

Rose picked up the bottle of whisky and two mugs giving Bet the bottle to undo as she placed the mugs in front of her, sitting down opposite her.

"Was it bad?" Rose asked watching Bet pour the drinks.

"Bad ain't the fuckin' word!" she replied passing Rose a mug.

"It was fuckin' hilarious!" she squealed dissolving into a fit of laughter.

Rose sat staring at her not quite sure what to do next.

"Ohhh!! I... I'm sorry!" Bet gasped dissolving again.

Rose still staring at her was getting infected with Bet's laughter, and was sipping her whisky smiling at Bet holding up her hand tears rolling down her face trying desperately to stop laughing, which in turn made her worse. Thinking, 'What a weird world we live in! There's poor Ros washing away her sins upstairs and Bet pissing herself laughing down here!'

"Fucking crazy!" she said aloud.

"You're tellin' me!" Bet squealed open eyed poking herself in the chest and claming her giggles down.

"Oh, I'm sooo fuckin' sorry Rose!" Bet said smirking at her again.

"Well, you gonna tell me whats so fucking funny?" Rose said resting her arms on the kitchen table.

"It's not funny about Ros an' Tommy!" Bet said smirking and shaking her head.

"Oh, no that's not funny! Shit! I'm sorry!" Bet cried dissolving into fits of laughter banging her hand on the table.

"Shit fuck I'm so so sorry Rose!" she cried wiping the tears from her eyes.

"It's just that she looked fuckin' hilarious sprawled on the floor fuckin' cream an' shit all over 'er an' a pair of fuckin' sandals adorned wif squashed plastic fruit where she'd thrown 'erself at Tommy's feet an' a fuckin' turban with a fuckin' pineapple in the middle pissed on 'er 'ead!"

Bet cried lighting another cigarette and tossing the pack to Rose before, both women looked at each other and completely collapsed across the table smacking each others hands and grasping for air.

"Oh, don't!" Rose screamed knocking Bets arm away and wiping the tears from her face.

"Whats so funny?" Ros asked standing in the doorway wrapped in a bathrobe and a towel wrapped around her head like a turban.

Rose and Bet swung round when they heard Ros's voice. Bet pointed to Ros's head wear and both women burst out laughing and screaming at each other every time they tried to look Ros in the eye. Ros caught on to their humour and dragged the towel from her head.

"Oh, yeh very funny!" she said in a seriously hurt voice.

Both women looked up from their giggles guilt waving over them as they turned to face Ros. They both mouthed "Sorry" to her. Ros seeing the funny side started to giggle, starting the other two off again.

"I'm sorry Ros!" Bet burst out holding up the whisky bottle and indicating to the mugs on the side. Ros grabbed a mug and stuck it under the bottle in Bets hand.

"Fill her up!" she ordered grinning at the two women and sliding on to the end chair between them.

When their laughter faded Rose put a motherly hand on Ros's arm.

"Darling we're both truly sorry about you and Tommy really we are."

Giving her arm a little squeeze.

Bet looked sideways at Ros then across the table at Rose,

bursting out laughing again.

"I'm soo sorry!" she cried burying her head in her hands and shaking her head.

Ros looked across to Rose who was trying desperately to stifle a huge grin spreading across her face. She shrugged her shoulders at Ros in an apologetic manner. Unable to contain her self any more burst out laughing grabbing Ros's arm to console her. Ros started to laugh so hard that she slid sideways off the chair landing with a thud on the floor, the tears turning to sorrow. Both Bet and Rose slid from their chairs wiping their faces with their hands, their laughter fading as they crawled either side of her on the floor.

"Oh, God Ros we're sorry!" Rose whispered kissing her head and putting her arms around her.

Ros leaned against her and Rose cradled her head rocking her slowly like a baby. Bet crawled behind Rose and Ros putting her arms around both women, nuzzling her head on Rose's shoulder and resting her chin on Ros's head giving them both a squeeze.

"Look Ros ya know me an' Rose'll be 'ere fer ya if the shit does 'it the fan don'tcha?" she whispered to the silent Ros, then bending her head kissed the top of Ros's head, leaning on both of them to get up she said.

"An I fink you two silly tarts 'ad better get up off that fuckin' floor, you'll 'ave bleedin' piles fer years! No wonder Doughy's legs fuckin' 'urt wif that draft! I'm gonna 'avft ta sort it out!" Bet carried on going back to her chair and sitting down.

Rose and Ros followed suit and all three sat around the table sipping their whiskey's in silence. Finally Ros opened her mouth.

"What am I going to do with this baby?" she asked looking down at her belly and taking another sip of her drink.

"I mean look at me! I'm a total wreck! How am I supposed to look after a baby when I can't even look after myself!" she sighed getting up and going into the girls room.

"Wot she doin' now?" Bet whispered across the table to Rose.

Rose shrugged her shoulders to say she didn't know looking towards the door dividing the kitchen and the girls room. Ros

173

banged through the door holding up a bag of weed.

"Tomorrow I start my life again! To night fuck it!" she said throwing Rose the bag and rolling material plonking down on her seat.

Ros, Rose, and Bet welcomed Doughy the next morning at six o'clock still sitting in their chairs. All three looked up and waved their hands. Doughy stopped in her tracks.

"You been 'ere all bloody night?" she asked her podgy hands on her ample hips.

"Uhuh!" they all said smiling with wide grins.

"Wan't a cuppa?" She asked filling the huge kettle for the first time that day.

"Yer a fuckin' angel you know that Doughy?" Bet said finishing the last of her whisky from her mug, letting her hand flop to the table the mug laying on it's side.

"You been on the piss all bleedin' night an' all," Doughy said firing up the old stove with a taper and a couple of hard blows.

"Nearly!" Ros sighed her eyes swollen from the night before and lack of sleep.

"Wot's 'appened?" Doughy turned from the stove looking at all three of them, her head to one side looking like a Blackbird after a worm.

"Tommy came 'ome earlie an' Ros 'ere was round Ben's 'ouse workin'. Fuckin' ironic fing is. It was gonna be 'er last fuckin' night! We 'ad it all sorted out didn't wc girl!" Bet explained.

Ros inturn nodded at Doughy adding, "An' I'm going to be staying here for a couple of days until I sort out my problems out aren't I Rose?" she said giving Rose a smile.

"Yep," Rose agreed nodding her head.

"Ros can stay as long as she needs to. Okay darling?" Rose added looking first to Ros then to Doughy.

"Fine by me!" Doughy mumbled knowing there was more to it than that. 'an wot about the baby?' she thought as she wandered into the larder pulling out two loaves of bread for the girls breakfast.

"You three want bacon 'n' eggs?" she asked poking her head around the larder door.

"Too fuckin' right!" Bet called grinning across the kitchen at her.

"Well, I'm just going upstairs to make-up my bed and have a wash," Ros said standing up and yawning.

"Okay darling sheets are in the airing cupboard," Rose said lighting a cigarette and taking a cup of tea from Doughy's hand.

"She in a bad way?" Doughy asked poking her thumb over her head.

"She was. That fuckin Tommy over reacted an' she finks it's all over! Me an' Rose 'ere told 'er that 'e'll come round in a few days, when 'e's calmed down an' starts ta miss 'er. Didn't we Rose?" Bet said sipping her tea and flicking her ash in the already full ash tray on the table wrinkling her nose at it.

"Yep Tommy'll be round soon enough. He knows where she is," Rose said carrying on from Bet, and taking the full ashtray emptying it in the bin.

"Does 'e know about the kiddie?" Doughy asked slicing the bread for toast.

"Yeh but I don't fink it'll 'it 'im till 'e runs through the nights events cos when she told 'im all 'e said was "Yeh and!" I feel sorry for 'im in a way. I mean fancy bein' told by yer old ladie she's up th duff as she 'angs off yer jeans, nufing on but a soddin' turban an' a bit of fuckin' cream!" Bet said grinning again.

Both Rose and Doughy nodded in agreement. Rose whispered to Doughy as she passed back with the ash tray.

"It's all right she's feeling guilty. I'll tell you later!" she said with a wink carrying on back to the table.

"You wanna hand lovey?" Bet called over to Doughy as the Bacon hit the hot pan.

"You just keep yer arse on that chair an' outta me kitchen!" Doughy grinned at her blowing her a kiss, turning her attentions to the sizzling Bacon.

"It'll be ready in five minutes, some one go tell Ros," Doughy called to the two women at the table.

"I'll go I need a wee," Rose said getting up.

"I'll get the knifes and forks. You eating Doughy?" Bet called opening the draw of the old farmhouse table.

"Later darlin' when the rush's over an' I can stick me feet up!" she replied turning the toast.

As Bet put the last fork on the table the front door bell went.

"I'll get it," she said as Doughy looked up from the stove.

As she went out of the girls room and into the hall she was met by Ros and Rose. Looking up to them she pointed to the front door.

"Just this sec rang. Dunno who the fucks knocking at this time in the mornin', but it 'ad better be fuckin' good!" she moaned as she reached the door and opened it.

Tommy stood on the doorstep four bags at his feet.

"Ya wanna see Ros?" Bet asked seeing the bags on the floor.

"Wot for? Nar just give 'er these will ya. Oh an' tell 'er the 'ouse's locked up an' the estate agents got the keys. Bye Bet," he said turning and walking down the path.

Ros barged past Bet running after him calling his name as she ran to him. Tommy never even looked back. He just raised his right hand level with his shoulder and spread his hand. Ros dropped to her knees along the path and begged him to turn around.

He just kept walking.

Chapter 16

"Push come on lovey give it ya best shot an' push the little fucker out!" Bet cooed in Ros's ear holding her hand.

"It's coming again ahh…"

"Go on Ros push! Push!" they called.

"You. Fucking push!" Ros said gritting her teeth looking around the bed at the five girls, Bet and Rose.

"Ahh,"Ros gripped Bet's hand like a vice and pushed with all her might.

"I can see the head!" Annie squealed jumping up and down, then promptly fainted.

"Oh, fuck! Wot do I do wif 'er?" Jude said looking down at Annie.

"Here wave this under her nose," Rose said handing Jude a small bottle of smelling salts.

"Don't ask!" Rose said seeing Jude's face.

"Here we go," the midwife said cradling a little head in her hands.

"One more push Ros come on darling."

Ros gave one more grunt and the baby slithered from her.

"It's a girl!" Bet cried giving Ros a kiss on the cheek.

"Well, done lovey," she said giving her a squeeze.

Everyone stood in silence amazed at what they'd just witnessed. A new life.

"Fuckin' 'ell!" Jude stood open mouthed.

"She's gorgeous!" she cried wiping a tear from her eyes.

"Ros your amazing!" Sal breathed into her ear.

"Well, done darling," she said kissing her fore head gently.

Kel stepped forward and peered into the blanket.

"They look so much bigger once they're out don't they?" she said grinning at Ros.

"She's beautiful. Really. Just like her mum," and giving Ros a kiss on the cheek and the baby a gentle kiss on the fore head, she rushed from the room totally choked up.

Annie poked her head up from the end of the bed.

"Oh, God I've missed it. What we got a boy or girl?" she cried scrambling to her feet and pushing past Misty, who was just about to have a look at the baby.

"Hey, slow down babe it's not going to go away."

Annie grinned.

"Sorry Misty. I just feel as if I've missed loads. What have I missed? Tell me! Come on tell me have we got a girl or boy?" Annie cried into Ros's laughing face.

"Oh, Annie calm down darling!" Ros soothed all motherly.

Annie stopped in her tracks and you could hear a pin drop. Ros looked around the room at the statues surrounding her bed. At one end she had Jude, dressed in one of her rubber get ups, nipples and fanny exposed looking gooy eyed at Bet then Rose, who were dressed one in an ice blue sequinned strapped top and long white skirt. The other a multi coloured caftan with the arms slit from shoulder to cuff, a long floating scarf wound around her neck and head band across her fore head respectfully.

She had Sal and Kel on one side of her. Sal dressed in a white halter neck cat suit the back scooped out to the top of her white backside. Kel had a ballet tu-tu on, the front of her leotard scooped so low her breasts were hanging out of it, both had silly grins frozen on their faces making them look like plastic dolls. Then to top it all she had little Annie and Misty on her other side. Misty filling Annie in on what she'd missed. Annie dressed in one stocking and a neck tie nodding intently as Misty tugged at her chains that wrapped either side of her hips and pulled on her pussy lips, stood legs apart, her hands in the motion of going down in front of her stomach to explain exactly how baby came out. The strangest thing of all was the midwife going about her duties of cleaning her up oblivious to the oddities going on around her.

"Oh, it comes with the pushing!" she said grinning raising her right hand, then looking around the room at her friends, she waved her hand in a sweeping motion and started to laugh.

Each woman in turn looked down at themselves, then at eachother. Giggles erupted from each of them as they pointed to one another. The midwife suddenly looked up from Ros's crotch to see what the laughter was about. She suddenly became the brunt of their laughter when Ros cradling her new born in her left arm sat forward and pointing to her midwife shook with fits of laughter hanging on to her stomach with her right hand unable to stop until Bet walked the midwife out the door. Ros calmed down after about five minutes and the midwife was told she could come back in. As soon as Ros saw the poor old midwife, she pointed and collapsed into fits of laughter. Starting the other girls off again.

"Smile you lot!" Rose called from the door clicking the camera as they turned to her voice.

"Fuckin' 'ell that's gonna be one fer the book!" Bet boomed laughing and putting her arm around the midwife giving her a squeeze.

"She okay ta be left now Marg?" Bet asked the midwife her other arm reaching out to Ros's shoulder.

"I've got to check the afterbirth and weigh baby," Marg replied scribbling in her journal.

"Right I'll just nip down an' let Doughy know ta bung the kettle on 'ow's that?" she said gazing down at the child.

"Cor old Doughy still 'ere?" Marg smiled looking up from her notes.

"Recon she'll go outta 'ere in 'er box that one!" Bet chuckled shaking her head slowly and tutting.

"You two go back a fair bit dontcha?" Bet asked her head on one side.

"About thirty years back!" Marge smiled.

"Ow many babies ya delivered?"

"God now your askin' before or after I retired?" Marg said raising an eyebrow.

"Retired. I'm interested 'ow many of 'em get in the Club," she said seriously.

Well we worked it out on an average my Jim an' me. An' we came up with approximately three a week! An' that's a ten mile radius of the island!" she said not looking up.

Bet whistled.

"Jeesus that's fuckin' loads! You'd fink wif this pill now you'd 'ave 'ardly any wouldn't ya!" she whispered remembering

179

the baby in Ros's arms, giving her a gooey grin.

"Well, I'm proud to have had you deliver my baby," Ros said looking down at her bundle.

"Too true!" Bet said as she walked out the room heading for the kitchen and Doughy.

"Six pounds three ounces!" Marg said proudly carefully lifting the naked child from the scales and passing her back to mum.

"She's a good size. I doubt you'll have any problems with this one," she finished scribbling down her notes.

"Thank you," Ros said graciously nodding her head and passing the baby to Rose, who on receiving her looked up like a proud grand mother.

"Oh, Ros she's beautiful!" she gushed.

"Wot we gonna call 'er?" Jude asked over Rose's shoulder clucking at the child.

"I really don't know! What do you think," Ros said stumped.

"I'm off downstairs now. Leave you an' the girls together. I'll come and see you before I leave okay?" Marg said closing her journal.

"How about Katie Jane?" Rose mumbled kissing the baby's sparse black hair.

"Katie Jane Carter," Ros said slowly repeating it several times.

"She does look like a Katie," Annic added leaning on Jude to get a better look at the child in Rose's arms.

"Katie it is then!" Ros beamed, then the tears rolled down her face.

Rose looked at the other five and motioned with her eyes to make them selves scarce. All five filed out of the room not making a sound. Rose went over to Ros sitting on the edge of her bed.

"Hey, come on darling," she said placing Katie in her arms and giving her a hug.

"I really loved him Rose I still do. And she's not even going to know him. Do you know where he is Rose? Please you would tell me wouldn't you?" she cried hugging her daughter her tears dropping on Katies little head.

"Ros if I knew where he was I'd have him know just what he was missing darling!" she replied wiping a tear away with her finger. Ros smiled giving a sniff.

"I think I'm just exhausted," Running her hand down her face.

"That's to be expected darling," Rose smiled in a motherly way.

"Rose have you ever had any…"

"Please Ros don't even go there!" tears welling up in her eyes.

"God I'm sorry truly I am!" she said trying to comfort Rose.

The door knocked three times Jude and Annie poked their heads around the door a bottle of champagne each.

"Thought we'd wet the baby's head wotcha say?" Jude waved the bottle from side to side.

"I say come on in!" Ros beamed and the five girls tumbled in through the door.

Rose laid Katie in her cot and tucked her in like a pro. The girls all sat on the bed holding their glasses together.

"Here Rose there's a glass for you darling," Sal breathed at her lifting a chilled fluted glass up.

"Not for me," she raised a hand.

"I'm going to nip down for a cuppa with the others," she said smiling at them all in their house robes sitting on the bed.

"See you in a while darling," Sal said getting up and helping Rose with the door and a bundle of sheets.

"Are you all right with those?" she asked picking up a tail trailing on the floor.

"Fine darling honest," Rose smiled closing the door.

As the door shut a cosy silence filled the room Ros broke it by a giggle.

"You wait until that photo's developed you all looked hilarious!" she chuckled.

"Funny no matter what the problem in this place you always have a giggle."

"Speak for your self!" Annies eyes widened.

"I had a gent in my room when you began to give birth. Poor old sod was just getting' his keks off when Misty here burst in yelling "She's 'aving it! She's 'aving it!"

"Noo!" Ros giggled.

"Ere where's the gent now?" Jude asked.

"Dunno when I went back ta get something on 'e was gone!" Annie shrugged her shoulders.

"I don't believe it!" Sal giggled.

"It's true! Who else was entertaining when it all happened?" she squealed.

Kel, Misty, and Jude slowly lifted their hands. They all looked at each other and collapsed across the bed.

"Do you mean to say we had four rampant hard on's and no where to put them?" Sal cried leaning onto Kel.

Aha! Jude nodded a huge grin on her lips as she uncorked the first bottle letting the golden liquid fall into Ros's glass then filling the others.

"Here's to Katie Jane and four 'ard dicks!" Jude raised her glass in the air.

"Katie Jane!" they toasted.

Katie gave a little snuffle in her cot and the girls raised their glasses in her direction.

"Well, she's gonna 'ave one 'ell of a story ta tell when she's at school an' they ask where she was born, especially if she takes the photo in!" Jude said and the rest laughed.

"Don't it hurts!" Ros cried.

Ros had been living in "The Club" ever since the day Tommy had dumped her bags at the door. She'd not seen or heard from him since. Bet, Rose and the girls had tried asking every one who knew him of his whereabouts. No one would let on. Ros became very low the first two months after that night and although pregnant was drinking heavily. Bet summoned her to her house one night to tell her, her fortune in a style only Bet could get away with saying, "Stop yer fuckin' mopin' or get out! I can't 'ave me gents upset wif your fuckin' face as long as a kite an' pissed every night it ain't good fer business!"

Ros took this as a warning and bucked her ideas up. Their little house was sold and Tommy sent a cheque through the post giving half to Ros, there was no note, letter or explanation, just an envelope and check. Bet gave the money to Rose to put in Ros's account and told her not to let Ros have it.

"It's so ya don't waste it lovey. Ya got yerself a nice little nest egg now. Don't blow it!" she told her and the matter was closed. Ros wondered what she was going to do when the baby was born. The girls were all begging her to come back with them on the entertaining side, but as far as Ros was concerned she was finished with that line of work now she was going to be a mum. It was her job that ruined her life with Tommy after all an' she didn't want it to ruining her life with her baby.

Now sitting in bed with the girls around her it came to her, what she was going to do! But she'd need Bet's help and the girls! When both bottles were empty Sal looked at her watch.

"My God do you realise we've been drinking champagne and the times four o'clock in the morning!" she giggled.

"How about we leave Ros ta get some rest with that beautiful baby, an' we carry on downstairs in the kitchen?" Misty said getting up from the bed and stretching.

"Bloody good idea champas breakfast wonderful!" Jude giggled tipping the last of her drink from the glass into her mouth.

"That all right with you darling?" Annie asked flitting from Ros to Katie in her cot.

"Fine darling honest. Could you do me a favour and ask Bet if she could pop up sometime I need to talk to her please."

"Sure no problem," Kel piped up.

"I'll tell her when we go down. You wan't anything brought up?"

"I'd love some tea and one of Doughy's BLT's!" Ros grinned.

"Fuck me! Ain't lost yer appitite 'ave ya but it does sound bloody lovely!" Jude joked.

"She's not sick Jude! She's just had a baby," Kel shook her finger at Jude smiling.

"Huh! Less of the 'just' if you don't mind! I'll have you know all that pushings a killer!" Ros grinned.

"Mind you I could do with a nap I must admit! Must be the champagne!" she yawned.

"Nothin' ta do with the pushin' then?" Jude asked raising an eyebrow.

"Oh, go on bugger off you lot! I vant ta be alone!" she said dramatically draping her arm across her forehead.

"Oh, and don't forget my BLT will you!" she called after them.

"Get you!" Jude poked her head around the door and winked.

"Be about ten mins okay babe?" she said and was gone.

Ros took a deep sigh how she loved this place and the girls not forgetting Bet and Rose' Your problems never seem so bad here. They always see the funny side of things no matter what!' she thought. She pulled herself up with her arms and leaned over to the cot. Katie was sleeping Ros could hear her little snuffles as she inhaled and exhaled, smiling to herself she slid down the pillows closing her eyes. She felt drained of all energy, but never happier. Bet slid the tray on to the bedside cabinet the smell of Bacon hitting Ros's nostrils waking her sense's before slowly she opened her eyes and smiled.

"That smells wonderful!" she whispered pushing herself up on her pillows and looking over at the tray then the baby.

"She's fine I've just checked her," Bet grinned.

"I can see I'm going to be sharing Katie a lot," Ros said without malice excepting the tray from Bet and sipping her tea.

"God that's the best tea I've ever tasted!" she said placing it back on the tray and pulling the plate of food in front of her.

"Trust Doughy!" she tutted and grinned when she saw another plate piled with her favourite cakes.

"She's a wonder isn't she!" her eyes getting wider as she bit into her sandwich, a smile spreading across her face.

Bet sat on the bed facing her and picked up her own mug on the tray, taking a sip she looked at Ros.

"Now wotcha wanna talk ta me about?"

"Well, I've been giving it a lot of thought since I gave up entertaining, as what I can possibly do to keep myself and Katie, and I've come to a decision,""

"Oh, yeh an' wots that?" Bet looked at her amusement dancing on her face.

"Don't laugh I'm serious here. I want to open my own gentleman's Club. With your help of course! Maybe we could be partners? What do you think?" Ros rushed, it not coming out as she wanted it to.

"Well, I thought you were gonna ask if it's okay ta stay 'ere wif little miss over there! I didn't expect this!" Bet said a little shocked.

"When did ya fink of this?" she asked.

Ros finished her mouthful then looking at Bet she said.

"A couple of months. Since I got that cheque. I've got to do something with it to make money! Living and working here, I've had all the insight I've needed to know how to run one! All I need from you is… some backing and help with sorting out which girls to hire. What d'you think?" she said picking up her mug and sipping the contents.

Bet was quiet for a couple of minutes and Ros could almost see her brain ticking over. She looked at Ros and picking up her mug, clinked it with Ros's.

"I fink you an' me'll make a fuckin' awesome team!"

"Is that a Yes?" Ros beamed.

"Wotcha fink ya silly tart! Course it is 'ow's about we go 50/50 ta start," Bet grinned.

"You seen anywhere ya fancy?" business taking over her.

"Only one so far a former bed and breakfast off the island. When I'm up and about I'll show you," Ros grinned picking up her sandwich and tucking in to it.

"It's a deal," Bet said putting out her hand. Ros took it but instead of shaking it Ros brought it to her cheek then kissed the back of Bet's hand.

"It's a deal," she said grinning.

Chapter 17

Two weeks after Ros had, had Katie she took Bet to see the old bed and breakfast.

"What do you think?" she said walking from room to room.

Bet nodded.

"Ideal. Plenty of room downstairs an' all the bedrooms 'ave a basin or en suite. So we ain't got ta fork out loads fer decoration. We can split this big room 'ere fer a 'box room' an' changing area fer the gents wotcha say?" she enthused.

"Definitely," Ros's eyes sparkled.

"The bar will have to be in this room, seeing we don't need much light in there," she said pointing to a long narrow room running along the back of the property.

"The 'girls room' can be the dinning room leading to the kitchen and our 'play room' will have to run along side that and the box and changing rooms. What do you think?"

"I fink ya got it all sorted lovey," Bet grinned placing a hand on her shoulder, lighting another cigarette and offering Ros the packet.

"Thanks. So is this…" she said waving her hand around the bottom part of the house.

"It, do you think?"

"Not arf Ros me girl! It's near enough ta the pubs an' Clubs, but far enough out ta be exclusive. Fuckin' perfect!" Bet said rubbing her chin thinking.

"I fink we'll be able ta keep all that wood panelling an' all, again savin' on decorators," she said running her other hand along the dark wood panelling.

"Ow much it up fer again?" she asked banging her feet on the parquet flooring. Don't seem it's riddled wif wood worm either!" she grinned.

"Twenty five thousand!" Ros said quietly.

"Wot I didn't 'ere ya?" Bet called still banging the wood on the floor and walls.

"Twenty five," she shouted walking into the room Bet was banging.

"Slap the guy's 'and off we'll 'ave it!" she beamed.

"Oh, Bet I knew you'd love it as much as me. Thank you you won't be sorry!" Ros ran over and hugged Bet in her cloud of smoke.

"Right let's go get some money out me bank fer a deposit. 'ow long ya got fer Katie?" she asked looking at her watch.

"As long as we need. She's with Doughy this morning. Jude an' Annie are taking her out this afternoon. So I've got as long as it takes!"

"Good," Bet answered still looking around rubbing her chin and puffing on her cigarette.'

If there's one thing Bet's got, it's a bloody good business brain!' Ros thought smiling to her self as she stood watching Bet walk from one room to the other mumbling to her self.

"Well, I've seen enough," Bet said coming to a halt in front of Ros.

"Shall we then?" she pointed to the door giving Bet an excited grin.

"Yep let's go get this business on the road now shall we," Bet replied marching to the door. Stepping out the door she turned.

"Ow about we do it up in deep red ta compliment the wood. Yer know leather chairs, chandeliers, open fire places real fancy?"

"Absolutely perfect!" Ros grinned visualising the old house in its glory.

"Well, wot we fuckin' waitin' fer!" Bet called unlocking her car door and getting in.

Ros walked backwards to the car gazing at the old house. Bet leaned over and unlocked the passenger side tapping the window.

"Get yer arse in will ya we got some business ta sort out!" she yelled in the car leaning back and starting it up.

Ros got in.

"Next stop the high street James!" she crooned in a posh

voice.

"Don't be so fuckin cheeky madam!" Bet grinned as she swung out of the drive heading towards the high street and a new partnership.

"No! I said fuckin' velvet curtains an' silk cushions! NOT the fuckin' uver way round ya dosy tart! Fuckin' 'ell it ain't that 'ard is it? I 'ope ya got the colour right! Yeh that's it fuckin' blood red! Well done!" Bet cried sarcastically down the phone.

"An let's make one fuckin' fing perfectly clear. I ain't payin' fer sumfink I ain't ordered okay! Good! Fine. Yer got two fuckin' days an' then I take me custom elsewhere got it? Good!"

Ros stood there biting her thumbnail.

"I can't believe they got it wrong!" she said as Bet threw the phone back down.

"Fuckin' gormless the 'ole fuckin' lot of 'em!" Bet said tutting to the phone.

"Right we've got the decorators in the bar at the moment, you ordered the glasses, ashtrays, drinks etc?"

"All coming tomorrow. The only thing I can't get delivered is the embossed towels for the girls rooms, and that's the only thing that's holding us up there or should I say down there seeing we're in the attic," she smiled.

"Yeh very funny! How long until they can deliver?" Bet looked up from their desk.

"They said three to four days!" putting her hand up to stop Bet, she carried on.

"Four days max! If it's any later we only pay for half that's the deal. What else needs ordering or done downstairs?" she asked looking at her lists of things to do.

"You're the one who likes the lists you tell me smart arse!" Bet smirked.

"It's only since I've had Katie my brain's gone! If I don't write lists I'm lost!" Ros said waving them in the air.

"Seems yer fuckin' lost even wif yer lists!" Bet replied raising her eyebrows and lighting another cigarette from her spent one.

"Huh! Just tell me!" Ros stood with her hands on her hips lists in both hands.

Okay the decorators 'ave just got ta finish wallpaperin' an' then we can get the sparkies in ta do the lights an' chandeliers, I recon they're be finished ta night so tamorrow they can finish off bungin' the shelves up in the 'box room'. An' we need a few 'ooks bunged in the wooden joists in the 'play room'. Apart from that everyfings done! All we need ta do then is stock up an' sort out the invites fer open night! Not bad fer six months work is it?" she smiled and patted her hair at the back.

"All right smart arse!" Ros said sticking out her tongue.

"I've been busy too you know. Do you know how hard it is to get good girls around here?"

"Tell me about it!" Bet said.

"Can't teach me ta suck eggs!"

"Oh, sorry Bet I didn't mean anything by it!"

"I know lovey," Bet grinned.

"Ow many we got so far?" she asked leaning across the desk.

"About eighteen so far, but half only want part time when their old men are working away," Ros said looking up and raising her eyebrows.

"Umm! Well I've 'ad a word wif the girls an' your lot are comin' 'ere wif ya. 'ow's that sound?" Bet slowly let out a grin.

"Oh, Bet I love you!" Ros jumped up and down running around the desk to give her a hug.

"Are you sure you don't mind them coming?"

"I'd rarver 'em come over 'ere an' work than fuckin' mope around the Club missin' you an' little Katie, cos that's wot it would be like! They all fink Katie's theirs anyway so I couldn't split 'em up!" Bet said looking up through her cloud.

"Your crazy do you know that! But I love you. Thank you Bet thank you so much," Ros cried as excited as a child at Christmas.

"No problem lovey lest the girls know 'ow ta act around the gents," she smiled.

" That reminds me, when's the first lot comin' ta the Club fer a trial?"

"The first five are coming tomorrow for two nights, and then as they leave the next four or five will come and so on until we find what we want."

"Any of 'em done it before?" Bet asked. It being her time to scribble notes down.

"A couple of them have for definite, they both came down on the train from a London Club."

"Um nice!" Bet replied thoughtfully.

"I've got a few who've done threesomes before, and a few who've done group. There's two lesbians, but the one I want to see is this one!" Ros said pointing to an application form.

"Say's she's got a snake in her act! What act I don't know! Seeing she's never done this type of job before!" she said giggling.

"Now that could be interesting!" Bet grinned.

"It always amazes me 'ow many girls that ain't done the job before know where ta apply!"

Ros looked naively at Bet and they both started laughing.

"You haven't sorted out the guest list yet right?" Ros asked through giggles.

"No. but I recon if we invite all the gents from the Club fer a free night, but only if they bring another male guest, then, that should give 'em some incentive ta come not that they'd need it!" Bet chuckled.

"No really I've 'ad a word wif some of our more influential gents about this place an' they recon by the sound of it that we're on a winner 'ere if we keep it totally exclusive ta those that can pay, if ya get me drift!"

"I couldn't agree more," Ros nodded.

"We need to get real class to work here. No tat!"

"Of course. Yer always gonna get wot yer pay fer in this game," Bet said very matter of fact.

"I fink the best of what we got at the Club will definitely pay a bigger fee ta keep it very private don'tcha fink?"

"I think you're a very cleaver woman Bet and I hope one day I'm as good as you," Ros said sincerely. Then taking a pad and pencil sat down opposite Bet in her cloud of smoke to write the names as Bet called them out.

"Ive got it!" Bet threw herself back in her chair.

"We 'ave two openin' nights! One fer our old gents from the Club, an' anuver for the new trade wotcha fink?" she beamed picking up the mug of coffee and drinking the last of it.

"Where does it come from?" Ros said amazed.

"Don't ask me! Just pops up from somewhere! So do I take that's a Yes then?" Bet said sitting forward smugly and shrugging her shoulders.

"Yes! Yes! Yes!" Ros yelled.

"All right lovey calm down! 'Ere there's just one more fing I've been meanin' ta ask ya."

"Oh, an' what's that?" Ros asked looking up from her list and putting her pencil on top of it.

"You gonna entertain in this gaff, you know wif the girls. An' if so 'ow much we gonna charge?"

Ros took a sharp intake of breath paralysed to the spot slowly her mouth opened.

"What!"

"What I do now!" Bet said throwing her arms up.

Ros stared at her.

"Fuck me Ros I was only askin'! I mean you could ask a lot of dosh fer yer services. Set yer up it would!" Bet said so matter of fact that even Ros's mind started to wander shaking her head.

"No Bet I can't! I've got Katie now! I couldn't even think about it!" she cried shaking her head.

"Maybe not the old gents, but ya could the new ones! They ain't gonna know yer history. Fink about it! Yer fuckin' good at wotcha do. Why not use it fer you an' Katie!"

She looked at Bets perfectly serious face through her cloud.

"I've never thought about it like that," she whispered as if she didn't want anyone to hear them.

"Well, that's all I'm askin' is fer ya ta 'ave a fink about it!" Bet smiled slowly getting up from the desk and walking around to Ros draping an arm around her shoulder.

"'Ow about we go an' get a fresh coffee an' see wot's 'appenin' down there?"

"Okay partner," Ros grinned clutching her pad and pencil.

"Fer fuck sake put those bleedin' fings down will ya! Yer fuckin' brain may 'ave gone but I fink I can remember a few fuckin' names wotcha say?" Bet cackled taking the items from her hands and banging them on the desk.

"All right you win!" Ros smiled raising both hands in surrender and headed for the door.

The two women wandered down the wide elegant stairs to

the bedrooms. They looked down the hallway then at each other.

"Put it there sister," Bet chuckled raising her right hand in the air.

Ros slapping Bet's raised hand grinned.

"It does look very grand doesn't it?" she breathed staring down the tall wide hall, the bottom oak wood panelling sending out a warm welcoming tone to the red painted walls above, covered where ever possible with gilded pictures and mirrors. Every door had a brass plaque on its panelling, yet to be engraved. (a later project of Bet's). The oak floor boards meeting the oak panelling, and a deep red and gold patterned runner carpet an inch thick deep ran to the far wall. At the end a tall sash window yet to be dressed in the heavy blood red velvet curtains. Three chandeliers sat on the floor under the spot they were to hang.

"It sure does lovey. I recon we're be in business in wot four weeks at the most. All we've got ta get now is anuver Doughy!"

"I think I know just the person. How would think the girls would feel to a guy cooking and consoling them?"

"Wot!" Bet looked horrified.

"No fuckin' bloke works in one of my gaffs! They all 'ave ta fuckin' pay ta walk in the door!" she said giving her head a sharp nod to end the conversation.

"I don't mean a straight guy. I mean Frankie!"

"Little Frankie? Fuckin' faggot Frankie? No. No way! Ros your fuckin' right yer fuckin' 'ead 'as gone. 'is worse than a naggin' old goat wif rotton fuckin' teef!!" the girls'll kill 'im! Nar yer can't be serious," Bet cried shaking her head.

"Have you ever tasted any of his cooking?" she said trying not to giggle splaying her hands on her hips.

Can't say I've ever 'ad the pleasure I must admit," Bet said giving Ros a sideways look.

"Well, I have an' he's bloody good. Let him cook you a meal and answer after. What do you say?" Ros said raising an eyebrow.

"Don't let it ever be said I don't give every bugger the benefit of the doubt," Bet said slowly.

"Is that a yes then?"

"Yeh," Bet sighed knowing she'd been beaten and grinned.

"That's me girl!!" and guided Ros down the next flight of stairs into the black and white tiled hallway.

Standing at the foot of the stairs the two women looked at each other again their excitement infectious. A huge double oak front door faced them with stained glass in the top panel.

"I just adore those doors," Ros gushed.

"I'll love 'em even more once we get some gents threw 'em!" Bet said turning right.

Facing her was the 'box room' door. Bet walked over running her hands over the oak panelling as she went. She reached the door and peered at the brass plaque that had been placed on it. Engraved was 'Box Room' in fancy lettering. Bet rubbed her forearm over it giving it a little polish.

"Fings like this make all the difference don'tcha fink?" she called over to Ros.

Smiling Ros walked over and opened the door for Bet swinging it all the way back. The smell of fresh paint hit their nostrils making Ros smile.

"Fresh and clean," she mumbled.

"Wot?" Bet asked turning towards her.

"I just said fresh and clean that's all," she said smiling and walking past Bet her feet sinking in to the thick carpet. She reached a second door the plaque was engraved 'gents room' in the same lettering. Ros pushed the door open. Both rooms were decorated exactly the same with the wood panelling carrying through but instead of red paint, both rooms were painted a dusky blue. The theme of gilded pictures and mirrors had also been carried through, with a huge mirror hanging behind the key counter reflecting the light from the two sash windows dressed in dark blue velvet curtains kept open with gold sashes. The boxes were yet to be stacked on their shelves each one with their own brass plaque number plate. A huge painting hung between the windows of the room. Bet walked over to Ros on the thick blue carpet the same colour as the curtains and they both looked into the back room the 'gents room' the carpet followed through but there was no windows in this room only another long gilded mirror at the far end reflecting Bet and Ros. There were gilded chairs with blue velvet seats behind elaborate screens scattered about the room, each screen capable of obscuring the largest of gents from his fellow comrades.

"Looks good don't it?" Bet said checking her hair and lipstick in the tall mirror.

"Never in my wildest dreams did I think it could look this good," Ros squealed.

"All down ta you lovey, you did this!" Bet smiled at her friend now partner waving a hand about the room.

Ros flushed with embarrassment and pride draping her arm about Bet they walked out shutting the doors behind them. As they were coming out one of the decorators waved at them making a cup of his hand, then grinning cheekily made a 'T' sign with his fingers putting his hands together dropped to his overall covered knees as if he was praying.

Bet and Ros chuckled.

"Where the fuck we get these guys from?" Bet said to her without moving her mouth.

Looking at the work man she called.

"Ya know where the fuckin' kettle is I'll 'ave two coffee's no sugar," then promptly opened the next room the plaque revealing 'play room'.

Ros looked at the man, who still on his knees didn't quite know if Bet was serious or not and wagged her finger at him. Smiling she stepped into the playroom.

"Wow!" she stood in the door way open mouthed.

The whole room was decorated like a cave. You would never have known it was a plain rectangle room. Even the floor covered in a thick earth coloured carpet, rose and fell in mounds. There were alcoves and boulders every where. In the middle of the room there was a pit fire surrounded by stones, a huge funnel hanging over it adorned with hundreds of church candles. Ros walked around it marveling at her creation.

"I never realized it would look this good," she whispered her hands over her mouth.

"I didn't want to see until all the equipment was in but I'm glad I have now. It'll look so different then won't it," she said to Bet, who was lying across a boulder. Ros collapsed laughing.

"I'll tell ya sumfing these fuckin' fings…" she waved her arms dramatically around to the other boulders.

"Are so fuckin' comfy I could stay 'ere all bleedin' day!"

"That's the business," Ros said wiping a stray tear from her grinning face.

Bet grinned.

"You're a fuckin' genius wif these you know that!" she said sliding off.

"There's nufink like a bit of comfort when yer fuckin'!" she said seriously making Ros stop in her tracks then burst out laughing again.

"Well... like... you... said you get what you pay for in this game!" Ros cried beaming at her.

"You learn fast lovey! Real fast!" Bet laughed shaking her head.

Calming down Ros started to look around again, her face getting more and more serious the more she looked about her. She visualized the chained cuffs embedded in the walls of some of the alcoves. The hidden cupboards full of love toys. Whips hanging on the cave walls. The boulder sex beds making it easier for the girls and gents. The blind folds all leather. Above, there was three spots where the huge hooks will be, to hold a girl in a sex harness, or to hold a gent by his arms for a little S&M. Ros's eyes burned bright and a slow smile ran across her face. She nodded her head agreeing with her self 'Yep this is one hell of a play room!' she thought turning she caught Bet watching her.

"Wotcha finkin' lovey?" she asked a smirk on her lips.

"I was just visualising it with all the stuff in. Thank you Bet for having enough faith in me to put your money in something like this," she said looking the older woman in the eye.

The smirk vanished from Bets face and her eyes softened.

"Oh, go on wif ya. You 'ad all the ideas an' I 'ad a bit more money than you. Partners remember?" she said giving her a motherly smile.

"More than partners," Ros said giving Bet a hug and walking her out thedoor. As Ros closed it the work man was just coming out of the corridor running along side the play room two mugs of coffee in his hand.

"Now that's wot I call service!" Bet smirked taking the mugs from the man and passing one to Ros then walking down the passage the man had just come from. Opened the next door on her left and walked in not giving him another look.

Ros looked at the decorator biting her bottom lip. Shrugging her shoulders she followed Bet shutting the door firmly behind her. She took one look at Bet sitting on a table swinging her legs, her red painted lips poking from a fresh cloud. Leaning hard against the door she broke down into a fit of giggles.

"You're a bad girl!" she said waving a finger at Bet.

"Oh, fuck off," Bet said sticking her tongue out, making Ros put her finger to her lips.

"Shh!" she grinned wide-eyed.

Bet smirked back at her and took a sip of her coffee placing her head on one side.

"Um not bad! Not bad at all!" she said amazed by her own honesty.

"This is nice," Ros said wandering around the little clusters of tables and chairs. Along one wall it was all mirrors with light bulbs surrounding them. Two hood dryers stood in the far corner concealed by a screen. 'It seemed so bare compared to the 'girls room' at the Club' she thought "Be even better when the girls put their mark on it," Ros finished.

"Once those get in 'ere it'll never look the same again!" Bet said craning her head about the room.

"That the door ta the kitchen fer the girls? 'ave a look Ros," Bet said watching from her perch sipping the hot coffee in her hands.

Ros walked over and opened the door. There in front of her was one of the latest kitchens on the market. Ros was speechless.

"My treat ta the 'ouse. Do it properly in the beginning an' it ain't gonna cost ya every year. Business!" Bet said tapping her nose.

"One of the gents at the Club. Me an' 'im did a little deal 'e gives us a discount kitchen an' we give 'im a discounted fee," Bet looked at Ros and smiled.

"We got the best deal!" she added, shrugging her shoulders.

"You never cease to amaze me!" Ros said again shaking her head at her.

"I know good ain't it," Bet smiled getting offf the table and walking over to Ros.

"I like the idea of the dining area down this end and the

kitchen up the other end with that lovely window its great. There's a door up that end as well, so really the girls are away, closeted."

"Yeh I fought the door from the kitchen ta the girls room was a good idea least they don't 'ave ta wander down the hallway to it. Yep two doors are a brilliant idea. Who's was it mine or yours?" Bet grinned.

"I don't know," she smiled finishing the last of her coffee placing the mug in the sink.

"Shall we go and have a look at the bar room they must be nearly finished."

"I don't see why not we've 'ad a butchers in all the uvers!" Bet replied placing her mug next to Ros's.

The two women walked out of the kitchen door. Ros noted even that door had a brass plaque and smiled to herself. They walked past the girl's room door and out into the square hall, turning left they headed to the double oak doors in the middle of the wall facing them. This time the plaque was above the doors still in the same lettering 'Gentleman's Bar' Ros had to admit it did give it class somehow. Bet gave one curt knock and pushed both doors open with a little too much force than was needed not giving anyone a chance to move if they were behind them. Ros giving her a sideways glance walked through with her the workmen stopped what they were doing and looked towards the two women.

"'ow much you lot got left ta do in 'ere then?" Bet asked taking a puff of her cigarette.

"Recon we'll be done 'ere ta day Mrs!" the portly older man called from behind a stepladder.

"Is that a definite," Bet barked back hating to be called Mrs. "An me names Bet okay!" she finished.

"Sorry. Yes that's a definite BET!" the older man said smirking.

"Fine. If ya do there's a drink on me fer all yer boy's ta morrow when yer done 'ow's that sound?" she nodded to each workman.

"Sounds good ta us Mr... er Bet!" the head decorator called back giving a nervous little cough making Bet smirk.

Nodding in his direction she walked over to the long bar

and sat on the first bar stool she came to. Looking around the room she saw the last of the wallpaper being hung on the wall. She called over to the portly workman.

"Ere John! Come 'ere a minute will ya," motioning the older man to the bar.

"Bet," he said curtly as he levelled with her.

"Ow much work ya got left in 'ere ta do really?" Bet asked lighting a cigarette blowing the smoke towards him.

Arthur coughed nervously.

"That's the last of the paper… cough! Umm we've just got ta bung a few 'ooks up fer the mirrors an' pictures in 'ere an' we're done. Just the clearing away. Oh an' we've got a couple of shelves ta knock up in the uver… cough! Room! An' me names Arfer not John! Bet," This time it was him that was smirking.

"Umm!" Bet said.

'Seems I've met me match 'ere. Intrestin'!' she thought a little flutter running through her body. Something that hadn't happened for a long long time. Smiling she said.

"Any chance yer boy's can finish ta day. I'll make it worf their while, bung 'em a few quid each!" Bet said business like but in a softer tone.

Ros walked behind Arthur raising her eyebrows at Bet and smiling. Leaving them alone she went over to the huge fireplace opposite the bar and turned scanning the room. The wood panelling ran all the way around the room finishing either side of the fireplace mantle. Above the wallpaper, in a deep blood red and gold gave the room an old gentleman's Club feel. The thin fanlight windows running across thee top of the walls either side had been replaced with stained glass allowing the minimum of natural light to break in, giving the room an evening feel no matter what time of day. The big studded leather armchairs stood about the room covered in clear plastic. Oak coffee tables sat at their sides sheets draped over each one. The bar faced her. The workmen had used the wood panelling from the cave room to cover the front of the bar. The big brass rail ran full length under the marble counter. Ros could see her reflection in the mirrored wall behind the bar, thinking as she looked at herself that there's definitely got to be a mirror over the fire place. She went over to the cluster of fancy lamps and shades lifting each shade and checking the colours for the room. The three chandeliers were stacked one on top of each other in their protective boxes. A foot of a leather chair caught Ros's eye and made her shiver, her past flooding in front of her, making her grab the edge of the panelling to steady herself. Bet dragged her eyes from Arthur as she heard a thud in the corner of the room.

Both Bet and Arthur rushed to the collapsed Ros sprawled on the floor backside exposed and legs akimbo. Bet looked at Arthur who knelt down straightened Ros's legs and covered her backside in a fatherly manner.

Bet felt the flutter run deep inside her as Arthur looked up at her then back to Ros sweeping her hair away from her face as a father would. Ros came round thinking it strange Bet and the workmen were in her bedroom and frowned at them. Bet dropped to one knee and took Ros's hand.

"You okay lovey?" she asked concerned.

"Y... yes I'm fine," Ros whispered propping herself up on one arm.

"Steady girl you 'ad quite a bump on the 'ead just then," Arthur said helping her to the covered armchair that put her on the floor in the first place, making Ros giggle nervously and Bet give her a worried look.

Arthur took control.

"Bet would you please get this young lady a glass of water while I check her head for any cuts," he said giving her a gentle smile.

Bet gave Arthur an elegant nod of her head returning his smile. Ros had never seen her like it.

"That must have been one hell of a bang on my head!" she said in Bet's ear as she stood to get her water giving her a sideways smile and wincing as Arthur ran his hand over her head.

Bet poked the top of her arm and winked making Ros chuckle wincing even more. Bet was away and back in seconds'fucking hell she's got it bad! Wait until I tell the others!' Ros thought giving Bet a smile as she took the glass of water as ordered.

"I'm fine now honest really I am," she said taking a sip of the water and smiling at them both in turn.

"I recon I just got a bit overwhelmed with it all," she said standing up and walking over to the bar placing the glass on the cold marble top and turning.

"Every things perfect!" she grinned.

"Just perfect," Leaving the room and heading up the stairs leaving Bet to sort out Arthur.

Bet grinned at Arthur.

"That's me girl!" she said lighting a cigarette.

"Now where were we?"

"You smoke too much you know that!" Arthur said walking past Bet heading to the bar again Bet for once in her life was speechless. She silently followed Arthur to where she was sitting before Ros's little bit of drama. She slid her backside on to the bar stool turned to Arthur exhaling the smoke in to his face.

"Let's get one fing straight. I pay yer ta decorate me fuckin' gaff. Not tell me what I do or don't do to fuckin' much got it mate!" she seethed only inches from Arthurs face, when something clicked in their eyes causing them both to burst out laughing Bet placing both hands on Arthurs shoulders to steady herself feeling that buzz run through her again. Looking Arthur straight in the eyes she said.

"Would ya like ta 'ave dinner wif me ta morrow night?" Bet felt her stomach flip and her heart was trying to escape through her throat, her mouth went as dry as a bone. Time seemed to slow to nothing, Bet couldn't take her eyes away from Arthur.

Suddenly Arthur's face wrinkled into a smile.

"That Bet old girl would be bloody lovely. Wot time an' where do I pick ya up from?" he said laughing and helping her back on her stool.

"W... w... wot? Really? You will?" Bet said feeling herself flush like a school girl.

"Yep where an' wot time," he said rummaging into his pocket pulling out a piece of paper and taking the pencil from behind his ear, wetting the lead with his tongue he held it poised over the paper waiting for Bet's address and the time to pick her up.

Bet regained her composure and waved her left hand over Arthurs.

"No need fer that I got ta sample a meal 'ere from a possible employee. Still fancy it?" she said placing her hands on her hips.

"Yer know old girl I don't fink I'd care where it was wif you," Arthur said giving her a wink and making her flush again.

"See ya 'ere ta morrow night wot shall we say eightish okay fer you," she said sliding off her stool, her left hand caressing her neck.

"All the lights 'll be done. Every fing finished?" she said trying to bring the subject back to the business.

"I'll get me boys ta get their fingers out a promise of a bung in their hands 'ill get 'em movin'" Arthur said watching Bets every move.

"Good! I always say yer get wot ya pay fer in this world. Ta morrow then?" she said heading for the double oak doors.

"Eightish," Arthur said watching her and smiling.

Bet reached the office door ignoring the 'please knock' sign and opening it without knocking. That being their rule, they were never to knock to enter their own office, that way they knew who ever was out side the door would have to knock be it friend or foe.

"Ya always 'ave ta pratect yerself in this game," she muttered to herself closing the door.

Ros looked up from a chair.

"What? Oh Bet! Hear me out before you say no," Ros said.

"I think we should have bar 'men' and waiters in the gentleman's room you know a Jeeves type very discreet what do you think?" she asked her eyes shinning bright.

"I think I'm in love!" Bet said sliding on to the chaise lounge behind the door.

"What…! OH… A certain gentleman down stairs could it be?" Ros grinned.

"Fuck I fink I've lost it! I really didn't like the stroppy little bastard at first! Now me! I'm sayin' I fink I'm in love in a matter of minutes! An' ta top it all 'e calls me old girl an' I don't care!" Bet cried tapping the back of her hair down giving Ros a hurt look when all she could do was laugh.

"Ohh I'm so sorry Bet," she said through giggles then crumpled again when she saw Bet's face. Holding her hand up she cried.

"Sorry!" before Bet couldn't contain her face any longer and dissolved on to the day bed.

When their laughter subsided Ros looked at Bet her face serious.

"So what do you think of my idea about having men in the gentleman's room?"

Bet raised her eyebrows and grinned.

"Yer get more like me every fuckin' day! Yes it sounds pucker very fuckin' classy," she said sitting up and turning back to business.

"An ya can tell old faggot Frankie 'e gets 'is chance ta prove 'ow fuckin' good 'e is ta morrow night 'ere," she said pointing to the floor.

"Tell 'im 'e can get in 'ere at six an' 'e'll be cookin' fer two. A three course meal. I'll pay fer the ingredients tell 'im. An' I'll give 'im the dosh when 'e gets 'ere."

Ros sat motionless staring at Bet eventually she managed to nod her head.

"Wot I said now!"Bet asked looking at her.

"Nothing," Ros said smiling and shrugging her shoulders.

"I'll give Frankie a ring now," she said reaching over for the phone and phone book.

"Any thing you want him to cook?" she asked finding out as much information to pass to the already hired Frankie.

Bet shook her head and looked at Ros.

"Whatcha up to madam?" her eyes beady.

"Nothing," Ros lied.

"Ros I know when yer lyin'. Wotcha up to?" she said squinting her eyes.

"Okay!" she said pushing the phone book away from her.

"I've already hired him! I'm sorry but I was in the local the other day an' saw a very depressed Terrance sitting in the corner and…"

"Fuckin' get ta the point." Bet butted in.

"All right well he was depressed," Ros put her hand up and opened her eyes.

"Soo when I asked. He said Frankie had been offered a job up in London some very fancy restaurant so thinking he must be good I offered him a job there and then."

"But 'e weren't there!" Bet said giving her a shroud look.

"NO he wasn't! But Terrance was so with his help he agreed to a smaller wage than his London job but the love of a good man is hard to find gay or straight an' Frankie realised that with Terrance," she said finishing her story.

"AH all very sweet Ros but I ain't 'appy wif the fact ya 'ired 'im wif out talkin' ta me first!"

"I know an' I'm sorry really I am, but I know the way you feel about men in general and he is a good chef an' would be a great friend to the girls Terrance as well!" Ros grovelled.

"All right you win," Bet said waving a hand and lighting another cigarette.

"Won't one?" she asked throwing the packet before she could answer.

"You've been right so far lovey I've gotta go wif yer wif the rest of it!" Bet said giving her a wink,

"This is gonna be fuckin' massive yer know that don'tcha?"

"Yep!" she nodded giving her a huge grin the excitement welling up inside her.

"Want me to stick around tomorrow darling?" she asked as a friend.

"Nar I fink I can 'andle meself don't you!" Bet chuckled.

"Anyways no doubt Terrance will be wif Frankie fer 'is big night!" Bet raised her eyebrows at her.

"So I won't be alone will I!" she said.

Both women grinned at each other Frankie was hired and that was the end of it as far as Bet was concerned. She'd had her say the air was clear.

Chapter 18

The invites had been sent out and the replies with fees came flooding back.

"Wot a fuckin' brilliant idea you 'ad wif them brochures instead of just invites! They can't wait ta give us their money!" Bet said opening yet another envelope with a cheque inside and shaking her head in amazement.

"It's "The Jones next door" syndrome," Ros explained.

"Probably the only thing I ever learn't from the old bastard!" she said smiling.

"What?" she asked a stunned Bet.

"It's the first time I've ever 'eard ya say anyfing about 'im!" Bet said quietly.

"Well, that's because I'm ready for him!" she said beaming at her.

"I've had enough sleepless nights. I want to face him. So I've sent him a brochure. I want to walk in on him sitting in one of those leather chairs, a pretty girl on his knee and then let him know what I know," she said very matter of fact. No emotion in her voice at all.

"Are yer sure about this lovey?" Bet looked concerned at Ros.

"Yes positive. I've got Katie now. I need to move on and the only way is to face the past."

"You 'ad a reply yet?"

"No not yet but we will. Be sure of that!" Ros smiled slowly.

"Wotcha put in that brochure Ros?" Bet said having an uncanny feeling Ros was up to some thing.

"Just a little extra some thing," she smiled.

"Wot little extra sum fing?" Bet asked.

"Let's just say some thing to wet his appetite!" she said

waving the conversation away.

"Okay I'll stop askin'. 'ow many we got fer tonight?" Bet changed the subject.

"About sixty of our old gents. All have taken the advantage of the reduced fee for their custom," she waved a wad of replies at her.

"Good girl. Now wot's faggot Frankie knocking up fer the grub? I 'ope 'e's doin' posh grub!" Bet said looking down at some papers.

"All gourmet stuff nothing but the best! Even better next week when we have the new gents. Seeing they're paying double!" Ros grinned.

"That a girl business first as always that's wot Arfer says," Bet said letting her in on their intimacy for a second.

"Well, every things sorted so I'm going to spend the afternoon with Katie before leaving her with Marg and Jim for the night, you know she loves those two, she never want's to come home the next day," Ros grinned at her.

"Strange init old Marg delivering all those babies but never 'avin' any 'erself," Bet said thinking aloud.

"I suppose it does,"She said.

"I'm just glad Marg is looking after Katie instead of going out to work. Now who else could look after her better than the woman that brought her into the world," Ros said raising both her hands as she stood by her chair.

"I'll see you and the girls five'ish okay with you darling. Oh is Arthur coming with you tonight?" Ros asked as if Arthur had always been around.

"Only til the gents start ta arrive. Said 'e didn't like the idea of stickin' around bless 'im!" Bet cooed.

"Okay darling I'll see you two later when the waiters and barmen arrive. Love to Arthur," she said blowing her a kiss and walking through the door of the office her daughter the only thing on her mind.

Ros turned up at the "ROSBETTE CLUB" at half past five. She stood at the double front door butterflies in her stomach, key in her hand. She took a deep breath calming herself down the brass plaque fixed on the side of the house simply said "ROSBETTE CLUB" "Strictly Members Only". It looked more like a Harley Street Doctors than a private Club. Ros smiled slowly to herself her nerves going, and placed her key in the door. She turned the key, then taking another deep breath opened the door.

'Weird' she thought 'I must have walked through these doors a couple of hundred times! But tonight is make or break for us and I can't stop shaking.'

Behind the doors the Club was heaving with girls, running from room to bedroom, some had curlers in their hair, others only one stocking on. A couple just had their robes on their face and hair immaculate. Ros nodded and smiled as they flitted past her and up the stairs. Josie stood in the door way of the 'box room' and draped an arm up the doorframe smiling at Ros.

"This place is amazing Ros. You an' Bet 'ave done us girls proud yer know that?" she said beaming at Ros hoping they'd keep her on in this club.

"An this get up's bloody brilliant!" she cried doing a twirl for Ros's inspection.

She was dressed in a tux with bow tie and waist coat the tails of the tux finishing at the top of Josies suspender and stocking legs.

"Wotcha fink?" she asked grinning.

"Stunning!" Ros nodded her business eye taking in every inch of Josies attire.

"I'd like to thank you for coming over for the opening night. If you enjoy it let me know. It's going to be totally different to the Club.

"That's okay Ros I'm quite excited to be in on the first night. The rooms are fantastic really they are!"

Ros thanked her blowing her a kiss and moving across the tiled hall to the 'girls room' passing the 'cave room' she'd look at that later, but first she had to see Bet. She opened the swing door of the 'girls room'. The scene took her breath away she just stared.

"Ros babe you okay?" Jude came over to her. Annie in tow took her hand leading her into the room.

Ros shook her head and beamed. That empty room she'd seen earlier was now a hive of activity.

"Ros lovey over 'ere!" Bet called from the far corner.

Every one stopped what they were doing and clapped her in. she didn't know whether to laugh or cry as Jude and Annie led her past the new and old girls to Bet's table.

"Wow 'ave a butchers at 'er Arfer don't she make ya proud!" Bet said standing to greet Ros.

"Sure does old girl. She sure does!" Arthur muttered, shaking his head in bewilderment as to how he got here, sitting in a 'Gentleman's Club' with a woman his only known a few days and considering asking her to marry him tonight!

"You look wonderful your self darling!" Ros smiled holding out both her arms to Bet.

The two of them kissed on both cheeks stepping back to admire the others outfit with an approving eye. Bet stood in a long black 'A' line dress, a ruffle running around the back and crossing over at the low cut neckline falling across the front to a split at the top of her left thigh, the garment fell to her ankles being finished with gold strap sandals and a gold choker at her neck. Bet's hair had been set and teased to perfection by Jude even her cloud about her head seemed somehow classier. Ros had dressed in a black silk Tux a gold lame halter neck plunged to her waist.

Under the trousers she had dressed her feet in black court shoes. She had tied her hair to the nap of her neck with a big gold silk scarf and finished everything off with a bowler hat tilted to the side.

"Very jaunty!" Arthur winked at her raising his glass to his lips.

"Wotcha 'avin' ta drink lovey?" Bet asked grinning at her and passing her the joint. Ros holding the cigarette between her finger and thumb said holding it up.

"I wasn't going to drink or smoke tonight. But I suppose one of each won't hurt me! So I'll have a red wine please and a lighter!"

She slipped into the chair opposite Bet and taking the lighter she inhaled the smoke closing her eyes enjoying the effect of her smoke of the day.

She opened her eyes and looked around. All the girls were indifferent stages of dress, the whole room was buzzing. Ros had, had every girl measured up and each had been given the option of colours but that was all they knew about their outfits for the night until they unzipped their named clothes bag. Ros and Bet spent a fortune on the girls dress. They wanted to keep with gentleman's Club theme and had old fashioned silk basque's made for them. Each one had something different to go with the girls personality and speciality! Jude and Annie came over to the table there eyes shining. Jude did a twirl in front of them,

"Wotcha fink?" she said beaming elbows bent hands out.

She had a black rubber basque covered with chain tassels attached to the rubber suspenders. Jude's legs were covered in fishnet stockings the seams at the back perfectly straight. Her slick heavy black hair swayed in it's bob and she had a black head band running across her forehead a huge ostrich feather bounced above her at the back.

"Me only problem is wot shoes ta wear?" she said looking down at her stocking feet wriggling them into the carpet.

Ros grinned at Bet then at Jude.

"You look wonderful darling! And definitely high stilettoed black court shoes. What do you think Bet?" she asked.

"Perfect. Now let's 'ave a look at little Annie. Come on girl give us a twirl," Bet said.

Annie jumped in front of Jude and dramatically throwing her arms out, spun around, bending her knees she placed her hands on them and straightened up sticking her backside out, which Jude slapped making her jump up her candy floss hair bouncing. Annie had chosen powder blue as her colour and was now standing there in her tight fitting whale boned basque laced up the front to her heaving breasts desperate to escape. Her little legs were covered in powder blue stocking, her feet in white laced ankle boots. Jude had put her hair up with mother of pearl combs leaving ringlet's bouncing about her made up face.

"Couldn't ya just eat 'er?" Jude gushed fiddling with a ringlet.

"That's the business girls!" Bet boomed and the all fell about laughing.

Ros finished her glass of wine placing the glass on the table and inhaling the last of her joint dropped it in the ashtray. Standing up and draping an arm about Jude an' Annie she said.

"Will you excuse us Bet, Arthur. I've got to see the other

girls and our Jeeves's over there in the corner," she pecked the two girls on the cheek and blow Bet and Arthur one, leaving them to their drinks.

"Where's Rose? I thought she'd been with Bet," she said to the two girls as they walked over to Kel, Sal, and Misty.

Ros straightened a new girls suspender as they went, giving her a wink.

The girl smiled and carried on her way.

"She was in the kitchen with Doughy, Terrance and Frankie last I saw," Jude said pointing to the open door from the girls room to the kitchen.

"Okay. You two go on. I'll just have a quick look won't be two tics," Ros said taking her arms from Jude and Annie smiling.

"Thanks girls I wouldn't be able to do tonight with out you lot!" she said patting their backsides and headed towards the kitchen.

Sentimental tart!" Jude called.

Annie smacked her on the arm and dragged her over to the other three.

Ros passed new and old girls, nodding, smiling an' adjusting as she went 'Every things got to be perfect tonight and tomorrow.' She thought as she straightened Sue's tail feathers to the centre of her backside and fluffed them up.

"Ros. Aren't they wonderful?" she beamed giving Ros a model walk and pose.

"They sure are darling. I'll be back in a mo," she said holding up one finger and walking into the kitchen.

"Doughy will you pleeese sit down sweetie. I have my kitchen under control. Now go on shoo," Frankie waved her away.

"Aright ya miserable old faggot!" Doughy called over her shoulder wiping her hands on her pinny.

"Ohh get you!" Frankie stood there his hands on his hips eyebrows raised as Doughy sat down opposite a laughing Rose.

Terrance spotted Ros at the doorway first.

"Wow! Sweetie look at yoou!" he said giving her a squeal jumping from his chair next to Rose clapping his hands as he circled her.

"What a boss lady!" he cried holding out both of her hands leading her into the kitchen raising one of her hands above her head guiding her through their clasped hands, her bowler hat tilting a bit more as she went under their arms coming out the other side. Ros pushed her hat back in place with one finger blowing the end of it as if it was a gun before taking a mock bow. Frankie threw both his hands to his face dramatically clapping quickly as Ros bowed.

"Darling!" he drooled.

"You look spectacular superb doesn't she Tel?" he gushed at his long time lover.

"Rose darling you look stunning!" she said to the now standing Rose hands out stretched.

Rose was wearing a deep red 1900's American saloon girls dress, plunging at the front in a laced bodice making her waist look like an hour glass. The skirts fell in layers to the bottom of her calves. She too wore black fishnet stockings and black square heeled lace up ankle boots. A black choker with a cameo pinned to the front of it adorned her elegant throat. Her red hair was piled up on top of her head. Pearl beads had been woven in to it. The finishing touch was the red evening gloves that finished above her elbow.

"Don't she look a picture?" Doughy said from her seat looking up at Rose.

"Doughy darling I wasn't ignoring you but she does take your breath away doesn't she!" Ros said rushing over to her bending down and giving her a kiss on the cheek. Doughy held her face with one podgy hand tears in her eyes.

"That she does! I'm so proud of all you girls!" she sighed burying her face in her hankie.

Ros gave her a hug. Frankie and Terrance stood together smiling at the scene.

"Wot's the matter wif you two old queens?" Doughy grinned at them blowing her nose.

"Tut nothings the matter with us sweetie just enjoying the nights excitement!" Frankie said smiling.

"You got sumfink burnin' Frankie?" Doughy asked very serious giving Ros and Rose a wink.

"Oh, shit! Pass me that towel "Tel," he cried over his

shoulder as he rushed to the ovens and opened the doors.

The three women started to giggle they winked at Terrance who catching on stopped rushing with the towel and was giggling as well delicately placing a manicured hand to his mouth. Frankie looked behind him for Terrance and the towel to find the three women and Terrance in fits by this time after seeing his face. He stood up and shut the ovens.

"You wicked old bats! An' that goes for you too Terrance!" he cried sticking his nose in the air instantly making them worse.

"Listen I've got to go. I'll see you all later all right," Ros said through her giggles.

She headed to the girls room taking a canapé as she went, leaving them to their banter. Ros headed over to the five girls who were now all sitting around a table drinking their Brandy and Babychams. As she neared them they all stood. Sal passed her a glass of the same.

"Oh, Sal I've already had a glass of wine and I promised myself not to drink or smoke tonight and I've broken both!"

"Fuckin' good job an' all!" Jude boomed leaning across the table waving a freshly made joint under her nose.

"Neat just 'ow we like it!" she said giving a growl.

They all burst out laughing.

"A toast," Kel said.

"To Ros and Bet. Rosbette Cheers!"

"Cheers!" they all toasted.

"Thanks girls. Can I just say this wouldn't be a Club without you. You lot are the best and I'm proud to know you all! Cheers!" Ros said meaning every word she'd spoken.

The girls toasted each other.

"Now Jude light that monster and I want to see Kel, Sal, and Misty.

Come on girls one at a time," she said sitting down next to Annie and giving her a little nudge.

Sal paraded in front of Ros first. She glided past her long legs were covered in sheer white stockings held up by two baby pink garter belts. She had a baby pink thong on exposing her tight backside, the front of them just covering her shaven fanny. Sal's baby pink and white basque started at her waist the front dropping to a point near her belly button. The top of it ran

211

strapless across her nipples exposing a crescent of pink flesh at the end of each heaving mound. The back had hook and eye fastening from top to bottom. Attached to the back at the top hung two sheer silk trains to the ground. Sal wore a gold serpent bangle on the top of her left arm and a gold band on both middle fingers. Attached to the rings was the end of each train, giving her translucent wings. Her straight blonde hair hung shining down her back. She wore a pink choker making her swan neck look even longer. Sal had a pair of white sandals on her feet to finish her out fit.

Ros exhaled her smoke.

"Fucking hell Sal you look like your flying!" Ros giggled passing the joint.

"That's great how do you do that?" Ros asked.

"Years of having to walk with books on my head darling!" Sal answered taking a drag of the neat joint and handing it to Misty who was waiting to show her costume.

"What books?" Misty asked nodding a thank you and looking confused.

Sal looked to the heavens and raised her arms in mock dismay.

"Fuck me it's the angel Gabrile!" Jude cried. No one said a word until Sals face broke into a grin and they all relaxed laughing.

"I still don't understand!" Misty said smiling.

"Was it the Bible?" she asked perfectly serious making the other five howl with laughter.

"Will you stop worrying about the bloody books and step up here and give us a twirl!" Ros grinned crossing her legs.

Misty stepped forward and stood in front of Ros a smile crossing her lips.

"Well?" she said giving Ros a little curtsy.

"Love it! Gold defiantly likes your skin!" Ros said admiring Misty's toned brown body.

She like Sal had garters holding up her sheer gold fishnet stockings. The garters were solid bands of gold metal held with a small golden padlock.

"I just love these don't you?" she said lifting the little locks with her fingers.

"And look!" she cried showing them the little padlocks one on the front of her gold thong, attached to a golden zip running down under Misty's crotch. The other attached to the gold zip running from top to bottom of her golden half basque. Misty's basque started under her breasts pushing them up. Her breasts were covered by gold chains attached to the basque and the neck band around her throat. She turned slowly for Ros's inspection. The golden thong ran up the crease of her brown backside ending at the bottom of her spine a gold chain attaching it to the front.

The back of the basque was very plain due to the wig Misty was wearing. A brown and gold mane hung from her head to her backside showing her tight cheeks when she walked. She had a plain gold tiara worn across her forehead. Her nails were long and painted gold making them look more like claws than nails. She bent and tugged at one of her thigh high gold leather boots giggling a garter pad lock as she went. Even her eye shadow and false eyelashes were gold.

"And to finish it off! Yes you've guessed! Gold lipstick!" she cried waving the lipstick in the air.

"Christ I've got the munchies!" Jude joked.

"You look like a fuckin' Toblorone!" she said licking her lips and chuckling.

"Oh, fuck off!" Misty grinned laughing with the others.

"Come on Kel your turn!" Ros called taking her drink from the table and having a sip.

Kel laughing stood up and pirouetted towards Ros.

"Ta da!" she said holding her pose.

Her long red hair half up half down swinging to a halt. Kel had an emerald green basque made of velvet that was heavily braided with black silk cord. It laced all the way up the front finishing under her breasts sheer black silk covered her pert nipples. The basque covered her stomach and down her back ending at the bottom of her spine, giving her the figure of eight shape. A pair of black silk g-string panties covered her milky backside the front of them crotchless and braided with more of the silk cord either side of the slit. Kel had a pair of sheer black silk stockings braided at the top in the same cord as the basque and panties, attached to four green velvet and silk suspenders.

On her feet she wore emerald green stiletto court shoes braided in the same pattern as the panties. The bottom of the basque had a frill of sheer black silk, giving it a tu-tu look.

"Wonderful!" Ros clapped her hands together and looking around the room as well as just the five girls she asked.

"How do you feel girls truthfully?"

"Fuckin' uncomfortable if ya must know!" Jude said making a face and lifting herself off one side of her chair.

"Why whatever's wrong darling?" Ros asked a look of concern on her face.

"Me fuckin' crotchless rubber draws if ya must know!" Jude said fidgeting on her seat again.

"Oh, I thought you'd got an itch or some thing!" Annie said now understanding Jude's fidgeting.

"Fuckin' itch!" Jude jumped up.

"More like a fuckin' pinch!" she said trying to look at her backside.

Annie squealed with laughter now she had her head level with Jude's crotch.

"I know what's wrong Jude darling!" she yelled through giggles pointing at Jude's crotch.

"Well, fuckin' tell me will ya!" Jude cried bending forward and looking where Annie was pointing.

"You've got 'em on back ta front ya dossy moo!" Annie burst out laughing, so much so she slid off her chair.

No one could help her for laughing them selves, as Jude did no more than tug the rubber panties down there and then at the table. Then proceeded to pull them back on, checking the slit in them was in the correct place and nodding to herself as comfort waved over her.

"Wot it ain't funny!" she said chuckling at herself.

"It's… the… way… you… checked… your… slit… that… done… it… for… me!" Misty cried lighting a joint and passing it to a now creased up Jude.

"Oh… fuck… off!" she boomed taking the cigarette and putting it to her lips.

"I… take it that's the only complaint! A pair of draws on back to front!" Ros said trying to keep a straight face getting up from her chair.

Every one looked up at her and nodded, suddenly bursting out again.

"Well, excuse me ladies! I have to check everyone else. And thanks girls," she said sincerely.

They all put their hands up unable to speak from their laughter. Ros tore herself away from them, still smiling as she reached the table of four gentlemen dressed in butler style suits immaculately pressed. Crisp white shirts, and black bow ties. Their black brogues polished to perfection. All four of them stood as Ros approached them.

"Please gentlemen sit," she said giving them a warm smile as she sat in the spare chair.

"Now how are you gentlemen bearing up under all this commotion?" she asked crossing her legs and reading their gold nameplates pinned to their lapels.

All four bowed their heads and gave her a little smile.

'I know I wanted discretion! But I hope they're going to speak!' she thought a wave of nerves washing over her. She looked around the table then over to her five friends taking her strength from them. She turned back to the table and taking a deep breath.

"Right," she smiled.

"Henry, James, Burt, and Jerome. Have I said that correctly?" she asked the last man, who in turn gave a smile and nod as an answer.

'Fuck here goes!' she thought clearing her throat she started again.

"Welcome to the first night of hopefully many more at "Rosbette". As you know from your interviews this is a very "Private" Gentleman's Club.

Discretion in this business makes or breaks it hence the confidentiality document you and the girls signed. If this is broken we as a business have the right to sue," she said giving each man a steely look her nerves disappearing.

"Is that understood gentlemen?" she smiled around the table.

"Your job will to be at the beck and call of the gents. I warn you now they will order drinks while a girl or girls are entertaining them! So no surprised looks please! I want

215

expressionless faces but not bloody miserable while you're on duty. Only two off on a break at a time and we prefer you to have them little and often due to the demand on your legs. You will be instantly dismissed if found anywhere but in here or the kitchen eating or drinking, unless your life depends on it! When on your break feel free to have what you want. But if found unable to do your job due to alcohol again you will be dismissed instantly. Apart from when your offered by either Bet or myself in the bar. I hope all seems fair to you gentlemen. Any questions?" she asked looking about the table at their expressionless faces.

Each man bowed his head to the side in a nod.

"Oh, and one more thing gentlemen," she said as she stood up.

"You can speak to me and the other girls! We're all on the same side remember, and you keep your own tips fair?" she smiled at them, bowed her own head, turning to see a group of new girls sitting around a table looking wide eyed and nervous.

"That's very fair Mrs Carter," One of the waiters said making her turn back to the table and look for the name tag to the voice.

"Thank you James," she said gratefully, and smiling at the others, left to speak to the new girls.

Ros watched the new girls expression as she approached their two tables. Everyone of them looked horrified at her descending on them.

"Good evening ladies! I hope your outfits are comfortable tonight?" she said with a smile spreading it around the tables. She pulled up another chair from a vacant table and sat down.

"Now before we start what are you ladies drinking?" she asked leaning over to a jug on the table and dipping her finger in tasting, her face a picture. All the girls gave a little giggle relaxing a little.

"It's bloody water! We can't have that! No wonder you all look so fucking miserable and nervous!" she cried jumping up from her chair and calling the five girls over. This made the new girls all stop in their tracks and look wide eyed at Ros.

"You girls need to enjoy your new job! An' believe me there's no way you can do that unless your relaxed and confident

216

in your selves!" Ros said softly to the frozen faces around her.

"Now doors don't open until eight thrity. So I think we've got plenty of time to get to know each other. Remember girls we've got to be here for each other, it's a closed business this one, and any problems. You've got to be able to tell any one of us. We all look out for each other understood?" she said smiling as Kel, Sal, Annie, Jude, and Misty all said in unison.

"Too fucking right boss!" giving her a group hug, making the new girls just stare even more, in turn making Ros and the girls start to laugh.

Jude raised her arms in the air and shimmied.

"How's about some champus then girls?" she boomed to the new girls No one spoke they all just nodded open mouthed at her.

"Fuckin' 'ell! Misty you'd better roll us a couple of joints!" Jude cried as she looked around the two tables.

"Annie babe come wif me will ya I fink we're gonna need some Brandy an' all!" she laughed giving the new girls a wink and grabbing Annie's hand they went off in search for the drinks.

"Ladies that was Jude and little Annie!" Ros said pointing in their direction.

"And this…" she carried on.

"Is Kel Sal and Misty."

Each woman nodded to the two groups of young women.

Sitting down in between them the girls started to chat to them putting the new one's at ease. They all heard Jude and Annie come back into the room by the deep boom of Jude and the squeal from Annie.

"Somethings tickled them!" Sal explained calmly as she saw the expressions on the table's occupants.

"You've all gotta 'ave a look in the kitchen!" Jude burst out as she got to the tables.

Annie threw herself on to a seat exhausted from laughing so hard. Every one looked at each other. Then as if some one had fired a gun there was a mass exodus to the kitchen door. The only people left at the tables were Jude, Annie, and Ros.

"Well, thank you," Ros said smiling in the direction of the disappearing group.

"I think they feel more at home with us now! Thanks as

usual to you two," she said giving both the women a peck on the cheek and a hug.

Jude hugging her back said.

"Yeh but you ain't seen them two when they start it's fuckin' hilarious!" she cried referring to Frankie and Terrance.

"And Bet thought you wouldn't like them!" Ros giggled remembering how the two men argue.

"God they're the funniest thing I ever come across. You've gotta love 'em!" Annie squealed falling into fits of laughter again.

Ros left the girls room to check the bar room, bedrooms, and playroom.

Everything was perfect! The barmen had already filled the ice buckets and nibble bowls. All the place needed was the Gents. Ros checked her watch as she came from the play room. 'half an hour!' she thought to herself smiling as she heard a crescendo of laughter from the girls room.

"Better get this show on the road!" she muttered heading towards the laughter. She entred the room scaning the scene. All the girls old and new were relaxed, laughing and checking their outfits one last time. Ros had chosen the same style basque for all the girls except Sal, Kel, Misty, Jude and little Annie. The only difference was the colours of each one. Seeing Bet, she walked over to her.

"Hello darling. I've just done a tour of the place and every things absolutely perfect! The girls seem a bit more relaxed now don't they?" she gabbled her nerves creeping up on her. Bet reading her like a book said,

"Ere do us a favour Arfer, go an' get Ros a drink would ya! Oh an' make it a bigern!" she took Ros's hand and pulled her down on to Arthur's seat.

"Ere 'ave a drag on that," she said passing Ros a freshly rolled joint.

"An fer fuck sake relax will ya! I know everyfings perfect!" she said grinning through her cloud.

Ros exhaled her smoke and smiled.

"I know!" she said her nerves fading.

"Recon we gotta say a few words when ya 'ad yer drink lovey," Bet beamed at her.

"Okay you doing it or me?" Ros asked taking another puff of the cigarette and flicking the ash in the ashtray.

"You start lovey an' if ya get stuck I'll 'ave a go all right?" Bet said smiling up at a returned Arthur with Ros's drink and a bottle in a bucket which he placed on the table next to them.

"What's that for?" Bet asked her eagle eye's never missing a trick, as she pointed to the bucket with a long blood red painted fingernail.

"Just ta toast you an' the yougan after yer speech that's all old girl," Arthur chuckled to her, turning to Ros he winked and gave her the 'OK' sign with his fingers.

Ros nodding swallowed her drink and said looking at her watch.

"Right let's get this show on the road then shall we?" she motioned to Bet to lead them off.

Bet stood up excepting a peck on the cheek from Arthur. She straightened her clothing put out her cigarette swallowed the last of her drink down and walked past a grinning Ros.

"Got every thing ready?" Ros whispered to Arthur as she got level with him giving him a hug.

"All sorted doll!" he replied giving her a wink, and tapping the top of her legs to shoo her on before he lost his nerve.

Ros stood next to Bet and draping her arm around her called for a little hush. When the room was silent and even Frankie and Terrance were stood in the kitchen doorway Ros began.

"On behalf of Bet and myself, I would like to wish you all long and happy days, or should I say nights, with us and we hope you'll all be very happy here. Thank you. Before we go to our posts as it were I have a gentleman here that would like to say a few words."

Everyone clapped Ros and Bet, then fell silent as Ros dropped away and Arthur came up to Bet. Dropping on one knee he said, "Will you marry me Bet old girl?" closing his eyes and holding her hands.

"Wot? Fuck me! Er I mean Yes! Yes! Yes! Ya silly old sod!" she grinned and there was a pop from the champagne bottle and a huge cheer went up as Bet pulled Arthur up hugging and kissing him.

Passing the two of them a glass of the amber liquid Ros said.

"Your Happiness!" as a toast.

Everyone repeated the toast and then Ros said clearing her voice.

"Ladies and Gentlemen! Your posts please. The gents will be here in five minutes or so and thank you people, have a wonderful evening and remember If You enjoy. They enjoy and come again! Pardon the pun!"

She giggled as the room collapsed into laughter.

"Now posts please," she called over the noise.

The only people that stayed behind when they'd all filed out was Bet, Arthur, Ros, the five girls, Rose, Doughy and Terrance.

"Oooh! Suppose you two will be scooting to your love nest now and leaving us!" Terrance purred his hands on his hips, his lips pursed and flicking his long locks.

"Yeh we will ya fuckin' poofter, an' I ain't tellin' ya whever I do or don't okay!" Bet said mimicking Terrance.

"Ooh your soo wicked!" he said holding his hand out in a feminine way.

"Well, we all fuckin' know you do don't we!" Bet boomed laughing so hard she had to lean on poor old Arthur for support.

"Com'on old girl let's go celebrate!" he said chuckling and giving the others a wink over her head walking her out as she waved and blew them kisses.

Rose came over to Ros and put an arm around her shoulders.

"Isn't it great to see her happy," she said smiling and waving to her friend.

"Want me to stick around?" she asked Ros face to face.

"I thought you'd never ask darling!" Ros's face broke into a huge grin and the two women embraced.

"Shall we ladies?" Ros beamed and they all walked out.

As they reached the hallway the first of the gents were arriving and Ros, Rose and the girls escorted them to the gentleman's room making them comfortable as James the only waiter that spoke to Ros took their orders. The lights were glowing amber, the fire was roaring in the hearth and all the girls were looking relaxed and horny in their basque's. Ros stood in the doorway with Rose smiling.

"They look good don't they?" she said more of a statement than a question.

"They sure do!" Rose replied then added.

"I need to go over just a few more replies that came today for Bet. Fancy coming up for a tipple and smoke before it all kicks off?"

"Why not!" Ros said relaxing as she saw how the gents were reacting to the new Club. She knew it wouldn't be every gent's ideal but a good seventy percent of the old gents had become a member.

The two women left the room heading for the stairs and the office.

Chapter 19

Descending the stairs a couple of hours later the Club was buzzing with laughter, music and anticipation. Ros said good bye to Rose and Doughy. She then checked with Terrance that Frankie was coping before going into the bar to see the girls perform.

She entered the room and all the lights dimmed, making her have a panic that they were going to have a power cut, then quickly she came to her senses as she heard the familiar music from the girls practice in the week. Ros slid on to the nearest bar stool excepting a glass of champagne from the bar man and lit a cigarette. Slowly every gent turned his head towards the girls, all eyes upon them. The five girls were in front of the fire, each girl was facing the fireplace slowly and seductively tapping one thigh very gently to the music. As the tempo of the music sped up. Kel was the first to turn and model walk over to a chair, grabbing it's back and dragging it towards the other four girls. Who by now had also turned and were seductively dancing, running their hands all over their bodies, to the wolf whistles from the men and the new girls. The atmosphere was electric and Ros could feel herself getting turned on. Kel was now on her chair and gyrating her body on to it and sticking her pantie clad backside out, the slit revealing a glimpse of her fanny lips every time she swayed her body. The other four moved in closer on her, their hands started to run over Kel's body, her nipples stretching at the sheer silk that covered them. Sal slid an elegant white hand between Kel's cleavage scooping her breasts form their confines and giving them a gentle tweak, making Kel throw her head back. The four girls turned Kel over on her chair so her backside was perched on the edge and her head tipped back over the chair back. Misty and Sal stood either side of her shoulders pulling her arms out, and running their tongues from her wrist to

222

her nipples and back again. They kept her restrained all the time making her arch her back and tip her head over the chair even more. Sal ran a long white fingernail from Kel's chin down her throat and across to one of her nipples that the girls had just left, making her shudder with pleasure. Jude and Annie ran their hands down Kel's legs from the outside of her thighs to her ankles, making Kel stretch her long legs taunt. Both Jude and Annie took a foot each and lifted Kel's legs in the air. The girls ran their tongues from Kel's ankles up the inside of her legs, making Kel spread her legs and expose her silk g-string crotchless panties to them. Annie looked at Jude for permission to run her tongue in between Kel's slit in her panties. Jude smiled at her and giving her a kiss on the mouth gently pushed her head down to Kel's wet lips. Jude was now standing to the side of Kel's hips undoing her panties. Annie stood up and let the panties fall. She scooped them up and flung them into the room, the cheers raising and falling with the garment and kissed Jude on the mouth. Jude then came round to face a trembling Kel ordering her to turn over and stick her backside in the air.

She then told Misty and Sal to go and pleasure themselves. Kel was her and Annies to the roar and cheers of the room. Annie ran off for a couple of seconds while Jude placed Kel in position and pinched and pulled her nipples that were draped over the chair back. Annie ran in with a huge black rubber Dildo and the room urged them on. Jude strapped the contraption on with expertise and sent Annie to play with Kel's nipples ordering only tongue and nails to be used. Annie licked her lips and did as she was told making Kel squeal with the anticipation of her touch. Jude entered Kel from behind, making deep hard thrusts into her. Kel's backside rose and fell with each thrust and her body shuddered as she came again and again. Annie nipped and sucked Kels nipples and Kel had pushed Annies panties aside and was finger fucking Annie with every thrust Jude gave her.

Some of the gents couldn't contain themselves any more and were sat in their chairs, their cocks up like flag poles, the new girls helping them out by either sucking or fucking these desperate erections.

Misty and Sal were pleasuring each other by the roaring fire. Misty's skin and outfit shimmering in the fire light against

Sal's translucent skin and ghost-like outfit. They were making such a show that some of the gents and girls were just staring entranced with the erotic scene in front of them.

Misty was crotching over Sal's face her booted feet and legs either side of Sals ears. Misty threw her wigged head back pushing her crotch further into Sal's willing face. Sal took hold of the padlock zip in her teeth and moved her head down freeing Mistys very wet fanny. Sal dipped her tongue deep into the opening, making Misty pump on to Sal's exquisite face. Misty threw herself forward and stood up and to Sal's delight crotched over her and pulling her legs apart pulled the thong panties to one side and buried her head deep into Sal's swollen pussy.

Sal grabbed Misty's metal garter belts pulling her onto her eager lips and tongue.

Ros feeling very hot and horny suddenly heard a commotion in the hallway. Sliding off her stool but still watching the girls she walked backwards to the doors, turning only when she reached them, to be confronted as she opened them, with Ben, John and the boy's from the band, along with four or five of the roadies.

Ros's face must have said it all.

"Yes gentlemen. Can I help you?" she asked as if she'd never met them before in her life.

"Yeh darlin' I'll 'ave a tequila! Wotcha 'avin' boy's?" John grinned at her from behind Ben.

"I'm sorry gentlemen this is a private Club. Members only I'm afraid," she said businesslike but smugly.

"Yeh we know," John piped up unable to keep quiet.

"I'm sorry?" she said tilting her head to one side.

"I paid Bet earlier this evening! Well I didn't some one else did! But we're all paid up for a years good time with you," Ben explained.

"I must say it's far classier than the Club! Congratulations Ros," he smirked walking past her to the gentleman's room, John and the boy's following him.

As John got level with a now white Ros he looked her up and down and whistled.

"Still worf payin' fer!" and blew her a kiss, laughing with the other guy's as they slapped him on the back and said something crude to him.

Ros turned abruptly and ran up the stairs to the office. She unlocked the door and went in slamming it behind her, leaning on it to catch her breath her temper raising. She went over to the desk and slumped into the chair.

Opening the top draw she pulled out a packet of cigarette's and a lighter. Numbly lighting one she inhaled the smoke, then picking up the phone dialled Rose at "The Club".

Rose picked up the phone on the third ring.

"Hello Rose speaking," she said dragging the huge appointment book in front of her.

"Can I help you?" she asked down the phone.

"Rose it's Ros what the fucks Bet playing at?" she rushed taking another puff of her cigarette and blowing out the smoke with a little more force than was needed.

Rose sighed.

"I'm sorry Ros but business is business," she said quietly as she flicked through their memberships in front of her.

"Tell me Rose was that the paperwork you had to sort out for Bet tonight?" she asked seething through her teeth.

"Well…"

"Rose fucking tell me! I'm not in the mood for shit!" she cried.

"Well… yes darling but…! Ros are you still there? Ros? Ros? Shit! Fuck! Shit!" Rose looked down the receiver as if she might be able to see Ros.

"Fuck I'd better give Bet a ring!" she said aloud picking up the receiver again and dialing her number.

"Fuck!" she said slamming the phone down.

"Ros must have already got through!"

Rose ran her hands through her hair trying to think. She dialled the 'Rosbette Club' to try to talk to Ros but it was still engaged.

"Bollocks!" she said lighting her joint.

"Now I'm gonna have to go round there before Ros does!" she muttered to herself throwing the cigarette in the ashtray and getting her keys from the desk draw and locking it after her.

"Bet it's Ros what the fuck you doing not letting me know Ben and the boy's were members?" she spat down the phone her knuckles white with temper.

"Oh, fer fuck sake! Ros it's business lovey! I only did it cos 'e's got contacts all over an' contacts is money. Now be fuckin' professional an' getcha arse back down there an' be fuckin' polite. 'e's paid 'is money 'is been vetted an' yer can't just say no because ya 'ad a rough time wif 'em even though, when ya fink about it it weren't even their fault was it!" Bet yelled down the phone her temper all too evident in her voice.

"Now go an' sort it out you 'ere me?" Bet seethed down the phone.

"Yer gotta be a pro Ros, an' yer actin' like a fuckin' school kid! If yer can't 'andle this then praps we'd better 'ave a fink about fing's ta morrow," And slammed the phone down not giving Ros a chance to say a word, leaving her spitting feathers.

"Wot's up darlin'?" John stood in the office doorway a huge grin on his face.

"What! How did you get up here!" she glared at him from behind her desk, unable to move. What she really wanted to do was thump him one and push him out the door.

"Used me legs babe!" he grinned pointing to his trouser covered legs, shutting the door behind him he walked over to the desk perching his backside on the edge of it.

"Get out!" she barked.

"You may be a member but the office is out of bounds!" she said trying to calm down.

"Got any booze up 'ere?" he asked totally ignoring her and looking around the attic room for a bottle of something.

"Didn't you hear me sir! This room is out of bounds. Only and I mean ONLY work personnel are allowed up here!" Ros said feeling her temper raising again.

All he did was raise his eyebrows and laugh at her.

"I mean it sir. If you don't leave this office I will have to call security!" Ros said summoning her courage and leaving her chair to walk over to the door and open it.

John watched her amusement on his face.

"Oh, com'on Ros! Quit wif the fuckin' sir crap! I gotta say ya look fuckin' horny in that getup babe!" he grinned as she swept past him to the door.

Ros ignored him opening the door and waving her hand to

226

show him the exit, breathing a sigh of relief when he slid off the desk and strolled over to where she was standing and walking past her, took the handle from her to shut it behind him. Only he didn't. He took the handle from her and instead of, as he made out he was going to do, he shut it leaning on it and smiling.

"I fink you an' me 'ave got some unfinished business babe!" he grinned grabbing her by the waist and pulling her to him.

"Wotcha say?" he said looking deep in her eyes.

Ros felt all those feelings come rushing back again and relaxed in his arms. John pulled her harder to him and she could feel his hard cock through his trousers, making her give a little shudder. She gave in as he kissed her deep and hard the passion welling up in both of them. John slipped her jacket from her shoulders and ran his hands down her bare back, making her nipples so hard they were pushing through her top straining to be set free. Ros grabbed at his jacket as he kissed, licked and nibbled her neck. Ripping it off she ran her nails down his spine and across his buttocks bringing her hand up around the front of him pulling his shirt out and ripped at the buttons as the passion welled in her. John ran his fingers around the band of her hipster Tux trousers, making her stomach muscles tense as he reached the fastenings. Ros slipped the tie from his neck dropping it to the floor with his jacket and ripped the shirt from his back, making his cock jump and throb through the restricting material. She stood away from him and pushed him against the office door, then, at arms length ran her nails gently down his neck, across his tight hard nipples, over his stomach muscles circling her nails around his belly button then fanning to his now thrusting hips. She ran them down the sides of his arse cheeks stopping at the top of his thigh and bringing them around and up to the fastening, never touching any part of his pulsating cock. Ros undid the belt buckle, button, and zip in a matter of seconds, letting his trousers drop to the floor around his ankles his cock standing to attention (John didn't wear pants). Ros stood back from him looking him up and down. She licked her lips, making him moan and his cock swell. She then ran her hands around the back of her halter neck slowly sliding the material down exposing more and more flesh as she went. When she had reached her nipples she let the cloth drop and fall to the floor, rolling her nipples between her finger and thumbs and tilting her head back. John reached for her breasts, but she looked him straight in the eyes and slowly smiling pushed his hand away, making him moan even more. He felt so restrained standing there and watching, his cock felt as if it was going to burst he desperately wanted to fuck her but she wouldn't even allow him to touch her. 'This bitch fuckin' knows 'er job!' he thought wanting her all the more. Ros ran her hands down her stomach and into her trousers letting her fingers slip into her wet lips. She pulled her hands out and sucked her left index finger glistening with her love juices. She then ran her right index finger across John's lips letting him taste her. John sucked her finger into his mouth licking and sucking each finger in turn. Ros pulled her hand away and unzipped her trousers letting them fall to the ground and stepped out of them. She stood in front of John in her black stiletto court shoes, black sheer hold up stockings and her bowler hat perched on her head. She turned right and with her left hand ran her index finger down his right cheek turning his head in the direction she was walking. Stepping out of his trousers, socks and shoes he sauntered over to Ros, who was by now laid out on the chaise lounge, her legs apart one hand opening her wet lips the other rubbing and pumping her hot hole. John dropped to his knees his face inches from her hands. Ros stopped and pulled his head onto her. He spread her legs and lips wide and buried his tongue deep into her pulling out he ran his tongue over her clit flicking it with the tip of it, making Ros shudder uncontrollably. He moved his body up on top of her and thrust his cock in deep, pulling at her hair, making her head tip back over the edge and her nipples point to the ceiling getting harder with every thrust. She pulled his head to them arching her back as his mouth closed over one, her body shook in waves as her orgasms hit her one after the other. John pulled her up and threw her over the desk her breasts slapping the wood as she went down. He stood behind her and pushed her feet apart with his foot, making her backside stick up in the air. He could see how wet she was as he spread her legs. He dropped to his knees and blew on her hot wet lips, making her moan and push her bottom out more the teasing unbearable. He then very gently ran his finger over her clit, making Ros push on to him.

"Wotcha won't then baby?" he said blowing on her swollen lips.

Ros groaned and grabbed her arse cheeks spreading her lips even more. John shook his head slowly and bit his bottom lip.

"Yer a dirty fuckin' whore ain'tcha bitch!" pushing three fingers into her hot wet lips and biting her erect clit. Ros cried out in pleasure as her body shook.

"Wot whore? Wotcha won't?" he asked pulling away from her and replacing his fingers with his throbbing cock and laughed.

"This wotcha wont?" he said pushing himself into her.

"Yes! Yes! Yes!" she cried urging him deeper into her.

"Well, whore yer can't 'ave it!" he said laughing and pulling away from her.

Ros's head was spinning.

"Noo.!" she cried.

"You bastard! You fucking bastard!" she spat turning to face him.

"You got it babe!" John replied smiling at her as he pulled on his shirt and tucked it into his trousers.

The door flung open John's jacket stopping it from banging into the chaise lounge. Dan stood there his face serious as he scanned the room. He looked Ros in the eye and smirked, making her shiver and sliding to the floor grabbed her clothes, her hat still stuck to her head.

"Yeh Dan mate?" John said bending over and picking up his jacket and tie dusting an invisible spot from them.

If Dan hadn't seen Ros spread across the table he would never have guessed by John's attitude that there had been anything going on. Only the smell of perfume and sex gave it away.

"Bus's ready," Dan said quietly leaving the room giving Ros one last knowing look.

"Cheers mate! Let the boys know I'll be down in five yeh," he shouted after the boy.

"That kid shouldn't even be here!" she cried pointing to the closed door.

"Well, 'e ain't now is 'e!" John smirked.

"Oh, an' bung yer fee on me bill wontcha darlin'. Bye Ros,"

he said smiling before he shut the door on her.

"You fucking bastard!" she screamed at him picking up the appointment book and throwing it at the door.

"I need a drink!" she cried through gritted teeth.

Pulling herself up she quickly dressed. She pulled on the top draw and rummaged in it for her cigarettes. Lighting one she inhaled deeply and placed it in the ashtray, she slipped her jacket back on picked up her cigarette walked over to the full length mirror in the corner and stared at the woman facing her. She fixed her hair and slanted her hat just right before applying some more lipstick and wiping away a little smudged eyeliner she stood up straight brushed a speck from her lapel took another puff on her cigarette before stubbing it out in the ashtray, picked up her keys and walked out the door locking it behind her.

She walked down the stairs passing girls and gents on the way, their giggles echoing in the hall below. She pushed the 'play room' door open and a wave of success came over her, the room was a mass of bodies all fucking, sucking, and licking. Ros allowed herself a hard smile.

"That's business!" she said under her breath.

Kel had a gent hand cuffed to a cave wall his cock bouncing every time she ran her whip across it. She ran the tip of the whip around the head of his cock making him squirt his cum in an arch as he slumped against the wall his arms holding him there.

"Ros darling! Did you enjoy?" Kel asked referring to her sex act with the gent.

"Loved it! You made me wet!" she grinned her old self again.

"You okay Ros? You seem different!" Kel asked giving her a strange look.

"Never better!" Ros smiled again slipping off her trousers and jacket.

Kel pulled her to the 'play room' door picking up her clothes as she went.

"You sure you want ta start entertaining again darling? What about Katie?" Kel hissed in Ros's ear.

"It's what I'm good at! Bet was right. I might as well make as much as possible while I can!" she replied coldly gently taking her suit from Kel and dropping it in a heap by the door and unclasping her halter neck and letting that fall also.

"Well, if your sure Ros. There's a joint between the candles over there. And happy fucking!" she grinned pecking her on the cheek and wandering off to release the gent from the wall.

Ros wandered over to the fire roaring in the middle of the room and found the joint lighting it from a candle flame her confidence getting stronger by the minute. Kel whizzed around the Club letting the girls know Ros had cracked and was standing stark naked in the 'play room' looking for a fuck. By the time all the girls got back to the room Ros had her hands cuffed to the ceiling chains, arms stretched high into the air and two gents were just clipping nipple clamps on to her. Ros's head flung back her bowler falling to the ground and her body gave a shudder. They all looked at each other and grinned.

"Seems Ros's back in business!" Jude boomed to the other four her hands on her ample hips.

"It does look like it!" Sal breathed sipping her drink and passing it to Misty.

"Well, wot do we do now?" Kel said her hands in the air.

"Stop her or let her get on with it?" she asked her voice high.

"Calm down Kel darling," Annie whispered taking one of her hands.

"Yeh she's a grown woman. She knows wot she's doin'. I say we leave 'er to it," Jude said placing an arm around little Annie's shoulder and looking over at Ros.

"Agreed then. We leave her to it and only mention it if she does yeh?"

"Agreed!" they all said touching hands.

Chapter 20

Ros checked the Club from top to bottom with her security man, locking up as they went. When they at last came to the front door, Ros said a thank you to him and locked the door behind him. Turning and leaning against the doors she ran her hands through her hair and sighed.

"Jeeesus have I fucked up!" she said aloud, pushing herself off the doors and walking over to the bar kicking off her shoes as she went and wrapping her robe around her again. She went behind the bar and placed a brandy glass under the optic letting it refill twice before she took her glass away. Taking a sip she slid on to the nearest bar stool, reached over the marble top and grabbed a bag of weed and Rizlas the girls always kept for emergencies. Pulling them out and sticking them together she silently rolled herself a joint. She took a sip of the brandy before she lit her cigarette. Ros reached across the bar taking a pen from the till and a couple of napkins from the dispenser. Taking another drag of her joint she placed it in the ashtray and picked up the pen.

Dear Bet,

Tonight I went back on my promise to myself. Even Kel tried to stop me! So I've decided to sell my half of the business…

Ros laid the pen down and picked up her cigarette lighting it again and inhaling. She didn't know where she was going to go. 'To a hotel I suppose' she thought to herself. 'I'll ask Marg and Jim to look after Katie for a couple of days until I find a flat' her mind raced as plans popped into her head. She placed the cigarette down again took another sip of her drink and picked up her pen.

I'm going to give Rose and the girls first option as an investment. I'll contact Rose with arrangements for the cash to be placed into my account.

I'm sorry to end our friendship like this but you knew Ben, John etc would be here tonight but you never warned me! But you managed to ask Rose to pick up their paperwork before you left with the man I helped to ask you to marry him! You're fucking low Bet.

What I don't understand Bet, is Why?

Why didn't you tell me Bet?

Ros.

By the time Ros had finished her, hand writing was as bad as her mind.

She carefully folded the napkin in half and laid it on the counter. She scribbled a simple BET on the fold.

Then taking her cigarette out of the ashtray she lit it inhaled and smiled.

"You sure your doing the right thing here Ros?" she asked herself.

"Yep!" she grinned answering her reflection in the mirror, lifting her drink she downed the last of the golden liquid.

Kissing her finger she tapped it on to the napkin and sliding off the stool headed to the doors. She turned taking in the room for one last time. Flicking the light switches she pushed the double doors open together and walked through. She locked the back door of the Club and walked to her little bungalow at the back of it.

Ros opened her wardrobe and started to pack up her clothes into the recently unpacked boxes. She then made a bag up for Katie and packed the rest of her stuff up in two boxes. She carried them to her car piling them on the back seat. Ros looked up at the sky, dawn was breaking and the memory of that first dawn of her new life flooded to her mind, dismissing it.

"No I'm going to get a way from this, I've got to. Revenge with you old man can wait," she said under her breath as she heard the dawn chorus. Ros wandered in to her home one last time and flicked the kettle on taking a mug from the hook. She spooned some coffee into it and waited arms folded watching the kitchen clock tick by, the only other noise the whirring of the kettle as the element heated up. The clock ticked by a quarter to six. Half an hour and Katie will be awake she thought. The kettle turned off and she poured the water into her mug. She sat down at the kitchen table and looked around asking herself if she was doing the right thing. Her mind going back a few hours. Yes she was doing the right thing. Ros sighed, she really thought she and Katie would be happy here.

'Now I've got to leave it all behind and run away like I've done twice before.' She thought.

"Oh, well third time lucky!" she said aloud toasting the air with her coffee mug.

After a bath and change of clothes Ros checked her watch and sighed.

"The time has come!" she said dramatically to herself in the hall mirror.

Walking into the kitchen she picked up the phone dialing Marg and Jims first. She asked if Katie had been good for them and asked if they wouldn't mind keeping her for a couple of days. Marg agreed to have her wondering what on earth could have happened to Ros last night if she had to sort some things out and she couldn't see Katie. Ros told Marg to give Katie a big kiss for her and told her she would ring replacing the receiver tears in her eyes.

"Now for Rose!" she said aloud picking up the phone again and dialing a groggy Rose answered.

"Rose speaking."

"Rose it's me Ros sorry to ring so early but.."

"Ros what's wrong you okay?" Rosa cut in as she came to.

"I'm fine, listen I've got a proposition for you. I know it's early but…"

"Ros what on earth, have you been to sleep yet?" Rose asked confused.

"Well, if you'd listen for a minute I'll tell you!" Ros chuckled down the phone.

"Go on I'm sorry. It's just a bit of a shock so early that's all," she said pulling her phone cord to reach the kettle and yawning.

"I've decided to sell my half of "Rosbette" and I'm giving you or you and the girls first option on it," Ros explained.

"Wh… what! Ros, last night was a huge success you can't sell you don't know what you talking about your tired you need some sleep your not thinking straight Ros!

"Hey, calm down Rose I'm not tired and I've given it a lot of thought I'm not mad I know the Club will be huge but Bet got you to take that paperwork last night and she as you know didn't tell me. I can't be in a partnership like that. I love Bet to bit's but she deceived me Rose and I went straight back to it Rose. I can't do that I've got Katie to think about now. So you see I know what I'm doing I just need to get Katie and me away from it."

"Yes I understand darling," Rose said, not at all understanding what Ben and the boy's could possibly have done to upset Ros like this.

"What happened last night Ros?" she asked quietly.

Ros told her about John and her in the office finishing it with.

"The trouble is he's right! I am good at my job. But worst of all I enjoy it too much. I loved it last night and that's what frightens me! I hadn't slept with any one since that night at Ben's. I'm frightened he's hardened me. I thought I was in love with him once you know? I even told Kel funny isn't it?" Ros chuckled then sighed down the phone at her.

"Oh, darling I'm sorry but you didn't exactly say no did you!" Rose said seeing both sides of the coin.

"No I know I didn't that's the point I wasn't working and he knew it. But he treated me like I was! If I carry on I'll never trust any one again. I now see why Bet's so anti men. Until she met Arthur that is. He accepts her for her. Her past present and future is her's he's just sharing it with her, and I don't want to wait as long as that for it to happen to me. I need to be loved. So do you want my half or not?"

Rose chuckled.

"Of course how much do you want for it?" she asked thinking of her interests.

"Only what I paid into it you've still got my book it will tell you in there," Ros said not caring about the money.

"Are you sure. You going to be losing one hell of an investment there," Rose said shaking her head down the phone.

"I know and I know it was my idea but why weren't you asked to be one of the backer's? I've always wondered.

"Did Bet ever come to you for backing only I left that side to her."

"No she didn't but I also didn't know she went out side for it either until she asked me to get involved with the paperwork by which time every thing was tied up," Rose explained.

"By the way speaking about Bet does she know your selling?"

"No I've left her a note at the Club," Ros said hardness in her voice.

"She's really hurt you hasn't she. I'm sorry Ros, I bet she doesn't even know she's upset you this much!" Rose said in a quite voice.

"I phoned her last night she knows."

"Oh!"

"Umm… look I'm going to have to go in a minute so can I leave the paperwork with you and if you can just put the money in my account and post it to this address I'll get all my post redirected is that okay?"

"Ye yes fine. Ros are you sue you don't want to give it a couple of days what do you say?" she begged her.

"No Rose I'll be in touch I'm not going far. But I do need to start again. Bye I love you."

"I love you too darling Ros ring m.," but Ros had put the receiver down.

"Shit Bet's going to go fucking mental!" Rose said aloud looking at the phone.

Ros wiped the tears from her face and picked up her keys walking out to her car. Grabbing the steering wheel tightly she took a deep breath then put the key in the ignition pulled the choke and started the engine.

"First stop Katie's clothes. Second stop new life! Not much to ask for in a day!" she said with a grin.

Chapter 21

Ros was now living off the island in a Hotel as the manager for Food and Entertainment. She and Katie had lived there for five years now and they were blissfully happy. Katie was getting on well in her school and Ros was happy with her solo life. She never contacted anyone from her old life or touched the money.

Since she had been manager, they were often booked up, bringing in more punters for the bar and very often they stayed the night, making the Hotel very popular for weddings and birthdays.

Ros checked the appointment book for any new bookings that had been taken by Jenny the receptionist. As she turned the pages her heart stopped. A band had been booked for a gig there was no name by the side just.

'Band 5-11.30 Function Room... 4 Beds reserved.

She picked up the phone in her office and pressed the intercom button to Jenny sitting at reception.

"Jenny," the voice said on the other end.

"Jen it's Ros."

"Oh, hi Ros what can I do for you?"

"This band that's booked. Have they got a name? Only I can't really invoice them as Band!" Ros said in a professional voice.

"Oh, it's okay they already paid when they booked. I've got the receipt here some where if you want it," Jenny said through the rustle of papers.

"No no it's okay if they've already paid," Ros said replacing the receiver and shivering.

"Two Days," she said running her hand across the page.

"I've got two days have I right," she said to herself getting up from her chair and walking around her desk tapping her long nails on the wood as she went.

"Who's going to know? Who can I ask? I know I'll start

with Pete he's bound to know!" she smiled walking towards the door and downstairs she found Pete the owner in the bar filling the optic's.

"All right Ros what's up mate?" he said turning and smiling.

"We've got a band booked for two days no one knows who they are! They've paid in advance and I wondered if you could put any light on it for me!" she said rubbing the counter down with a duster that was left on it.

"Yeh! They're a band from the island. Been overseas for a couple of years an' they're doing a promotional gig fer all these big wig producers something like that anyway. Why do you fancy having a boogie with me at the gig?" Pete winked and spun around.

"No no boogieing!" Ros laughed excusing herself.

"So that's where they've been," she smiled to herself. She liked to know things about people she felt it gave her an advantage when anything is said.

"Now to find out if there's any catering involved shall we!" Ros grinned to herself as she walked over to the reception desk.

"Jenny did the band leave a contact number. Only there wasn't any mention of catering and I've just found out there's a lot very influential people coming. Thought I might see if I can get some more money out of them!" she said with a wink.

"Hang on I had it when we were on the phone. Oh yeh here it is your in luck," she said looking at the receipt and passing it over to Ros.

"Thanks Jen, see ya later," she said with a wave of her hand.

She closed the door of her office and only then looked at the phone number scribbled on the cash receipt. She shut her eyes tight a slow smile spreading across her lips.

"Got you, you bastard!" she grinned rushing over to her chair and sitting down on her hands.

"I know it's them. They don't know it's me. ah!" she grinned.

Ros pulled a hand from under her leg and picked up the phone slamming it down as soon as she heard the dialing tone.

"Shit! Shit! Shit!" she cursed aloud reaching for her cigarettes. Lighting one she sat back trying to think. A smoke ring circled her head and she blew it away.

"Got it!" she said leaning forward and before she had time to think she dialled the number.

The last of the numbers clicked in her ear and then she heard the ringing tone.

"Come on pick it up," she said under her breath tapping her nails on the desk.

"Yeh?" the deep voice crackled down the phone.

"Ah hello this is the Grandee Hotel. I understand I am, talking to the gentleman whom booked our function room?" she said in a very posh voice.

"Yeh that's right darlin'," the voice came back.

"Wot's the problem?"

"Oh, no problem sir. The Hotel would just like to confirm the booking and make sure there was no catering needed for the evening," she replied.

"I dunno babe 'old on a will ya," the voice said not giving Ros a chance to answer before the hand was placed over the receiver and she could hear muffled voices on the other end.

"You still there babe?" the voice broke in on the line.

"Yes sir," she said trying to sound business like a smile creeping on to her lips.

"Wot kinda grub you do then?" the man asked.

"That depends on what you wanted and what the occasion was," she said making him do the thinking.

"Well, 'ow about some of that buffet grub back stage and a few beers and pop!"

"That would be no problem sir how many for?"

"Ow many fer wot?"

"How many for the food sit?" she said loving every minute.

"Fuck me I dunno 'ang on a minute. 'ow many fer the grub?" he shouted not bothering to cover the phone.

"Wot? Yeh! All right yeh. 'allo love fer about twenty okay wif you?"

"Fine sir any specific food?"

"WOT? Nar just bung it all on an' we'll 'elp ourselves!" the voice said and the phone went dead.

Ros looked at the receiver and grinned.

"Now to work!" she said aloud.

She picked up the phone again.

"Hello Sam. Can you and Maria see me in my office in a hour please."

"Yeh fine I'll tell 'er now," Sam said calling to her friend in the loo as she put the phone down.

"Ros want's us in her office in an hour."

"Wot the fuck we done now?" Maria came out the toilet pulling her knickers up.

"Dunno until we get there do I!" Sam said in a silly voice. Maria raised her eyebrows.

Ros was sitting behind her desk when the two girls knocked on the door. She checked her watch and smiled. 'Five minutes early! A good start.' She thought.

"Come in," she called her face straight her elbows resting on the desk.

"Sit down girls," she motioned them to the chairs.

Both sat down as lady like as they could.

"Right girls I'm going to get straight to the point as I've only got two days to sort this out," she said firmly.

"I need two girls, to be human buffets are you interested?"

Both sat there open mouthed.

"I'm sorry girls I'll ask some one else," she said opening her draw and pulling out her cigarettes giving the girls time to look at each other their looks saying more in seconds than words ever could.

Ros got up from the desk lighting her cigarette and walked around the desk and behind the girls. Maria turned first.

"Wot we gotta do Ros?"

"I need you to lay on a buffet table and be used as a serving plate," she said blowing out her smoke.

"Wot we wear?" Sam asked eyeing Maria.

"Nothing," Ros said, putting out her cigarette, giving the girls glancing time again.

"I dunno Ros is there going to be anyone there you know ta watch nothin' happens," Maria asked.

"Good question. Yes I'll be there all the time," she smiled at them.

"Wot if the men won't more than me food?" Sam asked.

"That's entirely up to you but they will have to pay you of course," she replied looking Sam in the eyes.

240

"How much we get?" Maria asked squinting her eyes.

"80% of any service you supply plus double a nights wages for doing the buffet," she said looking at the girls.

"But before you say yes I must confirm your eighteen years old girls," she added scribbling notes on a piece of paper.

"I'm going to nip this note down to Jenny it'll give you time to have a chat but I must have your answer when I come back. Fair enough?"

"Yeh thanks Ros see ya in five then," Sam said looking at the floor.

"I won't be long help your self to tea or coffee behind you," she pointed to a tray by the door.

"Thanks," Maria whispered looking at her friend.

Ros shut the office door behind her and screwed up the piece of paper. She checked her watch giving them ten minutes before she went back in.

She smiled to herself 'they're do it' she grinned as she headed to the function room and back stage just to refresh her mind.

"Perfect!" she whispered.

"What?"

"God. Pete you scared the shit out of me!" Ros grinned when she realised who it was.

"Sorry just checking there's enough of every thing," he mumbled from the store room.

"Pete I've been meaning to have a word and now seems as good a time as any. It's just that we've had a bit of a weird request from the band that's booked. They want a couple of buffet tables."

"Wot's weird about that?" Pete frowned.

"They want a couple of nude girls under the food," she said raising an eyebrow.

"Do they now?" Pete grinned.

"An how we gonna do that then? Got any one in mind?" he asked knowing her very well after five years of working together.

"Maria and Sam," she said.

"Well, don't hang around do you! They said yes yet?" he smiled.

"They're in the office now. I'm giving them ten minutes to have a think," she said, looking at him from under her lashes.

"And?"

"They'll do it," she grinned.

"You know wot yer doin' Ros?" he asked concerned.

"Oh, I think so," she smiled slowly.

"Fair enough I'll leave you to it then," he said ticking his checklist and shutting the store room door and locking it.

Ros checked her watch.

"I'd better get back to them," she said heading back to her office.

The little voice in her head asking her if she really wanted to do this. Ros dismissed it and walked into her office making the girls jump out of their seats. She didn't say a word until she'd sat down and lit a cigarette.

"Well?" she said leaning back in her chair and blowing out her smoke.

The two girls looked at each other then at Ros.

"We'll do it," Sam spoke for the pair of them as Maria nodded in her chair.

"Good. Be here tomorrow at three o'clock and we'll have a pre run."

Ros said sitting forward and smiling at them.

"Don't worry I won't be covering you in the food. But I will expect you to be able to strip off in front of me and lay on the tables."

They both looked concerned.

"Don't worry I'm not after you, but if you can't strip off in front of me, there's no way you'll be able to do it in front of a bunch of hyped up band members that's all," she said putting their minds at rest.

"Now any questions before you go?" she added.

They both shook their heads.

"Good. I'll see you tomorrow then girls don't forget three o'clock," she said smiling at them as they stood and headed to the door closing it behind them.

Ros breathed out a sigh of relief and pressed her hands together looking to the heavens.

"Please let me pull this off!" she said through her hands.

Chapter 22

"Hi Ros it's Jen. I've got Sam and Maria here, want me to send them up to you?"

"Please."

"Sure thing bye," Jenny put the phone down before Ros could say any more. She checked her watch a grinned, it was a quarter to three. A couple of minutes the girls came bursting through the office door grins all over their faces.

"Hi ya Ros I hope you don't mind but we've 'a a bit of Dutch courage before we got 'ere!" Maria blurted out sitting on a chair and grinning.

"Well, I'm glad you told me girls," Ros smiled.

"That's what I like the truth at all times, remember that won't you. Now shall we?" she said standing and waving her hand to the office door.

The two girls looked to each other for confidence and headed for the door. Ros smiled inwardly, 'I knew I wouldn't be wrong with these two!' she thought leading the girls to the function room and the room behind it.

"Follow me girls, it's this way," she said opening the back stage door for them. Sam and Maria walked into the small room and looked around.

"It's a bit bare init," Maria said wrinkling her nose at the square room with no windows.

"It is at the moment, but when the band, the roadies and all the kit comes. The room will be jammed packed," Ros said looking around as well.

"How da you know?" Sam asked impressed.

"Let's just say experience, shall we Sam?" Ros said giving her a little smile then turning to the two buffet tables, she pulled out a piece of paper from the folder she was carrying and said.

"Right let's get down to business shall we. Now I've worked

out the food to go on you. The only thing is how are we going to place you? Head to head, toe to toe, or head to toe?" she said biting her thumbnail as she turned to the girls looking them up and down as a designer would his creation.

"How about Sam an' me jump up an' ya can get a bit of an idea?" Maria said excitement in her eyes.

Ros seeing her excitement grinned and nodded.

"And once we've got that sorted, we'll try it with out your clothes shall we?" she said tapping the tabletop.

The girls rushed over giggling and sat on a table each swinging their legs. Ros stood back and looked at them. 'They could have been sisters' she thought looking at their features. The only difference was Sam had raven black hair and blue eyes. Maria had baby blonde hair and dark brown eyes. Both girls wore their hair in the same trendy style as only best mates can without any malice. Ros looked at their taut long legs hanging from the table tops and smiled to herself. What a picture these two were.

The girls stared at Ros and her expressions, not sure what she was thinking.

"Right let's try head to head first," Ros suddenly said coming out of her day dream.

The girls instantly swung their legs on to the table and laid down their arms by their sides, looking like boards staring to the ceiling.

"Come on girls loosen up you look petrified!" she chuckled resting a hand on their shoulders.

"Sorry Ros I just feel a complete and utter prat layin' 'ere!" Sam said being truthful.

"You feel a prat now! Wait till we're covered in fuckin' food!" Maria said quietly.

The room fell silent, then all thre of them burst out laughing.

"Your do fine!" Ros said through giggles.

"Head to head's perfect!"

"I suppose yer want us ta strip off now don'tcha?" Maria said a hand on her hip and one behind her head posing.

"If you wouldn't mind ladies," Ros said stepping back.

"I'm going to have to sit back here and watch you I'm afraid

244

girls. You've got to be able to take your clothes off in front of people," she said apologetically.

Both girls slid off the tables all the giggles aside now.

"Do you want us to try and do a strip or just whip it all off?" Sam asked trying to sound confident.

'That's a girl!' Ros thought saying slowly.

"How do you feel about stripping?"

"I dunno I ain't ever done it before," Sam said honestly pouting her face.

"So you wouldn't like to give it a go one day?" she asked her mind ticking.

"Maybe... I mean if I can lay stark naked covered in food 'avin' men pick it off, I recon I could give it a go!" she said her confidence shining through.

"What about you Maria? How do you feel?" Ros asked looking at the table and biting her nail.

"Wot about bein' a buffet or strippin'?" Maria said.

"Both," she replied smiling.

"Truth. Scared. Unsure. Excited. And Horny!" Maria said blushing.

"Darlings you'll be wonderful!" Ros beamed at them.

"You fink so?" Maria asked unsure.

"Not think so. Know so!" she told them.

"You've both got what it takes," she added looking down at her folder.

Maria and Sam gave each other a quizzical look and shrugged their shoulders not knowing what to say to that. Ros looked up a sadness in her eyes that the girls noticed before she could shake it off saying.

"Right enough of that! Time to see if you can really do it!" she smiled eyeing the girls up and down like a man would and pouted at them making them giggle and relax a bit.

"When you're ready ladies," she said sitting back in her chair and crossing her legs her eyes on the girls as they kicked off their shoes first, then looking at each other took the same garment off as if they'd been practising all night. Ros noted this in her mind and filed it. When the girls had slipped their panties down Ros spoke before they had time to cover themselves with their hands.

"Well, done ladies! Now could you please hop up on the tables as you were before. That's wonderful!" she encouraged them as they done as they were asked.

"Now, how do you feel?" she asked from her chair.

Both girls turned their heads towards her voice.

"Very sexy!" Maria said going red from the neck up.

"Yeh sexy and powerful!" Sam said grinning over to her smiling and nodding.

"Good. That's good now if you two ladies don't mind I'd like to see how the food's going to lay on your bodies."

"Yeh no problem," Sam said stretching a long leg into the air and grinning.

"I've got a problem Ros," Maria said not moving.

"Oh, and what's that?" she asked getting level with them pencil and folder in hand.

"Is it going to be warmer in here on the night. Only if it ain't I'm gonna want a wee every five minutes!" she said perfectly serious.

Ros and Sam never said a word.

"Wot! It ain't funny!" she said her voice in a panic.

Ros and Sam couldn't hold it any longer and burst out laughing! Tears rolled down their faces.

"It's true Ros she's always wanting a wee ain'tcha babe's?" Sam cried wiping the tears from her face and tapping her friends belly.

Ros's mind went back all those years to her and Kel.

Ros patted Maria's shoulder.

"Darling you'll have nothing to worry about I promise and the room will be bloody boiling I personally promise you that."

"Now if you young ladies would like to get dressed we can go back to the office and have a coffee, and if you've got any questions I'll see if I can answer them for you," she said walking over to the chair she'd been sitting on and pushing it in.

"Fuck! I forgot I didn't 'ave any clothes on!" Sam cried looking at her body then at her friend.

Ros smiled at them.

"I'll see you upstairs girl's," she said leaving them and walking out the door.

She slumped down in her chair and reached for her

cigarette's pulling one from the packet and lighting the end sat back, relief washing over her. Suddenly that little voice jumped into her thoughts 'you know this could get you back on it Ros. Be very careful it's been five years that's a long time!' she waved it away.

"I know what I'm doing! Tomorrow you'll see!" she muttered taking a puff of her cigarette and blowing smoke rings in to the room.

Ros told the girls she wanted them in her office at seven thirty the night of the gig. She checked her watch as she wandered into the Hotels kitchen. She opened the big industrial fridge and checked the food was all ready. It was five to five, the band and roadies would be arriving soon. Ros knew she'd have to keep out of the way while they were setting up. She came out of the kitchen and used the back stairs to her office so no one saw her.

Pressing her intercom she heard Jenny's voice.

"Hi Jenny, it's Ros. Do me a favour and buzz me when the band arrives would you," she said casually.

"Yeh no problem. You want me to send some one from the band up to you or some thing?" Jenny asked trying to be helpful.

"No! no that's not necessary thanks Jen. Speak to you soon," she said replacing the receiver.

As it was Jenny needn't have bothered to buzz Ros. When the band turned up they made such a commotion that the whole street knew they were there. Ros watched out of her window her stomach turning over.

"Fucking hell Ros, will you calm down!" she told herself pulling her eyes from the window and pacing the room. She went to her top draw pulling out a little bag of weed and a pack of papers tapping it in her hand she needed to calm her nerves. Finally she gave in and sitting down rolled a strong joint. She sat staring at it twisting it between her fingers the lighter in the other hand. She put them down and went to the window once more.

Just as she did a guy looked up at the building Ros couldn't tell who it was or if he'd seen her, but it was enough to make her jump out of her skin and rush back to the desk her heart pounding. She picked up the joint and lighter placing it between her teeth she bit off the end turned it around put it to her lips and flicked the lighter and inhaled deeply, she closed her eyes and let the smoke drift from her nose letting the little green bud claim her. She opened her eyes and saw her suit hanging in the dry cleaners bag waiting to do it's job. She smiled to herself. 'yep I've come a long way in those five years off the island!' she thought.

"So why bring it back now?" the voice but into her thoughts making her jolt up in her chair and look about her.

"You can always call it off you know!" it came again.

"No," she said aloud.

"It's going to happen end of. Any way it came to me did it not?" she argued with herself biting her thumbnail. She picked up the phone and dialled Marg asking if Katie was okay and to tell her she would be round in the morning to take Katie to school. She felt better after speaking to Marg and sorting out the normality of her life with Katie. Replacing the receiver she picked up her cigarette and lighter and wandered into her suite next door to run a bath coming back to her office while the water was running to order a beef roll and a bottle of red wine, then smiling to herself padded back to her bath water.

Chapter 23

She checked herself one more time in the bedroom mirror and smiled, all she needed was her lippy in the office and she was done. Picking up her earrings she clipped them on, then taking her wine bottle and glass she went to her office. 'the girls should be here soon.' She thought looking at her watch as she placed her glass on the desk. She could hear the thudding of the music as the band warmed up testing their equipment.

She had to admit they were good, really good as she tapped her feet to the beat.

"Knock. Knock. Knock.

Ros looked up to two grinning faces.

"God is it half past! My watch must be slowing!" she said getting up from her chair a little panicked.

"Nar calm down it's only seven. Wow you look fantastic!" Sam cried as Ros came around the desk to the door.

"Oh! Thank you," she said a little confused.

"We were so bloody nervous at 'ome so we thought if we got 'ere early well we'd kinda feel oh fuck I'm nervous!" Maria jabbered.

"Where's the loo?" she cried smiling at Ros.

"Down the hall," Ros grinned after her.

"Come on in Sam an' have a seat," Ros said going back behind the desk and opening her drawer pulled out the bag of weed and silently started to stick two of the papers together and build a joint. Sam sat stock still staring at Ros in amazement. Ros was just licking the papers and rolling it when Maria came through the door freezing to the spot. Ros looked up.

"What?" she asked sliding the roach down the narrow end and biting the other twisted end off.

"Is that what I think it is?" Maria asked pointing to Ros.

Sam looked up at her and nodded looking back across at

Ros as she lit it and a purple'ish haze filled the room for a second.

"Well, fuck me!" Maria said sliding into the other chair and whistling.

"A woman of many talents!" she breathed a sigh as she gazed at Ros.

"You girls fancy a drink to relax you?" Ros said pointing to the bottle of wine then to some glasses on the side taking another puff of her cigarette.

"Thanks," Sam said getting up and fetching two glasses and filling them topping Ros's up as well.

"A toast," Ros said placing her joint in the ashtray and picking up her glass.

"To entertainment," she said giving the girls a wink.

Entertainment!" they said together looking at each other and taking a sip of their wine.

"Do you girls smoke?" Ros asked offering them her joint.

Maria leaned over taking the cigarette from Ros and placed it to her lips taking a puff and passing it to Sam, who looking at Maria took a puff and passed it back to Ros. The drug hit them after a couple of minutes and a couple of puffs more. Ros watched them carefully not letting them have too much that they didn't know what they were doing or saying.

"You girls feel all right?" she asked holding the joint.

"Not spinning or anything?"

"I feel fuckin' brill! I'm ready let's do it!" Sam giggled.

"What's funny?" Maria grinned at her.

"Nothin'!" Sam laughed.

"Nothin' at all!" she cried laughing even more.

"Nothin'?" Maria giggled at her.

"Nope!" Sam said shaking her head, trying very hard not to laugh, pursing her lips together before collapsing over the desk holding her ribs as she laughed.

"I change that!" she gasped.

"Me fuckin' ribs are killin' me!"

"A small price ta pay ta be 'appy!" Maria's giggles erupting into fits of laughter.

Ros sat opposite the two girls a smile on her face as she watched them, their nerves flying out with their laughter. When they'd calmed down Ros leaned forward over the desk and said.

"It's nearly time to get you ready can you both go and get showered there's a couple of robes in the bath rooms and meet me in the kitchen would you. Oh and girls, no deodorant it affects the taste of the food. Okay I'll see you in a while. And take the back stairs please," she said all business like again.

She pushed her self up with her elbows, stood up, walked to the office door opening it and motioned the girls out shutting it behind her, and watched them down the passage to the bathrooms. Ros leaned back against the office door her fingers crossed by her side.

"Show time!" she said taking a deep breath and pushing herself off, headed for the kitchen. As she went down the back stairs she could hear the band just starting their gig and her stomach turned over with anticipation. Ros had just poured herself a coffee from the percolator when she heard the girls giggles floating above the music. Both Sam and Maria fell silent as they turned the kitchen wall and saw Ros. She motioned them over smiling.

"You girls okay?" she asked them as they got level.

They looked at each other and nodded.

"Ros before we lay down can we have another couple of puff's of your cigarette?" Sam asked quietly going red.

"Of course you can darling. But before you do can you both sign this from stating that anything you do here tonight, you agreed to before hand. It's only to cover the Hotels backside," she said waving a hand in the air.

"But it must be signed."

They both shrugged their shoulders and took the paper put in front of them and signed, handing it back to Ros.

"Lovely thank you ladies," she said placing the paperwork back into her folder.

"Now let's go and have a little smoke and get this show on the road!" she added putting the folder on top of a cabinet and putting an arm about both girls, leading them to the downstairs office. Ros sat them down their nerves creeping back because of the surroundings. This was Pete's office. Surley he'd smell the purple smoke!

"Listen girls I know this is Pete's office, but where do you

251

think I get the stuff from?" she said opening Pete's top draw and pulling out a bag full of the green weed.

The girls relaxed, sat back in their chairs and watched Ros expertly roll the cone.

"Where did ya learn ta roll a joint Ros?" Sam asked as she watched.

"Let's just say a friend showed me years ago and leave it at that shall we," she said twisting the end up.

Sam nodded sticking her bottom lip out in thought. Ros grinned to herself, 'they'd never believe me even if I told them!' she thought passing the cigarette and lighter to Sam.

"Enjoy ladies," she said standing and going to the door.

"Where you going?" Maria asked her eyes wide.

"Only to get the food taken into the room, so you don't have to lay buck naked in front of our waiters!" she said giving the girls a grin.

"Won't be long promise," she added quietly closing the door behind her and walking to the kitchen.

"Paul and Martin. Would you take all the food on the first two shelves in this fridge back stage for me. Oh and don't lay them out keep them on the trolleys and ask anyone in the room to leave until the foods has been prepared. Thank you boys," she said wandering off not giving them time to question her.

"Oh, and boy's when your done get Jenny to give me a buzz please," she called back to them heading to her office.

As she reached the stairs the music and noise from the crowd drew her over to the function rooms double doors.

"One peek won't hurt," she said under her breath reaching the doors slowly she pushed a door open an inch. The noise and heat exploded into the foyer making her shut it quickly and look around. No one was in sight they were all in there enjoying the band. Ros opened the door again, this time some one pulled it open.

"Oh, all right Ros?" Bert the bouncer said when he recognized who was coming through the door.

"Great ain't they?" he said grinning towards the stage tapping his foot.

Ros looked in the bands direction, then up to the lead singer and caught her breath. There he was as large as life singing his heart out, and God did he look good! All tanned and toned from all the gigs. Ros tore her eyes away and left quickly the old feelings rushing back. She tried desperately to push them away and calm down. She turned left in to reception passing the desk as Jenny looked up.

"Ros Paul told me to buzz you when every things ready. I've been doing that for five minutes! Ros you okay you look ever so pale!" Jenny said looking concerned at her.

"What? Oh thanks Jen. Yes yes I'm fine a bit hot that's all!" she said waving her away as she went past.

"Fine!" Jenny said raising her hands and tuting to herself like an old woman.

Ros reached the downstairs office doorway and could hear the girls giggling inside. Taking a deep breath she opened the door.

"All right Ros!" the girls said together grinning at each other. Standing up in front of her they flicked their heads back and dropped their robes. Ros stood in the door way a grin spreading across her face.

"Business as usual," she said under her breath raising her eyebrows at them.

"Wotcha say?" Sam asked pulling her robe about her.

"Nothing darling only Wow! You two amaze me!" she said.

"Time to have a rest girls!" she said holding the door for them.

All three snuck into the room behind the stage.

"Wot we creepin' about for we could scream in here an' no one would 'ear us fer the music!" Sam said looking around the room.

"See wotcha mean about it fillin' up!" Maria said going over to her table and having a look at the food soon to be on her body and wrinkling her nose.

"Why's our table covered in tin foil?" she asked running her hand over it.

"So I can put the food down the side of you without using plates and secondly it keeps you warm!" she said walking Sam to her table.

"Robes ladies please!" she said holding out her arms for their garments to be placed.

"Up you get and make your self comfortable, relax you'll love it!" Ros said grinning at them.

They heard the band finish a number and some one say that the next was the last in the gig.

"Shit when they gonna be here?" Sam asked through gritted teeth trying not to get up and make a run for it.

"Probably about twenty minutes, by the time they've encored etc!" Ros said calmly standing back to admire her work.

"How's it feel girls?" she asked grinning at them lighting the joint and holding it over their lips.

"Actually I feel a whole fuckin' lot better than I thought I would!" Sam giggled making the food on her jog about.

"NO! Don't Sam! You can't move or shake!" Ros cried laughing at the food on the girl.

"Ere Ros when that lot come in do we say any thing?"

"Like wot ya silly cow! 'ere boy's come an' 'ave a nibble!" Sam burst out biting her lips.

"No darling, don't say a word! Please!" Ros cried at her.

"Will they touch us. You know!" Sam said bending her head and looking down her body.

"That's up to you girls," Ros said business like.

"Wotcha mean?" Maria asked.

"Well, let's put it this way, you let them touch you. You get paid for it plus tips!" she said raising her eyebrow.

"An you'll be there all the time?" Sam asked.

"All the time so calm down. Think of your selves as a huge serving plate!" she grinned and the girls smiled back.

They'd just put their heads back in position when the back stage doors flung open making the three of them jump.

"Fuckin' brilliant night boy's! Did we fuckin' show 'em or wot!" John yelled as the four men flew through the doors.

No one noticed Ros or the girls, the high of the gig still in their veins the adrenalin rushing through them. Ros left her joint in one of the ashtrays and stood by the exit doors over the other side of the room she slid out of sight in the corner.

"Ere John some one's left us a billy bonus!" Paul the drummer yelled as he ripped his jacket and shirt off throwing himself into a chair putting the joint into his mouth and lighting it.

"Fuckin' jammy bastard give us a drag!" Al came flying over piling on top of him taking the joint from his mouth.

"Oi! Fuckin' give us that back!" Paul jumped up running and leaping on big Al's back laughing.

"Ere Gary won't this?" Al held up the cigarette in front of him Paul still on his back grabbing at his arm.

"Cheers Al 'ere cop this!" Gary said throwing a couple of cans of beer at them, Paul fell to the floor in a save two cans in his hands.

"Fuckin' 'ell Gary mate yer couldn't 'ave booted 'em any 'arder!" Paul yelled throwing a can to Al and laughing.

"Oi give us a drag," John came from the toilet taking the joint from Gary's mouth and catching a can from him with his other hand giving him a cocky grin.

Ben walked in with four other men behind him all five were suited and Booted "Gentlemen," Ben called from the door giving John and the boys time to regain their composure as the four men aging from forty to sixty walked into the middle of the little room talking, their conversation stopping as they entered.

"Gentlemen," Ben started again.

"May I introduce you to "The Jug Band" John, Paul, Gary, Al, I'd like to introduce you to your new production company "Blackout Vinyl's"," Ben said his business smile on his face.

Ros watched with amusement as John and the boy's just looked up from their antics and nodded as the four men all put out their hands to them retracting them as quickly as they put them out. Ben cleared his throat exaggerating the noise and staring wide-eyed at them, who were finding Ben's attempts to get them to behave hilarious.

"Ere Ben mate 'ave a drink!" Al said passing him a can of beer giving him a smirk.

Ben nearly hit the floor.

"You bastards!" he hissed in Al's ear as he took the can.

Al stepped back giving Ben a smile that said 'we ain't started yet!'

"Gentlemen would you care for a drink?" Ben said to the four men watching the boy's rolling joints and fighting playfully as they came down from the gig.

All four nodded politely to Ben who in turn went white

when he saw the buffet.

"Fuckin' hell!" he said under his breath walking over to the drinks.

"What can I get you gentlemen?" he asked turning to the four men.

"Looks like we've got everything," he said impressed.

"Fuck me you seen this boys!" Paul yelled over to the others.

"Who ordered that?" he asked with a grin on his face the other guys rushing over to see what he was pointing at as he put a grape in his mouth.

"Jeeesus fuckin' Christ!" Ben said slapping his fore head as not only the boy's went over so did the production company.

"All right darlin'? Ain't too cold fer ya is it?" Al asked Sam giving her a wink and looking at her erect nipples poking up from the lettuce leaf placed over her.

"'ave a butchers Al," Gary said nudging his friend in the ribs to lift the leaf.

Ros stood stock still a smile wide on her face enjoying the commotion until she saw the oldest of the gentlemen under the buffet table lights. Her hands flew to her face covering her eyes trying to block out that face. Slowly she made herself pull her hands away, the room seemed to spin. Ros reached behind her for the wall to give her support before she scanned the room again, this time she made sure no one could see her by first stepping way into the corner. Ben was talking to him his business laugh ringing across the room. He had his back to her, she couldn't see properly her eyes hurt from straining them. The band and other gentlemen were now talking and laughing together, slapping each other on the backs and telling dirty jokes, judging from the sudden roars that erupted every few minutes. Ben started to walk the older man towards the exit deep in conversation. Suddenly Ben and the man turned around huge grins on their faces. The man called to the other men that he was going to sort out the paper work with Ben and to enjoy themselves. Ros stood paralysed to the spot, unblinking or breathing, her eyes deep black holes.

"IT can't be!" she whispered to herself.

"Not now it can't!" panic welled up in her.

She had to get out! Get away! She felt trapped like an animal. Turning she clicked the fire exit bar down and pushed, she didn't care who saw her she just had to get away. The door banged behind her but no one looked up they were having far too much fun with Sam and Maria. Ros ran around the corner of the hotel stopping to catch her breath, she heard the roadies putting the equipment back in the van. Some one looked up from the back of the van at her. She tried to look away from him a shiver running down her spine as his eyes bore into hers, making her feel he was extracting every thing about her out, even from a fair distance. He closed his beautiful blue eyes and opened them sneering at her, flicking his blonde hair from his forehead he returned to his job. It was Dan. Ros covered her face with her hands biting the fleshy part of her palms to stop herself from screaming. She didn't know how long she'd been standing there before the cold air hit her and she started to shiver. She stood up straight and took a deep breath trying to compose herself.

"Come on girl pull yourself together. This is getting way out of hand!" she told her self as she clenched and unclenched her hands by her side. She walked slowly to the staff entrance using her key to get in, shutting it behind her, she sighed as a little security filled her empty heart. Ros held her head high as she walked through the kitchens. This was her show! 'I'll deal with the face later!' she thought as she got to the restaurant doors heading to the reception, Jenny wasn't anywhere to be seen much to Ros's relief. She passed the reception in a grand a manner as she could muster heading straight to the function room. 'He wouldn't know it was me anyway!' her thoughts went through her mind as she entered the empty hall. The smell of electricity still in the air made her nostrils twitch. She could hear the noise coming from the room back stage Sam and Maria seemed to be keeping the guys happy by the sound of the cheers suddenly erupting in waves. This gave Ros the confidence to stride across the room and stand in front of the double doors, her hand reached out for the handle.

"Here goes!" she said lifting her head up and opening the door stepping into a world she left those years ago.

"Fuck me don't I know you?" a drunk Paul stumbled past her as she was shutting the door.

"I don't know do you?" Ros asked raising one eyebrow and staring straight at him.

"Give us a minute an' I'll letcha know! But first I gotta take a slash!" Paul grinned disappearing.

Ros smiled walking into the middle of the room and straight up to John sitting on a chair watching Sam and Maria flit about the room getting the boys to eat the food from their bodies.

John's face froze.

"Good evening sir. Is everything to your satisfaction?" Ros asked her face and mannerisms not letting on how she was feeling inside.

"Fuckin' 'ell Ros! What! Yeh yeh every fings fine fuckin' great thanks," he said looking her up and down.

"Is there anything else we can get for you?"

"No. No everyfings fuckin' great! Ros ain't ya gonna ask where we've been or anyfink?" he asked the gig still buzzing through his head.

"That's not why I'm here sir. I'm here only to enquire whether every things to your satisfaction," she said loving every minute of it.

"Fer fuck sake Ros you gonna talk ta me properly?" John asked getting up out of his chair their eyes meeting.

"No!" Ros said gracefully turning on her heels and catching Sam and Maria's eyes.

"Girls please!" she called motioning them with her hand. Sam and Maria high on their success blew the guys kisses and floated out the room leaving their giggles behind.

Ros following out the door, had her elbow grabbed by one of the men from the record company.

"Yes sir?" she spun round a smile already on her lips.

"I'm Chas. I'm staying until tomorrow evening is there any chance you and I could have a coffee before I go?" Chas asked a warm smile spreading across his face.

"What?" she said, a frown on her face.

"No I'm sorry I don't think so," she said giving him a smile and walking on towards the door.

Chas caught her arm again. This time not letting go.

"Please just a coffee," he said giving her as pleading look.

"Okay. 11.30 in the lounge tomorrow, if your late I'll be

gone!"

"Fair enough 11.30 it is," he said letting her elbow go and watching her walk through the doors.

"Fuck Ros why'd ya take us outta there they loved us!" Maria wailed as she came through the doors.

"It's for your own good believe me!" she said.

"Now go and get showered and dressed." More of an order.

Both girls looked at each other not sure if they'd done something wrong and wandered off.

Ros strode off towards the reception desk hoping Jenny wouldn't be there. Her luck was in.

She went up to her office and poured herself a coffee and sat behind her desk trying to collect her thoughts.

"That face," she said aloud shaking her head slowly.

"Why now? How'd he get here?" she muttered opening her top draw.

"Wot face Ros?" John's face broke the silence of the office.

"What! How did you get up here?" her face full of surprise.

"You ain't answered me question yet!" he said a slow smile crossing his face.

"None of your fucking business actually! Now if you wouldn't mind I've got things to do," she said opening her second drew and bringing out some papers.

"Bollocks you 'ave!" John said waving the papers to the floor with one hand standing in front of her only the desk between them.

"Get out!" she said slowly through gritted teeth pointing the way with her finger.

"Your choice Ros," he said raising both hands and shrugging his shoulders and walking out.

She sat in her chair temper welling up inside her.

"Cheeky fucking bastard!" she yelled throwing a paperweight at the closed door.

"You say sumfing babe?" John asked poking his head round the door and grinning.

"No. Just fuck off John!" she screamed getting up her fists clenched.

"Go on get out now!" she yelled at a now laughing John.

"Okay babe. Chill out will ya I'm gone!" he said still

laughing as he shut the door again.

Ros screamed the tensions of the night coming out. she could hear John's laugh as he went down the corridor, making her even madder.

The two girls gingerly knocked on the door stepping into the room.

"You all right Ros?" Sam asked quietly.

"Yes fine darling you girls want a drink before you go home I know I could do with one," Ros said smiling at them feeling cold inside.

"Do you know what I think I'm going to have? Something I haven't had in years," she said more to herself than the girls.

"Oh, yeh wot's that?" Maria asked.

"A brandy and babycham it blows your head off just what we need I think!" she said looking at them and smiling.

"Well, I'll 'ave a bash at it!" Sam said.

"Yeh!" Maria agreed.

Ros poured them all the drinks and passed them around sitting on the edge of the desk and passing them a cigarette.

"Thanks for tonight girls you've done us proud," she said holding up her drink and toasting them.

"Now drink it up and go home an' have a good nights sleep," she said taking a long sip.

"That what your doin' Ros or ya goin' ta see that bloke that stopped ya?" Sam said grinning at Maria.

"No! Straight to bed it's been a long night!" she smiled slowly at them "I've already rang for your taxi it'll be here in about ten minutes so drink up an' I'll walk down with you."

"But I want to party!" Sam yawned.

"Yes I can see that!" Ros laughed placing her hand on the young girls back.

"Come on bed you two!" she said and they all stood up.

Ros tapped their backsides as they went out the door locking it behind her. And putting an arm around them walked them down the stairs.

"Ere Ros you gonna see that guy tamorrow or ain't ya gonna turn up?" Sam asked.

"Well, seeing you so interested yes I am we're having coffee tomorrow," Ros said smiling at them.

"I don't blame you one bit! He was absolutely fuckin' gorgeous!" Maria blushed her face scarlet.

"Any thing else you want to know?" Ros said laughing.

The girls could have stayed all night asking her questions God knows they had enough in their minds, but instead of saying so they simply shook their heads and smiled at her. Tonight was not the time.

"Good. Now go home!" she said blowing them a kiss as they reached the bottom steps turning in the opposite direction to the girls.

"Night Ros," they said in unison.

"Night girls."

Chapter 24

Ros woke early the next day so that she could take Katie to school from Marg and Jim's. When she returned from the school run she went straight up to her office and pouring a coffee sat down to do some ordering before meeting Chas in the lounge. She was just finishing her phone order when Pete walked in with a tray of BLT sandwiches in his hands.

'Oh fuck what's happened!' she thought as she waved him to a seat and smiled unconsciously sitting up in her chair.

"Thanks Ed, and it will all be here by the 15th at the latest?"

"Great speak to you soon."

"Yeh bye. Bye."

"Pete this is a surprise what do I owe the pleasure?" Ros asked resting her elbows on the desk.

Pete grinned at her.

"Ros wot did you do last night?" he asked offering her a sandwich.

"What do you mean. What did I do?" she said waving the plate away.

"Nothing bad pet!" he said putting a hand up and smiling as he tucked into his sandwich.

"What then?"

"It's just that I've had a lot of people coming up to me and congratulating me on a great buffet!" he said raising an eyebrow and attacking his sandwich again.

"Ah!"

"Yeh Ah!" Pete smirked.

"Why didn't you say how well it went?" he said smiling and putting his food down reaching for her cigarettes.

"I didn't think you really liked the idea," she said honestly taking the packet offered to her.

"Well, I've got to say I did have my doubts about it yeh but what a success!" he boomed lighting his cigarette.

"Sorry. But I could have got you in a lot of trouble last night couldn't I?" she said giving him a little warning and taking the lighter from him.

"Let's just say next time let me know when they're gonna do that! Now eat ya fuckin' food will ya!" he grinned.

"Definitely I'm really sorry Pete I didn't know they would jump off and feed the men from their tit's! God I only left them for a minute!" she tutted.

Pete coughed nearly choking on his bacon, making them both laugh.

"Wotcha doin' now then Ros?" he asked accepting a coffee from her.

"Well, I've got a coffee date with one of the men from the production group last night his names Chas."

"'e one of the guys that stayed last night?" he said nodding at her.

"I don't know who stayed last night. There was no names with the booked rooms! Which I might add turning to business for a moment is very unprofessional when we don't know who's staying! You can't really go up to someone and say "Oi mate wot room yer stayin' in only we ain't gotcha name down!" can you?" she said to a chuckling Pete.

"Okay I'll 'ave a word, no name no bookin' 'ow's that?" he said. Seriously taking what she said in.

"Great thank you. It'll make all our lives easier you'll see," she replied sipping her coffee and checking her watch. She wanted to change before she met Chas.

"Wot's the matter Ros got sumfink ya wanna do?" he asked.

"I just wanted to get tided up before meeting this Chas bloke that's all," Ros said telling Pete the truth.

"Fuck me 'is one lucky guy!" Pete whistled giving her a wink.

"'ave a nice mornin'!" he grinned putting the plates on the tray and his cigarette out.

Ros stood up and walked around the desk to the door opening it for him.

"Cheers doll. See ya later yeh!" he said over his shoulder as he passed her.

"Of course bye!" she called shutting the door and walking into her suite. She changed into a cream trousers suit with a black and gold shirt underneath. She tied her hair back with a black and gold scarf that matched her shirt. She checked herself in the mirror and wiped an eyebrow with her index finger, before turning and heading out the door to the hotel lounge.

As she walked into the room Chas stood giving her a smile of approval. Holding out his hand.

"Good morning Chas," she said holding out her hand to his.

Chas held her perfectly manicured hand gently in his leading her round to one of the chairs opposite him. Letting her sit down before he opened his mouth.

"I'm sorry I don't know your name," he said his brown eyes glinting with amusement.

"No I'm sorry it's Ros," she said removing her hand from his slowly, never taking her eyes from his.

"Ros would you like some coffee?" he asked turning his head to one side and nodding slowly.

"Please," she said sitting back in the chair and crossing her legs.

Chas motioned the waitress over.

"Two coffee's please," he said as she came to take his order, then sat down opposite Ros and looked at her.

"I'm sorry have I got something on my face?" she asked putting her hand up.

"No not at all! I was just looking at you you're a very attractive woman Ros," Giving her a smouldering smile.

Ros nodded a thankyou to him unable to speak, trying to compose herself when all she wanted to do was lean over the table take his face in her hands and kiss him hard on the mouth. Chas gave her a knowing look, making her breeth in sharply.

"Now tell me Ros did you organise that little show last night?" he asked snapping her back to reality.

"Yes I did I'm sorry if it offended you Chas," she said defending herself and the girls.

"Who said I was offended? I'm more interested!" he said a smile in his eyes.

'Oh fucking typical of all the men an' I get the perv!' she thought saying, "What do you mean by interested?" sitting forward just as the waitress brought them their coffee's.

"Thank you Mary," Ros said politely to the girl and smiling at her.

"Oh, Mary," Chas called the girl back putting his hand in his pocket.

"Yes sir," she said pulling out her pad.

"Here," Chas said standing up pulling a pound note from his pocket and giving it to her.

"Oh, sir I can't," Mary said beaming.

"Yes you can thanks love," Chas said pushing the note in her hand and giving her a wink as he sat back down to a smiling Ros.

"That was very good of you. The girls live on their tips. It's a known fact in this business," she said picking up her cup and saucer taking a sip of the black liquid. Placing the cup back down she said.

"Now what were we talking about? Oh yes you were interested! In what my I ask?"

"You the girls and what they do!"

"What do you mean Do?" Ros asked frowning.

"Look Ros I'm a business man just like all the others last night and I've got my fingers in a lot of pies so to speak and I might be able to offer you and your girls some kind of deal."

"Let's get a couple of things straight shall we. First they're not my girls. Secondly I don't care how many pies you've got your fingers in. They are not going anywhere near whose type of girls. And Thirdly they are not some two bit hookers. Last night was the first time they'd ever done any thing like that ever! So no slimy little deals are reaching their ears understood?" Ros said getting up from her chair.

"I was right a fucking perv or pimp all the bloody same!" she cursed under her breath.

"Hey, calm down I've certainly hit a nerve there haven't I!" Chas said his eyes staring deep into her a smile on his face.

"Yes you have as a matter of fact! I hate blokes like you taking advantage of young girls like them if you must know," she said quickly tearing her eyes from his getting the feeling he could see deep into her.

"So do I," Chas said picking up his coffee.

"That's why I thought I might be able to help you and them in some way! By Christ if that was their first night they've got promise!" he said aloud catching her agreeing with him and cocking his head to one side.

"You saw it too yeh?"

"Yes I mean no! No I didn't!" she lied squirming in the chair.

"Sorry my mistake," Chas smiled.

Ros nodded picking up her coffee silence eloped them.

"So. You married?" Chas asked, making Ros cough on her coffee.

"Divorced."

"Kids?"

"One. Katie she's five. You?"

"One. He's about nineteen twenty."

"You don't know?"

"Divorced his mum ten years ago or so and we're just getting it back on. He's the reason I'm here actually.

"Oh!" she said silence slipping over them again.

"You live local?" he asked.

"UM you?"

"About half an hours drive down the dual carriage way. So what do you do here?" he asked waving his hand about the room.

"Don't laugh," Ros said a wicked grin on her face.

"Promise!" Chas said giving her a puppy dog look his hand on his chest.

"I'm in charge of the food and entertainment!" she burst out laughing the tension in the air gone.

"Fuck me! Your not," he cried laughing with her.

"Umm," she nodded.

"Ros."

"Yes."

"Would you come out to dinner with me tonight?" Chas asked looking her straight in the eyes.

Her giggles stopped.

"I don't know. I don't think so. Any way haven't you got to see your son?"

"What's the matter Ros? Scared you might enjoy your self?"

266

Chas said still looking in her eyes.

"No no it's not that, it's."

"That's not what they're telling me!" Chas but in, pointing to her eyes. Ros looked down a wave of excitement washing over her.

"Okay!" she said looking up and across to Chas giving him a smile. "What time?" she said.

"How about eight. Okay with you?" he asked reaching over the little table and cupping her hand and kissing her fingers.

Ros sucked in some air. She suddenly felt very hot and flushed. Her body trembled and she closed her eyes for a couple of seconds waiting for Chas to release her hand. When he didn't, she slowly opened them. Chas was just sitting staring at her. She could feel the passion building up between them. It was electric!

"Do you by any chance fancy changing that dinner date to lunch?" he asked cheekily.

"Umm I must admit I do feel a little hungry!" she grinned giving him a wink.

Chas raised his eyes to the ceiling and sighed deeply.

"Where d'you fancy going?" he asked his voice deep.

"I know just the place. Good atmosphere! Good food! And good wine!"

"Sounds great!" he said still holding her hand, neither taking their eyes from each other.

"Good. Follow me!" she said uncrossing her legs.

Chas stood up still holding her hand.

"Lead the way!" he said helping her up, running his other hand down her spine.

Ros walked him through the lounge and up the stairs.

"I've got a feeling this is going to be one hell of a lunch!" he said following her up the stairs.

As they got to Ros's door Chas took both her hands and turned her around.

"Are you sure Ros?" he asked passion burning in his eyes.

Ros didn't answer. She cupped his face in her hands and kissed him, letting him know her answer. She reached up behind her and clicked the door open walking backwards into her suite. Chas kicked the door shut behind him. Ros pulled away from him and taking hold of his tie pulled him through to her bedroom.

Pulling him into the middle of the room she let go and stood in front of him. She slipped off her jacket slowly undoing the buttons on her shirt looking him deep in the eyes as she went. As she got to the bottom she carried on to her trouser fastening undoing the button and zip only her hands held them up. She slowly lifted her hands to the neck of her shirt letting her trousers fall to the ground, gracefully stepping out of them as she slipped the shirt from her shoulders, letting that also drop next to the jacket and trousers.

Chas tore his eyes from Ros's, letting them wander over her body. She didn't move, she just stood there in a black lace bra, black hold up stockings and a tiny black thong showing all but nothing!

Ros smiled kicked off her shoes and walked the five paces between them. She ran her finger down Chas's cheek and neck taking hold of his tie again she draped it over her shoulder and led him to the bed. Turning to face him, she sat down on the bed releasing the tie from her grip. She let her hands run down to his trousers and pulled at his belt buckle pulling it through the loops of his trousers and dropped it to the floor. Chas ripped off his jacket, tie and shirt, kicking off his shoes as Ros undid his trouser fastening and zip pulling them over his taunt arse. Chas pulled them off his legs taking his socks with them. He stood in front of her his boxers between her face and his cock.

Chas pushed her back on to the bed and stood between her legs. Leaning over her he smiled as he ran his hands down her bra covered breasts. Ros arched her back wanting more of his touch, Chas grinned and ran his hands down over her belly to the top of her panties. Sighing she pushed her hips on to his hands. He ran one finger inside the top of her panties going from one hip to the other, as his other hand ran down her right thigh and up again with both hands resting at the top of her legs. Chas ran his index fingers down the inside of her panties either side of her crotch, Ros gasped opening her legs wider willing him to touch her now very wet lips. He cupped her bottom cheeks in both hands lifting her legs off the floor so that her backside was perched on the edge of the bed. He rubbed a finger over her covered fanny the material wet from her juices. Kneeling on the floor he rubbed his face into her pussy poking his tongue inside her panties either side of her lips, then grabbing the material either side of her hips ripped them off throwing the ruined garment to the floor and buried his tongue deep into her. Ros pumped herself on to him coming as soon as his tongue touched her. Ros grabbed at Chas's head and pulled him on to her. He ripped off his boxers letting his pulsating cock free. Ros cupped his balls in one hand and ran the other the full length of his manhood. Licking her lips she rubbed the tip of his cock over her swollen clit pushing on to it, slipping him into her and wrapping her legs tightly around him. Chas pounded into her, making her gasp with each stroke their rhythm rushing to a crescendo as they came together.

Chas laid on top of her, his cock not wanting to leave her. Ros gently rocked herself onto it having one last orgasm smiling at him.

"You're one hell of a woman Ros!" he said shaking his head slowly, looking deep in her eyes.

"And you're one hell of a man!" she said meaning every word she said. She'd fallen badly for him and she didn't even know who he was!

"Drink?" she asked sliding from the crumpled bed.

"Love one," he grinned stretching out across the bed.

Ros padded out of the room to fetch the drinks. As she walked through the bedroom door with two glasses in her hand, Chas was laying propped up on the pillows with the biggest hard-on Ros had ever seen in her life, she couldn't take her eyes away from it!

"That was your starters baby. This is your main course!" he said running his hands up and down his cock.

"Well, I did say I was hungry!" she giggled putting their drinks down and climbing on to the bed for an afternoon of hot sex.

It was dark when they got out of bed and ventured in to the kitchen starving hungry.

"Omelette?" Chas asked looking through her sparse cupboards and fridge.

Ros picked up her phone.

"Room service!" she grinned.

"Perks of the job. Now what would you like?" she giggled.

"Don't you ever cook?"

"Never had to," Ros said thoughtfully.

"Now what do you fancy?"

"You!" Chas grinned feeling eighteen again.

"NO to eat!" she cried holding the phone and pointing to it raising her eyes to the ceiling.

"Yeh. You!" he carried on.

"I'm gonna bash you in a minute! Now what do you want to eat?" she asked her hand on her hip waving the phone about.

"All right! I'll have a steak and horseradish sandwich!" he said kissing his fingers.

"Oh, and a trifle!"

"What a whole trifle?"

"Yep!" he said grinning.

"Fine!" she said dialing to the kitchen and ordering for them.

"Come and sit down," she said wandering into her little lounge and turning on the stereo.

"Got any of "The Jug Band". I thought they were bloody brilliant last night! Nice bunch of guy's as well, didn't you think?" he said watching her body movements as he spoke.

'If only you knew!' Ros thought to herself flicking through her records finding their first album and pulling it from it's sleeve.

"Yes I have. And yes they do seem a nice bunch," she said turning and giving him a smile.

"Sorry I thought you knew the singer. Only he seemed to know you," Chas said quietly.

"Why what's he said?" she asked a little too quickly.

"No nothing. It's only that he called you by your name that's all!"

"But you said you didn't know my name!" Ros jumped in.

"I lied! But it was only hear say. It wasn't as if you told me your self was it!" he said in a clam voice.

"No I'm sorry. Look I did know them a while back, when I was younger," she said sighing.

"Thanks for telling me the truth Ros," he said as he tapped his foot to the beat and smiled.

"It's nothing. Perhaps you could tell me something," she said sitting down opposite him.

"Sure what you want to know?" he said sitting up.

"The three other men with you last night."

"Yeh."

"Who are they?" she asked casually.

"That's Jeff and Russ the producers and the old guys the money. Wot's his name! Shit it'll come to me in a minute!" he said rubbing his chin.

"That's it! Edward Chambers! Yeh that's it!" He said slapping his knee and grinning at her.

Ros expecting it to be the man's name still jumped when he said it.

"You all right Ros you've gone real quiet all of a sudden!" he asked confused.

"Yes fine," she said smiling at him, then frowning.

"So what have you got to do with the other three men?" she asked praying he had nothing to do with the said mister Chambers.

"Oh, I found the band, or should I say my son found them. I'm the guy that gets everyone together. That's my job."

"Oh, I see," she said not seeing at all and showing it on her face.

"Look I've got the contacts certain people need, to make a few quid, and I earn in the process. Understand now?" he said smiling at her.

"I think so," she said sensing it was time to stop asking and time to start enjoying. But she had one last question she couldn't leave.

"Chas."

"Yes?"

"The old guy."

"What about him?" Chas asked bored.

"Nothing it doesn't matter," she said trying to relax. He hadn't seen her and Chas wasn't interested in Mr Chambers!

"Where's that food got to I'm starving!" Chas said taking his drink from the table and emptying it in one a huge grin on his face.

Chapter 25

Ros and Chas had been together for six months. Katie loved him as much as Ros did. She could never remember being so happy with her life.

Sam and Maria were now working for Chas in a very exclusive strip Club in London, and Ros watched over them like a hawk, even though Chas promised all they did was strip, and got well paid for it! She'd even taken up cooking and although she'd had a few disasters even she had to say she was pretty good.

Chas hadn't moved in with them officially! But spent most of his time with her and Katie in their little suite at the top of the hotel. Pete didn't mind as Chas had filled the function rooms every week there'd been a gap with all the local Bands jamming together. The Hotel was getting quite a reputation for good gigs and sessions with the music mongrels. Bringing with it big money! A couple of the big names had even had their birthdays there because people could stay over the night. Chas seemed to be a lucky charm to Ros, Katie and the hotel. Everything fell into place when Chas was about. He even had a joke with old Mrs Tatler the Hotels oldest employee, who never did anything but moan about every body and every thing!

Ros grinned to herself as she put the chicken back in the oven and checked the time as she shut the door.

"Chas'll be here in an hour darling," she said to Katie as she wandered past the child, heading for the bedroom door, turning she looked at her playing with her Barbies and smiled. Yep for the first time in her twenty six years she was finally happy.

Ros walked through and shut the door behind her. She'd laid out her clothes earlier, and walking over to them dropped her robe to the floor.

She slipped her dress over her bra and panties, going over

to the dressing table she picked up her brush and checked her make-up before attempting her hair. She checked every angle until she was happy with the face in the mirror and smiled.

Picking up her robe she hung it on the back of the door and opened it. Giving the room one more scan checking everything was in place before she shut it a warm glow running down her body as she thought of Chas the night before.

Walking into the lounge she smiled at Katie.

"You look nice mum," she grinned looking up from her dolls.

"Thank you darling. Dinner won't be long."

"You did say Chas was coming round tonight?" the little girl asked pulling Barbies top on.

"Yes baby, any minute now he'll be coming through that d…" Ros said pointing to the already opening door.

"There you go magic!" she grinned at her daughter as Chas came through to the lounge a big grin on his clean shaven face.

"And how are my girls today?" he asked scooping Katie up in his arms and tenderly kissing her cheek before leaning towards Ros and pecking her on the lips.

"Good day darling?" he asked as he followed her into the kitchen Katie still in his arms.

"Wow something smells good!" he said grinning at the little girl and sniffing the air like a dog.

"Mum's getting good isn't she?" Katie said as Chas put her down.

"She sure is darling!" he said winking at her and crotching out of the way of the flying end of a tea towel as Ros flicked it at him.

Katie ran off to her Barbies leaving Ros and Chas alone.

Chas turned around slipping his arms around Ros's waist and kissed her neck as she checked dinner. Ros tipped her head to one side saying.

"God I've missed you today," As she turned from the meal into Chas's arms kissing him full on the mouth.

Chas pulled away.

"Ros I've got something to ask you."

"What's that darling?" she asked a quizzical look on her face.

"Well, you and I have been seeing each other for what six months now and well I've been thinking…"

"Yes darling?" she said leaning into him and draping her arms around his neck.

'Here we go.' she thought running her tongue along his jaw line.

"Ros!" he said laughing and pulling away holding both her hands looking in her eyes.

"Listen! I've been thinking. You, me and Katie well we've almost become family. And well since I've been coming down here to see you. I've… well I've been seeing my son also!" he said waiting for her reaction.

"Well…" she said slowly.

"Well, that's wonderful darling!" she smiled drawing him to her.

"Oh, that's good," Chas said pulling away from her again and looking her in the eyes. He kissed her full on the mouth this time it was Ros's time to pull away.

"Don't tell me you were worried to tell my you were seeing your son for all these months!" she said looking towards the lounge and Katie.

"Well, yes. I thought it would be too much. I thought you might think I'm only seeing you because of seeing my boy and somewhere to stay. But that's not the case Ros I love you and Katie. Ros I want to marry you and I want us 'ALL' to be one big happy family now that I've got to know my boy. Chas cried, the most insecure she'd ever seen him.

"Chas do you mean what you've just said?" Ros asked giving him a chance to change his mind.

"Ros I've never been so sure about anything in my life. I know we're right for each other and I know you'll love my boy as much as I adore your baby!" he said his deep brown eyes glinting as they did the first day they met.

"Oh, Chas I love you too! Madly! So does Katie," she cried tears in her eyes.

"I know. Why don't you give him a ring and invite him over tonight. I'm doing a chicken so there's going to be plenty! And I'd love to meet him!" Ros said excitement in her voice.

"I dunno Ros what if he isn't in?" Chas asked doubt in his

voice.

"Well, there's only one way to find out!" she said taking the phone from it's cradle and passing it to him.

"Are you sure Ros. I mean about every thing?" Chas said holding the phone in his hand.

"Every thing?" Ros asked.

"You know. Will you marry me?" he asked looking deep in her eyes.

"Oh, Chas of course I will! I love you more than I've loved anyone else on this planet!" Ros said smiling at him.

"Now dial!" she ordered giving him a kiss on the cheek and pinching his bum as she went past him to check the chicken.

Chas dialled the number and Ros left him to it sitting in the lounge with Katie until he wandered through. Ros looked up and stood as he came to her side.

"Well?" she asked her nerves as tight as a drum.

"He'll be over in about half an hour!" Chas said beaming.

"And he can't wait to meet his stepmum to be!" he cried picking her up and swinging her around the room to a clapping Katie.

"I love you Ros truly I do!!" he said in her ear.

"And I love you too. Now let me check our dinner and set another place!" she said pulling away and rushing about the room pumping up the cushions on the sofa and chairs.

"Hey, slow down! If you make him too comfortable he might not want to go!" Chas said laughing as Ros whizzed about the little suite clearing and tidying as she went.

"I just want it to be perfect. Is that wrong?" she asked disappointment on her face.

"No darling it's wonderful! But all he's going to be looking at is his beautiful step mum!" Chas laughed at her.

"That's not funny Chas!" she cried heading for the kitchen.

"Sorry but when I'm nervous I take the piss!" he said shrugging his shoulders giving her a grin.

"Well, go take the piss in the loo!" she grinned lightening the heavy room.

"Ha! Did you hear your mother Katie?" Chas called to the giggling child.

"Shit he'll be hear in about ten minutes!" Ros cried rushing into the lounge checking the place settings again.

Katie looked up from the floor at Chas, who shrugged his shoulders and pulled a face, making her giggle again.

"I'm just going to sort my hair out," Ros said as she headed to her bedroom and shut the door behind her.

Leaning against the door she took a couple of deep breaths. Exhaling the last breath she ran her hands through her hair and walked over to the dressing table, picking up the brush and running it over her head smoothing any stray hairs and tucking them into her hair band. She held the brush in limbo as she heard a tap on the door and Chas's deep voice welcoming some one in. Ros was frozen to the spot the brush in the air, her other hand on her head band. Suddenly there was a knock on the door and Katie's voice trailed through.

"Mummy Chas's son's here," Katie called through the door.

"Okay darling I'm just coming," Ros said to her daughter standing up from the table and straightening her dress.

Slowly she walked to the door the sound of men's laughter echoed through. Taking the handle she opened the door and walked into the room.

Chas turned towards her a huge grin on his face.

"Darling I'd like you to meet my son!" he said motioning for the lad playing with Katie on the floor to stand up.

Ros froze her smile was fixed to her face as the lads head appeared from behind the sofa.

"Hello Ros," the lad said staring at her, making her shiver.

Roslynn threw her hands up to her face.

"Hello," she whispered as the lad stretched out his hand.

"Do you two know each other?" Chas asked confused from the scene he was watching.

"Oh, yes we know each other don't we Ros?" the lad grinned.

"From the band dad," the young man explained to his father smiling at him.

Chas nodded at his son and smiled back. Looking at Ros he said, "Are you all right darling you look a little pale?" as he walked to her side.

"Yes yes fine," she replied pulling herself together.

"You just look so alike!" she added rushing in to the

kitchen and their dinner.

"Ros darling calm down it's only my son!" Chas soothed in her ear wrapping his arms about her waist.

"I'm sorry I'm just so nervous at meeting him! He must think I'm crazy!" she rambled on.

"Believe me he's as nervous as you are! And he probably won't remember anything you said anyway you know what young lads are like!" he said trying to calm her down.

"How about I open that wine an' we all start again whatcha say?"

"Okay just let me check the dinner and I'll be right out," she said giving him a reassuring smile and thinking 'Shit! Fucking Shit! How the hell I'm I going to get through this he knows me he knows what I was who I am oh God!' she felt a rush of panic run through her.

"Pull yourself together Ros!" she told herself taking a deep breath and turning the oven down she turned to face her past and future.

"Ah there you are darling!" Chas said as she walked in holding out a glass of wine for her.

"Young Katie here has been entertaining us in your absence," he added winking at the little girl sitting crossed legged on the floor a snakes and ladders board in front of her.

"Do you know mummy they cheat!" she said grinning at the two men.

"Oh, I dare say they do darling!" Ros laughed giving Katie a sympathetic look.

"She's a lovely child Ros," Chas 's son said looking deep in her eyes for what seemed an eternity but could only have been seconds. Enough for Ros to feel he knew exactly what she was thinking.

Ros felt a chill run down her body having to move before she could reply to him.

"Thank you," her voice raspy.

"Dinner will be ready in a couple of minutes. I hope your hungry!" she added smiling at him but adverting her eyes from his.

"Well, I am!" Chas butted in rubbing his stomach and pulling a face at the child, making her dissolve into fits of giggles.

Ros and the lad looked at the pair of them quizzical looks on their faces.

"It's private!" Chas said unable to look at the laughing child and shrugging his shoulders at his son.

"Umm I'm sure it is!" Ros said sternly, then smiling at them, she turned to the kitchen to dish up dinner.

"If you'd like to sit up dinner will be through in a tick," she called from the kitchen as she stirred the gravy on the stove.

Dinner went far too slowly for Ros and her nerves felt raw. Chas made most of the conversation trying to bring the others into it. Katie seemed to be the only willing participant enjoying his attention.

After dinner Ros cleared the table and told Katie to go and get washed for bed and Chas and his son to relax and have a father to son talk with a brandy while she washed up. Katie ran into the kitchen nighty on and a huge grin on her face.

"Oh, mummy, Chas told me he's going to be my new daddy and I'm so pleased I love you mummy," the little girl beamed.

Ros bent down to her daughters height and said.

"I love you too darling and I'm so very happy that your happy!" grinning at her popping some washing up bubbles on her daughters nose and kissing her forehead.

The little girl yawned.

"And I think it's time for bed young lady!" she laughed standing up.

"Can Chas put me to bed. He's more fun than you!" Katie asked giving her mother the puppy dog eyes that Chas had taught her.

"I don't think so tonight darling. Chas has got his son here remember," she said to the pouting child.

"What don't you think?" Chas's voice came from behind her making her give a little jump.

"Mummy said you couldn't put me to bed tonight," Katie rushed on before Ros had a chance.

"Oh, I think I could tear myself away for that!" he grinned at the child saying to Ros.

"Leave that darling go and have a drink while I put this little madam to bed," Turning her to the kitchen door and giving her backside a little tap making her move.

"Yes go on mummy. I'll help you tomorrow," Katie cried jumping up and down.

Ros gave Katie a gentle smile and bending down she kissed her on the cheek.

"Thank you darling... Good night darling and God bless. I love you."

Turning to Chas she blew him a kiss with one finger and walked into the lounge and his son.

Ros picked up the Brandy and a glass offering a refill to the lad. She poured herself a large one and sat down opposite him.

"So do you work full time for the Band now?" she asked him taking a sip of her drink.

The lad stared at her his expression unchanging.

"Remember. I know what you are," he said slowly.

"I beg your pardon!" she gasped her hand flying to her throat.

"Tell him or leave him."

"NO! No please!" she whispered her heart breaking already.

"Good bye Roslynn," he said standing up.

He looked down at her and gave her that knowing smile she remembered all those years ago.

Ros sat motionless in her chair. She was drained of all colour and trembling all over.

"Ros darling are you all right?" Chas asked distress in his voice at the sight of her. He didn't even notice his son wasn't there.

"Please talk to me!" he pleaded on his knees in front of her.

She just stared straight ahead unseeing. Chas put her Brandy to her lips and tipped a little into her mouth, making her cough and splatter back to life.

"Darling are you all right what's happened?" he rushed, slowly she averted her eyes to his voice.

"Ros darling speak to me."

"I... didn't... feel... well," she said slowly. Her mind fuzzy and confused.

Chas looked about the room.

"Where's Dan?"

"I... sent... him... home," she said quietly, staring into

space.

"What! Why didn't you get him to fetch me?"

"He's gone."

"Here drink this," Chas said putting the glass to her lips again. This time Ros held the glass herself and took a trembling sip. The liquid burnt hot down her throat as it went down calming her and bring her back to her senses again. Taking a deep breath she sat up slowly before exhaling and smiling at Chas's worried face.

"How you feeling now?" he asked.

"Better much better," she smiled taking another sip of her drink.

"I think the panic of tonight just caught up with me. Sorry darling," she said giving him a sad smile the pain coming back to her.

"Why didn't you get me Ros?"

"Katie," she answered the tears close to the surface as she thought of her little girl. 'God she's going to be as heart broken as me!' she thought.

"I see," Chas nodded.

"Chas."

"Yes darling?"

"Make love to me."

Chas stood up scooped her up in his arms and carried her to the bedroom.

'Good bye my darling I'll always love you," she silently said to him as she ran her tongue down his neck feeling his body tense.

Chas laid her on the bed slowly bending he kissed her tenderly on the mouth until she could stand no more and grabbed his head pushing her tongue into his mouth and arching her back. Chas slowly undid her dress slipping it over her shoulders and kissing her neck. She freed her arms from the material and ripped at his shirt, the buttons flying about the room. She needed to touch and smell him, needed to remember.

Chas climbed onto the bed taking the rest of his clothes off as he went. Ros moved to the middle of the bed and he ran his hands over every inch of her flesh. It was as if he knew. Slowly he ran his hands up the inside of her thighs spreading her legs as he went. Ros closed her eyes and prayed for time to stand still. Slowly he pushed his fingers into the flesh either side of her thighs Ros writhed her body onto him hoping to move his teasing fingers nearer her silk covered love lips. She ran her hands down over her hard nipples poking out of her bra, across her body to her mound slipping her fingers inside her panties. Chas lifted his head and smiled at her and pulled himself on top of her kissing her hard on the mouth. His cock pushing into her covered wet lips, his chest rubbing on her swollen nipples. He pinned her hands above her head with one hand and with the other he slid it under her back and released the clasp of her bra pulling it up and above her head tying her hands with it. Ros gasped her breasts heaved up and down as he traced his fingers very gently over them, pinching her nipples just as she thought she was going to go mad. He replaced his fingers with his mouth sucking and biting her. He moved his hands to her panties and ripped them from her slipping his fingers deep inside her feeling her come instantly on him with a shudder. Lifting his head from her breast he slid over her body and buried his head between her hot wet lips. Ros moaned and licked his balls taking them one at a time into her mouth and ran her tongue over them, she slipped her tongue around the base of his hard cock, making it jump and pulse she then took him deep in her throat and rocked her head in rhythm with Chas as he licked, sucked and finger fucked her. He suddenly flipped her over her arms still above her head. Pulling her backside up so she was on her knees, he pulled her arse cheeks apart and rammed himself into her releasing her hands from their confines at the same time. She reached behind her and grabbed his arse pulling him deeper inside her. She never wanted the moment to end knowing only too well that pretty soon it would be. Tears welled up in her eyes.

Good bye my darling.

When she said goodbye to him the next morning Chas had no notion that it would be the last time he'd see her or little Katie.

Ros took her daughter to school, kissing her good bye at the gate and waving her into her classroom. Turning she walked briskly away keeping her head down so no one could see the pain on her face.

Finally she reached her suite and shut the door before she crumbled. Sobs wrenched her body as she told herself it was for the best. She loved Chas so much, that to tell him her past would make him think of her as a different person and she didn't want to lose his love that way.

"No it's for the best!" she cried into the room looking about it. Chas seemed to have his mark on everything in it.

"I can't stay here we're going to have to move!" she cried aloud pulling herself up from the floor by the suite door and wiping away her tears, the sobs dry now but still wrenching her body.

Ros walked into the bathroom and cleaned herself up, her mind ticking all the while.

"Abroad!" she said smiling in the mirror and sniffing.

Ros walked down to Pete's office and knocked on the door clenching her fists with nerves.

"Yeh come in," Pete yelled from behind the door.

Ros walked in giving him a little smile and sitting down.

"Pete I've made a decision I'm taking Katie and myself abroad to live."

"You fucking what!" Pete stared openmouthed reaching for his cigarettes.

"Since when Ros?"

"Oh, about five minutes!" Ros said smiling at him.

"Talk to me Ros," he said passing her the packet.

"I can't see Chas again. Please don't ask me why I just can't and I've decided it's time Katie and I moved on. I'm going to need your help though."

"Sure what?"

"Well, could you give your old friend a ring for me and ask if we could stay at his villa for a couple of weeks while I find some thing for us?"

"Well, I'll give him a ring for you. Ros are you sure about this I mean what ever has happened with you and Chas you don't have to leave the fucking country!" Pete said giving her a pleading look.

"Yes I'm sure it's time we moved on," she smiled slowly at him.

Pete pulled out his draw and found his address book

clicking through until he found his friends number.

"Thanks for every thing Pete I will keep in touch I promise. I'm going to pack our bags and I'll book the flights when I come down. Even if your friend can't help me I'm still going to day," she said with determination in her voice knowing Pete wouldn't ring if he didn't think she was truly serious which she was.

"Ros."

"Yes?" she said turning back on him.

"I'll sort out the flights after I've rung Tony and go down an' pay for them it's the lest I can do after what you've done to this place!"

"Thanks Pete," she smiled walking out the door looking forward to telling little Katie that they're going on an adventure.

Two hours later Ros walked into Pete's office smiling as he looked up.

Pete poured two whisky's handing her one, placing his drink on the table he said.

"Your flights are booked for seven tonight I've just got to pop out and pay for them in a minute Tony's getting some one to meet you at the other end it's all sorted!"

"Pete you're an angel!" she cried leaning over the desk and kissing him.

Chapter 26

Ros and Katie loved Spain and using the money from "The "Rosbette Club" Ros brought a little bar with a flat above it in a popular haunt for the ever increasing Britsh expat's. Ros kept in touch with Pete and he came to visit them every year with Marg and Jim. These were the only three people Ros wanted to know from her life in England and made them swear not to tell a soul where she and Katie were. The past was finally behind her, and after six years of hard work by herself Ros had become great friends with one of her locals. He was a widower who, as she had, had come over to start a new life. Their friendship had grown over the time Ros had, had the bar and she felt at ease with him, which was why she had excepted his invitation to dinner knowing that Richard wanted more than friendship and so did she. That was a year ago now and in a months time they will be celebrating their first wedding anniversary.

It had been hard for Ellen and Louise, Richard's daughters when he told them he wanted to move abroad giving them the option to come out with him. Louise was eighteen at the time and decided to take the chance. Ellen was twenty in a steady job and engaged, her wedding planned for a month after Richard had to move from the family home he'd sold. The wedding went ahead but Richard was unable to attend leaving Ellen feeling very resentful. She'd lost her mother and now her father. So she severed all contact with him and her sister Louise.

Richard had the shock of his life when he received a letter from her. It read.

Dear Dad it's Ellen!

God I don't know where to start I want to say so much!

My marriage to Phillip only lasted as long as my job did. Two years to be exact. All my dreams of being a successful businesswoman and mother came crushing down around me at once! Sending me down the wrong path for a while, but unbeknown to me there was a reason! And his name is Daniel. He helped me through the tough time I was having not caring what I'd become, but seeing what I will be.

It took me a year to sort out and decide what I wanted out of my life, and Daniel was behind me all the way. The day he asked me to marry him was the happiest day of my life and has been ever since.

We're now living up the road to you. Well 300 miles actually! We've been here for three years and have loved every minute. I am that business woman I dreamed of being years ago. Unfortunately due to my business children are not an option. I'm not sad I've got Daniel and our love is so strong that all we need is each other. It's down to him that I'm writing this letter. I've wanted to do it before, but never had the courage. So here I am, I know it will be a shock to you after all this time and I'm sorry.

Also ashamed of my behaviour towards you. I was totally out of order I acted like a spoilt child. I realise now how you felt you needed to get away and start a fresh. Perhaps that's why my marriage and job went. To make me realise just what you were going through, but yet again I didn't learn did I.

I've waited another five years before I could write this letter because of my own stubbornness and I can't say how truly sorry I am.

I know it's probably to soon but I'd dearly love to see you and Louise again.

Your daughter.

Ellen.

Richard showed the letter to Ros. Who told him to contact her and make arrangements to see her. Louise didn't want to see her sister, she needed time and said she would write first.

When he came off the phone to Ellen he seemed as if a weight had been lifted from him, putting Ros's mind at rest that the advice she'd given him was right.

Ellen had invited him and Ros to visit her and Daniel. Richard had accepted on the spot, making arrangements for that weekend, surprising every one involved, including himself considering the weekend was the next day.

"I need to do it now!" he explained pacing the floor.

"If I don't I could lose her again! She seemed so... Oh I don't know!" he sighed giving Ros an apologetic smile walking over to her burying his head in her hair and inhaling her scent.

"Every thing will be just fine, you'll see," she said running her hands up and down his back.

"I hope so Ros. I truly do," he said above her head.

Ros pulled away from him giving him a smile and holding both of his hands saying.

"Well, if I'm going to meet my new stepdaughter tomorrow I've got to go and have my hair done!" grinning at him.

"Oh, and pack!" Ros cried her mind on what to do.

Richard laughed at her and thanked God above for his beautiful wife.

***

"Well, how did it go?" Daniel asked seeing her face as she replaced the receiver.

"Not bad she replied running her hands through her hair and looking at him.

"They're coming tomorrow!" she rushed biting her nails.

"What your dad and Louise. That's great," he beamed at her.

"Louise? No dads new wife!" she cried panic in her voice.

"Hey, come on baby," he said reaching out for her.

"It's still good he's coming isn't it?"

"I suppose," she whispered looking into his eyes letting them calm her nerves.

"That's my girl," Daniel smiled kissing her forehead and holding her tightly.

***

"How long until we're there do you think?" Ros asked tightening her scarf about her head to keep her hair in place from the warm wind rushing past her in their MG.

"About half an hour," Richard said giving her a nervous glance.

"How about we stop and have a drink before we get there?"

she said casually.

"God I thought you'd never ask! I'm so nervous."

"Ah but what you've got to remember is she probably is as well," Ros said smiling her own nerves racing.

"True my love. True!" Richard replied reaching over and tapping her knee and smiling back.

***

"For fuck sake!" Ellen yelled down the phone.

"No I can't!"

"No… You know why. I've got my dad coming and his new wife!" she said exhaling her smoke.

"Yeh very funny…! Try an' sort it out if you can't it'll have to wait until I get in okay?"

"Fine."

"Yeh see you later bye."

"Jeesus I can't believe it!" Ellen said coming off the phone and stabbing out her cigarette.

"What?" Daniel asked looking up from what he was doing.

"Only had an old sod die on us!" she replied picking up her wine glass and taking a sip and looking at Daniel her other hand on her hip.

"Don't! Don't laugh it's not funny!" she cried smirking at Daniel.

"I'm not!" he grinned biting the end of his joint and lighting it, clearing away the loose tobacco and dropping it in the ashtray.

"If it can't be sorted out I'm going to have to go in tonight!" she said pacing the floor.

"That's okay we can give your dad and step mum a tour!" he said seriously.

Ellen stopped in mid pace and stared at him open mouthed their eyes connecting.

"Oh, don't!" she cried waving a finger at him as they both collapsed laughing.

***

"Seems we take this road to the top," Richard said looking at his map.

Ros placed her hand on his.

"Richard please! We've gone over this five times now!" she said chuckling and picking up her drink.

"I know and I'm sorry," he said picking up his drink and swallowing it in one.

"It's okay. I can't stop to imagine what it must feel like!"

Richard looked into his empty glass.

"Ros. I've just thought are you okay? I'm so wrapped up in my own thoughts I forgot that you haven't even met Ellen before!" he rushed looking in her eyes.

Ros looked at her husband taking his hand from the glass.

"I don't mind admitting I do feel a little left out but only because it's your past not ours. Yes I'm nervous. I want to make the right impression and I know nothing about the girl."

Richard tightened his hold on her fingers.

"I'm sorry Ros. If you can't go through with it we'll go home. I really didn't think did I?"

"No you didn't think you listened to that little voice in your head for once!" she said squeezing his fingers and smiling at him.

"We've got to go. To put your mind at rest that you've finally found her again," she added lifting the last of her drink to her lips.

Richard gave her a "Thank you" smile leaning over the little table between them and kissed her full on the mouth.

"I love you Mrs Cooke," he said looking into her eyes.

"And I love you too," Ros said back meaning every word.

***

"You want me ta get it this time babe?" Daniel called to Ellen.

"No I've got it but this is the last time!" she shouted back at him.

"What is it now?" Ellen asked down the phone.

"Ellen is that you?" the voice on the other end asked.

"Dad! Is that you?" she asked back thinking 'shit what must he think of me!'

"Yes. Yes it's me," he said chuckling.

"Listen we've just stopped at a bar for a drink and should be with you in about half an hour or so… is that all right?" Richard asked.

"Fine. That's fine we'll see you then… Lovely. Bye then," she said quietly replacing the receiver and going into the lounge.

"Dad's gonna be about half an hour," she said plonking down next to him taking the joint from his hand and inhaling the smoke.

"You okay?" he asked pulling himself up and looking at her.

"As okay as I'll ever be," she replied resting her head on his shoulder.

***

"Bloody hell!" Richard exclaimed as they drove up Daniel and Ellen's home.

"What she marry a millionaire?" he said looking at Ros.

"Well! It is a lovely place,"sShe said nodding.

***

Darlin' they're here!" Daniel said quietly to Ellen as he heard a car pull up.

"Wh… what!" She cried pulling herself upright.

"They're here. Yer dad an' his wife they've just pulled up."

"Shit shit why the fuck did you let me sleep?" she cried jumping to her feet running her hands through her hair and straightening her clothes.

Daniel grinned at her as he pushed himself up from the sofa and took her in his arms.

"Hey, calm down."

"Fuck their coming now!" she said pulling away from his clasp and moving to the window for a better look.

"Jesus she can't be much older than me!" she gasped motioning Daniel to take a look.

As he came up behind her there was Ros walking arm in arm with Ellen's father up to the house.

'Well, well, I wondered what happened to you!' he thought

a smile creeping on his face 'Well are you in for a shock Roslynn.'

***

As Ros walked up to the house she wondered what kind of business Ellen and Daniel could be in.

Richard stood poised at the pullie and look at Ros.

"Ready?" she asked squeezing his hand and smiling at him.

Richard took a deep breath.

"Ready," he nodded pulling the cord.

As they heard the bell ring, Daniel could feel Ellen tense.

"Hey, baby shall we do it together?" he whispered in her ear kissing her neck.

Trembling Ellen turned.

"I don't think I can do it!" she cried holding him tightly.

"Ellen it's your father behind that door. He wants to see you!" he reasoned pulling away from her and holding her hands.

"Now let's go open the door.

The bell rang again, making her jump.

"Open it darling," he whispered.

As Ellen reached for the latch Daniel stepped back away from her. Looking at him for support she took a deep breath and opened the door wide.

Both father and daughter stared at one another, the silence seemed endless. Giving Richard's hand a squeeze Ros pulled away taking a step back. Richard quickly turned his head to her. Ros smiled at him. Quickly he took a step forward towards Ellen.

"Darling," he whispered holding out his arms.

Ellen threw herself in to her father's arms tears falling down her face.

Pulling away Ellen wiped her tears with the back of her hand and smiled at Ros in the background. Following her gaze Richard motioned Ros over.

"Ellen darling let me introduce Ros. My wife," he said his arm about Ellen's shoulder.

"It's a pleasure to meet you," Ellen smiled wiping a stray tear.

"You too," Ros said holding out her hand and smiling.

Catching a movement behind Ellen, Ros looked up seeing the face of her past. Her smile froze she was fixed to the spot. Panic seared through her. Feeling Ros's hand go tense Ellen quickly turned to see Daniel's calm smile.

"Oh, God," she cried realising. Her hand covering her mouth, "I'm sorry," she gasped.

"Dad, Ros, this is my husband Daniel," she said taking a step back to allow Daniel to meet her father and Ros.

"Nice to meet you Ros," Daniel said calmly as he held out his hand.

"Y... you too Daniel," Ros said slowly as she held out a trembling hand.

Taking hold of Ros's cold hand Daniel bowed his head and kissed the back of it. His blue eyes bore into her as he lifted his head. A cold shiver ripped through her body as he smiled at her.

"You too Richard," he smiled extending his hand to Ellen's father.

"Are you okay Ros your very pale," Ellen asked.

"Just a little tired from the journey and the excitement," Ros whispered.

As Ellen led her into the house followed by Daniel and Richard deep in conversation.

Ellen walked Ros into their cool lounge.

"Please take a seat and I'll fix us a drink how's that," she said wandering over to the bar in the corner.

"Hey, I'll do that," Daniel said as he walked in with Richard.

"Go on scoot," he said giving her a kiss as they passed.

Ellen went and sat opposite her father and Ros.

"So how long have you two been married?" she asked tucking her feet up under her and lighting a cigarette offering the pack to Ros and her father.

"A year," Richard replied adding, "But we've known each other quite a few years haven't we darling?"

Ros nodded and smiled the shock of seeing Daniel still with her.

Daniel brought a tray over with four glasses and a bucket containing a bottle of champagne. He placed it on the table taking the bottle from the ice and twisted the metal clasp holding the cork and popping it open, making Ros jump in her chair and Ellen and Richard cheer.

"A toast," Daniel called passing the glasses around.

"To the past present and future."

"Past present and future!" they called.

Ros unable to take much more slowly raised her glass.

The phone rang and Daniel turned towards Ellen who gave him a pleading look.

"Don't worry I'll get it," he said touching her shoulder as he passed.

After a few minutes he came back and excused himself and Ellen for a minute, explaining it was work.

"Sorry darling we've got to go in to night they won't release the body until we sign some papers.

"Oh, fucking brilliant!" Ellen hissed turning around.

"Look we can nip in for a drink early and sign the papers before we have dinner," Daniel said.

"An what about dad and Ros?" Eleen cried.

"They'll just have to except that that's our business. I don't think their be as shocked as you think," he said, smiling at her.

"Well, okay I suppose they are grown adults an' if they don't like it then I'll have to except it. I haven't seen him for a few years so a few more won't be too much of a problem will it," she said calming down.

"Good girl now let's go and tell them shall we?" he said kissing her nose. They went back in to the lounge and told them that they had a problem at work and did they mind if they stopped for a drink there before they had dinner.

"Oh, we know how it is don't we Ros?" Richard smiled at a quiet Ros.

"Ros has a bar herself. Don't you love so we know what it's like," Richard explained.

"What's yours like?" he asked.

"Actually Richard it's a very private Club," he said looking Ros straight in the eye and smiling.

"Oh!" Richard said nodding slowly.

"Is that a problem?" Daniel asked him.

"No son I think we're adult enough to know that this type of thing goes on, and I must admit I am quite intrigued," he said picking up his glass to hide his embarrassment.

"So you wouldn't be offended if we had a drink there first Richard? Ros?" he asked.

"Well, I'm fine about it," Richard said grinning.

"What about you darling?" he asked Ros.

"Yes fine," she said quietly not daring to look in Daniels direction.

"Hey, that's great you'll be able to meet my father he's using part of the Club for a business meeting.!" Daniel said smiling as he topped every ones glasses.

Ros's heart stopped.

Ellen showed them to their suite and left them to change for dinner.

Chapter 27

Ros was just going to tell Richard to go to dinner without her when.

"Oh, God Ros I have you to thank for this!" he said waving his hand towards the door as he dropped to his knees in front of her.

"I love you desperately darling! I could never have done it with out you. I need you by my side you're my strength!" he cried holding both her hands and kissing the palm's.

Tears welled in her eyes as he looked up at her and she cradled his head.

"Come on we've got a Club to visit you soppy sod!" she cried wiping away her tears.

Wrapping her towel around her Ellen stepped from the shower a smile across her face.

"I feel so much better now dad knows about the Club. Isn't he wonderful," she said kissing Daniels chest as she passed him.

"Ros doesn't say much does she?" she added thoughtfully.

"D'you think she was more shocked than she let on?"

"Much more!" Daniel murmured under his breath smiling.

"Sorry darling I didn't hear you?" she said taking the towel from her head.

"I said no," he grinned turning from the sink and tutting at her.

Grinning Ellen turned and walked into their bedroom.

"Wow you look fucking great!" Daniel whistled as he walked into the room his erection showing through the towel around his waist.

"Thank you," she said twirling around in a blue lacy gypsy style dress her shoulders bare.

Daniel walked over to her pressing his body hard against her and kissed her bare neck and shoulder.

"Oh God Dan we can't!" she moaned tilting her head back with his caresses. Pulling away from her he looked deep in her eyes.

"It's either this!" he said dropping his towel.

"Or a joint? Your choice!" he smiled.

"A joint I'll have that later!" she laughed.

"Good choice darlin'!" he laughed with her.

Ros walked into the lounge and straight up to the drinks cabinet. Richard walked in as she was opening it.

"Are you sure you can handle that?" he grinned as she held up a bottle of scotch.

"Please darling," he said doing up his cufflinks.

Ros poured two large scotches handing Richard his as he came up to her.

"Cheers," he said clinking their glasses.

"I must say I'm quite excited about tonight aren't you darling?"

Ros smiled wishing she could be any where but where she was. She glided across the room and picked up their cigarettes and lighter offering Richard one. She clicked the lighter inhaling as she waved the flame under the cigarette. As she passed him the lighter he held her hand.

"Ros do you know how stunning you look tonight my sweet," he smiled releasing her hand.

She had piled her hair high on her head letting the stray hair fall and chosen her lilac silk suit finishing it off with chunky gold jewellery and gold strap sandals.

"Thank you," she said bowing her head. Her body shivering as she glanced at her watch.

"Nervous darling?" Richard asked downing his scotch.

'If only you knew!' Ros thought her hand trembling as she moved her glass to her lips. It felt as if her world was falling about her.

"I'm so nervous!" Ellen cried slipping her feet in to her sandals and doing them up.

"Why darling the Clubs fantastic some thing to be proud of! Your father can meet mine and then we're have a wonderful dinner," Daniel said exhaling the last of his joint and dropping it in the ashtray.

Ellen gave him a disbelieving look then laughed as he raised his eyes innocently.

"Bollocks! It'll never go that smoothly! We've got an old boy laying dead in the Club to sort out remember!" she laughed tapping his backside to signal she was ready.

'Not that smoothly, no!' Daniel thought grinning as they walked out into the hall meeting Richard and Ros just coming out of their suite.

"Wow!" Richard called seeing his daughter.

Grinning Ellen went over and hugged him.

"Shall we?" Daniel said jangling his car keys smiling at Ros.

Ellen opened the front door and slipping her arm through his, guided Richard out.

"Ros," Daniel called waving his keys in front of her and smiling.

"Please!" she whispered pleading in her eyes.

"What's the matter Ros can't run this time?" he asked gently his eyes looking deep in side her.

"Dan please not now!" she pleaded her lips trembling.

"Let me guess," he said stepping towards her and taking her arm.

"Richard doesn't know does he?" he tutted.

"Don't you know the past has a funny way of catching up with you? When will you learn Ros!" he sighed closing the door behind them and smiling at Ellen and Richard waiting by the car. Ellen pointing to a particular view and Richard nodding.

Ros walked robot like by his side.

"Ah there you are darling," Richard called to Ros.

"Isn't it beautiful?" he asked.

"Beautiful," she said her smile fixed.

Daniel unlocked the car and started the engine eager to get moving. Ellen got in the front with Daniel. Richard and Ros in the back. Turning in the front seat she pointed out interesting spots telling them little stories of the different locals in their village until they turned off the main road on to a dirt track.

"Well, this is it!" Ellen said smiling as they turned the corner. Facing them was a square castle. Lights shone up the walls giving the whole building a halo of light around it.

"What d'you think?" Ellen beamed from the front seat at Ros.

"It's superb Ellen lovely setting," Ros croaked licking her dry lips.

"Wait until you see the interior!" she cooed proudly.

Ros smiled as a shiver ran down her body remembering the Club's interior.

Daniel pulled into the reserved parking spot and turned off the engine. Getting out he went round to Ellen and Ros's doors opening the front and back together and holding his hand out for Ros smiling.

Slowly and gracefully she exited the car with out his help, pulling herself up to her full height, her head high. Taking a deep breath she took a step towards Richard her smile fixed on her face. Inside she was in turmoil. Ellen locked arms with Daniel and they headed to the castle door followed by Richard and Ros.

When they reached the door Ellen held Daniels hand before he put the key in the door turning to her father and Ros she said.

"I didn't want you to know about this place when I first contacted you but now I'm pleased you know about it and are going to see it. It means we're starting on the right foot no secrets an' all that!" she grinned.

"One more thing. Please don't show your shock when we go in these gentlemen are paying customers," she finished pecking her father on the cheek and smiling at Ros.

"Oh, I'm so nervous!" she whispered to Daniel without moving her lips.

"It's okay honey, we understand," Daniel said out loud with a grin, putting the key in the door and turning it in the lock.

"Let's go and have a drink," he said pushing the heavy door and waving them in. As Ros passed him he smiled at her closing the door behind him. They were stood in a huge hall with sandstone floors and walls decorated with suits of amour, shields and swords. Huge church candles dripping wax onto the floor was the only lighting in the room. In the middle of the room was a round table carved of stone. On it, a large red leather bound book with a gold pen in it's holder next to it.

"Please," Daniel said pointing to the table and book.

"All our visitors have to sign in."

"Even us!" he smiled heading to the table.

As Daniel signed in for himself and Ellen, Louisa, a short tubby Spanish woman of sixty'ish came out of the archway to their left.

"Ah Daniel, Ellen!" she cried rushing over and pecking Ellen on both cheeks.

"Oh, mucha problems!" she wailed waving her hands in front of her oblivious of Richard and Ros.

Ellen hugged the older woman.

"Louisa calm down we're here now," she said holding the woman's shoulders and smiling at her, her eyes wide.

"I'd like you to meet my papa Richard and his wife Ros," she said introducing them.

"Ah bella bella!" Louisa grinned nodding at them.

"A pleasure to meet you," Richard said extending his hand to her.

"This is my wife Ros," he added placing his hand at the bottom of Ros's back and guiding her forward.

"Bellisimo!" Lousia cried clapping her hands together and going up to Ros and pecking her on the cheeks.

Richard excused himself going over to the table and signing his name in the book taking the pen back with him.

"Your turn honey," he said passing Ros the pen smiling at the little group.

Ros glided over to the table her body disguising what she felt inside. As she wrote her name on the line below Richards she quickly scanned the other page. What she saw took her breath away, the name seemed to jump out at her.

'No! No this can't be happening!' she cried inside as her body trembled.

Lifting her head she saw Daniel watching her from the little group, his blue eyes dark and threatening as he gave her a slow smile. All the faces from her past flooded before her she grabbed the cold stone table for support. Hearing Richards laugh brought her back to the present. She closed her eyes tightly and took a couple of deep breaths to calm her self down. Slowly she turned to face them still holding the table behind her.

"Come on Ros darling, we're waiting for you!" Richard

called waving her over to him his face flushed with excitement.

Ros pushed herself from the table and headed towards them her legs felt like lead weights as she forced them forward.

"Ellie! Dan! Thank fuck yer 'ere!" the voice boomed as a door behind Ros opened.

"'Ave we 'ad a fuckin' nightmare or wot! An' it's all yer fuckin' fathers fault!"

Ros froze in her tracks not daring to turn and see the face of the voice she knew so well.

"Oh, shit! Sorry I didn't know ya 'ad company wif ya!" the woman said seeing Richard and the back of Ros as she strod towards them.

Richard put his hand up.

"Don't worry no harm done," he called to the woman, laughing.

As the woman's footsteps got closer panic waved over Ros. Suddenly the footsteps stopped and the hall fell silent.

"Fuck me! I'd know that arse anywhere!" the woman boomed taking a step closer to Ros.

Ros flinched. With pleading in her eyes she looked straight at Daniel.

"I'm sorry?" Richard called a confused expression on his face as he looked at Ros and the woman, then Daniel and Ellen for some kind of explanation.

"I don't know Dad!" Ellen whispered shrugging her shoulders.

"I 'ave ta say yer lookin' fuckin' good babe!" the woman said as she stepped in front of Ros and grinned.

"Hello Jude," Ros whispered, tears welling up in her eyes as Jude embraced her trembling body.

Richard, Ellen and Daniel walked over to the two women.

"Well, well and how d'you two know each other?" Ellen asked a smirk spreading across her face.

"Long story babe!" Jude grinned.

Richard stared at Ros a look of disbelief on his face.

"I think we all need a drink!" Daniel said breaking the silence and catching Richards arm.

"Y… yes I think we do!" Richard said looking over his shoulder at Ros as Daniel led him away to the bar.

"Well, ladies shall we?" Ellen asked walking ahead of Ros and Jude, her mind swimming.

Jude smiled and locked arms with the silent Ros and dragged her behind Ellen.

"Ros I need to talk to you!" Jude whispered quickly to the numb Ros as they walked into the bar.

Ros stared at her, her eyes vacant.

"Now Ros!" Jude hissed through gritted teeth, as she smiled at a customer passing them.

Jude put a hand up at Ellen, Richard and Daniel as they were taking a seat at a table.

"Look I'm gonna take Ros ta freshen up we've both 'ad a shock ta night!" Jude told the seated group as she looked at the zombie Roslynn. Jude led her away before anyone could comment on her decision and walked Ros through to the girls dressing room. Jude led her to a chair, turning she shut the door behind them.

"Shit Ros 'ow the fuck yer get 'ere?" Jude asked running her hands through her bobbed hair and wondering how she was going to tell her.

Ros looked up at her blankly not saying a word her eyes staring. Jude walked over to a dresser and poured them a scotch each. She opened the top drawer and pulled out a tobacco tin. Picking up the glasses, she walked back to Ros staring into space. Jude handed her a glass and sat down opposite her.

"Ere drink it! It ain't the only shock yer in fer ta night!" she said downing half of the amber liquid in her glass.

Opening the tin and resting it on her lap she pulled out two rolling papers and proceeded to stick them together. Ros took a sip of her scotch feeling it's warmth and closed her eyes leaning her head back.

'I've already seen the name. Why do you think I'm like this!' she said to herself.

Suddenly Ros opened her eyes her heart pounding. 'But Jude doesn't know!' she thought.

"Ros you okay?" Jude asked looking at her old friend in a concerned way.

"You said you're not my only shock tonight! What do you mean by that?" she asked slowly sitting forward in her chair her heart pounding and her mind racing.

"Jude!" she cried.

"Okay!" Jude said lighting her joint and exhaling the smoke.

"Yer ain't gonna like it babe!" she said warning her.

"But all the guys from the Band are 'ere fer the night sumfink ta do wif Dan's father Chas an' some meetin'!"

Ros nearly fell off her chair as the room spun. Jude leaned forward clasping her hand.

"I told ya yer wouldn't like it!" she said passing Ros her joint.

"You don't know the half of it!" Ros moaned.

Taking the joint she inhaled deeply forgetting it had been a few years since she'd had one.

"So why ya 'ere Ros?" Jude asked downing the last of her drink and wondering what Ros meant by not knowing the half of it.

Ros took another puff of the joint passing it back to Jude.

"I'm married to Richard, Ellen's father," Ros said picking up her drink.

"Well, fuck me! So 'ow long ya known about this place?" Jude asked getting up and heading for the dresser.

"About six hours," Ros sighed looking about the dressing room as she came back to life.

"We're supposed to be having dinner," Ros said slowly frowning.

"Oh, shit!" Jude cried.

"What is it?"

"I totally fergot seein' you! WE 'ad one of Chas's old boy's snuff it taday! That's why Dan an' Ellie 'ad ta come in. Ta sign some papers ta release the old git!"

"So that's why it couldn't wait," Ros said quietly sighing.

"'e's still laid out up in one of the girls room's. Fuckin' off puttin' if yer ask me!" Jude said coming back with the whisky bottle and pouring their drinks.

"Did you know the man?" Ros asked the name in the book blazing in her mind.

"Yeh 'es been 'ere before, with Chas an' the other blokes when there's a meetin'. Fuckin' loaded 'e is! Or should I say was!" Jude frowned.

A shiver ran down her spine.

"Jude. What's the old boys name?" Ros asked putting her hand up.

"No questions asked here," she said taking the joint from a nodding Jude and inhaled.

"Edward Cham.."

"Bers," Ros finished for her nodding.

Slowly a smile spread across her face and she started to giggle uncontrollably.

"Yeh dirty old bugger! Only 'ad one of our yongest girls in the room wif 'im when 'e copped it! Fuck knows wot 'e was gonna do wif 'er but there ya go!" Jude rushed not really taking in that Ros knew this man somehow.

"Ere Ros 'ow did ya know?" Jude suddenly asked her friend a confused look on her face.

"Well, it had to be didn't it!" Ros cried collapsing in her chair a groan coming from her body leaving Jude speechless and very confused.

"Oh, fucking Jesus! What a fucking day!" she said shaking her head and wiping the tears from her face the shock still sinking in.

"I don't understand Babe!" Jude said staring at Ros.

"You don't! My whole life except for Tommy is here in this castle!" Ros said. Then she saw Jude's expression.

"No don't tell me he's here as well!" she laughed.

"Fraid so 'e works fer the Band now!" Jude said quietly looking down at the floor.

"Well, I'll tell you what. You roll me a joint and you can see my whole world fall down around me when we go in there," she cried pointing to the door they had come through.

Silently Jude rolled Ros's joint and handed it to her along with a lighter.

Ros stood up and lit her joint a cloud of purple smoke floated to the ceiling. Draining her glass she walked over to the dressing mirror and checked her hair and makeup her eye's were void of emotion. Slowly she smiled at her reflection and a shiver ran through her.

"Ros don't do it! Go out the back door. I'll say you felt

faint! Please babe!" Jude pleaded.

"I've got to do it. I can't run away for ever," Ros cried.

"I've got to face the demon's," she said heading for the door.

Jude ran in front of her.

"No! yer in no state ta go out there Ros yer don't know wotcha sayin'!"

"That's where your wrong Jude," Ros smiled.

"That's where your wrong!" she said standing tall and moving Jude aside and opening the door on her Past, Present and Future!